Angel on the Great Medicine Trail

By

Marty Young Stratton

To Karen
with a grateful heart
for how you helped our
dreams come true,

Marty

This book is a work of fiction. Places, events, and situations in this story are purely fictional. Any resemblance to actual persons, living or dead, is coincidental.

ISBN: 1-4107-8504-1 (e-book)
ISBN: 1-4107-8503-3 (Paperback)

Library of Congress Control Number: 2003095843

This book is printed on acid free paper.

Printed in the United States of America
Bloomington, IN

1stBooks - rev. 02/02/04

Dedications

This story is dedicated to the memory of my mother, who believed in letting the heart rule; to my family, extended and nuclear, every one of whom is far more talented than I; to Nikki for believing; to Andrew, Elizabeth and Nikki for saving the computer when I threatened to hit it with a stick; to Angela Angel Smith; to Tom who gives me wings to fly.

Notes of Interest

1789	The position of Federal Marshals established.
1812 – 1846	Fur trade along the Great Medicine Trail.
1824	The Bureau of Indian Affairs established.
1830	Indian Removal Act.
1834	Fort Hall established.
1841	John Fremont given an appropriation from congress to map the Oregon trail.
1848	Elizabeth Blackwell is the first woman in the United States to graduate from Medical school.
1849	Fort Laramie bought by the army.
1850s	Oregon Donation Act.

Part 1

Marty Young Stratton

Chapter 1

"Life is nothing if not a great adventure."
                        Helen Keller

"Wishing you were somehow here again
Wishing you were somehow near
Sometimes it seems if I just dream
Somehow you would be here.
Wishing I could hear your voice again
Knowing that I never would
Dreaming of you won't help me to do
All that you dreamed I could"

                        Andrew Lloyd Webber

"Wishing You Were Somehow Here Again"
                "The Phantom of the Opera"

Angela peered up into the wagon, her high-laced black shoes neatly planted on one of the rough planks that served as steps. She had to look over the wooden sides and through the opening made by a flap of canvas tied back. This was not what she had imagined. She had seen in her mind's eye a stagecoach, set high on four spoke wheels, iron-framed steps going up, large windows for viewing. From such windows she imagined the frozen faces of wide-eyed women staring horror-struck out at pursuing savages. The interior of this odd conveyance was dark, the air close. The dark shapes of assorted trunks, carpetbags and barrels were barely discernable. There was a smell of something unpleasant, dirty. She felt a little shiver-shudder and tried not to think of the long journey in this cramped dark wagon with its eerie shapes and bad smell. Her young brother Ben was running around and under, poking his head

3

inside the canvas thrilled beyond containment. Her mother, Clara Harrington, was in an ongoing argument with their driver. Her dutiful sister Lillian stood beside their mother.

They were starting late in the season for a trip to the western territories. They should have left as soon as the grass was up in Missouri, but Mother had her own ideas and functioned on her own time expecting the rest of the world to follow. They were lucky to find a driver at all, and their arrival two weeks after the planned departure date hadn't pleased him. The wagon was another bone of contention between her mother and him. Clara had been horrified when she first saw it yesterday afternoon. It was not the stage with plush seats she had requested, nor was it a Conestoga wagon that most families used to travel west. The vehicle was a large four-wheeled farm or military supply type wagon. It had been adapted with a rib-like frame built over the top and canvas covering the frame, resembling a Conestoga, but shorter, wider and square. The driver's seat was a simple wooden bench, set outside the canvas covering and higher than the main body. Two sections of canvas hanging behind the seat were tied down and nearly joined except for a small gap. The tied-back flap of canvas on the front right side and two wooden steps built to aid the ladies climbing aboard, served as an entryway.

The driver, her mother explained to her children when she returned from her first meeting, never intended on taking this trip by stage according to her written instructions. He said she was a foolish woman who didn't know what she was talking about. She said he was terribly rude and rough and she didn't know what she was going to do.

The contraption was ugly, Angela thought now as she examined it, but it did seem more reasonable than a coach. The luggage would never have fit in a smaller conveyance; they would have had to hire another wagon for their things. The two, her mother and the driver, had been arguing for more than an hour outside the hotel, her mother doing most of the speaking, the driver replying with terse one-word statements.

How could her uncompromising, proper Bostonian mother endure this journey? The journey? What about the destination? The wilds of some western frontier? What was her father thinking when he invested in some piece of untamed land? She remembered seeing him

4

at the head of the dinner table, seeing the excitement light his eyes and color his cheeks as he spoke of the wondrous possibilities of this growing country. Did he actually intend on taking his family to dangerous primitive places? Angela only knew that no trace of fatigue could be seen on him even after a long day of seeing patients, when he'd launch into stories of a new world in the West. Her mother would never have agreed to go. But, here they were five years after his passing; grimly facing this voyage into the unknown, ill equipped mentally and physically, only resigned. Ben, who had been three, barely remembered his father. Lillian would never dream of leaving Boston. He had planted the seeds of interest in his middle daughter however. She sought out newspaper clippings and journals of people who had traveled west and memorized every detail of the accounts.

Only recently could Angela think of her father without flashes of intense pain. She remembered being in his office alone a few days after the funeral, numbly going through his things when a silent scream gripped her. It felt as though iron bands clamped around her middle were tightening and tightening. Her mouth opened in a scream of anguish, but no sound came from her. She was screaming, screaming from her very center, but no sound reached any ear save heaven's. For a year she pretended her father was away on a trip. She wrote him letters, which were now tied up and hidden away in a trunk of her private things. Her rational mind knew he was gone, but she wouldn't listen to it. She went about the world insensitive to the world until one year after her father's death. Walking one beautiful spring morning the clear call of a phoebe bird cut through her dulled senses. This one voice spoke directly to her calling insistently until she stopped to listen. She suddenly believed in her heart that this voice calling to her was her father's spirit, or an echo of his spirit. He had loved nature, always pointing sights and sounds out to her. It was beautifully calling her to live, to feel. The numb suspension ended and the real pain began. She allowed the memories to slip into her thoughts. Sometimes they were a comfort, sometimes hugely regretful. She began to think that she must do something, something important with her life to what purpose she wasn't sure, maybe to honor her father to keep his spirit going. She took many of his medical books, hid them in her room and studied them in secret.

When he was young Angela's father had reluctantly accompanied a free-spirited friend Adam Barnard, to hear Dr. Whitman speak. Dr. Whitman, some years back, was organizing what he called the "Oregon Emigration Society." He was stirring up people from Massachusetts to travel the trail along the Platte River to the rich land in what would someday be the Oregon Territories. Her father, a doctor who loved learning and exploring new things, was immediately fascinated. His interest did not wane. Later, when he shared stories with his family he assured his wife that this would some day be a well-used trail, after all the fur trade organized by John Jacob Aster (a name he hoped would impress her) had established posts along the route. At first Clara would not hear of these wild stories, but Angela, an inquisitive youngster, who liked the excitement and the animation with which her father told them, would ask questions in order to bring the subject up at dinner. Eventually he and Adam Barnard (who Angela never met because her mother did not approve of him) formed a partnership. The partner went out and claimed the land. They compromised on the location, the partner wanted to go still further west, but he left the trail finding suitable green land off the Bear River. He was to establish a ranch and maintain it. Maybe her father had hoped to move his family there. He talked hopefully about the railroad expanding and complained that Boston was no longer a healthy place for a family. The streets were crowded and the air was heavy with soot and ash. Sometimes Angela felt little prickles on her arms when she thought about this journey and her eyes filled with bittersweet tears feeling they might very well be fulfilling her father's dream. Would he be pleased or would he be scared for them doing it without him?

She saw her mother standing rigidly straight, her dark hair coiled up behind her neat little black hat, her wool dress, also black had lace at the collar and sleeves and was hemmed with a ruffle, elegant, yet proper. Lillian standing behind her wore a soft gray print dress with a high lace collar, long ruffled skirts. A sweet bonnet framed her delicate face and she wore lace gloves.

Clara was pointing out all the trunks, belongings and furniture she still wanted to bring. In Boston the man who made the arrangements and hired the driver had explained to her that it was not possible to carry so much baggage because of room needed for necessary supplies. Many boxes were taken and put in storage, yet there were still too many. Angela looked at their remaining possessions, neatly piled beside the dusty street. Then she studied the driver with keen observance that sometimes embarrassed her sister, who would chide her not to stare. He had thin white hair partially tucked behind his ears; long strands strayed forward. She smoothed her own hair back self-consciously, frontier or not, her mother would not tolerate her children looking less than respectable. The man wore a flannel shirt that had most likely been blue, but now was faded gray, suspenders, dark woolen pants and worn boots. Would this little crooked legged man be able to see them safely through uncivilized lands? She had noted that he moved stiffly on bowed legs with a bent spine as he pointed at the luggage. Oh, this was going to be difficult. More of their things would have to be put in storage or sold. Was there any trustworthy place to store them here in this gateway to the West?

They had lost so many things one by one. Her father, a generous man with his fees, had not made a lot of money in his practice. Angela heard her mother complaining that her father was only a doctor, not born to wealth and he did not leave them secure. She told her daughters she knew nothing of managing money, nor did she want to. It was vulgar to discuss money. In spite of her mother's tears and words there were always new things coming to the house and entertaining was not curtailed.

Also her mother had a beloved nephew who borrowed and borrowed from her, promising each time he'd pay back double with earnings he would make from investments. He would come to the house and they would talk in muffled tones behind closed doors. He had lived fashionably, as her mother's side of the family had been accustomed to. He was the youngest child of elderly parents and they both died; other relatives tired of his careless lifestyle and he had no one to turn to but Clara. Through gambling and extravagant living he drained both his inheritance and his aunt's investments.

Their father's office was rented, then sold, the same with the horse and carriages. Then jewelry and pieces of furniture disappeared and finally the house itself was sold. The Harrington's went to stay with generous relations, but her mother's pride could not endure charity for long. After meetings with her dead husband's lawyer she discovered that all they had of substance was the land, her father's dream - ranch.

7

The adventurous partner had long since abandoned the property. He had at least left a letter, complaining about encroaching civilization and stating his need to move on. Staying in one place for long did not suit his wanderlust heart.

David Harrington's brother, a doctor like himself, but not burdened by a family had gone to see the land some years back. Finding the territory to his liking and his services greatly needed, he stayed, helping start a young township. The lawyer advised Mrs. Harrington to write him and have him hire someone to make the home ready and manage the land.

Clara's sapphire necklace caught the sunlight and flashed. Angela wondered if she should tuck it under her collar. This did not seem to be a place where people wore gems. There were many sinister looking characters around this town. And shouldn't they dress more like the women she saw walking to the general supply store and riding in wagons with their families? They wore looser, shorter skirts coming to the tops of their sturdy boots. Their skirts provided greater freedom of movement for climbing in and out of wagons. The blouses they wore were light colored and a hardier material than what the Harrington women wore. The blouses appeared comfortable and free for this heat. Her mother had insisted they purchase hats, bonnets more like, to protect their faces from the sun. Still in his dark city suit, Ben was happily unaware of the passing children turning to look at him twice.

One of the four large workhorses stamped his feet impatiently at flies biting his legs and the wheels of the wagon rolled. Where was her brother? It would be just like him to be exploring under the wagon.

"Ange!" he put a hand on her shoulder as he jumped alongside her before she could move to look for him. "Did you know there's someone in there?"

"Ben, lower your voice," she said.

She turned toward her mother and the driver and saw a large-bellied man was now standing with them. Other passengers? She hadn't thought of that. How crowded would they be? When they were first making arrangements she had hoped there might be other girls, not silly loud shrieking girls that would be dreadful. Clara would need to be sandwiched between Lillian and herself or Ben. She couldn't

8

stand to have strangers touching her. Ben? Would he sit still or would he aggravate the other passengers with his questions and fidgeting?

The new man's throaty voice carried clearly to her. A large, heavyset man, he stood legs apart, hands on his hips, his wavy, sandy hair slicked back neatly trimmed. His shirt was flannel like the driver's only new with a vest over it. He also wore loose dark woolen pants, his held up with suspenders and a belt. On his feet were tall boots. He and the driver wore the western hats men seemed to wear here, the kind Ben had pleaded with his mother for, but was stuck with a more moderately brimmed hat; Mother insisted he would be a gentleman even on the frontier.

The large man took her mother's hand to his mouth and then Lillian's. His movements, voice and appearance, all seemed big and loud, as if deliberately calling attention to himself, but this kissing of the hand was incongruous with his other gestures. Ben hopped down from the step and ran around to the other side of the wagon.

"Angela," her mother called.

"This is my daughter Angela," Clara calmly introduced her to the two men. The driver inclined his head and toddled away without a word. Angela got a glimpse of a leathery face and a bit of blue sparkling through the wrinkles.

"That is our driver," her mother said. "He calls himself Lou."

The large loud man thrust his hand at her; "I am Barton Finch, Miss. Delighted to be traveling with such lovely company."

Angela in her surprise at the suddenness of his gesture drew back.

Her mother's pale cheeks flushed at her behavior. "I am sorry Mr. Finch. My daughter Angela is … shy."

He laughed humorlessly. "As I was saying, you are in good hands with and old guide like Lou here and myself, seeing as I'm a lawman. No need to be shy or nervous."

"You are a lawman?" Clara looked hopeful.

Looking up from the tips of her toes, Angel saw him take a piece of paper out of his shirt pocket. He ceremoniously unfolded it and handed it to her mother who glanced at it politely, but did not seem to understand it. Her brow wrinkled faintly in question.

"Yes Ma'am, I guess you could say I work independently for the government of the Territory of Oregon. You know there is a governor now? You see, outlaws figure it being newly settled country, they can

9

do whatever they want or hide out. Men like me keep the territories safe for settlers like yourselves. I seek out and find outlaws, then transport them to circuit judges for their fair trials."

The driver made a sort of "humph" sound.

Angela, noticing the red, puffed face of the speaker, wondered if he was a drinker.

"It will be a great comfort to have you as a fellow traveler. Won't it girls?" her mother was saying.

"Oh yes indeed," Lillian said, stepping forward with a brilliant smile.

Angela saw her mother's posture had indeed softened with relief and she regretted her own negative reaction to the man.

Lou grunted and spat as he hoisted a trunk.

Ben reappeared. "Can I help Mr. Driver?" he asked cheerfully. "How are you going to get everything to stay in place? I read these wagons bounce and bang around. And there's no roads where we go. And we have to go up and down hills and through rivers. What if we have to gallop away from Indians?" As usual when he was excited, Ben gave no time for answers to his questions. His voice increased in tempo, loudness and pitch until he was interrupted by his mother's sharp, "Benjamin."

Lou simply ignored the boy's chatter and continued slowly, steadily loading trunks.

"Come stand by me. Let the driver do his job," his mother directed.

"This is my son, Benjamin," Clara introduced him. "Benjamin, this is Mr. Finch."

The man reached out and patted the boy's head.

Ben wandered back to watch Lou, who was now tying down assorted barrels and boxes with thick ropes and tightening the canvas. Angela heard her brother ask, "Who is in there?"

There he goes, imagining things and making up stories, she thought. She had seen no one. A little trill of fear passed through her mind. It was dark and dingy inside. What if Ben is right? What if there is a person in there? Why is he or she skulking in the shadows? She glanced back, half thinking to have a look for herself when Mr. Finch's voice invaded her thoughts.

10

"Now Ladies," he boomed. "Let me set your minds at rest concerning this trip. You will be completely safe with me."

"I'm certain now," Lillian said delightedly and clapped her gloved hands together.

The man smiled at her.

"Excuse me sir. Have you made this trip before?" Angela asked timidly.

"Angela do not interrupt," her mother said. "Do continue Mr. Finch. I apologize for my daughter."

Clara was relaxing more into her habitual ways, her gestures becoming more, in Angela's eyes, affected.

"Not at all, a ma'am," Finch said chivalrously, "a very good question from the young lady. Miss, I have been across to the territories more than a few times, even beyond our current destination."

"Do you know about Indians?" Ben asked. He was drawn back by the rapt attention his family seemed to be paying the man.

"Why yes, I'm quite familiar with savages. I've been privileged to accompany parties whose job it was to drive savages away from civilized settlements. I suppose you've heard many stories, but things have changed along these trails."

This talk of Indians was scaring her mother and sister. Her mother's spine appeared rigid again. Lillian was fanning herself and whispering, "Oh dear, oh dear." "As I was saying," he continued, dismissing the conversation pertaining to Indians, "I have made this trip many times. I am an expert in this business. I don't want to sound boastful, but after many years of observing others in my line of work I've figured just how to handle criminals my own way. Things go smoothly for me now. This particular one has been difficult." He gave a laugh under his breath to show how confident he was in his work, "But I have plans for every situation, every possible type of ruffian, including this one. I can make them farm dog obedient. Yep, I could get them to lick my hand."

The women listening attentively understood nothing of the significance what he was saying. They watched his face with puzzled expressions. Slowly a heavy feeling began creeping into Angela's limbs. Was he preparing them for something? She looked at her mother's face, but saw no signs of suspicion, only trust.

"Yeah, this one's been tricky, but I have my ways of making them submissive."

"Mr. Finch, are you saying you'll be picking up one of these criminals on our way?" Angela asked, finding voice for her fears. She was interrupting again. This time her mother didn't correct her. Instead Angela heard her breath catch.

"As I said," Barton blustered on, "You ladies have nothing to worry about. I'm not picking one up on the way." He shook his head as if weary. "Can you believe it? I had to drag the cur all this way, from where we caught him out in the territories in early spring. I dragged him east to find a judge. I get nearly to Missouri and figure I'll just take him to a judge here in Independence. The judge says he's too busy, not his problem. Now I have to haul him back to the territories and wait for a circuit judge to come through and try him. The fellows who want him brought to trial are paying me a bonus when he's hung. They'll pay extra if they can witness it, but I was so tired of dragging him around I thought I'd just be rid of him and return to civilization myself. Didn't work out that way. I didn't know how I was going to get a ride back out and here you people are going in the same direction."

"Do you mean to say we are traveling with a criminal?" Clara asked. Her voice lost its customary authority.

Ben leapt in the air with excitement. "A criminal? Where? Is it a robber? A murderer? What? Is that who I saw in there? Is it?" As he turned to run and see the curiosity in the wagon Barton Finch grabbed his arm.

"Boy, don't you go near my prisoner!"

The aggressiveness of his action stunned the Harringtons. Angela reached out and put protective arms around her brother.

"I apologize," Barton said. He quickly recovered his open-faced expression. "It's a matter of the deepest importance that everyone, I mean everyone, follow my orders about the outlaw. You'll be perfectly safe under my expert management. I've developed a system for controlling these varmints. I may even publish my ideas for others in the business, if I can find the time."

Ben's eyes recovered their curious gleam. Angela met his gaze and frowned at him, trying to impress upon him the seriousness of what was happening here. Lillian suddenly went limp. Angela and

12

Mr. Finch caught her elbows and led her to the wagon, sitting her on a barrel.

"Ma'am, I have complete control," he said to the anxious Clara while fanning Lillian with a handkerchief. "You see he's been in there all this time and I have no fear of him escaping. My methods are foolproof. I swear he doesn't dare so much as breathe without my say so."

Clara was making little sighing noises.

"You won't have to so much as look at him. And he won't look at any of you. He wouldn't dare. Honestly it's a science the way I control him. I don't have to be near him to keep him in order; he's that cowed."

Angela's legs felt wobbly.

"We must find another ride," Clara said weakly. "I cannot have my young son and daughters traveling with some sort of villain."

For the first time Barton Finch looked agitated. "You ... can't do that ma'am. There are no more rides to hire at this time in the season. You'll be getting into winter conditions if you wait for another. As it is, we're cutting it close. Isn't ... isn't that right Lou?"

Lou, who was resting on the wagon's steps squinted at them and nodded.

Clara's head ached. Whatever could she do? They could not go back. It would be expensive. What would they go back to? Could they stay here? It did not look like the sort of place where decent people made their homes. She did not have money to waste on rented rooms for an extended length of time. A good portion of what was left had gone to the expense of this trip. She'd never dare ask the driver to return his fee. She could just see him slapping the reins on the horses' backs and trotting off with their money.

Barton Finch took her hands. "Ma'am, I promise you this outlaw won't be any trouble to you at all. If there is any sign of mischief I can't handle I'll put an end to him, money or not." Saying this he pushed back his vest and showed the handle of a gun tucked under the folds of his shirt in a leather holster. "Lou, he's got a big old rifle up there by him and I've got one stowed in the back."

13

Guns? Criminals? Clara sighed, collecting herself. She looked at her daughters. Angela, she shared her father's fascination with horrid earthy things. Angela's mouth formed a smile to say, "It's fine mother. We'll be fine." Lillian sat on the barrel next to her. What would her fiancé's family think if they returned to Boston? Then they would know the dire financial straits of the Harringtons.

"Benjamin," she called her son to her. "You must listen very carefully to Mr. Finch. You must do exactly what he says concerning the criminal and stay away from him."

"It might be a good lesson for the young tyke," Barton said hopefully. "He'll see what happens to boys who go astray. Believe me, watching me in my work should convince any young rascal to stay on the straight and narrow. And he seems a bit of a restless one."

Angela's eyes jumped to the man's face as he said this. Was he seeing Ben as one of his future charges? Was this his way of implying that her brother wasn't well behaved? True, he was mostly left to his own devices, or she was given the responsibility of watching him. Ben didn't take insult from the man's remarks in fact he seemed awed by him.

"Mr. Finch, will you teach me how to catch robbers and bad men? Can I help guard him? Maybe I better have a gun too."

Barton smiled with his teeth at the boy, but he was looking at Angela. She realized she had been staring and looked away.

Chapter 2

"Where in the annals of history can we discover a movement of this scope, essentially conducted by individual initiative... And in a world which seems to move steadily toward greater suppression of the individual, when shall we look upon its like again."

George R. Stewart - on the westward emigration of the people of the United States

Lou was creakily climbing the wooden ladder-like steps leading to his bench. He bent to sit and spat brown liquid over the side. "Git in," he growled.

"Oh dear," Clara said, "I specified no driver who drank, but I never thought of spitting. I will have to speak to him at our first stop."

"I don't think you should mention it Mother," Angela suggested. They were in an unfamiliar world, yet her mother seemed to think she could direct everyone as if she were queen and they her servants.

"I hope that driver secured everything. This contraption will bang and bounce terribly. We will be all bruises." Clara complained nervously as they hurried to the wagon.

Before the opening Barton explained that the prisoner was sitting to the left of the doorway. He said not to look at nor speak to his charge, who was asleep anyway. "I keep them too weak to cause any trouble, so mostly they sleep."

He explained how they would enter: First he would escort Clara to the same side as the prisoner, but further down, this way she would not have to see him. He himself would sit between her and the offender. Lillian would be across from her mother, then Angela and Ben. Ben was delighted, knowing from the seating arrangement he would have the best view of the outlaw, but he managed to stay silent as instructed by his mother. Barton backed up the two steps then

15

squeezed himself in the small opening from which he offered Clara
his hand. She held back, so Angela took his outreached hand to climb
in first and find her place within the shadows. Her throat closed, she
bunched up her skirts in her free hand and cautiously stepped up each
plank. He walked backwards, holding her arm firmly. "Watch your
step," he said lowly as she was about to place a foot inside. In the
dusky light and her nervousness she thought she saw something on
the floor and carefully stepped over it, sliding deeper into the recesses
to sit down against the opposite wall. Barton squeezed past her, barely
avoiding her feet. She could see nothing for a moment except the
bulky shape of his departing back. The air was dull and smelled
sourly. She tried to breathe through her mouth only.

As her eyes slowly adjusted she could see blankets covering the
floor; they smelled of horses. The stronger odor permeating the
interior reminded her of the times she'd accompanied her father to
poor areas of the city to attend to the medical needs of some of his
charity patients. It was the smell of stale sweat and urine. She put her
hand on the canvas to feel possible openings for air and light.
Barton's shape was blocking the light once more. He was assisting
Lillian now. She prattled nervously and minced her way saying, "Oh
dear, Oh my." After settling her, he left to escort their mother.

Straining to see, Angela could just make out a jumble of shapes if
she looked along the floorboards where the light came through under
Barton's legs. She could see the outline of his legs, one of her
mother's little pointed shoes and what looked to be a foot coming
from a leg extending out of the shadows on the opposite wall. Clara
entered grasping both of Barton's forearms and looking neither left
nor right, only staring straight into his face.

What happened next was confusing. There was a noise, a
breathless gasp of, "ahhh." A dark shape stretched upwards and
shadows flailed. Clara screamed. Barton pushed her back with one
arm and with the other lashed out at the shape. Angela heard the dull
thud of a head hitting the wall, then only her mother gasping and
Lillian crying, "What is it? Mother?" The shape was motionless.
Frozen to her spot against the wall briefly Angela recovered and
reached to help her mother. Clara huddled in her place opposite
Angela. Mr. Finch was breathing heavily. He sat beside Clara with a
loud thump. Angela moved over to put her arms around her crying

16

sister. The big man leaned close to Clara. "Mrs. Harrington, are you hurt?"

"Shakily she accused, "I thought you said … everything … under control. I stepped on something. It was horrible."

"I'm sorry, ma'am. You must have stepped on him and startled him. You will remember I warned you to mind your step."

"Mother, Lilly, Ange! Are you all right?" Ben called. "What's wrong?" His anxious face peered in.

"Excuse me just a moment ma'am while I fetch your boy," Mr. Finch said. He patted her arm then made his way to where the boy and Lou were looking in.

Barton kept himself between the boy and the slumped figure and guided him to his place. Angela slid from her sister and mother to sit next to Ben. For once he was speechless and still. Regaining her dignity, Clara smoothed her skirts and took a breath as a prelude to speaking.

Finch jumped in, "Ma'am, honestly if you all just do as I say everyone will be fine. I cautioned you to watch your step. It appears you stepped directly on him. He was startled is all. He wasn't going after you."

Then why did you strike him? Angela thought.

"Well," Clara was shaken, but indignation was replacing the fear, "you assured us that there would be no trouble that we'd hardly know he was here. We certainly know he is here. What violence!"

Angela braced herself for a confrontation, but at first puffed with insult, Barton seemed to deflate. She could see him in a thin stream of dusty light. He smiled and said, "I am terribly sorry. And again I say there will be no more trouble from him. See? He wasn't attacking you. He doesn't know you are here. He doesn't even know where he is."

To emphasize this he grabbed the back of the prisoner's head and pulled it up by his hair. The head lolled back, he was quite evidently unconscious. Angela gasped and Ben leaned forward curiously.

. . .

17

Can't move, can't open my eyes or lift my arms? Heavy, everything feels heavy. All sensation deadened. Not all. The drum beating in the leg won't stop. Thud, thud, thud, no end.

Then suddenly, the leg explodes piercing the benumbed world. Grabbing for it, his head is knocked back and the relieving blackness returns.

The driver startled everyone by shouting something unintelligible down through the opening behind his bench. He had climbed back to his seat. Whatever he said must have been about being underway. They heard the slap of the reins on the broad backs and the wagon began to sway noisily forward. They all grasped the sides to steady themselves. Angela felt about the canvas once more to find an opening however small it might be to ease the closed - in sensation. She did find a hole in a seam where she could see through to the bright outside. Her mother was sniffing distastefully and fussing with the blankets. "When we stop, we must get some of our own blankets and pillows from the trunks," she told them.

Lillian was crying softly. Ben was staring across at the outlaw.

"Ben," Angela nudged him.

"I understand you are from Boston," Mr. Finch said casually. "I haven't been back East in years. What brings your family this way?"

Angela breathed more easily as her mother and their companion started conversing. Lillian joined in with names and places familiar to her, stopping now and then to fan herself and exclaim she was going to be ill. Clara paused frequently to frown and sniff at the uncomfortable surroundings. Barton sympathetically acknowledged that ladies such as they were not accustomed to traveling like this, although this was luxurious compared to his past trips. He described how he would do things differently if he were in charge of this journey. How seats with cushions could be designed along the sides or furniture could be nailed down rather than lashed together uselessly in the back storage area. But, this was not his line of work; his line of work was altogether different. These lands where they were headed to were newly declared territories, he and others like him would keep these lands clear of troublemakers. His descriptions distracted the two women from their discomforts.

Their voices blended to background noise. Angela examined the interior more closely. She saw Ben leaning forward, oblivious to all

18

others, gawking at the person fallen against the far side. She followed the line of his intensive study. The head of the figure rolled slowly from one side to the other with the movement of the wagon. Long shallow breaths were coming from him, and then they changed to sharp catches. He was regaining consciousness. With an excruciatingly slow effort he leaned over, taking his outstretched leg in both hands, he carefully repositioned it. His head seemed loose on his neck, long dark hair hung down hiding his face. From his half sitting, half-slumped position he rubbed the calf of his right leg. Angela's mother caught the movement from the corner of her eye, her voice faltered then she continued, deliberately not looking in that direction.

"Mr. Barton?" Ben spoke, not taking his eyes off the criminal. "I think his leg is hurt." Barton not pleased to have his discourse with the charming ladies disrupted answered curtly, "That's right boy, it's broken."

"Broken?" Angela gasped.

"Oh, your mother didn't do it. I told you this one gave us a hard time arresting him. Didn't I?"

"His leg got broke when you arrested him? He put up a big fight?" Ben was caught up in the story.

Seeing he had sparked keen interest, the lawman was only too happy to pick up the thread of the story. "He did. He was fast too. Took five of us to hold him and he still got away a couple of times. There was only one way to stop him or he would have been gone again. He was mighty determined."

"What did he do? Is he a murderer?" Ben leaned towards his new hero, his eyes aglow.

Finch chuckled patiently, "No, no."

"What did he do? Rob a bank?"

Finch answered in a formal tone, "He is in my custody for kidnapping and being a horse thief."

"What will happen to him?"

"He'll have a trial, then they'll hang him." Barton said emphatically.

"Hang him?" Ben's mouth was open in amazement.

"That is enough on this matter," Clara broke in, "Benjamin you will have nightmares. We will leave this subject to our expert."

19

"Thank you ma'am," Barton beamed and pulled his stout torso a little taller.

The wagon rocked roughly and they all braced themselves. The injured man's breath escaped abruptly at the jarring, then his body sank sideways, unconscious again.

"Can I be your partner? Can I help guard him?" Ben began as soon as equilibrium was established. "Are you a sheriff or something?"

"Benjamin, it is a far too dangerous a matter to involve a boy," his mother responded. Barton chuckled, patted her hand and said with a wink, "Sure the young fellow can help. On the condition you do as I say and don't mess with him when I'm not supervising. Remember I've made a study of this management of criminals, like a doctor studies medicines and the workings of the body."

"My father was a doctor. I can do it. I can help. Can I have a gun?"

"Certainly not," his mother said. "Enough of this, you are giving me a headache."

"Ben look," Angela said, coming to her mother's rescue. "You can find places where the canvas doesn't quite come together and see outside. Maybe you and I can observe changes in the landscape as we travel. Let's see what kind of animals there are."

Ben was reluctantly diverted.

Angela showed Ben the larger opening she had made in the seam of the canvas with her fingers. When he put his eye to the hole, she fell into her own thoughts. *What is wrong with me? Why does Mr. Finch make me so uncomfortable? It's good to have a big strong man aboard; the driver looks rather old and unsteady. Something bothers me about this man. He changes rapidly from one demeanor to the next. I think my mother critical of people, and here I am looking for reasons to dislike the man, I'm no better then her.*

She took a turn at the window hole. Blinding sunlight mingling with dust kicked up by the horses hindered her view. Occasionally a rider or another wagon could be made out as they passed. Her mind wandered back to Barton Finch's charge. *How did his leg get injured? The explanation seemed odd. In a struggle how would a leg get* broken? A hand, arm or shoulder injury while being restrained made more sense. She wondered also about the crimes. Kidnapping? Who did he kidnap? Some poor woman or child? Why? She shook her head at herself. *I'm as fanciful as Ben. Too much reading of silly fictional novels.* She was irritated with herself and wished she'd kept out some books on medicine or articles on westward travels, to pass the time.

They had traveled for a half a day when their driver pulled out of the wagon wheel ruts into a field. He set the breaks, climbed down and began preparing buckets of water and feedbags of oats for the horses. Barton Finch carefully assisted everyone outside. The prisoner didn't stir as they tiptoed by. He lay in the same position as he had for the past few hours. Every so often a lurch of the wagon had slid his body to the side and Barton would shove him back against the wall.

Ben ran about happily free now. It was a great relief to be on solid ground and move around at will. Barton Finch, leaning against the side of the wagon, lit a pipe. After the ladies found a discreet place to relieve themselves Clara shaded her eyes, unsure of what to do, where to go.

"Shall we sit under that tree and have something to eat?" Angela asked.

Her mother answered, "Yes, first let's ask the driver to get blankets for sitting not those dirty blankets from the wagon, some of ours."

"I'll get them. He seems to be occupied with chores."

Happy to have a purpose, Angela went with her mother and sister to inspect a little grove of trees. Then she called Ben and together they went to the back of the wagon where the canvas came together. He climbed in following her directions and found the blankets. After spreading the coverings on the ground they set out baskets of food. They had biscuits, a little butter, milk, jam and strawberries. Angela's mother served the meal. Mr. Finch thanked her heartily and praised the food. The driver nodded his thanks and took his tin plate to sit, his back against a tree.

This playing hostess, she could do well Angela noted, but she worried that in general her mother and Lillian still seemed to expect others to do for them. How would they adapt to this new life? Not that

21

she had any experience either, but she did not love the city life and had some hope and excitement along with the anxiety. She would miss the changeable Boston weather, the tangy smell of the ocean and the light feel of the salty mist on her skin.

Mr. Finch 's chin dropped to his chest and he snored. The driver pulled his hat down over his eyes. Ben played in the grass nearby. Angela closed her eyes and stretched out her legs, lulled by the cheerful hums and chirps of crickets and birds. She woke when the driver stood up and began to put away the horses' buckets. The Harringtons took this as a signal it was time to pack. They did not doubt for a moment that he would leave them behind if they tarried. Angela gathered the tin pails, cups and baskets while her mother and sister shook out the blankets. Mr. Finch rose laboriously then walked around the trees studying the ground until he found a large fallen limb. He tested it for size and strength. Ben, who had disappeared for a while exploring, reappeared from the vicinity of the wagon. Angela handed him the pails to pack. Turning to gather the remaining supplies, she thought Ben would need closer watching. His curiosity about the criminal might get the best of him. She was on her way to the wagon with her arms full, when Lou took her burden from her without a word. This helpful gesture from a man she'd assumed was an enemy of sorts surprised her.

"What's the stick for?" Ben asked Mr. Finch.

"It's a walking stick, boy," he replied as he offered an arm to Clara and Lillian.

"I'll get one too!" With a shout the boy was off to find his own walking stick.

Lou stood waiting by the steps as Barton Finch helped each of the apprehensive women inside. There was no incident this time. Ben came running back with his stick.

Going from the bright sun to the interior of the wagon made for difficult visibility again. Angela's window hole let in a dusty trail of light, as did other openings. The slumped shape showed no sign of movement. Lou climbed stiffly to his seat, said something back to the passengers and off they started.

Frequently the wagon lurched so hard they all grabbed the sides for support. Lillian complained each time with cries of "ouch and oh," and bunched blankets for softer cushioning. Ben, who had amused himself with his walking stick for a while, began to fidget, kicking one leg, then another with hard thumps. Barton frowned across at him. As for herself, Angela sympathized with Ben's restlessness. It was a bruising achy ride. Searching for ideas to occupy her mind, she thought of keeping a journal. Although it would be impossible to write while traveling this way, at least she could plan what to write later. She reminded herself to get the paper and ink she'd packed with her books when they stopped for the night. The family's fellow traveler dozed off quite soon in spite of the rough rocking. While Clara and Lillian closed their eyes and rested as best as they could, Angela told Ben of her idea. He thought it was a great plan.

"I'm going to start a journal too."

"Yes, like the great explorers' journals," she encouraged him. "Like Lewis and Clarke, we could record our observations."

"I could write about Indians."

Angela tried to change the topic while glancing at her mother who was sleeping and didn't hear Ben's chosen subject. "Or you could write about the wildlife we see."

"Yeah, like wolves, coyotes and bears!"

Angela began her journal in her mind. Ben aimed his stick at the prisoner, pretending it was a gun. He was busy practicing various shots, shutting one eye, squinting both, holding the stick rifle out on straight arms or on his shoulder, when the outlaw's head moved up slowly off his chest with a soft moan. Both hands moved to the bad leg, long hair hanging about his face and shoulders. Ben froze. He glanced around, everyone was sleeping, even Angela.

"Don't move. I've got my gun on you," he said lowly in the deepest voice he could muster.

There was no response. His curiosity stronger than his fear, he asked, "Can you talk?"

The man seemed aware that someone was speaking to him. Ben could see the shine of his eyes through the dirty stringy hair. He didn't move except for a slight lift of his head trying to locate where the voice was coming from.

"What does a broken leg feel like? Does it hurt? Did you know your head is bleeding?"

The outlaw put his hand slowly to the back of his head. He did understand. Encouraged, Ben scrunched forward on his seat. "Did you ever kill anyone?"

Was there a tiny sideways movement of the head?

"Did you really kidnap someone?"

This time, no question, there was a barely perceptible incline of the head.

"Who was it? A lady? A kid? A man?" Ben paused, waiting for a response.

"Hey! What are you doing?" Barton shouted.

At the sound of his voice the prisoner's body jolted.

"Oh! What is the matter? What is it?" Ben's mother awakened by the shout asked.

"I said what are you doing?" Barton Finch demanded of Ben.

"He was awake. I just asked him something." Ben was nonplused.

The lawman peered into the hidden face of his charge, looking for signs of alertness.

"Benjamin!" Clara gasped. "You understood you are to have nothing to do with that person. It is terribly important."

"I'm sorry. I was just asking him a question."

"You must obey instructions," his mother ordered severely.

"Yes ma'am," was the repentant answer.

Angela heard him grumbling under his breath, "I wish this was a real gun."

She glanced over at the prisoner who was collapsed, asleep or unconscious.

"Ben," she whispered, "This is not a game. That's a dangerous criminal."

Clara was turned to Barton. "I am not happy with this situation at all. Couldn't you tie him up or move him back with the furniture, not so close to us?"

"Well I could tie him I suppose, but honestly, you'll see as time goes how my methods make restraints mostly unnecessary."

About an hour later Ben nudged Angela and pointed with his stick. She saw the figure shivering in spite of the heavy hot air. "Mr. Finch, Mr. Finch I think our outlaw is cold," Ben called.

24

Barton turned away from Clara and Lillian to look. "No, he's not cold. He does this every afternoon."

Angela felt a quivery fear inside. "Excuse me sir, he isn't sick with anything contagious is he?"

Why was Finch taking these symptoms so lightly? Barton didn't hear her. But Ben persisted for her, "Why does he shiver in the afternoons?"

The lawman hesitated then leaned close to Ben and whispered something. Angela looked at Ben questioningly. He blurted out, "You mean he has to go? Should we stop? I kinda have to."

"No, we don't stop for him. You see it's part of my strategy. He's at my mercy for everything, food, water including his own er … Excuse me ladies, bodily functions."

"But what if he has an accident," Ben continued. "He already smells bad."

It wouldn't be the first time, Angela thought.

Clara tssked with disgust.

"Ooh horrible," Lillian turned away.

Barton laughed, "Nah, I don't think he will, not with ladies present." He grabbed him by the hair, twisting his head up in their direction. Angela saw the light of eyes through the hair before the head dropped when his captor released him. As they continued she could see his hands clenching and unclenching. The shaking became stronger and stronger until his very breath came out shakily. He moved his arms restlessly. She gazed out her window trying to avoid looking at him, her own anxiety growing. To calm herself she tried to think from a medical perspective. What would happen to a body under these conditions? Would systems shut down? What would her father say to these questions?

. . .

Voices? Somewhere through the fog he heard voices. He'd dreamed a voice was talking, asking questions. He could hear the sounds. Then words came to him. In the dream he saw a person. A boy? No dreams. Let the fog close in again. No, there would be no escape into the fog, not for a while. He knew it would get worse and worse until he ached and then the shakes would start. He'd fight it. He wouldn't give Finch the satisfaction. Here come the shakes. Hope he doesn't start nudging, making it harder to stay in control. Voices? His head was yanked up. Through the pain and shaking a word, "ladies." Outlines of people in the shadows? He'd thought Finch couldn't reach him, couldn't penetrate the dull aching numbness. There were women around? Was this another of Finch's punishments? The humiliation was being taken up a notch.

The sun was beginning to lower. Her face at the hole in the canvas seam, a soft breeze touched Angela's wet forehead, stirring her hair. When younger she used to imagine that an unexpected, refreshing breeze caressing her forehead on a hot summer day was the loving touch of God's hand. She turned back to the stuffy interior and just as she did they bumped to a stop. The prisoner was shaking hard by this time, his head thrown back, his arms wrapped around his middle. Ben jumped out before the others could get to their feet. Barton Finch offered Angela a sweaty hand and helped her out. Then he did the same for Lillian. They waited for their mother. From inside they heard her say, "Please take that man out first. I do not want to have to pass him."

There was the sound of movement.

"Come on you," Finch commanded as he backed out, pulling his charge's head and shoulders through the doorway. "Come on!"

Barton yanked him completely out. He collapsed on the ground just outside the wagon. Angela stared, shocked.

"How disgusting!" Lillian shrieked. She sidestepped away; her hands flew up to her mouth.

"Damn," Barton complained, stooping over his charge.

"Well too late for you. Saves me from having to drag you off somewhere." Finch dragged the body out of the way of the steps and there it lay in a crumpled heap.

"Well, what should we do now?" Clara said wearily stepping down, pretending not to notice the unconscious body on the ground.

Finch was walking off, his wide back to them.

"We'd better ask the driver."

They walked around to where the old man was unbuckling the horses' harness.

"Um, what would you like us to do?" Angela asked.

He raised an eyebrow at her. Continuing his work, he said in a craggy voice, "Do what you have to then git supper started."

Get supper? How exactly do you get supper out here? Angela asked Ben to take buckets to the river for water. She and Lillian spread blankets on a pleasant rise of the ground several yards from the wagon and got food from the supplies. They had to eat their fresh foods first, before they spoiled.

Mr. Finch strolled back. Watching him walk by the prisoner's still form without a glance, Angela had a horrifying vision. She saw the injured man laid out dead among their possessions, arms flopping with the motion of the wagon. She shuddered; sometimes she had these little visions, usually they didn't come to anything. She hurried to help Ben returning from the river with two sloshing buckets. Barton Finch dropped himself down on a blanket with a grunt.

"These days the Oregon Trail is well used," he informed them. "You see those wagon wheel ruts? It's a regular road now, not like it was. Folks had to make their own way then, no posts to stop at and re-supply, savages all along the way stealing and killing. There is many a grave along this trail."

"Please," Clara stopped him.

Too late though, Ben had already heard, "Really?"

He put down his bucket and sat by Barton. Clara put her hands up to protest.

"Ben, maybe you could see if our driver needs any help," Angela suggested.

He was putting hobbles on the horses so they could be free to walk around and graze.

"Sure!" Ben jumped up.

"Angela, I do not think that is a good idea," her mother remarked. "Our driver is being paid to do his job. I am sure he does not want a child in his way. Benjamin stay here."

When Lou finished with the horses he brought an armful of kindling and started a fire. Next, from the wagon he brought an iron frame and two black pots. He hung one over the fire and poured water into it. With a knife he pulled from his belt he cut the meat and

27

vegetables the women had set down haphazardly, letting the pieces fall into the water over the fire. He stirred everything around with a large ladle. Angela stood awkwardly nearby. When he paused she said, "I can do the stirring if you like." He put the ladle in her hand. When it was hot and the vegetables tender she and her mother dished the stew out for everyone. Lou lifted the pot off the fire and put on a smaller pot of water to boil for coffee. Angela observed all he did. Barton did not move from his spot on the blanket. They handed him his supper of stew, a biscuit and coffee. Angela dipped her cup in a water bucket. Lillian did likewise and gave a shriek, "There are things floating in my water!"

Angela looked into her cup and carefully picked out any objects, living or non. Delicious, she thought as the cool water ran down her dry throat. Ben finished eating quickly and while the older people were enjoying their coffee, he marched around the prisoner at a safe distance, pointing his stick. Barton glanced at the boy, every once in a while and smiled indulgently.

Angela worked up her nerve and asked, "Excuse me Mr. Finch, have you ever had a criminal die in your care?"

He looked at her quickly. "Die? No, I've never had one die."

"Would it matter if they died?" she asked. "I mean…"

"Matter? Yes, it would matter a great deal. I'd only get half my money."

"What would you do? Bury the body out here somewhere?"

"Oh no, I'd have to bring him along as proof. It's not like there is a judge or coroner to certify the fact." He looked at her with his face flattening with concern. "The gentleman who hired me would be very disappointed. He wants him brought to trial and punished."

Clara said, "There will be no body inside the wagon with us. I will not permit it."

Lillian was staring wide-eyed.

"No … no I'm sure I could devise something if I had to." He answered distractedly, not turning his gaze from Angela. "Why do you ask? You worried he won't make it? Is that it?" He laughed loudly. "Don't you worry Miss. He'll make it. He's a tough one."

Angela thought his laugh sounded nervous, "Without food or water?"

28

Clara shot her a look, telling her she was overstepping her bounds. She explained by way of an excuse for her daughter, "I'm sorry to say, Angela's father, the doctor took her to his office and on rounds. Now she fancies herself an expert on these things."

Angela's breath caught in her throat to hear her mother speak of times so important to her as something to apologize for. Barton smiled, but shifted his weight uneasily. "What, in your expert opinion, makes you think he could be dying, young lady?"

In spite of her embarrassment she couldn't stop herself from going on. "He's injured and the injury hasn't been treated, I'm guessing. He's not eating or drinking, so starvation is a possibility. The lack of water necessary for the body to do its work combined with the fact that he's not allowed to … relieve himself may cause serious internal problems." She stopped abruptly; realizing this was a long lecture to people who were her elders.

"Really, Angela." Her mother expressed her disapproval, and then she added hopefully, "It might be easier for us if he did die. Providing you could make some sort of cart for the body to be pulled outside the wagon."

Barton clearly did not like this idea. "No, no," he said, "I'd only get half my money. After all the trouble this one's put me through," he shook his head. "And the fellows he wronged are paying a bonus to see him hanged. I'm fully aware of the necessity of nourishment for human beings. I do feed him, Miss Doctor. Feed him every night. Just haven't got to it tonight. What with making sure you ladies are all settled." He stood.

Ben, who had been keeping his self-appointed sentry duty from a safe distance saw his partner standing and ran to his side. "When is he going to wake up?" he asked.

"You want to see how to feed a prisoner?" Barton asked.

"Yes sir!"

"Watch carefully," he grinned. "It seems a simple thing, feeding a prisoner. But even in this simple thing you've got to show who has control."

"I do not think Ben should be involved in this," Clara said.

"He'll be safe, ma'am. You can come along too," he invited Angela, "satisfy yourself about his condition."

29

Maybe he isn't making fun of me, she thought. Curious and a little flattered to be involved, she followed. She expected her mother to forbid it at any moment, but Clara only warned her to watch her brother and stand back. When they came close to the prone figure, Barton handed Ben a biscuit saying, "Here, toss this at him."

With his stick in one hand, Ben threw the biscuit, hitting the man's head.

"Good shot boy. Come on, wake up!" Barton shouted, thumping the ground with his walking stick.

"Yeah, come on, wake up," Ben imitated his new hero's tone.

The head lifted off the ground. Lying on his left side he rose dazedly on his elbow and reached slowly to position the injured leg. Barton batted the food with his stick until it touched the prisoner's hand. He looked at it disinterested.

"Eat it or I'll force it down your throat," Barton ordered.

When the prisoner put his dirty fingers around the biscuit and shoved it in his mouth, Finch elbowed Ben confidingly. The man tried to swallow, his throat working hard; he tilted his head back showing his dirt-streaked neck. Choking and gagging, pieces of biscuit flew out of his mouth.

He can't swallow, Angela thought. "He needs water," she cried, and turned to get some.

"Here," Finch plunked down a cup he'd been holding.

The man snatched it up in both hands and still choking, gulped the water as best as he could. Breathing hard, he eased back down to the ground, shoving the last crumbs of biscuit from his fist into his mouth. Barton Finch clapped Ben on the back and turned back to the fireside, but Ben stood staring at the man on the ground. He looked at Angela.

"Why did he eat like that Ange? Why was he choking? Was it because he ate too fast?"

Sickened she said, "No he ate like that because he is starving. Remember how it feels when you are sent to bed without supper? This is one hundred times worse. Imagine how would you feel if all you ate all day was one biscuit? He can't swallow because he isn't getting enough water, his throat is all dry."

"You mean like when your throat gets really dry on a hot day like today."

30

"No, it's much worse than that. Not only does your mouth and throat feel miserable, but your body can't do the things it's supposed to do because it's not getting enough fluids. It can't cool itself, can't work like it needs to."

Ben was solemn. "It makes you sick, not having enough to drink?"

"Exactly," Angela nodded, "a person dies faster from no water than no food."

They walked back to pick up the supper things.

"Don't leave nothin' around to attract bears," Lou grumbled.

Angela had wondered about the sleeping arrangements. Would they all sleep cramped together in that stuffy wagon? Her questions were soon answered. While she and Ben packed up, Lou set up a small tent next to the wagon. "Men'll sleep here," he explained motioning with his chin.

The air was now soft, cool and smelled sweetly of the grasses. An evening bird sang out. The katydids and other insects had hushed with the setting sun. Clara rose and suggested they turn in.

"You people sleep in there if you want," Lou motioned with his chin towards the wagon. Angela dreaded going back inside.

"You want first watch?" Lou asked Barton Finch.

"It's probably not needed. Not like the old days when Indians would come and steal the horses or wolves would scare them off," he replied.

"Indians?" Lillian squeezed Angela's arm.

Clara stopped, before entering and asked Barton, "You will tie the criminal for the night? I will not be able to rest knowing a kidnapper is out there unrestrained."

"I'll be right here ma'am. He won't move anyway. You'll see in the morning. He'll be in exactly the same position."

She was about to insist when Angela said wearily, "Mother, he's too sick to move."

"What did you say Angela? I do wish you would speak clearly."

"He's too sick to cause any trouble," she repeated, guiding her mother up the steps.

31

Perhaps Mr. Finch's methods do work, she thought. I just wish I could be more at ease about him. As tired as she was, Angela could not fall asleep easily. The floor was hard through the blankets and she was bruised and tender. She lay her head down, but her eyes would not shut. In the dusky dark she could see her mother's outline sitting upright. Loud snores could be heard from outside, and inside Ben breathed evenly.

Chapter 3

"Pourquoi me Reveiller"
"Why do you wake me, o breath of
spring?
Tomorrow, into the valley, will come
the traveler,
recalling my former glory.
And his eyes will look in vain for my
splendor:
they will find only misery and grief!
Alas! Why do you wake me, o breath of
spring?"

"Werther" Act 3

"There's always a reason to feel not
good enough
And it's hard at the end of the day."

Sarah McLachlan

She must have slept because she opened her eyes to the soft morning light. Ben had been watching for her to wake. He whispered, "Ange, will you come out with me. I can't wait any more."

They slipped out into the summer morning celebration of bird songs. Barton and Lou's tent was a vague shape. Lou's silhouetted form was before it, sleeping his rifle on his lap. The outlaw lay, an unmoving lump on the ground. Angela and Ben walked to the creek, each carrying their own toiletry supplies: soap, a hairbrush and toothbrush, all wrapped in a towel. They startled a family of ducks. The mother scolded them and paddled off, her children all in a neatly disciplined row behind her.

"We better not stay long. Mother will be upset if she wakes to find us missing. Wash quickly," she urged. She dipped her hands in the quiet waters, washed her face and shook out her hair.

This was nice, just herself and Ben in the peaceful morning. She felt relaxed for the first time in days. He threw rocks in the river. With the brightening light, objects were becoming more sharply defined now. The light would be calling the people in camp from their slumbers; she and Ben had better head back.

The camp was indeed stirring. Lou fed the horses oats and stirred up the fire for coffee. After breakfast he caught the horses and led them in his stiff slow gait to hitch. Barton ate, stretched and did not help pack any gear. When they were ready to depart, he walked heavily over to the prisoner asleep on the ground. Ben followed happily, but stopped short when the lawman took his walking stick and jabbed the sleeper in his gut. He woke with a violent start, arms swinging blindly. By luck he caught the stick. Finch yanked it out of his hands and stabbed him harshly in the middle again. The prisoner doubled up on the ground. After a moment of no sounds, a long wheeze came from his lungs and he began gasping. Ben turned his eyes from the man to stare at Finch. The big man saw his expression and explained, "You don't want to get too close. You see how viciously he wakes? If I used a hand or foot he could have grabbed me and pulled me down. The stick gives me a safe distance. You see?"

The boy nodded, satisfied with the explanation. Angela watching in horror wondered if he woke "viciously" because of the manner in which he was awakened.

"Come on. Get up!" Barton Finch ordered. The prisoner pushed up on his arms, palms against the ground. Mr. Finch smacked him across the shoulders with the stick, knocking him flat again. He struggled pushing his hands against the ground, but didn't have the strength to rise. Barton pulled him up with a grunt of effort and half carried, half dragged him towards the wagon, thought better of it and took him off out of sight. Upon returning he shoved the prisoner's upper body through the opening of the wagon's canvas flaps. Then he shoved his legs and feet the rest of the way in. Angela and Ben heard the injured man's breath hiss through his teeth.

34

"Is it necessary for that person to ride with us?" Clara asked. She stood waiting to climb into the wagon.

"Please, he smells horrid," Lillian added wrinkling her nose. "Couldn't he ride with the driver?"

"I should keep him with me." Barton smiled at them. "After all this is my responsibility, not Lou's. I'm the one with experience handling prisoners."

Angela saw Lou roll his eyes. Apparently their driver was not impressed with the scientific methods of the lawman.

"I'll clean him up a bit as soon as I get the chance," Barton promised.

Underway, they were bounced and banged. Angela noticed the prisoner would mostly sleep except when jarred into consciousness by the wagon's rocking. What she could see of his skin between strands of hair and streaks of dirt was an unhealthy yellowish color. Finch's methods may have some merit, awful as they were to witness. He didn't have to tie this poor wretch, for he didn't appear to be a threat to anyone. Barton's confident assurances concerning their safety seemed to be true, she reasoned. The wagon jolted over rough ground, the passengers braced themselves. The prisoner rocked from side to side. When he stopped moving his breath came in little catches, his head lolled weakly against the wall behind him. Barton saw her studying his charge and ceased his enjoyable conversation with her mother and sister.

"What symptoms do you see now, Miss Doctor?"

Angela, busy with her own musings, ignored his sarcastic tone. "Pinch a little skin on his arm. Not hard, just a little. Now let go and see how long it takes to go back," she said.

He reached over and did as she suggested, skeptically watching the spot on the arm. "It's staying pinched up," he said.

She nodded. "That shows he isn't getting enough water. His color isn't good either."

"Really Angela, you are not a doctor. Enough of this," her mother broke in.

Abashed at her own audacity, she was silent. She saw Barton pinching his own arm and observing the result. "Doesn't mean anything," he muttered to himself.

35

Later that morning, Ben suddenly pointed to the prisoner. "Mr. Finch, I don't think he's breathing."

They all looked. His head lolled loosely against the wall as before.

"Of course he's breathing. What are you talking about boy?"

Angela leaned forward to see. Her stomach tightened. Ben was right; he wasn't breathing. Was this it then? Barton slid closer. Just then the prisoner took a long rasping breath and his head dropped forward. All was quiet inside except for the wagon's creaks and groans and the rapid breathing of the prisoner. The lawman felt about and found amongst his belongings a canteen. He pulled the prisoner's head back and forced water into his mouth. The man choked and moved his head away weakly.

Ben asked, "Maybe he could have just a little more food and water?"

"Well I can't have him dying on me. If I make any changes I'll have to watch carefully for any changes in his strength," Barton said.

Angela saw Mr. Finch's forehead was wet with sweat and he breathed as if he'd been running. He had really been worried. She relaxed with relief that they weren't riding with a dead man.

"If he has more to eat maybe he can talk more. Maybe he won't sleep all the time," Ben was thinking this would make for a much more interesting captive.

. . .

What and odd young woman, Barton Finch thought, different from the mother and sister, both charming. The mother is elegant even on a rough trip like this; the older daughter is a beauty. This other daughter is plain and outspoken. Not very sociable either, most times she seems to be somewhere else. She takes interest only in subjects that are not very attractive in a young woman. And that boy, he runs wild, does whatever he pleases, says whatever comes into his head. He needs the firm hand of a man. He shook his head to himself. And this damn troublemaker, his thoughts turned to his captive, better not die and cheat me out of my money. I'm getting too old for this line of work, need to settle down on some nice place. Could teach my methods to others and live in a home with a wife to take care of me.

That would be nice. I could use the money from this one to set myself
up in a little town. He better not cheat me out of my money and deny
me the satisfaction of watching him hang. He folded his hands across
his large belly and smiled to himself.

Gazing out her opening at the endless blue sky, Angela believed
that no human could reproduce the colors of nature no matter how
they tried to imitate her with paints and dyes. And the grasses below
with their infinite shades of greens, yellows and browns make an
intricate carpet that no weaver could match. The scenes passing by
lulled her to a doze until the wagon jolted to a halt for the half-day
break. The passengers stepped over the outlaw into the blinding sun.
He was asleep or unconscious, a state that he sank more deeply into
when the bone jarring motion ceased. Mr. Finch left him in the wagon
during the lunch break.

During the light midday meal, Angela brought out her journal and
started it between bites. The prisoner weighed heavily in her mind;
instead of writing a traveling log she found herself describing his
condition to her father. She also wrote descriptions of Barton Finch
and the driver.

"What's that you're writing Miss?" Mr. Finch's voice startled her.

Self-consciously she put her hands over her work. "A journal of
our trip," she replied, She hoped he would ask no more.

He nodded his head approvingly, his face serious, "you writing
about everything? I mean the people and all."

"I haven't quite decided. I've only just started. I've never written
one before."

"I'm going to keep a journal too," Ben said, remembering their
plans. "Will you help me start Ange?"

She was thankful to Ben for drawing the attention away from her
writings. "Let's find you some supplies to get started." She stood up
to take him back to the trunks.

"Hmm," Barton mused, "You got paper and pen. Do you have a
neat hand? You could be a help to me for recording my ideas on
prisoner control."

She smiled vaguely back at him and left with Ben. They found the
supplies by climbing through the back opening: a pen for writing,
some ink and paper. They were taking Ben's writing tools back to the
blanket when Barton came to the wagon. Oh no, he wants to know

more about our writing, Angela thought, but he started up the steps a mug of water in his hand.

"He's giving the prisoner water. I'll help," Ben said losing interest in his journal already.

"No, you can help later. Let's start our writing."

"Will he be sick now? He's getting more water?"

"I don't think it will be enough to make him well, but it is not Mr. Finch's intention. I believe he wants him close to dying. How many cups of water have you had today?"

He thought, "Two this morning, four when we stopped. I was very thirsty. It's awfully hot here, no breeze like at home."

"Um, if you had just one cup of water today, how would you feel?"

"My throat would be scratchy."

Barton came back to the blankets, but not before helping himself to a double portion of biscuits and jam. Lou was dozing; hat over his face.

Ben wrote for all of five minutes, then ran off exploring after snatching a biscuit and heaping jam on it. Happy to be on solid ground and hypnotized by the hot sun, the others were dulled into forgetfulness about him. Approaching the wagon, he glanced back at the adults then he went to the horses' heads. They were munching oats in feedbags. He put his hand on the white stripe of a giant face and watched them chew rhythmically. He climbed the steps to the driver's seat still holding the food. After pretending to drive for a minute or so, he went down and through the parted canvas into the wagon, first with a backward glance at the adults. He slid on the seat of his pants until he was directly in front of the sleeping form and waited. The body was limp; head bowed towards the left shoulder, left leg bent the right resting on it. Ben held out the biscuit.

"Prisoner," he whispered. No response. He inched closer. "Hey don't you want to eat?"

The head straightened slightly, still down. Ben could see the light of his eyes. He reached for his stick, he'd left there. "Don't try anything, I've got my gun." He waved the stick.

The prisoner shut his eyes.

"No, don't go back to sleep. Look, I brought you something."

38

Ben thrust his hand with the biscuit toward him. He waved it about. Slowly the eyes seemed to see the food.

"Go ahead. Take it."

The eyes looked at Ben's face. He lifted his hand with the biscuit. Slowly a dirty scratched hand reached for the food, took it, stuffed it whole into his mouth, chewing quickly. He wiped his arm across his mouth and swallowed with effort.

"Aren't you afraid you'll get sick eating so fast?" Ben asked.

The eyes refocused on Ben, then the head slowly moved back and forth once.

"I knew you could swallow this time because I saw my partner give you a drink. Did you ever kill anyone?"

Again the slow movement of the head.

"Did you really kidnap someone?"

The head slowly tipped down in the affirmative.

"Wow," Ben whispered to himself. "Did you steal a horse?"

Yes, the head indicated.

"Are they going to hang you?"

The nod again, hair hanging down. Before he could recover to ask another question Ben heard voices.

"Benjamin!" His mother's voice, filled with panic made the man jump.

"Don't worry it's just my mother," Ben said.

He quickly climbed out shouting, "Here I am!"

They were looking off by the river and didn't see him leaving the wagon.

Angela was the first to reach him. Holding her skirts with both her hands, her hat swinging by its ribbons, she came running.

"Ben you frightened everyone. You cannot wander off like that."

"I'm sorry. I wasn't far."

Seeing her face, he truly felt bad for the fuss he'd caused. Their mother joined them, the muscles of her face tight with fear. Barton came, sweating profusely and too out of breath to say anything for a few seconds. Even Lou had been on his feet, scouring the horizon.

"That boy," gasped Barton Finch when he could talk, "needs discipline."

"You may be right Mr. Finch," Clara said. "I have been too easy on him. It is so difficult without my husband. A boy needs a father."

39

Angela wished her mother wouldn't mention her father, not in front of this person, who never knew him.

"Time to move on." Lou rasped at them.

"Angela," whispered Ben as they made ready to leave, "would father be angry with me?"

She saw tears in his eyes.

"No Ben, he was not much of a disciplinarian, but please be more careful."

During the afternoon's ride Mr. Finch and Clara lectured Ben on possible dangers to young boys: wild animals, falling into rivers and other such misadventures. Barton told stories of bear attacks and how he saw a man terribly maimed by one of these creatures. This seemed to upset Lillian more than Ben, so he changed to examples of wayward boys.

"You see what happens," he concluded indicating the prisoner. "It starts off with disobedience, not minding your elders and before you know it you've gone completely bad."

Ben listened soberly. He did not want to be sick from no food and water or have broken bones. He sat quietly for a long time, vowing to himself to follow the rules. Angela resented Barton for trying to scare Ben. This was not his place. Everyone was quiet for a while, lost in their own thoughts.

Rattling along Angela remembered apprehensively how the prisoner shook the afternoon before. She watched him from the corner of her eye; he had begun to shiver again. Would he make it to their stop? Would they have a terrible scene with Lillian shrieking and everyone staring? It was sad and pathetic to witness the poor creature's misery. As the afternoon went on, his condition didn't progress beyond shivering. She recalled Barton disappearing with him for a while in the morning. She wondered about his chances for survival. Could there be gangrene in his leg?

"Mr. Finch?" Ben asked timidly. "Mr. Finch, are you really going to hang the prisoner?"

"Not me, personally," he chuckled in reply. "He'll have a trial first. We're lucky to be in a great country like this, where even rotten souls such as this one can get a trial."

40

"But they'll hang him after the trial?" Ben continued, "because he did it?"

"Oh yes, he's guilty. He'll hang as justice dictates."

Ben mulled this over and then asked, "Why did he do those bad things?"

"Doesn't much matter why, he has to pay for his crimes."

"You reap what you sow," Clara added in agreement.

. . .

Jolted back to the ceaseless drum-pounding throbbing, he heard voices. The boy's voice again. Finch's loud words, "He'll hang."

Hang? Kill me now. His eyes closing again. In the blackness he saw Finch looking small, standing a long way down. Standing below him with a huge grin on his big red face, Finch was pointing up and shaking with laughter.

The afternoon and evening of the second day were the same as the first. When they finished the day's travel Barton Finch pulled the prisoner from the wagon and he collapsed on the ground, his breath escaping in a long sigh. Barton Finch lifted and dragged him out of sight this time. Then they returned Barton released him and he fell in a crumbled heap. The lawman sat himself in a shady spot to wait for the meal.

Angela, knowing a little more what needed to be done, prepared for the meal, directing Ben to help. Their mother was exhausted from the worries and strains of the past few days. She dished the meals and Angela passed the plates. Lillian was too emotionally and physically worn to do anything, but tidy her hair and dress as best as she could. Later, serving as Mr. Finch's assistant, Ben carried the tin cup of water to the prisoner, set it down and backed away. After watching his charge gulp it down, he reached for the biscuit Finch had thrown on the ground, inched forward with bent knees and handed it to the prisoner, who didn't look at it or brush the dirt off it before eating it.

"Here, I brought you another," Ben said when his partner looked away. He pulled it from his pocket.

41

The hungry man crammed it into his mouth and eased his head and shoulders down, but not before whispering a single word only Ben heard, "Thanks."

Angela fell asleep quickly despite the aches. She woke some time during the night realizing with dread that she needed to make a trip outside. They had talked of wild animals again that night during the meal. Disturbed by this information, Clara had told her children not to move about after dark unless accompanied by one of the men. Lou had mumbled from under his hat, "No need. Stay in pairs. Make noise if you're not right close by."

Now Angela sat up wondering if she should risk the trip alone. She was not about to ask one of the men to go with her. Ben, sensed someone was awake, sat up, felt around and touched his sister. "Ange?"

"Ben will you come outside with me?"

"Sure, I need to go too."

The stars filled the sky until it seemed more and more were being created as they gazed; softer stars just behind the brilliant glittering lights in the foreground. Angela had never seen the sky looking so immense, so filled with jewels generating their own light. The enormity of creation gave her a strange vulnerable feeling for the all-powerful force beyond earthbound life, yet part of everything.

"Watch out!" Ben warned.

She looked down to see that she was about to step on the prisoner's arm. His head was resting, cushioned on the upper arm, the rest outstretched. As she hopped lightly over it, her skirts brushed his face. He made a quiet noise, like a soft question or a sigh, and pushed himself up to a half sitting position. Angela grabbed Ben's hand and hurried away a few steps.

"You woke him up," Ben whispered.

"Sorry, go back to sleep," she said nervously over her shoulder.

The man on the ground, disoriented, not sure what woke him, saw two figures walking away. Had one of them spoken to him?

"That was a stupid thing to say," Angela spoke aloud to herself.

"No, it wasn't. You were just being polite. Mother says you should be polite to everyone," Ben reminded her.

"I do feel bad waking him. Sleep is the only relief he gets; I'm sure."

On their way back, giving the prisoner a wide girth, they saw he was propped up on his arm and looking in their direction. When they moved beyond where he was, Angela whispered, "Is he still watching?"

"Yeah."

Ben looked back before he put his foot on the step.

"He's lying down now."

Angela and Ben were the first of the family to awake to the wispy light. Something about early mornings triggered memories of special times when she would visit her grandparents. Rising from bed, she would take the steps down to the kitchen one stair at a time, savoring the sense of peace and comfort. She could hear her grandparents' voices in their cozy kitchen, warm and cheerful like the new day itself. Large glasses of milk, thick slices of bread and a small pitcher of sweet molasses were set on the table. Their smiles of greeting told her she was truly loved. No one else and at no other time in her life had ever made her feel so loved. Ben had never known their father's parents, hard-working people, who had made their own way. They were gone now.

She stepped out of the wagon, followed closely by Ben. Lou was up checking the horses. The brother and sister picked up a bucket to bring fresh water from the river where they were headed to wash. They carefully worked their way down the embankment. Ben pulled off his shoes and socks to wade. Angela scooped water to scrub soiled spots off her dress and then washed her face and hands.

Mr. Finch was just out of the tent stretching and fastening his suspenders when they returned. Their mother and Lillian were on the far side of the wagon brushing their hair and dressing. Lou had started the fire for coffee. They poured the water they carried between them into the pot and brought the rest to their mother and sister for washing. Clara's face was drawn, showing no signs of rest. Lillian helped put up her mother's hair in the tight coil she always wore.

"Angela, you will get calluses, let the men do the heavy lifting," her mother said.

43

Angela didn't bother saying that soft hands were probably not important, or possible, in frontier living. When they had breakfasted and were ready for the day's ride, Barton Finch approached his still sleeping charge with his heavy tread, walking-stick ready. Angela tensed for another stomach churning scene.

"Mr. Finch," Ben called from his chores, "You don't have to hit him. My sister and I, we ..."

Angela was alarmed for a moment that Ben was going to reveal their nighttime adventure.

"Ben, leave Mr. Finch to his own business." His mother took his arm. "Please, haven't you learned?"

Remembering the trouble he had caused the day before, he renewed his resolution to behave better.

Angela turned away from the impending scene. She heard the thuds, the prisoner's lungs' long wheeze trying to get air. In spite of herself, she turned and saw him doubled over. She felt nauseous. This time Barton didn't strike him again when he was slow to get up, for Clara miss-stepped while carrying two satchels back to the wagon, and with a cry she fell. Barton huffed and puffed to her side. Angela rushed to her and tried to convince her to remove her boot and stocking and soak the ankle she was rubbing. Clara would have none of that, even though Barton ordered Ben off to get water. Seeing there was nothing to be done, Lou turned away muttering something about "silly citified shoes."

After Barton helped her mother inside and Lillian followed, Angela looked for Ben. He wasn't far this time. She saw him by the prisoner, who had got himself to a sitting position and was looking up at Ben. She walked cautiously closer, ready to pull her brother out of reach. Ben had brought a dinner pail of water scooped from the larger bucket.

"Here," he said. "Maybe if you wash, they wouldn't think you're so scary. You'll smell better too."

The prisoner was staring at Ben through his hair, which had grass and twigs in it.

"Go on, take it," Ben ordered.

Holding it in both hands he raised it to his mouth and drank with long gulps. Then he set it down with a deep breath.

"That was for washing!" Ben exclaimed in surprise.

44

The prisoner gazed at Ben, then at the bowl, then back at Ben, his arm across his mouth.

"Oh, that's ok, I guess. You were really thirsty."

Angela was too fascinated to interfere. She saw the man blink and swallow. Was it surprise she could see in the partially hidden eyes? What she could see of his face was colored with purple and yellow bruises as well as dirt. His lips were blistered and cracked. She felt an odd quiver of pain.

"Ben, come away," she said quietly.

Once Clara assured him that she was fine, Barton Finch left the wagon to returned to his charge. "Get up," he ordered, stick held high. The man pushed himself up on his palms, drawing up his left foot on the ground for support. His guard struck him across the shoulders, sending him flat against the ground. With supreme effort he pushed up on his hands once more, bent his left knee then rose on his left foot, both hands pressing against his knee for balance. He stood, leaning on his left leg and wavering. The lawman grabbed him before he could fall and pulled him off.

Angela dreaded riding in the bruising wagon all day. She wondered if she could walk alongside. Timidly she asked Lou if people sometimes did.

"Many folks do," he answered looking at her shoes. "Saves the animals."

She smiled at the idea. To walk out in the sun and air would be a wonderful change.

Lou noticed her smile of delight. He thought, "This one's not so bad. She don't complain like the mother and sister. She helps too." His wrinkled face softened.

Angela decided not to ask to walk just yet. She ought to see if her mother needed her.

Inside, her mother let her feel of the ankle through the stocking, but continued to refuse a closer examination.

"Angela, a little medical knowledge is useful for a woman, but you dwell on these things far too much."

She said this with a little superior smile. The words and the smile stung almost physically, making Angela's eyes fill. Why did her mother always make her feel stupid and ridiculous, even when

45

discussing a subject that interested her that she had some knowledge and a small degree of competence in? It was so much better to not express opinions and feelings. When would she ever learn to stay quiet and mind her own business?

When they stopped for the midday break, they were all anxious to get out into the air. Barton made his way out first, waiting at the steps to help the ladies. Ben scrambled out next, then Lillian. Angela followed her mother. The canvas roof wasn't high enough for a person to stand up straight. They had to walk bent at their waists. Clara's skirts swept after her as she tiptoed by the prisoner, slumped in his place. As her mother went out the opening her ruffled skirts floated behind her. Angela saw the criminal's body suddenly become rigid. He started to reach out, stopped clenched his fists, his head was thrown back, strong white teeth clamped down on his lower lip. Angela's breath caught in fear when she saw her mother's trailing skirts had caught his right foot. The leg usually bent and resting on top of the other, was pulled straight, disappearing under the dress.

"Mother, stop. You're caught," she called. She went forward on her knees and lifted the skirt, freeing the foot.

"There, you're free," she said shakily.

The prisoner's body was still arched, fists closed, eyes shut. Angela carefully put both hands under his calf and bent the injured leg to rest on the other. His eyes flew open. He reached spasmodically for the leg, then stopped himself and put his arms at his sides, fists pushing on the floor. Breathing hard he looked up in her face. She caught the expression in what she could see of his eyes, and was held for a few seconds in amazement before hurrying past.

"Mother, you should be more careful of your skirt. It caught the man's foot. We could have had another incident," she warned. Her cheeks were red. What have I just done? That was foolish, it could have been dangerous. She acted stupidly again. Think before you act or speak, she told herself. She'd never be dignified like her mother or smart like her father.

There was something else troubling her as well; the disconcerting sense of guilt that she'd just done something rather intimate. She'd touched a stranger, someone she shouldn't have been close to, never mind helped. In her mind she changed the scene. She imagined that she had waited, the skirts freed themselves and the man pulled his

46

own leg back. She sometimes did this, correcting in her mind something that had gone wrong. But then she saw another scene; she saw the leg not pulling free, the prisoner grabbing at the hem, frantic with pain to free his leg. She saw her mother screaming, Barton Finch running, his walking stick raised. She shook her head to clear these fancies.

Sitting on the blanket after eating the midday meal, she saw again those eyes staring at her. They were dark. It was difficult to see them clearly behind all the hair, but she was certain of their expression, and that was what had held her. It was not hateful, angry or clouded; it was a look of shocked wonder, hardly an expression she would expect to see in the eyes of such a person. For the first time she thought of him as a person, not a wild criminal or a medical case.

"You're awfully quiet over there," her sister interrupted her daydreaming.

She blushed at her own secret thoughts as if others could read them.

"Not writing in your journal I see," Barton said. "What do you think of the shape of the patient, I mean prisoner, now?"

He was mocking her.

"He's not shaking so much," Ben volunteered, "but I think he's still sick."

"Yes, his survival is in danger from lack of food and water," Angela said, ignoring Barton's taunt.

"I wish you would have him wash. We would gladly donate soap," Clara said.

"I can oblige you there," Barton replied. "About the food and water, you don't understand. I have to be careful, it's a delicate balance. Don't want him getting his strength back."

"Then you'd have to tie him?" Ben asked.

"Yes, and I'd have to keep watch night and day."

"What if it was only a little more?" Ben continued.

Lou pushed his hat back. "I could use him. If he weren't in such sorry shape you could put him to work." He climbed crookedly to his feet. They all looked at him in surprise, not accustomed to hearing whole sentences from him. He walked off without another word.

Clara added, "If he was a bit stronger he could walk outside rather than sit inside with us."

47

Angela couldn't imagine him being healed well enough to walk any time soon. Barton shook his head slowly as if to say it would be too difficult to explain to them why their suggestions were mistaken.

"Mother," Angela remembered what she had asked Lou that morning. "I would like to walk outside rather than ride inside. I understand it is customary."

"Me too," Ben joined in.

"It is much too hot. You'll get sunburned and ruin your feet," Clara answered.

"Really Angela! You'll get freckles and hideous color," Lillian said.

"Exercise and fresh air are healthy. We would wear our hats. We could get back in if we were to tire."

"Please, may we?" Ben asked.

Clara gave an exasperated sigh, "I suppose, you may try it."

"Yea!" Ben whooped.

Watching Lou toddle to the horses standing in their harness, Angela thought of his remark about needing help. He struggled to lift and check each of the plate-sized hooves for rocks and other debris. He did this at least twice a day. And catching them in the morning in spite of the hobbles was a slow task. Starting late in the season as they had, the ground was quite dry. The wagon got stuck only once so far, but the powerful horses had pulled it out with extra effort. What if they got stuck deeper? How would they get out? Lou didn't seem to have the strength to push the cumbersome wagon. Mr. Finch, would he help?

Barton Finch seemed troubled by the idea of Angela walking although he was relieved to have Ben removed from the wagon. Angela was odd and cold, but he was enjoying his audience of ladies and bringing her down a peg or two gave him satisfaction. He questioned Clara about her daughter walking.

"You think it unwise? Is there any danger?" she asked.

He opened his mouth to answer when Lou gave a loud, "Ha." He reconsidered what he was going to say.

"You'll keep a close eye on them, driver?" he asked sternly.

Lou ignored him.

Thrilled to be free, Ben was running and jumping alongside the wagon. Lou leaned over from his seat and said to Angela, "You might wanta keep on the shady side or put charcoal on your face." And he added just before slapping the reins, "Let me know if you git tired."

She waved her thanks to him.

In spirit she was running and jumping with Ben, though she walked calmly. There was something reassuring about the steady clomping of the horses' hooves, a solid, steady sound of progress toward a promise. Little clouds of dust puffed from each hoof like a cloud of lady's powder. The harness jingled and the creaking of the wagon sounded pleasant from the outside. Angela felt a tickle down her back. Alarmed, she thought an insect was crawling under her dress; she wriggled until she discovered it was only sweat running down her spine. She smelled the honest sweat of the horses, the rich summer grasses and clean air. Ben joined her on the shaded side of the wagon, matching her strides. His face was wet. She felt an impulse to take off her shoes and feel the prickle of the grass and powder-soft dirt. At intervals they could see the river sparkling and undulating lazily. Birds flew across the bluest sky she'd ever seen. She thought of the people who'd first made this trip, explorers and missionaries. How brave they were, going forward into the unknown; These people who forge in all things, cut the trails for the rest of us, these inventors, innovators who expand our world with better medicines, new thoughts, new discoveries. And here she was, content just to be safe and comfortable.

She was tired, her face hot and her feet sore when they finally stopped for the night. They were falling into patterns now. They set up, ate, washed and prepared to sleep. Barton Finch took the prisoner off, returned, leaving him in heap on the ground and threw his food and water at him. Tonight when the meal was finished he asked Ben, "Boy why don't you go fill another bucket for me."

Ben complied willingly, proud to help his partner. He brought it back and set it before Mr. Finch, who carried it over to where the prisoner lay. The prisoner, hearing the heavy steps, lifted himself onto an elbow. When he saw the lawman holding the bucket over him he threw an arm across his face. Finch dashed him with water and then walked away.

49

The man lay on the ground, his arm still over his head, not bothering to wipe at the water. Little rivulets whirled around him quickly soaking into the earth. Once again Angela was taken by surprise at Finch's sudden, brutal methods.

"Wouldn't it work better if he gave him some soap?" Ben asked her. "Now he'll smell like an old wet dog."

Chapter 4

*"... one of those delightful solitudes of
the New World, which almost led
civilized man to regret the haunts of the
savage,"*

Alex De Toqueville

Ben and Angela enjoyed a second dawn by the river. It was a
brief time of relaxation before a long day. By breakfast
Angela's middle was already tightening with dread anticipation of
Mr. Finch beating the miserable man. How she wished someone
would intervene, no one did and sure enough the scene was repeated.
Attending to chores, she kept her back deliberately to the lawman and
prisoner. She saw Lou watching them. He shook his head, spat and
turned away. Ben did not turn away, but he flinched.

Camp equipment packed, the wagon ready, Barton led the
prisoner to the wagon and left him there. He clung to the side for
support, his weight on his left leg, his shoulder and head against the
wood. The lawman escorted Lillian up the steps and to her place
inside.

"Wait, I forgot something," Ben told Angela. He ran to the trees.
In the bright light she saw the prisoner's buckskin pant legs hung in
tatters from the knees down. The right foot was purple and distorted.
The sleeves of his shirt hung loosely open and shredded. Barton Finch
had just given Clara a helping arm up the steps and was about to
climb the stairs himself when Ben charged back into camp carelessly
plowing into his back.

"What?" The big man swung around, his uplifted arm ready to
strike. He caught a blur of Ben and tried to stop himself, but it was too
late. Before Angela could yell, "no," the prisoner hopped to the left
placing himself between the boy and the blow. He took the partially
checked strike and went down. Ben caught him but couldn't hold him
up; the prisoner slipped to the ground.

51

"I'm sorry, I'm sorry," Ben blurted. "I saw an animal. A bear or something. I'm sorry I bumped you Mr. Finch."

Finch's face was flushed with anger and surprise. "You see what trouble your ways cause. When are you going to learn, boy?"

Ben was crying. Now it was Angela who put herself between Ben and Barton.

"It was an accident. He was scared by something over there." She spoke softly, but her voice shook with anger. Barton recovered his composure with some difficulty.

"No harm I guess. Excuse me ladies," he said to Clara and Lillian who were peering out through the opening. "Nothing wrong. If you'll move back…" They scurried back to their places as he grabbed the prisoner sitting on the ground head bowed, boosted him up and shoved him into the wagon.

It took a while for Angela's heart to slow down. Lou had leaned over to see the commotion. He'd even swung a leg over to climb down. Now he looked at the brother and sister before moving the horses forward. They could hear their mother's and Barton's voices inside. *I wonder how he's explaining this?* Angela thought.

"I'm sorry Ange," Ben said tearfully.

"I know. Please be more careful."

"He shouldn't have hit Prisoner. It was my fault."

"I know," she said.

Over and over that day she kept seeing the prisoner put himself between Ben and the blow. Did he do it deliberately? He sure saw things quickly if he did. Why protect Ben? Was it just to aggravate his tormentor?

"Did you see, Ange?" Ben said in wonder. "Prisoner got in front of me. Maybe he likes me because I give him food sometimes." He looked at her anxiously, "and I talk to him. Don't tell, please."

"I won't," she assured him. Then she asked, "He speaks?"

"Oh yeah, he talks a little."

Of course, she thought. Why wouldn't he talk? Then her stomach fluttered and she felt cold, seeing again Barton's sudden aggressive reaction to the accidental crash. There was something hidden just beneath the surface of this man, something awful, maybe dangerous. She had convinced herself that he was added security for them, not danger. She didn't quite understand his line of work, but he was indeed in complete control of his charge. Still there was something in her that reacted strangely to him. Now she was nagged by anxiety she couldn't reason away. She argued with herself, perhaps working with dangerous men made him overreact. He probably thought it was the prisoner who knocked against him. After all, he did try to check his arm when he saw it was Ben. That was it, of course. She was being terribly unfair to Mr. Finch just because of some unfounded feeling. It was wrong of her to judge him so unsoundly.

It was easy to be more hopeful In the light of the world outside the canvas as she walked alongside the wagon. She noticed Ben trudging along, looking at the ground and scuffing his feet. Angela looked for a distraction to lift his spirit

"Look Ben, wild rabbits."

Little brown shapes appeared along the edges of the wagon wheel road, then flashed out of sight into the tall grasses. Her thoughts circled back to that morning's incident. She felt angry and frustrated at herself for not reacting. Freezing in a situation that required immediate action, she'd been helpless to aid her brother. Of what use was she? The prisoner, even in his feeble state, had reacted better than she had. She promised herself to stay more alert and be quicker to take action.

After the evening meal Angela and Ben soaked their tired feet in the river. Her eyes burned and her head ached. Ben's eyes were closing as they sat. The sun began to sink and hordes of insects disturbed their reveries, driving them to return sleepily to camp. Angela slipped Ben an extra biscuit to give the prisoner before he went with Barton to feed him.

Just as the darkness slid in and they were making their way to their sleeping quarters, eerie howls echoed across the land. Clara started, dropping her satchels. Lillian cried out and clung to Angela's arm. Angela listened one way, then another, trying to decipher from which direction the sounds came. There were cries answering cries out of the earth itself, and the sounds bounced off heaven's ceiling and back to earth again.

"Coyotes," muttered Lou, bending to enter his tent.

"Nothing to worry about," Barton added. "They're a long way off."

"Whew," Ben breathed, "scary."

53

"They sound lonely," Angela said. She looked all around before going in the wagon.

The long cries somehow expressed the vastness of the open land around her. The beauty engulfed her, tickling her skin and entering her when she inhaled. At the same time she felt a keen sense of loneliness. These wild creatures responding to each other were finishing each other's sentiments across great distances. Well, she was headed to a new life, new possibilities, maybe aloneness would be left behind.

Except for the beautiful temperamental ocean and shadows of loved ones gone, she was leaving little. Never comfortable at formal dinners and parties where politeness and manners were masks, she'd sat invisible. In the crowded streets of Boston with its carriages dashing by, and strangers brushing past she was just another body in the frantic motion of the city. The young men and women introduced in quieter settings were uninterested, uninteresting and only increased her self-consciousness. She was happiest doing rounds with her father, meeting people from all walks of life. There was something to learn from everyone. There always is. She recalled one patient, a nervous meek little woman. She talked too fast, her eyes shifting, her hands wringing. People withdrew from her because she lacked smooth social graces, a sad woman, afraid of her husband, of life, not someone you would think to emulate. Yet, Angela came to know this woman's authentic qualities. She had a loving heart. Not wealthy herself, like the woman with the few coins in the Bible story, she gave more than her share to charity, donating her time as well as money.

There was the woman with luxurious long silver and white hair. In ill health and having fallen on hard times, her beautiful face lit with inner beauty when she spun wonderful stories of parties and events she had attended at the homes of statesmen when she was married to an important, though cruel diplomat. She had no bitterness for the difficulties she endured past or present. "I've got my knitting and my painting," she'd say.

In contrast to this truly lovely woman, she thought of a friend of her mother's. She and her husband owned a few imposing homes. She could always be called upon for advice on proper social customs, whom to seat where, what to serve. The sort of woman who would greet you with an embrace, call you "dear" and stab you in the back (figuratively speaking). Angela had heard this woman, whom her mother considered a friend, saying very cruel remarks about her family.

Then, there were the tired, work-worn men with hands from which no amount of scrubbing could remove the dirt of their genuine labors. The grandfatherly man with huge capable hands and the merry laugh, he always had a teasing twinkle in his eyes, never a complaint though he toiled from dawn to dusk six days a week all year. When he finally came to the doctor, for breathing trouble, it was too late.

"Just a little out of breath," he'd say, "It's nothin'."

It wasn't "nothin'." His lungs were diseased.

I whine about the least little things, she thought. He was, strong inside and out. She admired these self-sufficient working people, who could thrive anywhere in any situation.

To amuse herself she tried to picture some of the young gentlemen from parties carrying firewood and fetching water from rivers with their gloved hands. One in particular, who had slighted her, came to mind. He had been friendly at first. They had enjoyed long conversations and he had looked into her eyes when they spoke. His mother, the very woman whom Clara claimed as a friend, had put a stop to their children's friendship. Angela overheard her in her own home, telling the son she, Angela was not attractive, not even pleasant. She had some common tendencies and it was time he turned his attentions elsewhere. Besides the family was not as well bred as they would like you to think. After that he ignored her, canceled plans they'd made together and pretended not to see her when they passed on the street.

That night the Harringtons experienced their first prairie thunderstorm. The lightening flashed, glowing through the heavy canvas. Water trickled through holes and loose seams, forcing the crowded inhabitants of the wagon to huddle in the few dry spots they could find. Luckily the storm moved on quickly.

In the morning the ground was slippery when Ben and Angela approached the creek. She caught Ben's arm and pointed. Standing as still as a pillar was a crane, its long delicate legs disappearing in the water. They watched it, whispering to each other until the shy crane, offended by their intrusion, rose smoothly out of the water, coasting on silent wings to a more private spot.

As morning mists rose from the river, the brother and sister finished their morning rituals and headed back to the campsite. Lou, particularly stiff in the morning, was nevertheless at his chores. Barton Finch hadn't emerged from the tent. Ben and Angela paused near where the prisoner lay unaware of the dawn. His left arm was outstretched, pillowing his head, dark hair streaming over his arm and face. His right leg rested on his left where he had carefully placed it before easing his upper body to the ground. His feet were bare and grimy. His clothes were sodden. The earth around him was darkened from the night's rain. Angela could see his shoulders moving up and down with each breath.

"Ange, do you think we could wake him? Would Mr. Finch be very angry?"

"Well, he couldn't be angry if the prisoner just woke up accidentally on his own," she said thoughtfully.

"Yeah," said Ben catching her idea. "It is morning isn't it?" he said loudly. "He could just wake up!"

No change in the prisoner.

"Good morning Ange! I sure am hungry for breakfast!"

Still no change.

"Try whistling," she suggested.

They both tried, no effect. Angela glanced around. They were going to attract unwanted attention if this continued.

"You woke him up that night Angela. Remember how you did it?"

"I'm not going to step on him," she answered adamantly, but she remembered something. She took her towel and trailed it as she casually passed, brushing the man's outstretched hand with it. Again, no reaction. She hesitated, moved closer and brushed his face with the end of the towel. He moved his head slowly, saying a word that they couldn't quite hear. He propped himself up on his elbow, not accustomed to waking peacefully on his own, he tried to make sense of his surroundings and the two figures moving away.

Angela and Ben exchanged anxious glances, waiting for Barton Finch's reaction to his charge's consciousness. He was bending his knees to sit for his breakfast, when he happened to look in the prisoner's direction. Seeing him sitting, the lawman strode over. He circled the man menacingly. The outlaw didn't move anything except his head, watching his keeper's face. From their places at the blankets, Angela and Ben could only watch. Still puzzling, Barton returned to the fire. He asked Ben, "You wake the prisoner?"

Before Ben could reply Angela jumped in, "No sir, he didn't. Ben didn't do a thing. He was with me."

The big man ate his meal watchfully. It was an anxious morning, but not nearly as difficult as witnessing those past morning beatings.

When they were walking later that morning, Ben and Angela saw three large deer in the distance.

"You should write about them in your journal," Angela suggested.

"Sure. What kind of deer do you think they are?"

"I'm not sure. They're bigger than the deer we used to see in Massachusetts. Maybe our driver will know."

Ben ran to the front of the wagon and shouted to Lou, pointing to the deer. Lou cupped his hand to his ear, not able to hear the boy over the creaks of the wagon. He squinted at what Ben pointed to and shouted, "Mule deer!"

Lou considered stopping to shoot one, but they still had plenty of supplies and that would be more meat than they could carry and keep fresh. He had been watching the boy and his sister these past few days as they walked, talked and pointed excitedly. Their interest refreshed his tired old spirit and helped him forget his aching bones. As long as his back didn't freeze up, it'd be all right. He watched them again. This time their faces were turned to the sky as they watched an eagle, its wings spread to catch as much air possible, float across the blue. He remembered how he himself had been struck by these lands when he first came.

"Do you think we'll see any Indians?" Ben asked his sister as they watched the bird circling. "I thought we'd see some by now. Why haven't we?"

"I don't know. Maybe it's better not to have," she answered.

"Mr. Finch knows about Indians."

"Ben, be careful not to bother Mr. Finch too much," Angela warned.

57

He looked disappointed, so she added, "If he's in a talkative mood, he might tell you things."

"Yeah, he might, he tells good stories," Ben said hopefully.

Ben forgot to ask the lawman about Indians when they stopped. He went off exploring, taking the last of his meal with him. He came back to ask, "Can I have a bucket?"

"Benjamin, what do you want with a bucket?" his mother asked.

"To pick berries."

"You don't know which berries are poisonous. They may be different than the berries from home."

"I'll go with him to see that he doesn't eat any," Angela volunteered.

They came back with a bucket of berries, but by then everyone was too busy to risk irritating with questions. Angela was fairly certain the little red ones were currents and the larger bush ones were gooseberries, but she warned her brother to wait to ask someone more familiar than herself. That afternoon they rode inside the wagon to rest their tired feet and legs. When the others napped, Ben held out a handful of berries and whispered, "Prisoner, Prisoner."

The man could only escape into sleep between the harsh bone jarring bumps of the wagon. Ben waited until a lurch jolted him. When it did, he whispered again, "Prisoner, here."

He could see the shine of the eyes. He didn't move his eyes off Ben's face, so he did not see the hand holding the berries even when Ben pumped it up and down. Ben took the man's hand, opened the fingers and put the berries in it.

"Berries," he whispered. "Be careful," he warned as the prisoner brought his hand to his mouth, "I don't know what they are. They could be poison. Can I eat them?"

The man brought his hand close to his eyes. He nodded his head and held the handful back to Ben.

"No, those are for you since they're not poison. I have more," the boy told him.

The prisoner swallowed the handful. Ben passed the time alternating between eating and passing handfuls to the prisoner.

Angela woke and saw the bucket was empty. "Ben, you ate them all? You should have waited to have someone identify them for you."

"It's alright Ange. Prisoner told me."

58

She looked doubtfully through the murky shadows to the sleeping man across from her brother. "Ben," she said shaking her head in disbelief.

"Does a broken leg hurt bad?" he asked her already moving to his next thought.

"Yes", she answered.

"Did you ever see anyone at Father's office with a broken bone?"

"Yes."

"Did they cry? I think I would cry. Why doesn't he make noises? Maybe his leg isn't really broke, just hurt."

"That could be," Angela agreed, "but I think it is. He can't put any weight on it. It could be he doesn't make any complaint because he's too weak."

"Oh, it's broke all right," Barton's loud voice startled them.

The prisoner started in his sleep, but didn't wake.

"It took four of us to hold him down. The doc swung a big old iron bar with all his strength. Smack! Right on the lower leg there. It made a cracking sound to set your teeth on edge. He made noise then, I tell you. He yelled like the wild Indian he is and blacked out."

Angela and Ben were stunned by this story. Angela felt sick in her stomach. She asked, "A doctor broke his leg?"

"Yeah, we figured he'd know best how to do it."

Angela said something softly to herself.

"What's that?" Barton asked.

"My father use to say that a doctor mustn't do harm."

"Now before you get all soft hearted, let me ask you, would you rather we had shot him then and there? If we couldn't bring him under control that's what we'd have to do. And Miss while you're thinking we were too rough, that doc was the very man he kidnapped."

Angela looked out through her canvas hole. The whole story made her stomach flip around. She didn't wish to hear more.

Ben was quiet for a while, but a word in the story made it impossible for him to keep his curiosity to himself. "Is Prisoner an Indian?"

Barton was only too glad to continue his tale as all the family was attentive. "He's a half breed. That's what makes him so dangerous. You see, Indians don't feel things like you and me. They're more

59

savage. You have to deal with them harder than your regular outlaw. They're tougher."

Ben hung on every word, entranced.

"Why wouldn't they feel as we do? They are humans like us," Angela challenged.

"Not exactly, Miss. They may look the same, arms and legs and all, but years of conditioning and hardening makes them tougher to physical hardships. They're conditioned by the way they live out in the elements, by their savage games and customs."

Ben's eyes were huge. "What are savage games?"

"They torture each other just to see who can stand the most pain. Yep, conditioning and the way they think makes them different."

"What kind of Indian is he?" Ben asked.

"Shoshone, I think. He was raised by a Shoshone mother. Apparently the father was a white trapper. He set the kid and mother in a cabin outside a settlement, and sent them money and supplies off and on."

The story was interrupted by shouts. Lou had caught up with another wagon.

Chapter 5

*"My Gentleman, said one, "You've got
a lucky face."
... and I paid nothing then,
As I pay nothing now with the dipping
of my pen
For her brother's music when he
drummed the tambourine
And stamped his feet."*

"The Gypsy" by Edward Thomas

The Harrington party pulled alongside a covered wagon. It was
nearly time to stop for the night so they decided to make
camp together. A broad dark-haired woman greeted everyone with a
boisterous laugh and a hearty handshake. She looked each person
deeply in the eyes and introduced herself as Rose. Her husband Alex
was tall and wiry with a lot of salt and pepper colored hair. He was
quiet, but smile wrinkles deepened in his tanned face when he shook
hands. There were three tall, broad-shouldered sons, Michael, Vincent
and Tony, three giggling daughters-in-law, and a beautiful daughter,
Rosita. The young women wore kerchiefs over their heads, blouses
and wide colorful skirts. Two daughters-in-law carried round-faced
babies on their backs, one also hung a toddler off her hip, while still
another small child happily chirped around her legs. It was difficult to
tell whose child was whose because the women seemed to hold and
care for them all indiscriminately. The daughters-in-law were Esther,
Katherine and Marie. A cow was tied to the back of their wagon her
calf followed her.

"You'll have fresh milk for supper." Rose announced, seeing the
Harringtons had no cow.

Rose and Alex's family set about making camp vigorously. There
were fresh berries, milk, dried fish, bread and coffee. Angela was
carrying a bucket of water and Rosita grabbed the handle. "Let me

help." Her beautiful brown eyes twinkled with good humor. Clara was rather taken aback by these exuberant people.

"You look tired," Rose said to her. "And you, so pale, so fragile," she patted Lillian's face. "Rest here, both of you. We'll make supper tonight."

The young women fussed over Ben as he helped gather wood for the fire.

"What a strong little man," Esther said, ruffling his hair as he passed.

"You are going to be such a handsome man," Katherine teased and swished her skirt.

Ben dropped his wood, embarrassed by the attention. Tony threw him up on his shoulders and picked up the wood himself. He continued to go about his own work as if Ben wasn't there.

While the women were spreading the blankets and setting up for the meal, they noticed Barton Finch coming back from the woods with the criminal.

"Who is that?" Marie asked Angela.

She looked over and answered with a frown, "An outlaw."

"Yeah," added Ben as he was finally lowered to the ground. "Mr. Finch has him under arrest and he's taking him to trial. Mr. Finch is an expert lawman, so you don't have to be scared. Besides, I don't think he'd hurt anyone."

There were sad headshakes and clucks of the tongue.

After the dinner, Alex played the harmonica. His children and grandchildren danced, sang and clapped their hands. The women wore no stockings and their skirts flipped high when they skipped. Angela and Lillian were pulled reluctantly into unfamiliar dances until they saw their mother signal them to come away.

Barton Finch stood apart smoking his pipe, openly suspicious. When they finally sat quietly by the crackling fire, he asked questions pointedly. "Where are you people headed?"

"We're taking advantage of the government's offer: work the land for a few years, then you own it," Alex answered.

"Aren't you a little late?" Barton continued. "That land is well west of Fort Hall. There's a lot of rough traveling ahead. You're not in some kind of trouble are you?"

Alex smiled. "We're not in any hurry. We like looking at the land along the way. If we see anything we like, we may just set down then and there."

"Aren't you worried about bad weather towards fall?"

"Nah," he said, "We've plenty of strong backs if we need to build a house, we build a house."

"Our ancestors were gypsies," Rose added, "wandering is in our blood."

Gypsies, Angela thought, That's what they look like. I once saw a painting of gypsies. They seemed delightfully exotic. She blushed when her mother said, "Oh my, I wasn't aware that there were gypsies in this country. That certainly explains the behavior and dress."

If the family was offended by her remark, they showed no sign. Rose stood up, shaking out her skirts, and the whole brood drifted sleepily off to retire for the night.

The next morning Angela and Ben found Rosita already washing by a nearby creek. She had taken off her dress and stockings and was sitting in the water wearing nothing.

"Come in," she called waving an arm above the water.

"You'll never get clean dabbing at yourselves like that."

Ben looked at his sister.

"Can I?"

"I don't know if you should," she responded hesitantly.

He chose the positive side of her ambivalence, threw off his outer clothing and waded into the water, politely keeping his back to Rosita.

"Ben, be careful," she called. "Don't go deep you don't know how to swim."

"It's not deep. Come in," Rosita called, "It's only cold at first." She rubbed her hair vigorously between both hands.

"Come on Ange!" Ben splashed at her.

Angela looked around timidly, pulled off her dress, shoes and socks and tentatively picked her way through the water. It wasn't as cold as she'd expected. She was used to the ocean, which first stung, and then numbed her feet and legs when she waded. Rosita laughed, her beautiful broad smile was infectious. What joy and pleasure this family found in the simple things around them.

Lillian had come to stand at the riverbank.

"Come on in Lillian," Ben called.

She shook her head content to dabble at the water's edge.

"Mmm, this feels nice," Angela said sitting down.

"Don't you feel like a queen dressed in velvet? The water is like soft robes flowing off me." Rosita closed her eyes and let her arms float.

When they finished Rosita and Angela sat on the bank and brushed their hair while waiting for their clothes to dry in the sun. What a luxurious feeling, to be clean, Angela thought. Rosita was right, she felt rich as a queen.

Rosita wore her hair loosely tied back.

"I couldn't wear my hair like yours," Angela said. "It would just hang dully flat and then get stringy. It isn't pretty colors like yours or wavy. At home Mother makes me curl it every day."

"Yes it is pretty," Rosita protested. "Mine is heavy and difficult. Yours lies smoothly. Look closely." She held the ends of Angela's hair for her to see. "It has many shades and colors. It's like looking at the prairie. On the whole it seems one color, but look closer, you can see many of different browns and golds. Here try this." She arranged the hair softly around Angela's face and braided the rest in one braid down her back.

When they walked back to the wagons, Ben touched his sister's arm. "Ange, can we wake Prisoner again?"

"We could try," she said.

"What's this?" Rosita asked.

"We wake Prisoner so Mr. Finch doesn't hit him," Ben explained. "It's kind of a secret."

Rosita smiled and put a finger to her mouth. They stepped softly to where the person lay on the ground.

"You have to wake him in a special way," Ben explained. "He's hard to wake up. If you poke him he gets a little wild."

Rosita, not at all scared by Ben's warning, tiptoed close. Angela explained how she had used her towel before. Rosita knelt next to him and brushed the hair back from his cheek with one finger. As before his head moved slowly, giving them time to step back. He sat up slowly. Confused, somewhere between sleep and consciousness he saw people walking away again.

64

The next few days went by quickly for Angela. The openness of the family was both disconcerting and disarming. They touched, hugged and complimented guilelessly. The young women told her she had beautiful gray eyes and a sweet face. She felt flattered and then foolish to almost believe their compliments. Ben thrived in the attention. Michael carved his stick to look like a rifle and it was his most precious possession. The brothers insisted on helping Lou with the horses and wagon. But Barton, Clara, and Lillian grew more openly hostile. The first night together, Barton had loudly warned the Harringtons to hide their valuables. Clara and Lillian kept a physical distance from the others, expressing disgust with lifted brows and pinched lips. Barton would comment aside to Clara, but Angela noticed with an inward queasiness that he watched the young women closely, staring at their bare legs.

They passed the babies freely to any willing arms, including Angela's. She enjoyed the new smell and warm feeling of their little bodies molding into her arms and against her chest.

One night instead of coffee, Rose offered tea. It tasted flowery and of mint.

"Mother has teas for aching bones, fevers, headaches, everything, even bad temper," Rosita declared laughing at Angela's surprised expression. "Not that you would ever need a tea for bad temper."

"And they work, don't they?" Rose declared, her hands on her ample hips.

"Sure do," Esther said, "Mama and her magic teas."

After tea, there was music and dancing. The skirts whirled and the young men clapped and stamped to keep time. Barton joined in the midst this time, where before he stood aside disapprovingly. When they took a break to catch their breath, Angela saw the men together off in the shadows sharing a flask. She hoped her mother did not see. Rosita put her arm around her shoulders, and seeing what she was watching said, "Don't worry, they're just playing a little. They can hold their drink. We have to save most for medicinal uses. More music! I want to dance!" she called across to them, breaking up their meeting.

Rosita skipped away to dance with her brothers and sisters-in-law. Watching the dancers in the firelight as she picked up the supper things, Angela was suddenly shoved by something heavy. She turned to find Barton Finch's fleshy face in hers. His expression was angry, his eyes bloodshot. He put his hand on her shoulder. "You, you should be nicer, Miss Know-It-All. You'd be a damn sight prettier if you didn't have such a sourpuss all the time, you know. Smile. Let me see. Go ahead."

Angela's heart raced. She slipped out from under his fingers and went to sit close to her mother and sister.

The dancers finally stopped, collapsing breathlessly on the blankets.

"Read our friends' palms, Mama Rose," Esther suggested.

"Yes, tell them their fortunes," Katherine shouted from where she sat, both babies on her lap, the toddler curled on the blankets like a puppy.

Rose stood up.

"I think not," Clara said, "We do not believe in that sort of thing."

"Go ahead Mrs. Harrington." Barton came out of the shadows. "It'll be entertaining. Here, I'll go first," he thrust out his hands, palms upwards. He was swaying on his feet.

Rose looked at his palms for a moment, then at his face. "Later," she said. She sat down in front of Clara, fluffing out her skirts.

"Oh really," Clara said resignedly.

Angela wandered away, watching the scene from a distance. Ben was playing with his gun at the edges of the firelight. Lou had turned in earlier after Rose gave him ointment for his back. She rubbed it on him herself, laughing off his protests. Katherine carried the babies to their tents. Angela helped settle them in blankets. She was watching them sleep when Rosita found her.

"Come, you haven't had your fortune told."

She pulled her by the hand.

The others had moved from the fire and were crowded near the wagon. Angela and Rosita made their way through.

They were crowded around the prisoner. Barton Finch and Rose stood over him.

"I'll prove this is bunk," Barton was saying. "Tell his fortune."

Angela moved closer to them. The prisoner was sitting with his back against the wagon his head was turned away. It was as if he were trying to press himself into the wood and disappear.

"Let her do it," Barton commanded.

Angela could smell the alcohol on his breath. He grabbed one of the prisoner's hands.

"Leave him be," Rose said.

The prisoner didn't turn his head when she took his hands. She gave a little gasp and dropped his hands. She put a hand on his forehead. Angela heard her whisper, "You're a hurting one, aren't you?"

"Go on, read his hands," Barton said with a laugh.

Rose ignored him. She sat in front of the prisoner, took his hands one at the time and wiped his palms with the ends of her apron. Then she began tracing a line on one with her finger. "The love line is clear and straight," she said.

His chest and shoulders rose rapidly. He stayed turned away. Angela wished they would all leave him alone.

"Ha," said Barton. "What about his life line? Tell us what you see? Is it short?" He winked at Angela.

"Noo," Rose responded slowly. "There is a bump here and it takes a turn here, but it's quite long. Longer than yours," she answered.

"Ha, that proves there is no truth to this hocus pocus. A long life line! He'll be dead at the end of a rope before winter." Barton laughed and walked away, bored with the game.

Rose studied the man on the ground. "We'll see," she said, more to herself than anyone. She got to her feet.

They all meandered away to retire for the night except Angela. She moved a little way off and looked back. The prisoner held the wheel of the wagon beside him, breathing hard, his head bent down.

The next morning after breakfast Alex announced they were going off the main trail to explore different routes. Clara sighed audibly with relief. Surprised and disappointed, Angela wished the morning chores would go much slower, but all too soon the wagons were hitched. Rosita found Angela waiting by her own wagon. They said good-by, fighting tears. Rose strode to them.

"I didn't do your palms last night," she said.

Instead of turning Angela's hands over she held them and shut her eyes for a few minutes. Opening them, she smiled. "I saw you. You were sitting under a tree watching two little boys play in the grass."

Angela looked into the woman's earnest eyes. Though she wanted to pull her hands back and say this wasn't possible, she couldn't. Rose

67

dropped her hands and searched the depths of her apron. "Here, have some of my teas," she said putting parcels into Angela's hands. "This one is for general pain and this one is good for old bones."

"What would I do with these? ..." Angela started to ask.

"Use them sparingly, when really needed. You'll know when." she turned briskly away, taking her daughter with her.

The raucous family's wagon drove off. Their shouts of "good by" and "good luck" could be heard long after they were out of sight. When the shouts were no longer heard, Angela felt alone and small in the enormous quietness.

Chapter 6

*"Now the snake was the most cunning
animal that the Lord God made."*

Genesis

While Angela and Ben were filling buckets that evening, she
noticed how brown her hands were. She smiled and showed
her brother.

"Mine too," he laughed, showing his. "I guess I can't be a
gentleman now."

"I don't know if being a gentleman is what you need to be in the
territories or if the color of your hands makes you a gentleman," she
said. "I suppose there's different kinds of gentlemen," she added as
she thought more about it. "Sometimes a person can look like a
gentleman on the outside and not be one where it counts, on the
inside."

"And the same for ladies," Ben added.

"Oh, of course," she agreed.

They were taking their time filling buckets and talking when they
saw Mr. Finch downstream dragging his charge. Alternately pushing
and supporting him, he didn't want him to actually fall because it was
too great an effort to pick him up off the ground. He resented the
labor of lugging him around, but the man was too weak to get around,
especially on one leg. The big man shoved the other, who stumbled
and fell forward at the river's edge.

Knowing the violence that Barton Finch was capable of when
others around, Angela had a sudden fear of what he might do when he
thought there were no witnesses. She couldn't decide if she should
make their presence known to him or not. "We'd better go back,
Ben."

"Yeah," he said, turning away from the spectacle.

She had secretly hoped to see Barton Finch fall in the water.

69

On their walk back to camp something sticking out of the grass caught her eye. She and Ben went to get a closer look. They found pieces of a wagon, wheel spokes and broken sideboards.

"We found parts to a wagon," Ben shouted to Lou when they saw him.

Lou with a habitual tobacco spit, stopped. "Where?" he asked.

They pointed to the spot. He walked over, kicking away the grass.

"Hmm, he seemed interested. "Should get pieces for when wood's hard to come by."

"I'll help. Want me to get some now?" Ben asked enthusiastically.

"Nah, later."

During supper Ben asked, "Want me to get the wood from the wagon?"

"I'll git it in the mornin'," Lou replied.

"What happened to the wagon? How did it get broken?"

"The wagon is broken?" Clara asked.

"What are you talking about?" Barton demanded.

"Boy saw remains of a wagon," Lou explained for him.

"Wagon parts break, horses go lame, people need to lighten their loads," said Barton, "or they have accidents along the way; wagons overturn in soft mud. The river was higher earlier in the season. People just give up or turn back for different reasons. We'll be coming across more than old wrecked wagons. We'll see bones of horses, mules and oxen that didn't make it." Barton helped himself to more meat.

"People bones too?" Ben asked.

"Now, really," Clara protested.

"Not likely," Barton said smiling indulgently, "plenty of graves though. Old people, sick people," he added quickly for Clara and Lillian.

They did not find this comforting.

"What about Indians? Were any of the dead people killed by Indians?" Ben moved on to his favorite subject.

"Not much anymore. The Indian Removal Act back in the thirties helped put end to a lot of the trouble in the East. Problem is it pushed them west. Wasn't far enough. These days more and more civilized folks are heading farther west, especially now that gold had been

70

discovered. They're running into Indians and there's bound to be trouble."

"The Indians are moving west looking for new homes just like us," Ben concluded.

"Not exactly just like us," Mr. Finch laughed.

Angela was thinking of how he had looked the last night with Rose's family. His close-set eyes were red and watery and his voice was slurred and rough. Here he was now, speaking in a mild manner, enlightening them with his knowledge. She'd heard once that a person's true colors came out when drunk. She wondered if this was true. She knew some people became silly, some loud, some weepy and some mean. She was glad her mother had insisted there be no drinking on this journey. Hopefully there would be no more and that side of Mr. Finch would stay hidden.

"Angela, come with me. I'm afraid to go by myself and mother has already been," Lillian said the next morning. She linked her arm in Angela's as they walked. "Let me fix your hair in a pretty fashion tomorrow," she volunteered. Her foot twisted. Angela caught her. "Oh, this ground is rough!" she protested.

"It's your shoes, Lillian. They are designed for man-made footing."

"I just couldn't bear to buy those ugly boots. I suppose I should have, I've nearly sprained my ankle a few times already."

Her sister being so agreeable gave Angela hope that they might be better friends on this trip. Her hope increased later that morning when Lillian, upon finishing her morning toiletry, insisted on doing her sister's hair. Angela hid her brown hands. Looking at Lillian as she fussed, she thought how lovely she is, her skin so beautifully smooth and her hair soft and wavy, although it was dirty now. They saw Ben and Lou heading to collect the pieces of the broken wagon. Angela couldn't help smiling at the sight of craggy old Lou engaging Ben in an adventure. He probably just needed help carrying the supplies. They were all a bit afraid of Lou, unnecessarily, she was thinking.

Angela and Lillian talked and picked flowers in the open meadow between the wagon and the trees. Realizing that time was passing they returned to camp quickly. Something was not right. There was no sound of voices; Clara and Ben were standing stock still as if frozen in mid action.

71

"Mother?" Lillian started to dash to her side.

"No, stay … where … you are," Clara said.

"It's a snake, a rattler," Ben stage whispered. He stood, half way between them and Lou, who was at the back of the wagon where he'd been loading pieces of wooden wagon parts.

"It bit Lou. It's going to bite him again," Ben whispered fearfully.

"Benjamin, quiet," Clara ordered.

Lou stood motionless. Coiled on the ground was the rattler, its head and tail up, trapping the driver against wagon.

Barton Finch came back into camp with the outlaw. Seeing trouble, he stopped abruptly. He let go of his charge and pulled out his gun aiming it at the brown and yellow scales roped in loops.

"How good are you?" Lou asked quietly. "It's close. You'll git my foot."

While Barton held the gun poised, waiting for a better opportunity. Angela caught movement out of the corner of her eye. The prisoner slowly, so slowly, hopped closer to Lou and the snake, looking at the ground as he made his way.

"What are you doing?" Barton said. "Stand." He switched his aim to the prisoner. Then back to the snake.

The prisoner picked up a rock. He hopped closer, holding it in both hands, balancing on his good leg.

"I said stand," his captor snarled.

"Shut up Finch," Lou said.

The snake turned its head to face the new intruder, who was now as close as Lou. The reptile caught between them must make a choice of its victim. The outlaw raised the rock over the snake's head and dropped it in one smooth movement. It landed with a loud thump. The coils writhed for a minute then lay motionless.

The effort of dropping the rock knocked the man off balance, and he fell to the ground. He sat, leaning back on both arms, breathing hard from the effort.

"Good work, kid," Lou said. He slid to the ground to examine the bite.

"Is it dead?" Ben asked.

His mother caught his arm preventing him from moving closer. Barton lifted the rock and pushed the snake with his rifle butt. He fired into it, making its lifeless body jump. Lillian shrieked.

He snickered. "Just making sure, Miss." He draped the snake over his rifle and held it up. "At least we know what's for dinner tonight."

"Ooo," Lillian hurried away.

"Lou got bit. I saw it bite him! Will he die?" Ben exclaimed.

They all drew in around the old driver, who pulled up his pant leg. He took out a knife and nicked the punctures. Then he tried to bend over, but his stiff back wouldn't allow him to reach the spot above his ankle.

"Damn," he cursed. "Someone's gotta come here and suck the poison out. I can't git to it."

"I will," Ben stepped forward.

"Absolutely not!" His mother dug her nails into his arm.

"Sorry old man, I've got a bad back. I can't bend over that far either," Barton said. "Pour alcohol on it and hope for the best."

"Look," said Lou angrily, "if I get sick, who's gonna drive you all. If we git held up much longer we're gonna run into bad weather. Someone's gotta do it."

Terrified, Angela stepped closer. It will have to be me. She braced herself for the task.

"He'll do it," Barton said, shoving the prisoner's head down to Lou's leg. "Go on!"

"Alright Kid. Hold my leg up a bit," Lou said.

The prisoner put his two hands under Lou's leg and lifted it a few inches.

"Go on," Lou said.

The prisoner bent over the leg, his hair falling around it. He put his mouth on the tiny wound and stayed that way for what seemed like a long time.

"That'll do," Lou said, putting his hand on the man's head.

He lifted his head and looked at Lou's face. Lou looked back for a moment and then shook his head. "Spit it out. Most likely won't kill you. Just make you sick and more miserable than you already are."

The prisoner turned his head aside and spat.

Clara and Lillian had drawn away. Barton Finch and Ben were examining the snake. Only Angela remained to witness this exchange between Lou and the prisoner. The prisoner wiped his mouth with his ragged sleeve. Lou pulled out a flask and poured some of its contents on his wounds. He then took a deep swallow from it and waved it at the prisoner. "Here take a swig."

He only stared blankly at Lou.

"Go on," Lou said.

He reached for the flask hesitantly, took it and raised it to his mouth. Almost immediately after swallowing he began sputtering and coughing, his arm across his mouth, the flask bounced in his hand. Lou laughed and grabbed the container lest it spill. "Never had liquor before?" he asked.

The man, forearm still across his mouth, looked at Lou in surprise. His coughing drew the others' attention.

"What did you give him?" Barton asked.

"Little nip to clean out the poison."

"He can't drink. He's a half-breed. You know Indians can't handle liquor," Barton said. He grabbed the prisoner and pulled him up roughly. "Come on, get up"

Clara stepped forward, her arm out. Angela realizing she was going to demand Lou hand over the flask or pour it out said quickly, "Mother, alcohol is needed as medicine. Did you see how he poured it on the bite? Don't say anything, please."

"I hope I will not regret this," Clara said. She turned back to Lillian who was crying.

Ben picked up the remaining parts and threw them into the wagon. Then he followed the summons of his mother. Angela asked Lou, "Are you alright? Is there anything I can do?"

"No," he shook his head. "Thank you Miss," he added, climbing to his feet.

They packed to start the day's journey. Barton brought his captive to the wagon and pushed him against the side. "Don't move."

The man supported himself unsteadily by grasping the side with his hands. Angela and Ben were discussing their upcoming trek. They stopped and watched him. Barton returned to the wagon and grabbed the prisoner to shove him inside for the day. Lou spoke, "How 'bout the boy riding with me?" He stood, one foot on the rung leading to his bench.

Barton shook his head. "No, he's my responsibility. I should have him in my sights at all times."

"Suit yerself. Up here the women won't be bothered by him."

74

The lawman shook his head. Angela watched curiously. What was this all about? Clara heard Lou's suggestion. She approached Barton Finch. "Mr. ...our driver is armed after all. You mentioned that he has his rifle."

Barton hesitated.

"If I get sick from the venom, he can signal you people," Lou said nonchalantly.

"Lou has a point," Angela said to her mother. "Someone ought to ride with him. What if he gets sick and faints?"

"I will," Ben chimed.

"Absolutely not," his mother said, visions of vulgar things he might learn from the driver passing through her mind.

Barton was tempted. It would be a relief to have a break from this miserable burden, but he didn't want to relinquish control.

"You'll be able to see him through the break in the canvas, if we open it more," Angela noted.

Her mother nodded in agreement.

"Ah, he ain't gonna give me no trouble," Lou grumbled.

"Please Mr. Finch," Lillian put her little gloved hand on his arm. "It would be much more pleasant for all of us."

"Don't try anything. I'll be watching behind you," Barton Finch warned the outlaw.

He pushed him to the ladder steps. Lou climbed ahead and leaned over from the bench to help. The prisoner put his hand on a rung and looked up. He was trying to muster the strength to pull himself up the steps.

"Turn round. Pull yerself up back'ards. Put the good leg on a rung," Lou directed.

He pulled himself up the three rungs, placing his left foot on each until he reached the wooden bench. There he lifted his right leg in.

"Better secure yerself. Pretty rough riding up here," Lou advised, bracing both his boots against the buckboard.

The young man put his good foot against the buckboard, but as Lou slapped the reins and they lurched off the deep grass into the wheel ruts he was tossed from side to side. He slowly righted himself, breathing in catches. He braced his arms down on the seat, left foot against the buckboard once more.

75

Bouncing along, he would doze often, but nearly as soon as his head would fall on his chest a lurch would jolt him awake. His defenses down, soft moans escaped from him.

Lou glanced at him now and then. He felt bad for the kid and figured getting him away from Finch for a time was a way of saying thanks for the help with the snakebite. A few hours into ride Lou pulled out a canteen and took a long drink. He thrust it towards the young man, who flinched away.

"It won't bite. Take a drink," Lou urged. "It's water."

His body held defensively away, he turned his head to look at the canteen.

"Take it," Lou said.

He took it and drank long draughts. Looking down, not at Lou, he handed it back.

"Here, eat some of this. Damn, you could be of some help if you weren't weak as a babe." Lou held out a piece of dried deer meat.

He hesitated then took it, chewing and swallowing rapidly. Later Lou picked up an empty tin can from the floorboards. Turning his body slightly away from his companion, he fumbled with the buttons on his pants. When he finished, he tossed the can over the side. He picked up another can and handed it to the prisoner, who just stared at it.

"Go on, take it. Use it and throw it over. Just make sure you don't hit them two kids walking over there. Ha!"

The eyes shone through the hair fearfully.

"You'll be a sight more comfortable," Lou said, turning himself as far as possible in the opposite direction, his arm out.

The young man took the can, hesitated then pulled at his clothing.

"Just throw it over when you're done."

Lou turned back to sit straight when he heard the can thump on the far side.

"Maybe you won't die on us. Could even be useful," Lou said with a spit of tobacco for emphasis.

When they stopped for the midday break, Lou climbed down alone. Barton looked up, considering making the climb to inspect his charge.

"He's dead to the world," Lou said brushing past him. "See fer yerself if my word ain't enough. Rough ride up there's pretty hard on him. Went right out soon's we pulled up."

This was true, the instant the wagon stopped its movement the prisoner fell into an exhausted sleep. From the ground he could be seen slumped against the side. There he stayed, not aware when Lou returned and took up the reins. When they swayed and creaked underway he woke, bracing himself as best as he could against the battering ride. The rest of the afternoon he slept off and on, drank and ate when Lou offered. Once in sleep his head slipped so far it rested against Lou's shoulder. When a bump awakened him, he jumped and pulled himself as far as possible to the other side.

"That's alright kid. I've had worse than the likes of you lean on me."

When the wagon rocked to a stop for the day, the prisoner's head dropped to his chest and he fell into the deep sleep that he had been fighting since he found himself on Lou's shoulder. Lou set the brakes and swung his leg over to get down. "Wake up kid," he said, but there was no response. He didn't want to shake him awake, having seen how he reacted to that with Barton, so he left the sleeper. The passengers were out by the time Lou reached the ground.

"Get down here!" Barton bellowed from the ground.

Lou waved a hand. "Wasting yer breath. Can't hear you. He's out." He went to unhitch.

Barton paced back and forth then with curse under his breath he mounted ladder rungs. They creaked under his boots. He reached across the bench and grabbed a fistful of the prisoner's shirt. The sleeper's arms flung out, knocking the lawman to the earth where he sat recovering his wind for a moment. Awake now, but confused as to what had happened, the prisoner leaned over the side. Lou came back from the horses and looked up at him. "Better git down," he said. "Come on yer good leg, facin' out. Slow and easy now."

The outlaw lifted his right leg over the side then swung the left over. He paused there, looking down at his keeper, who had risen and was glaring with hard glittering eyes. He braced himself on his arms and lowered his left foot rail by rail until he stood facing his jailer. Finch struck him across the face, spinning him around to face the wagon. He clung to it to keep from falling, his forehead pressed against it. Angela, standing nearby, gasped. The prisoner hung on until Finch pulled him off.

Lou made a disgusted snort, which drew Angela out of her trance. Her heart pounding and her eyes stinging, she followed him to the horses. She had to say something.

"How are the horses holding up?" she asked, trying to sound calm. She shyly stroked the near horse's long sloping shoulder, not looking at Lou.

"They're plenty strong," he answered defensively. "Made this trip before. They'll make it again."

"Oh, I'm sure they're fine," she said quickly. "I didn't mean to question their ability." She paused. "Um… you can wake him just by brushing his cheek with your hand or something."

"What?"

"The prisoner," she said. "He won't wake violently if you touch his face gently."

"Oh yeah?"

He looked at her and though the lines of his leathery face she saw his blue eyes sparkle.

Searching through her belongings for her journal, Angela found the sacks of tealeaves Rose had given her. She sniffed the contents and examined the leaves, trying to identify them in the waning light then tucked them amongst her things.

The next morning when she and Ben came back to camp, casually waking the prisoner as they passed, Lou was not at his chores. He was sitting in front of his tent, elbows on his knees, chin in his hands. Barton came out of the tent and started to walk by when Lou stopped him, "Gimme a hand up. Will ya?"

"Something wrong with you?"

"My back's froze up."

Barton pulled him up by the arms. Lou stood with an "umpf", but he remained bent over.

"Walk around a bit. Work it out," Barton said over his shoulder as he headed off.

Lou tried to walk a few feet, made it to the steps of the wagon and sat back down, shaking his head. Angela was worried. How long would he be like this? Could he drive the team? Her mother finished with her morning absolutions, came around the wagon. "What's wrong?" she asked, seeing Angela's face.

"It's Lou's back." She indicated the driver.

"He will be fine. He's always a bit stiffer in the morning. It is quite normal for older people," Clara said.

They had breakfast. Angela brought Lou his meal, "Is there anything we can do?" she asked.

He shook his head, "I wish I had some of the stuff that woman put on my back, but I'm all out."

Thinking of the tea, Angela said, "Pardon me," and squeezed past him into the wagon. Feeling around she found the cloth sacks. She tried to remember which one Rose had said were for which symptoms. She climbed out of the wagon with her best guess and went to the fire. She picked up a cup and ladled hot water into it from the pot. Then she carefully shook some of the tea greens into the cup. Mixing it as she walked, she brought it to Lou.

"This is some of Rose's tea. I don't know if it'll help. I don't even know how much to mix in."

He squinted up at her, "I'll give it a try."

He cupped it in his gnarled, work twisted hands and sipped for a while as the others went about their routines. When he finished he called to Barton, who was sitting, spreading jam on another biscuit. "Finch, 'less yer gonna help me, I'm gonna have to use that kid of yers."

The heavy man stood up, looking at his charge as he mulled this idea over.

"Either that or we'll have to sit here a day or two 'til I can move," Lou continued.

"I'll help!" Ben shouted.

"No, you are too young," his mother said from her place, "I forbid it. Please, Mr. Finch, that person may as well be of some use. You could oversee his actions."

Angela was doubtful. He could barely stand. How helpful could he be?

"Give him somethin' to eat and let's see what he can do, for God's sake," Lou growled. "We can't afford no delay."

"I will," Ben said, "I'll give him breakfast."

"Wait, Ben." Angela caught up with him. "Give him some of Rose's tea." She mixed the leaves into the hot water. "Be careful, it's hot," she warned as Ben nearly ran with the mug in one hand and biscuits in the other.

The prisoner had heard Lou ask for his help. He sat straighter. Ben set the meal down and backed away. "Be careful, it's hot," he cautioned as the man reached for the cup.

The eyes looked up at him. He lifted the cup and paused with it under his nose for a few seconds before taking a cautious swallow.

"It's not poison, drink it," Ben encouraged.

Meanwhile, Lou was trying to loosen his back: walking, stopping, stretching and walking again. He made his way to Ben and the prisoner. "You think you can help?" he asked leaning his hands on his thighs.

The man nodded.

"Finch?" he called over his shoulder.

"Very well," Barton answered, frowning. He came over as the outlaw worked himself to his feet. "I'll be watching you," he menaced in his ear.

"I'll bring the horses over. You wait there to help me with the harness," Lou instructed.

The man hopped to the front of the wagon and waited, one hand holding on for support. Angela and Ben watched as they packed. "I could have done that," Ben grumbled.

"You can't reach over those horses' backs for the straps, Ben. You're not tall enough."

She saw the prisoner take a horse as Lou backed it into place. He leaned his back against the massive chest, the headstall in one hand, the other hand on the horse's face. He slid the bit into the obliging mouth, then the crown piece over the ears. He worked slowly and smoothly, hopping on his good leg, leaning against or holding onto the horses for balance. Then the driver said, "Over here, let's check the canvas."

The prisoner took the rope Lou handed him and they tightened the canvas in various places. When they finished, Lou ordered, "Everyone that's gittin' in better git. You go on up." The outlaw looked and up to the high seat; his hair fell back from his face. Standing near him, Angela gasped involuntary. He was young. He had

80

to be about her own age. His head turned at the sound and she saw for a moment large dark brown eyes, framed with thick black lashes. He turned away quickly and climbed painstakingly to his seat.

Walking with Ben that morning, she couldn't get those eyes out of her mind.

"I had no idea the prisoner is so young. I thought he was much older."

"Why did you think that?" Ben asked.

"I don't know. I just did."

"You can tell he's Indian," Ben said. "Do you think it's true, what Mr. Finch says?"

"What do you mean?"

"I mean about Indians and the things they do? And they don't have the same feelings as us?"

"Well, they live differently than us, so I suppose they have some different ways of looking at things. They must have families and friends just as we do. They need the same things, like food, water, shelter and family."

"Do you think Prisoner has a family? Maybe a little brother?" Ben wondered.

"Mr. Finch mentioned a mother and a father, didn't he?"

"I wonder if he knows how to shoot a bow and arrow," Ben asked.

When they stopped for the break, Ben thinking no one was looking, put a foot on the rung to climb up to the driver's bench. He was full of questions.

"Where do you think yer goin'?" Lou asked, catching him in the act.

"I just wanted to ask Prisoner something."

Lou shook his head, "Don't go botherin' him. Let him rest."

Disappointed, Ben walked away.

Chapter 7

*"No man had ever touched him except
to bruise him. All his contact with men
had been by blows... Through suffering
upon suffering he gradually came to the
conclusion that life is a war and that in
that war he was the vanquished."*

<u>Les Miserables</u> *by Victor Hugo*

When they stopped to make camp for the night, Barton was
displeased to find the prisoner swinging his leg over before
he ordered him down. "What are you doing? Did I tell you to move?"
he yelled.

"He's comin' to help me," Lou grumbled. "You wanta wait all
night?"

Angela had ridden inside that afternoon to rest her legs and let the
blisters on her feet heal. She was stepping out, squinting in the setting
sun when Barton's shouts made her look up to see the prisoner's foot
and tattered pant leg dangling over the side of the ladder steps. Lou
gave her a wink as he passed by. The young man lowered himself
down the steps, then using the wagon for support, he hopped to the
horses to help Lou unhitch. Lou put his hand on his shoulder to point
out a piece of equipment. The prisoner flinched at the touch. Lou
pulled back his hand, shaking his head.

The next few days followed smoothly. Lou's back relaxed more
each day. The young man helping him seemed to stabilize too, not as
weak as when they first began, but not well either. He'd fall asleep the
moment he hit the ground every evening, as well as sleeping when he
could in the wagon seat. Ben would have to wake him to eat.
Sometimes when Ben put the food on the ground he would sit an
arm's length away and talk to the young man. Angela watched her
brother apprehensively. Mr. Finch didn't object and the prisoner
didn't have the strength to lift his head, never mind harm him. She

figured he was asking the many questions that came into his head. Whether or not the prisoner answered, she couldn't see. One night when Ben was busy questioning the captive and Lillian and her mother were sewing Angela did not want to bother anyone to accompany her on her evening toiletries, so she went off on her own. The sun had dipped below the horizon; its rays still coloring the skies. Wisely or not, she felt safe going off alone. There was no river nearby, so she sat by a small creek, slid her blouse down to rinse away the grime and sweat. The earth was warm not willing to release the warmth the sun had beaten into it all day. Taking her time, enjoying the cooling air and water, she forgot to be aware of her surroundings. The grass rustled nearby. Her heart pounded, she hoped it was just the breeze stirring the grasses, but it sounded like something more, like a large animal rummaging over there by one of the cottonwood trees. Trying to remain calm, she sang to herself while she dressed to alert any wild creature to her presence. Forcing herself to walk, when she wanted to run, she headed back to camp. Was that pipe smoke she smelled? Barton Finch must be near. She could always yell to him if there was trouble.

Back at camp she didn't mention her experience and no one asked her where she'd been. Barton came whistling into camp and Angela felt a sickening flip in her stomach. Where had he been? He was sitting on the blanket when she'd headed off. Next time she would scout her area more carefully. He saw her studying him and smiled. She shuddered remembering how he'd stared at the young women's legs and wondered which was more alarming, a large wild animal or Finch.

Another evening it was Ben who was careless. He wandered out of sight, forgetting himself in his explorations. The light was fading when Clara looked up from her sewing. "Where is Benjamin? Lillian, do you know where he went? Angela? Benjamin!"

Angela jumped up from where she'd been sewing buttons.

"That boy will get into real trouble one of these times," Barton complained. His face darkened.

Angela didn't like his expression, she assured them, "I'll get him. He can't be far."

She found him easily. He was kneeling in the grasses.

"Look Ange," he said solemnly.

Coming closer she saw a rough cross made of cottonwood branches, much weathered and falling over.

"Do you think this is for a traveler like us?" he asked sadly. "Do you think the person was killed by Indians or an animal?"

"Could be this person was sick or very old and it was just their time," she answered.

"Prisoner is sick, but he's getting better I think. I hope none of us get sick. You brought Father's books didn't you?"

"I sure did."

"I wish he were here with us. He'd know what to do if anyone got hurt or sick," he said wistfully.

"I wish he were here too," she said. She choked on the words. "This was a dream of his, you know, to come to the frontier." She felt her eyes filling. Her voice faded to a whisper, "Now we're doing it for him. Let's go, it's getting dark."

They heard their mother calling as they walked away from the lonely cross. Barton stood next to her his arms folded across his chest. Before either of them could begin to lecture Ben began, "I found an old cross, Mother. Someone is buried out there. Is it a traveler like us? Or an Indian, Mr. Finch?"

"With a cross? Of course not. Didn't I tell you boy? Indians are heathens."

"What's a heathen?"

"A heathen isn't God fearing, that's what a heathen is. Another reason they're savage."

"The children and ladies? Are they savage too?" Ben asked.

The lawman, happy for a chance to show off his wisdom, forgot about disciplining the boy for the time being. "Ladies? Yes they are female, but not ladies like civilized women. Nasty creatures the squaws. What? ..." Something across the fire had caught his eye. It was the prisoner, awake and standing, facing their direction.

"Sit down!" Barton marched over.

The family moved closer to the security of the firelight. Finch kicked the young man's good leg out from under him then strode back to the family. "You see that? You people think he needs more food, more water! Now, I've got to keep a closer eye on him! He's getting strong! You see?"

They huddled together under his wrath.

The prisoner lay collapsed on the ground, slowly reaching to reposition his right leg, and breathing hard. Barton turned as if to go back and kick him again. Angela nervously spoke up, "I heard Indians ... well some anyway, believe God lives in everything."

Barton stopped and looked at her.

"You said they are heathen," she continued.

He gave her his patronizing smile. "Now Miss, that's hardly the same thing. Is it?" He escorted her to the blanketed area, continuing the discussion. "They pray to spirits, spirits in rocks, trees, animals. They think creatures are holy. Some think beavers are holy, others think turtles are," he laughed his scornful laugh. "Can you imagine beavers as God?" he said to Clara and Lillian.

Lillian giggled at the thought and with nervous relief that his rage had passed.

"Well, isn't believing that there is a spirit in all things similar to our belief in the Holy Spirit? ... we believe God is in all things, at least all living things. Aren't all things his creation?" She countered partly out of her own thoughts and partly to distract him as Ben slipped the prisoner his supper.

"Angela!" her mother was shocked by her speech. "What are you saying?"

Barton shook his head at her naivete. "What kind of god-fearing creature would scalp women and children? I ask you? Do you know what they do to prisoners? They... "

"Mr. Finch please, I do not care to hear anymore," said Clara. Her face was white and she held her hands up.

That night when they lay in their bedding Clara spoke sternly to her daughter. "Angela, why do you challenge Mr. Finch? This is a world, which he is far more familiar with than you are. How can you be comparing godless savages with good Christians? You worry me terribly. The way you think, I just don't understand. You'll never have a husband if you persist in acting inappropriately for a young woman. What will happen to you?"

"I was simply asking," Angela whispered. "Mother, there is something about Mr. Finch that bothers me. He..."

"Enough of your foolishness. I do not want to hear another word," her mother cut her off.

Lying in the dark, Angela thought of the tiny grave. She felt insignificant, they were insignificant and nature heartless.

Expectation was rising over the next few days because they would soon reach Fort Kearney. Lou whistled, Lillian complained less, Clara's face softened to almost a smile at times. Ben plagued Mr. Finch with questions about the fort. Finally it was the morning of the day they would reach it. Civilization was a day's ride ahead. Though they were not terribly short on supplies, thanks to Lou's wise planning, it would be exciting to meet people and comforting to be within strong walls.

Upon reaching the fort that afternoon they were intercepted by two soldiers on horseback. There were a few scattered tents around the outskirts and not much traffic except for the two horsemen. The family stood close to the wagon while Lou climbed down. He and Barton Finch met the men. The discussion became heated. The Harringtons heard Barton's raised voice, "All healthy. My word's good enough!"

Then Lou's, "Don't make things worse."

Barton shouted, "You have no right to tell us where we can stay! We can camp wherever we want!"

"What are they saying? We can't stay?" Lillian said. "Mother?"

"Sh," Angela said. She tried to hear the conversation.

Then she heard a word that chilled her, "Cholera."

Returning to the family, a flustered and angry Barton Finch tried to explain, "It seems there's been a lot of sickness amongst the emigrants. It's got them all spooked."

"Cholera?" Angela said softly.

He glanced at her quickly, as did her mother. "There were some cases a while back." Then he added belligerently, "They can't tell us where we can camp."

Lou finished his conversation with the men and returned to the group. "We'll be movin' on. No sense taking chances. They've had sickness in the fort. Don't want no emigrants campin' close or stayin' too long." He saw the frightened faces of the family and added, "We'll keep a distance from recent campsites, put charcoal in the water, boil it good."

With these words of little comfort they started back on the trail. Discouraged and tired, they traveled until dark and made a quiet camp for the night.

The next morning Ben and Angela began their walk sadly. Without the anticipated respite at the first fort the journey now seemed endless. The sun burned brighter, its heat a personal antagonist pushing down on Angela's head and shoulders, pulling at her arms and legs. She lifted her eyes from the dust to see an expanse of open land ahead and in all directions. A gift to her eyes, there was color everywhere. She had imagined the western country to be all dry barren desert, not the rolling fields of red, blue, yellow and white blossoms before her. The Trail now followed the Platte River; there would be plenty of water. The delightful scene combined with the company of Ben, who was returning to his normal happy state, made it hard to stay gloomy.

Lillian had cried the night before and complained all morning, but she was out of hearing now.

"Emigrants. He called us emigrants. He may has well called us riffraff," Clara had despaired. Their bemoaning long into the night gave Angela a headache that persisted when she woke in the morning. Now, tired as she was, the land lying ahead looked as if it would enfold her into its verdant, comforting breast.

Unexpectedly Lou pulled the horses to a stop. "Whoa, whoa you."

Ben ran to the front of the wagon. "Why are you stopping Mr. Lou?" he shouted.

"The Kid sees somethin'!" Lou shouted back.

The outlaw's attention was fixed, staring in the same direction.

"What do you see?" Ben shouted to Lou. Ben and Angela could see nothing out of the ordinary.

He shook his head, "Nothin' yet. Hold on. Could be, I see it."

As they watched, a cloud of dust appeared on the western horizon. Lou picked up his rifle. Barton Finch lumbered out of the wagon. "Why are we stopping?"

No one answered. The prisoner and Lou stared intently at the cloud. Seeing it himself, Barton hurried back into the wagon to dig out his rifle. Lou readied his. "Hostiles?" he asked the young man, who didn't respond, only kept his eyes locked on the approaching shape.

Men on horses were now distinguishable. The young man said a word to Lou.

"Get inside," the lawman ordered the brother and sister.

"This one thinks it's just hunters," Lou said spitting.

Angela and Ben climbed inside, but kept their faces to the opening. They heard riders pull up and greet Lou and Barton with Halloo's, a good sign. The riders stayed in shouting distance. "Any you people got the sickness?" one asked.

"Nope," Lou answered. "First we heard of it was at the fort yesterday."

"Could be you folks have missed the worst of it. Where you headed?"

"Fort Hall," Barton answered.

"That so. Little late aren't you?" Both parties moved closer as they spoke, feeling safer.

"You going to Kearney?" Barton asked.

"Yep, I suppose they didn't encourage you people to stay around, did they? Because of the cholera they're movin' folks on. Seeing as we're not with a party, they let us camp nearby. We're keeping to ourselves. Good luck. Watch for prairie fires, been kind of dry." They touched the front of their hats and galloped east in the direction of the fort. This reminder of their disappointment did nothing to help the spirits of the family.

After being turned away at the Fort, the next few evening meals were eaten despondently quiet, not even Barton Finch was talkative. He watched the outlaw more carefully. While he ate, smoked or conversed with the women his small eyes gleamed in his direction. Sometimes instead of sitting comfortably he would stand nearby, arms crossed, legs apart, while the prisoner tended to the horses and wagon with Lou. When he finally shoved the prisoner down for the night he would sit heavily by the fire with a loud sigh and wipe his face as if he'd been toiling at hard labor all day.

"Ah, thank you ma'am," he said wearily to Clara when she handed him a cup of coffee.

"Mr. Finch?" Ben asked tentatively. "Do you think we'll see more graves?"

"Very likely boy. Keep a sharp eye out and you'll see signs."

"Signs?" Ben whispered. His eyes were wide with fascination and a little fear. He considered for a moment then he asked, "Mr. Finch do you think I could find Indian stuff, like bows and arrows?"

"You might find arrowheads."

"Truly?" Ben's face lighted.

"Benjamin, Mr. Finch is tired. Do not bother him," Clara said. She passed a plate to the lawman.

Barton smiled at her. "Thank you ma'am, I am at that. I don't mind educating the boy, not at all."

Ben beamed, grateful for the attention from this important man. "Do Indians have families?" he asked.

"Depends what you mean by family. Indian men hunt and fight. The squaws do all the work, skinning their kill, gutting, cooking, most everything."

"Do they love their families like we do? Do they love their squaws and children?"

"I told you they don't have feelings like us. To an Indian any squaw will do. She's just his slave. She can be replaced if she doesn't work hard enough. Indians will steal women, not because they like them, but to make them their slaves."

His voice rose louder and louder with particular emphasis on the word squaw. Angela looked up from her journal. He directed his words not to Ben, but to the prisoner sitting several yards away. The prisoner was not sleeping as he usually did as soon as he hit the ground. He was sitting, his arms straight by his sides. His hair falling about his face didn't hide the fact that he was staring at Barton Finch. Her mother and sister were sewing in the fading light and Ben was listening with rapt attention. Angela was the only one noticed the hateful antipathy.

"The squaws, they are as cruel as the men. God help the captive who is given over to them. You can hardly call that a family, the men using women as slaves and the squaws so vicious and cruel they can hardly be called women!"

The rising passion in his voice made Clara and Lillian look up from their sewing. They too saw Finch and the criminal; eyes locked across the space.

"Mr. Finch, why is he staring over here?" Lillian asked. "He's scaring me. Mr. Finch, please. Make him stop."

Barton hefted himself to his feet, fists closed at his sides. Angela jumped up and caught Ben to prevent him from following his admired partner. She held him tightly, though he tried to shake her off.

"Ben no. It's going to be ugly."

He stopped, realizing she was right. They stood halfway between their mother and sister and Finch and the prisoner, dreading the impending violence, unable to prevent it, or pull themselves away. To their surprise, instead of going to the prisoner the lawman climbed inside the wagon. They glanced apprehensively at the prisoner. He wasn't waiting for Finch's wrath with trepidation. In fact as soon as the lawman had broken the stare his chin dropped towards his chest and he slept where he sat, too tired to lie down.

They heard a jingling and Barton Finch emerged carrying thick chains. On the ends were iron cuffs. When he stood over the prisoner he was calm, unnaturally calm. Angela thought the calmness was as disturbing as his anger.

. . .

Sensing danger through the dark world of sleep, the prisoner woke to see his captor towering over him; something jangled. Slowly it came to him what it was and what it was for. He shook his head and pulled back.

"Looking to challenge me?" Finch bent his knees to thrust the chain in his face. "Are you? Get uppity with me? This is what it gets you."

The prisoner shook his head adamantly and pushed back further. Finch swung the chain at him, hitting him in the chest. "You will wear this. You will offer me your leg real nice. Slide your foot forward now."

Still he refused. Finch shook the chain at him. He looked over his shoulder and saw the others watching. He put his face close to the young man's, "You let me put it on willingly or I'll strip you and drag you in front of the women and kid. You know you haven't the

91

strength to fight me. I'll drag you before them and spit on you and offer you for them to mock you"

The prisoner slid his left leg forward.

"You'd like that wouldn't you," Finch scoffed.

The prisoner looked at him, confusion showing in his eyes.

"The other one."

He hesitated, then put his hands under his right calf and lifted it slightly.

"That's more like it," Finch gloated. He grabbed the right ankle and roughly locked the cuff around it. Then yanking the chain so the broken leg was pulled out straight, Finch locked the other end of the chain around a tree. The prisoner fell back against the ground, his back arched in pain, his hands frantically digging at the earth. Finch walked away from the young man stiffened in pain, his chest heaving, his breath coming out in gasps. Finch brushed off his hands on his pants.

Angela was sickened. She wanted to turn away; she wanted to help him. She stood staring. Her mother rose, calmly saying, "Come children, let's attend to other matters. This is not our concern."

Lou stood up with an "argh" of disgust and went to the tent. Angela couldn't take her eyes off the prisoner, who was excruciatingly slowly sliding his body along the ground to slacken the chain's pull. Lying on his side, he reached for the thigh of his right leg, bent it at the knee and lifted it to cushion it on top of the other leg. She stood with her hand over her mouth until Ben turned and ran. She followed where he ran under the wagon. "Ben, come out. It's time to go to sleep. Ben please you'll only get Mother and Mr. Finch angry." He crawled out for her and they went into the wagon. Neither spoke of the incident.

"I know I'll sleep better tonight," Lillian said from her blanket that night.

Angela's heart was still racing and her stomach churning. Ben was curled in a ball, his back to everyone.

The birds, sensing the sun rising before humans could detect any brightening of the sky, woke Ben and Angela. As was their habit, they tiptoed out into the deliciously cool morning. Most nights they camped close to a river or stream. Angela and Ben washed from buckets dipped in barrels of stored water when there wasn't time or a fresh source available, but they preferred to go to water and watch the waking day. Splashing their faces clarified their sleepy senses.

The campsite was a collection of odd shapes coated with rosy light. Ben hesitated before the prisoner. "I wish Lillian didn't make such a fuss. Then Mr. Finch wouldn't have chained him." He bent to wake him.

"Better let me." Angela was worried that he might react differently, after last night. She walked closer and timidly reaching down brushed his cheek with her hand. She skipped back quickly as his head rolled and he sighed a word. A name? She almost caught it this time. Rising to his elbow, then a straight arm, he sat up slowly. He carefully adjusted the leg, breathing in short catches. Angela and Ben walked away.

. . .

The numbing fog had lightened lately. He could make out people, feet, voices, faces, women's faces grimacing, the open face of the boy asking, asking, making him think, making him remember. The boy gave him food and water. The old man too. Probably why things were clearer. He wanted to stay in the fog, go deeper and deeper until he was no longer. Awareness was misery. The drum throbbing in his leg was his lifeblood mocking him that he still lived.

Helping the old man, feeling the warm moving horses wasn't bad, though he was almost uselessly weak. It felt as if stones were tied to his shoulders, arms and legs, pulling him down.

He could bear Finch's games, tripping, pushing and laughing as he struggled to get to his feet and make it to their destination. The threats, the insults, the blows, one breath at a time he could bear it. Whatever came at him didn't matter. He was dead, his spirit already in another place waiting for him. Then the night before he caught a word, intruding into the sleep world, then again the word thrown at him across the fire, "squaw," and with it more insulting words.

Finch could do what he wanted to him, it didn't matter. Last night was different. It was his mother and grandmother Finch was reaching out to strike. The best people he ever knew, the kindest and wisest. This loud clumsy white man could not be allowed to insult their ghosts. He had to defend them, protect them. He wanted the strength to rise and fight, he told him with his eyes. He challenged though his body refused to help him. Finch heard his challenge and turned away.

It was over he thought. Then the chain …. The idea of being chained, to be totally defenseless to Finch, he couldn't submit, not to this, but the faces were all staring, he could feel their eyes. He called all his inner strength to fight the senseless urge to defy Finch. It was a fight he couldn't win. Still he wouldn't let Finch win. It would be his own power to choose.

He saw the chain was meant for legs and that was more bearable than having his arms tied. Then unbelievably, Finch wanted his bad leg. It didn't make sense. Why chain the weaker leg? There was a flash so intense he couldn't see. He wouldn't let Finch win. He would not cry out. He bit his lip. The flash wouldn't go out. Blindly he tried to relieve the leg by moving it. Then losing what little strength he had, he could do no more, the leg still burning to its own fire all went dark.

Ben brought the prisoner his food that morning when Barton nodded his permission. He sensed this was not a good time to ask questions of Mr. Finch or Prisoner, although he had so many. It was hard to get all the information his curiosity demanded from a person who only nodded, shook his head or answered with one soft word. Ben was ambivalent. Sometimes, like today, he felt sorry for Prisoner. Sometimes it seemed to him that Mr. Finch was the bad person. Mr. Finch scared him when he was angry. The anger was always there, hiding in the red of his face. You just never knew when it would come out. It wasn't a nice red, like the red in people's cheeks when they are out on a windy day.

Was he a bad person for feeling sorry for Prisoner? He had stolen someone's horse. Worse than that he had kidnapped a doctor, a doctor like his own father. He even admitted it when Ben asked. The fact of the prisoner worried Ben. If you were a bad person, you could end up like him. That was a scary thought, to imagine yourself chained and hungry with a broken leg. Ben vowed to himself almost every night to be a good boy, but it was hard to remember; it seemed he was always making mistakes. He set down the mug of water and held out the biscuits with jam.

The young man was trying to ease his chained leg when Ben appeared above him. He stopped, looked up in Ben's face and waited.

94

He wouldn't take the food from Ben's hand. He wouldn't make a move towards the boy or anyone; Finch had conditioned him well. Ben took his filthy hand and put the food in it.

After finishing breakfast Lou was anxious to hitch, but his help was still chained. Barton strutted over to his charge. Lillian was gathering the last of her things. She stopped before climbing in the wagon to criticize her sister. "Angela, for goodness sake put your hair up. You wear it like a little girl or an Indian. I don't know which."

Angela was relieved to be distracted by her sister's nagging. She always felt a nervous tightening when Barton approached the prisoner. Still she could not resist looking past her sister when a scuffle began. Barton squatted by the end of the chain attached to the tree. Not satisfied to simply unlock it, he yanked the chain, sending the prisoner on his back, his hands reaching for the leg. While the young man was locked in pain, Finch unlocked the band from around his ankle with deliberate clumsiness. He took his time, watching the prisoner writhe. Lillian turned to see what had Angela's attention. "Ooh," she shivered, "It's a good thing Mr. Finch knows what to do. That man is frightening."

While the criminal lay on the ground, holding his leg and breathing hard, Finch put the chain away. Angela did not share Lillian's sentiment; on the contrary she felt a fierce anger building inside of her. She saw Ben turn away from the scene and wipe his eyes. Lou hobbled over to the young man and leaned over him, "Think you can help?"

The man on the ground looked up quickly. He struggled to his feet, stood unsteadily for a moment then hopped after Lou.

While walking that morning Ben told his sister, "I don't think I want to be a lawman anymore. Hurting people makes my stomach feel funny."

"Yes, I know what you mean," she agreed, "but I don't think all lawmen hurt people."

"Ange? Do you think Mr. Finch will chain Prisoner every night? I heard him tell Prisoner it would serve him right if a coyote gets him in the night. What if a wild animal comes in the night? He won't be able to get away. Can you talk to Mr. Finch?"

"I don't think I can influence him."

"Isn't there something we can do?"

95

"Well, let's think about it and see if we come up with any ideas."

During the lunch break Ben tried to bring up the subject, "Mr. Finch, do you think if we took turns guarding Prisoner, then you wouldn't have to chain him?"

"Wouldn't have to chain him? What? No boy, I need sleep you know. I can rest without worry, if I know he's restrained. You wanted him to have more food. See the difference in him?"

"I'm certainly comforted to know that criminal is restrained," Lillian spoke.

Barton smiled and patted her hand. "I'm glad of that Miss."

Their mother nodded her approval then gave Ben a stern look.

"Perhaps," Angela began. She cleared her throat nervously and ignored her mother's look, "perhaps the chain you're using could be greased, the bolts or lock that is. It seems difficult to remove. I'm sure Lou has some extra grease for the wagon axles..." she trailed off.

"No, no I can get the leg irons off. I don't usually have to use them, but I'm happy to since they're such a comfort to the ladies," he smiled at Clara and Lillian.

Angela, embarrassed for having an interest and for speaking up, blushed. Lillian watched her curiously and her mother glared.

Before entering the wagon for the afternoon, her mother warned her sternly, "You are not to question Mr. Finch's judgement anymore. It is rude of you, Angela. Also, your interest in these matters is completely coarse and inappropriate. I do not want to have to speak of this again."

Angela looked down at her shoes; they were scratched, scuffed and dusty as if they were years old.

Ben said gallantly, "It's my fault mother. I asked Ange to say something. It makes my tummy feel funny when Mr. Finch hurts Prisoner."

Lillian came up behind Ben and gave him a hug. "Oh you sweet little man. Remember what Mr. Finch said about Indians not feeling the same as us. It's not as bad for him as it would be for you."

Clara was neither touched nor amused. "If it bothers you Benjamin, then don't look," she gestured for them get into the wagon.

Later that night when their mother and Barton had fallen asleep on the blanket, Angela asked her sister, "Isn't there something about Mr. Finch that makes you feel uncomfortable?"

"What do you mean?"

"He has an explosive temper. And one time when I went off to wash, I think, maybe, he followed me."

"Followed you? Why do you think he followed you?"

"I heard a noise in the bushes and I thought I smelled his pipe."

"Angela, you can smell a pipe from a long way off. Besides he watches out for all of us. That's a comfort, not a concern. Our driver certainly doesn't watch out for us the way Mr. Finch does. It's fortunate he is on this trip with us."

Angela did not feel the same. She couldn't shake the recoiling instinct she had when near Barton Finch. And she was sure her sister's assessment of Lou was wrong. Lou did all the work, and many times when it appeared he was asleep she had seen a watchful blue eye under his hat.

Lillian unwittingly provided Angela and Ben with a plan for Finch's roughness when attaching or detaching the chain. He was fastening the iron cuff over the prisoner's ankle when Lillian's clear musical voice called, "Mr. Finch, Mr. Finch. Would you help us start the fire? The driver is off doing something or other, and I'm afraid I'll faint from hunger. Mother and I can't seem to get it started."

Distracted by a lady in distress Barton quickly bolted the chain and hurried to the rescue. The prisoner winced and slid closer to the wheel for less pull on his leg. It was over.

The next morning when Barton went to unchain his captive, Angela was ready. When he bent over, she called fearfully, "Mr. Finch, there is an animal, a large animal over there. What is it?"

He swiftly detached the ankle cuff and puffed over to her.

"I'm afraid it's gone now," she said, shading her eyes and pointing vaguely.

"Where? What animal?" Ben came to look. She smiled and winked over her shoulder. He smiled and winked back. On the day's walking they plotted to take turns distracting Barton every morning and evening so he would make quick work of chaining and releasing the prisoner.

Chapter 8

"A dog is a comfort,
An ally in a sometimes unfriendly
world.

A dog hears your secret needs and
sympathizes
Or artfully distracts you from your
woes.
A dog defeats loneliness, defies
unhappiness
And teaches the hard humans the virtue
of play."

"Truest Friend" by Gail Peterson

A few days later they overtook two covered wagons plodding
along. They were pulled steadily by oxen. The lead wagon
was driven by a thin man, who raised a long arm in greeting. The
woman sitting beside him nodded her bonnet solemnly. Beside the
wagon four scruffy little boys about Ben's age and younger stopped in
their tracks and stared at Ben and Angela. They were followed by a
yellow dog and her four fat pups. In unspoken agreement the three
wagons traveled together for the rest of the afternoon. The boys
pushed each other and generally showed off.

When they stopped for the night the tall man, with shoulders
hunched shyly mumbled introductions. "Thompson, Charles
Thompson. Mary my wife." Mary, a gaunt faced woman with hard
eyes, halfheartedly called the boys to introduce themselves. They
ignored her and she made no further effort. The man from the second
wagon approached with an extended hand. Jacob was the younger
brother to Charles, also tall though not as angular. Both men had full
bushy beards. Jacob's wife Edith was a stout woman with a baby in
her arms. She dimpled as she greeted them. "This is my oldest
Abigail." She pulled the hand of a short plump girl, hiding behind her.

Abigail smiled shyly. Angela guessed she was younger than herself, but older than Ben. Edith shouted, "Caleb, you come here!"

Caleb ran to his mother, grinning, hat in hand, his blond hair raggedly sticking up like a scarecrow's straw hair. He said his hellos quickly and ran off to join his cousins and Ben.

Camp was set up with little conversation except for off-hand assurances of good health and to reach agreement on where to build the fires. Abigail beamed when Lillian took her aside and brushed out her long thick blond hair. Her mother laughed good-naturedly. "Abigail, there isn't time for vanity. Come help with the supper."

Barton Finch pointed out the prisoner who was helping Lou, to the men and explained the situation. Both men took their wives aside and informed them about Barton and his captive. They all stared when Barton brought the young man back to the wagon, shoved him down and chained him. The boys came close to stare, but Barton shooed them away. Charles Junior, Jonathan, Sam and Caleb followed Ben and peppered him with questions.

Ben relished the audience. He sat with a sleeping puppy in his lap and proudly told them all about the prisoner and the special business of guarding him. Edith asked the Harrington women if they weren't afraid of having an outlaw with them. Lillian told the story with animated hand and facial gestures. Her voice rose and fell dramatically. "At first as you can imagine we were dreadfully frightened. Traveling like this is a dreadful hardship. Then to have to suffer the presence of a criminal… Well it was almost too much, but as the trip went on we saw how adept Mr. Finch is at handling dangerous criminals. He has made us feel quite secure. Hasn't he mother?"

Mary stared first at Lillian and then at Clara as if she'd never seen the like of them. Then without comment she turned to prepare the meal. Ben showed the boys his prized stick gun. They shared stories of their adventures and things they had seen along the trail, trying to outdo each other with tales growing more outrageous in the telling.

"Are all these dogs yours?" Ben asked.

"Yep," said Charles, "They're gonna protect us when they get big, if the coyotes or Indians don't get them."

"No coyotes are gonna get them!" yelled little Sam. He pushed his brother.

"Quit," shouted Charles. Then his voice dropped to a conspiratorial tone, "Let's go see the outlaw."

"Yeah," the others joined in.

Ben glanced in Barton's direction. "I don't think we should."

"You said he was your prisoner too," Jon said.

"He is."

"If it's true take us to see him," Charles challenged.

"You can have one of the pups if you do," Jon said.

"You mean it? Follow me and do what I say. Be quiet about it."

"Bring your gun," Charles said.

They circled around the back of the wagon and came out to the side facing the camp. They stood staring at the young man sleeping with his back against the wagon. Not content to simply look, boys picked up sticks and aimed their pretend guns at the unknowing sleeper. This wasn't exciting enough. One picked up a rock and threw it, hitting the sleeper on the shoulder.

. . .

There was a jumble of legs moving around him. He heard young voices. He tried to pull himself more tightly against the wagon, but the chain caught at his leg. Growing bolder, they moved in, poking him with their sticks. He turned his head away from the prods.

Ben didn't like this turn of events. "No," he whispered putting his hand on a stick about to strike. "Don't hit him. Stop," he hissed as another stone fell. "He won't hurt you. Stop or I'll yell. I will." His voice grew louder, threatening to alert the adults. The boys looked nervously toward the campfires and backed away. Gradually aware that they had left, their victim slipped back to sleep.

When Ben came in for bed that night Angela noticed the bulge under his shirt; she said nothing. Lillian however turned just in time to see him take a fuzzy bundle out. She shrieked, "Ben, get that animal out of here! Mother, he's got one of those mongrels!"

"She's not a mongrel, only a pup," he protested.

"Benjamin, it is liable to give us all fleas. Put it out," his mother commanded.

101

Uncharacteristically, Ben snapped at Lillian, "You're mean, just mean!"

"Now," his mother said, unyielding.

"Please," he begged.

She sighed, "Take it Angela. Set it outside the door."

Wrapping her shawl around her shoulders, for the nights were surprisingly cool, Angela touched her brother and they went out together. Ben was sniffing. Her heart ached for him.

"The puppy is tired from walking all day. I'll bet if we wrap her up in my shawl and put her under the wagon, she'll sleep through the night."

"I don't know," Ben hesitated.

She wrapped the sleeping animal and placed it gently under the wagon. The pup lifted her head, but didn't crawl out of her bed. Angela guided the reluctant boy back inside.

She woke at their habitual time. Sensing that something was wrong, she felt around in the poor light whispering, "Ben."

There was no answer. She went outside, whispering his name. Under the wagon she saw only the shawl. Her heart beat rapidly. She peered through the vague pre-dawn light. Then she made out a shadowy figure on the ground. As she looked more closely she could see a smaller shape bouncing around it. "Ben, you scared me," she whispered.

"Oh, I'm sorry Ange," he said, looking up. "My pup was just waking up when I found her. She might have got lost or eaten if she wandered off."

"She probably would have just gone to her brothers and sisters. Come on. Bring her with us. We're up now, we may as well get ready for the day."

When they returned to camp the pup waddled ahead. She sniffed around Barton and Lou's tent, then wandered farther, nose to the ground. The puppy came to the prisoner, sniffed around his feet and up to his face before Ben could catch her. "Puppy," he whispered.

Reaching the young man's head, the pup wriggled delightedly, her little pink tongue flicking over his face. Angela held her breath. His eyes opened, he put a hand up and touched the little animal gently. Ben breathed a sigh of relief knowing his pet wouldn't come to harm by startling the prisoner. He tucked her up in his arms as the prisoner worked himself to a sitting position.

Clara noticed her son feeding his breakfast to the puppy. "Benjamin, do not give your meal to that animal. Put her with the others."

"She's mine. Charles gave her to me. I have to take care of her."

His mother looked at him wearily. "You cannot keep a dog. It is out of the question."

Barton mumbled through a mouthful, "It'll be a nuisance boy. Eating food we can't spare, getting into things. It'll just get carried off by some animal anyway."

Charles Senior looked up from his coffee and drawled, "A dog's a good thing to have around. When she gets bigger, she'll bark and scare off critters. She'll follow the boy around. You'll always know where one is the other is."

"Please mother," Ben pleaded. His eyes were brimming with tears.

Angela couldn't bear Ben's disappointment. She reinforced his plea, "I'll help him with her. We'll make sure she's no trouble."

"Oh very well." Clara rubbed her forehead.

"Mother, you're not going to let him keep a dirty dog," Lillian began, her voice rising with dismay.

Angela shot her an angry look. How could she be so heartless? It struck her how out of place Lillian seemed on this trip. Her gestures, her voice, and clothes all seemed false against nature's settings.

Angela tried to imagine Lillian and her husband-to-be Phillip living in a cabin in the territories. Clara had kept the truth of their financial situation from him, even going as far as to imply this journey west was a business trip she had to attend too personally. Although he had not deigned to make the trip with them, he did not seem too concerned about his fiancée making the difficult journey. He managed his family's finances. He might join the Harringtons once they were settled, then decide whether he would stay or bring Lillian back East. Angela believed he was happy to have a year or two more of bachelorhood.

The boys fought each other daily, rolling in the dirt, punching and pulling hair so fiercely Angela feared they would seriously injure each other. They shouted at each other all day and howled back at the coyotes at night. The older people were serious and distant, but being with fellow emigrants made their small party feel less vulnerable and the days pass more quickly.

One afternoon Angela had found a quiet spot to write in her journal, she saw Mary lugging a large bundle of clothes to the river. She had made the boys remove their shirts and socks to give them a good scrubbing, now she would do the same to their clothing. Angela, felt guilty for being at such a frivolous activity as writing and went to see if she could help. "Many hands make light work," she said.

The woman stared at her with no change of expression. Not knowing what to do, Angela walked with her. She could at least get a little water to mix with her ink if the woman didn't want her help. She returned to her writing until it became too dark.

In camp the boys were wrestling, rolling on the blankets spread for dining and sending supper things flying. Clara was resting with a damp cloth on her forehead. She had a headache every night since meeting the Thompsons otherwise she would have not have allowed the boys' behavior to go unchecked. Lillian and Mrs. Edith Thompson were putting away their mending.

"How can you stand the noise?" Lillian moaned to Edith. "Do make them stop."

"The sounds of children playing keeps a person young," she answered jovially.

Not the sounds of these children, Angela thought. They were abrasive and rude. They never helped with any chores, ran rampantly, and ignored all reprimands.

"I'm afraid the noise has an ill effect on our mother," Lillian said, scowling in their direction.

"Poor dear," Edith sympathized. "I wish I had some headache powder for her. Caleb, come here! Time to sleep!" she hollered making Lillian cringe and Clara put a hand to her head.

When Ben and Angela placed his pup in her nest under the wagon, she asked, "Have you thought of a name for her yet? Maybe you could call her West or something pertaining to the trip."

104

"I know! How about Traveler? She's a traveler like us. I think I'll name her Traveler."

"That's a good name. She looks like she's going to stay put. Let's turn in ourselves."

"Yeah Traveler gets up early, like us. Hey Ange, you know how we kind of do something in the morning so Mr. Finch doesn't hit Prisoner? And you know how Traveler did it for us today? Maybe it could be her job? I was scared at first when she went right over, too scared even to chase her. He didn't mind; he liked her."

"That's true. I don't see why that can't be her job." She smiled back at Ben's happy grin.

They were pleased with their new secret. Every morning they let the pup wake the prisoner. They simply aimed her in his direction as they walked by, feigning innocence and ignorance.

Ben wasn't sleeping well now that he was the proud owner of a dog. He would toss and turn at night, worrying that she had wandered off and gotten eaten by a wild animal. He rose before sun up each morning. Angela worried about him out in the dark. She tried to sleep light so the sounds of him rising would wake her. She hadn't mentioned it to their mother for fear she would force Ben to give up the puppy. Lillian bothered by his agitation that night, scolded him. "Ben, lie still."

Clara asked, "Benjamin are you feeling well?"

"Yes ma'am, I'm fine," he answered.

"Then stop squirming."

One morning when Angela went out, she couldn't find him. No puppy under the wagon either. He knew better than to go off alone, she thought. Finally she saw him coming towards her in the dark.

"I can't find Traveler," he cried.

"Maybe she is with her mother and brothers and sisters."

"No, I looked. I looked all under the wagons. She's not anywhere."

"I'll help you look under the wagon again."

She searched carefully around the wagon. When she was passing the prisoner he moved. She stopped. He'd never wakened on his own. There was something strange about the movement. She looked closer. It was the puppy curled against him. When she heard Angela's footsteps she thumped her little tail and waddled to her. Angela scooped her up and brought her to Ben.

Mornings while the adults prepared for the day's long travel the boys were to wash and help pack, but they wandered off, hunting for animals with sticks and rocks. They sometimes wandered out of sight. No one worried; they could be heard even when not seen.

"Come Abigail. Let's do our hair," Lillian said. She and her young admirer went off giggling to attend to their morning grooming. Barton slowly heaved himself up and meandered off in the same direction. Angela saw him and felt that tightening in her stomach. She got up and headed in the same direction, unsure of what she suspected. Most likely a coincidence, she thought. My uneasiness is more reflective of my own untrusting nature than of him. I should just stay in camp and mind my own business. She almost walked straight into Barton, who had stopped to light his pipe. Startled, he dropped the match. He stomped it out with his boot and ground it into the dirt. "Nice way to start a brush fire, sneaking up on people like that," he huffed.

"Uh, sorry. Just looking for my sister," she mumbled and plowed forward.

He said nothing for a few seconds. Then he called after her, "Good, that's good. Your sister needs protecting. She's not suited to this rough…" She outdistanced the sound of his voice.

Angela didn't want to startle the two girls. She rustled the grass and called out their names.

"Oh I'm glad you are here Angela," Lillian said. "Let Abigail practice on you. We can at least do our hair in these primitive circumstances."

When they returned to camp, Angela noted that neither Barton Finch nor the prisoner were in sight. Good, that meant he was with his charge and hadn't been lurking somewhere near them.

"Benjamin!" Clara called. "Angela? Lillian? Is your brother with you?"

"No, mother," they said. The Thompson boys charged back into camp with the dogs barking and running under foot, but no Ben or Traveler.

"Have you seen Ben?" Angela asked them.

"Nope," Charles answered.

"I don't believe you. None of you have seen him?"

"Not since breakfast," Jon answered.

"Do you know where he went?"

"Nope."

"Benjamin, where are you? Come here at once!" Clara called.

Lillian sang out, "Ben! Oh Ben! Where are you?"

"Don't worry, he can't be far," Jacob Thompson passed them leading his oxen.

The Harrington women went from person to person asking if anyone had seen Ben. They scanned the area and called.

"I'll help you look," Abigail said.

"Stay in sight of the wagons," her mother called. She grabbed Caleb's hand as he tried to follow his sister. "You stay here with your cousins, one missing boy is enough. Your sister and I will look."

"Ben, Benjamin!" A chorus of women's voices sang out.

Lou released the horse he was leading and joined the search.

Barton hurried back into camp, pushing the prisoner ahead of him. "What is it?" he shouted to Clara. "What's the boy done now?"

"We cannot find him."

"Uh ha," he said as though it was expected, "I'll find him." He shoved the prisoner down and stomped off calling.

Angela stood in one spot, trying to control her rising panic. From what direction had the boys come when they returned? She couldn't remember. Fear was mixing her logic into a batter of nonsense. "Think," she said out loud, trying to calm her reason. Her mother and sister ran back and forth, their calls becoming hysterical cries. Lou, Barton Finch and Jacob were moving in different directions out of camp, trailing out of sight and still no happy voices announced finding Ben. Where could he be? Why wasn't he answering? Rushing off haphazardly, she saw the prisoner out of the corner of her eye; his body language stopped her. He had pushed his hair out of his eyes, and was searching the horizon with every fiber of his being. Barton bellowed off in the distance, other voices were fading away. Lou disappeared down by the Platte River.

"Can you find him? Will you?" she asked desperately.

He nodded and struggled up on his good leg.

107

"I think they were playing over there." Her voice wavered.

She started to race off then stopped to look back at him. He was standing still, his dark eyes taking in everything. Then he limped after her. She had to slow her pace because he moved slowly. The thick jungle of grasses was difficult for him and he paused frequently to look, listen and examine the stalks. Please hurry, she pleaded silently. Lou saw them making their way along. He watched curiously then followed at a distance. The prisoner focused on a direction moving right and north purposefully. He progressed unsteadily, losing his balance more than once. Angela fell in behind him, calling her brother's name. This time when the prisoner paused she noticed the flattened grass.

"Do you see him?" she asked.

He didn't answer, only continued on, as slowly as before. What have I done? Where is he taking me? Over the noise of their legs rustling grass Angela heard a new sound. She stopped to listen. He continued to pick his way forward. She followed. Now she heard it clearly. It was yips and barking. Traveler.

"Ben, where are you?"

Then with relief melting over her she heard him. "Ange, come here! Hurry!"

They pushed through the grass and found him sitting on the ground, restraining Traveler, who was barking excitedly. In front of him something furry and orange was thrashing.

"It's caught in a trap Ange. It won't let me near to help," Ben explained. His face was streaked with sweat and tears.

It was a fox snapping its sharp white teeth in fear and pain. Its hind legs were caught in a rusty metal trap. Angela gingerly reached for it. A hand firmly pulled her back. The prisoner moved in front of her, an arm's length from the flashing teeth. He lowered himself to sit, holding an arm out to keep Ben from getting any closer to the animal. Leaning his upper body back as a barrier between them and the animal, he pulled his torn shirt off. He looped it over the animal's head, quickly tying it, covering the eyes and shutting the jaws. Then he grasped the trap with both hands and tried to pull it open. His arms and shoulders quivered with the effort, but the jaws would not budge. He looked around then pointed to a rock out of his reach. Ben jumped up and retrieved it. The young man pounded at the bolt where the

108

jaws of the trap came together. Lou walked up behind them. He cupped his hands around his mouth and called back several times, "He's here! The boy's here!"

Ben, Angela, and the young man were oblivious to the relayed shouts of the others and to their arrival as they followed Lou's voice. Barton appeared just as the rusted joint of the trap gave way. The prisoner cradled the fox and Ben opened metal the jaws, releasing the delicate legs.

Barton drew his gun. "What is it? Fox? Leg's most likely busted. Better shoot it."

"No!" yelled Ben. He realized for the first time the others were there.

"Put it down and back away," Barton ordered.

Jacob Thompson said, "It'd be most merciful son." He put his hand on the boy's back.

"No, I won't let you." Ben stood and faced the men.

"Fox pelt is pretty fair trade," Barton said. "You could get something nice for it."

"I don't care," Ben yelled. "Don't kill it."

Lou peered over Angela's shoulder and shook his head, "Naw, it's just a kit. Shootin' it would mess up what little pelt there is."

"I'll snap its neck," Barton suggested.

"A wild critter can't make it on broke legs, son," Jacob explained to Ben.

Angela had remained sitting next to the prisoner watching as he held the tiny legs in his hands. He gently moved them between his fingers. The skin was torn and bleeding, but they moved freely.

"The legs are not broken," she declared excitedly.

"Of course they're broken." Barton leaned closer.

Lou picked up the trap they had tossed aside. "Legs must have been small enough to slip between the teeth, held them, but didn't bite down hard enough to break. This is for a bigger animal, not as tight as it oughta be. In pretty bad shape at that, look at the rust. Lord knows when it was put out here. Let it go Finch."

While the men discussed its fate, the young man pulled his shirt off the animal with one efficient motion. With outstretched arms he held back Ben and Angela, who were on either side of him. The little

109

fox didn't turn on them; it limped off, disappearing in the long grasses.

"Might have got yourself a nice knife for the pelt," Barton grumbled.

"Let's get you back to camp, boy," Jacob said.

"Yes Ben, please hurry," urged Angela, "Mother's terribly worried about you. Go to her."

The Thompson men led Ben away with his pup, and Lou started slowly after. Angela looked down at the prisoner in wonder. He was gazing in the direction the fox had taken, his right hand unconsciously rubbing his bad leg. She picked up his rag of a shirt to hand to him. The sight of his torso shocked her. His ribs stuck out, his body sunk away from the bones. He was all sinew and skin. A purplish bruise spread over most of his left shoulder blade, scratches and welts covered his back and shoulders. She looked away quickly. He put on the shirt and struggled to his feet.

The sight of Barton, gun drawn, face darkened, made Angela realize for the first time what she'd done.

"Mr. Finch, I was so scared. I didn't think. … I thought being an Indian, he might be a good tracker. I'm sorry. I was so scared for Ben." She was shaky, but she had to do this. "I'm so sorry. I'll never do it again."

He was looking at her, his face a mask of anger, his eyes glaring into hers. She suddenly feared the repercussions the young man would face because of her actions.

"I asked him to help. I know it was a stupid, dangerous thing. But this is proof of … of the effectiveness of your training. I was safe because you've made him … so obedient."

She didn't dare look at the prisoner. She was ashamed of herself, saying these things in his hearing. "I'll help you record your ideas, if you like."

Barton's face went blank, then relaxed. He reached forward and put an arm around her. "It was a dangerous position you put yourself in Miss. I hope now you'll trust my ways more and mind yourself."

He squeezed her closer. She held her breath and closed her eyes tight. At that moment the prisoner stumbled against him, causing the lawman to release Angela. Barton grabbed him by the arm, but did him no further violence.

Clara had finished scolding and crying over Ben when Angela reached them. Lillian was hiccuping little sobs. "Oh Angela, how did you find him?" she asked.

She was relieved to see that they did not know what she had done and she was not about to tell. Barton Finch was not likely to upset Clara by admitting he'd left the outlaw unsupervised and unrestrained.

As punishment Clara ordered Ben to ride inside with her. Lillian rode in the Thompson's wagon with Abigail, where she could pass the time filling the happy girl's head with visions of parties, dances and beautiful dresses. Angela would walk without her brother's company today, but it would give her precious time to herself to recover from the morning's events.

Ready to get underway, Lou and the prisoner were up on the driver's bench. They were surprised by the sudden appearance of a bundle, then Angela's head and shoulders popped up behind it.

The prisoner turned his head away.

"I ... wonder if you have room for this up here," she asked from the prisoner's side. "It's crowded inside. I thought ... maybe ... if there is a little room up here, you might be able to fit this here for me."

Lou's wrinkles deepened with bafflement, but he said to the prisoner, "Go on. Take it."

His head down, the young man took the bundle of linens tied up in a blanket and set them by the ladder-steps.

"Umm... it's quite light. I'm afraid it might fall out. Would you mind putting your leg over it?" she asked.

He looked at Lou, who shrugged his shoulders and said, "Go on. Help the lady out." He lifted his right leg with his hand and placed it to rest on the soft bundle.

"I hope it's not too much trouble. Thank you," she said quickly and disappeared down the rungs.

The prisoner gazed after her until Lou startled him with a loud laugh and hand slap on his own thigh. He turned, looking at Lou curiously.

"Go ahead, get comfortable. I think the lady is tryin' to say thanks."

In spite of the tangle of hair Lou could see disbelief in his eyes.

111

"Yer gonna need it, pretty rough up ahead." He slapped the reins, chuckling as they started off.

With his bad leg cushioned, for the first time the prisoner was able to sleep much of the day. Lou met Angela when he climbed down for the first stop.

"Much more restful today, Miss," he said with an upward jerk of his head.

She blushed and looked down. Lou watched her walk off with a twinkle in his eye and a humorous shake of his head.

The outcome of her transgression in the fox incident was that Angela's precious time for writing was lost. Barton took her up on her offer to document his philosophy on the management and transportation of criminals. Her evening spare time was spent using her treasured writing supplies to record his pompous diatribes.

Ben was very quiet the next several days. He played with Traveler, who rode inside with him, his one comfort in his restricted activities. They drifted ahead of the Thompsons, though they could often see them a few miles back. The distance was comfortable, close enough not to feel alone, far enough to give each other peace. Soon they outpaced them by a day and they no longer shared campsites. Angela observed the prisoner was more lucid. He sat up longer in the evenings. Stronger, he helped Lou to repair the wagon and to pick pebbles out of the horses hooves and wash their harness sores.

Chapter 9

"The bear being so hard to die reather intimedated us all. I confess that I do not like the gentleman and had reather fight two Indians than one bear."

Merriweather Lewis

"And I don't want the world to see me Cuz I don't think that they'd understand."

"Iris" Goo Goo Dolls

One night the skies opened up in a terrible thunderstorm. Barton and Lou dashed into the wagon with the family for whatever protection it could provide; their tent was no match for the howling wind and torrential rain. Water dripped steadily through the wagon's canvas seams and the wind gusted so violently Angela thought it would pull the entire canopy off the wagon. Between white lightning flashes Ben asked, "Mr. Finch, what about Prisoner?"

"What about him, boy?"

"He's not coming in here, is he?" Lillian exclaimed.

"No, don't worry," he assured her. "A little rain won't hurt him, only clean him up some." He nudged Ben with an elbow.

Ben crawled to the doorway, pushed back the flap and stuck his head out.

"Benjamin! Inside now," his mother commanded.

He pulled his dripping head inside. "I can't see him."

"He didn't go anywhere," Barton said.

Eventually everyone managed to sleep in the driest spot they could find, despite the rippling canvas, crashing thunder and occasional cracks of tree limbs breaking.

The night was long and uncomfortable, but the morning brought a world reborn. Mist floated mysteriously above the river in the early

113

gray light; the air smelled fresh and clean. Ben and Angela poked their heads out and Traveler squirmed past them to jump out.

That was when they saw the tree. The wind had uprooted it. It had fallen near the wagon a few feet closer could have meant disaster. A large limb was wedged against the wheel where the prisoner had been chained. They climbed down and pulled aside branches and leaves until they found the end of the chain, still attached to the wheel. The rest disappeared under a tangle of leaves, branches, and sticks. The prisoner was nowhere to be seen. They pulled at the tree, but their efforts only caused scratching and thumping against the side of the wagon disturbing its occupants. Lou was the first out, hobbling as quickly as he could. Barton followed more slowly.

"The tree! It's on Prisoner!" Ben shouted. He tugged frantically.

"Stand aside Miss," Barton said. He took a hold of the limb with Lou and Ben. Angela picked up the puppy, who was making a nuisance of herself by barking and getting underfoot.

When they managed to pull the tree back, Angela turned away. Then she peeked back. There was no crushed body under it. In fact there appeared to be no one at all, only the chain trailing under the wagon. Barton kneeled with a grunt to peer beneath. Ben dropped down and squirmed all the way under the wagon on his belly while the lawman tried to see.

"Benjamin!" Clara had emerged from the wagon just in time to see him disappearing beneath. "Get him out of there! Is that man under there?"

"He'd better be," Barton said. Angela saw the sweat on his brow in spite of the cool morning air.

He reached to pull Ben out by the feet, but the boy popped out, grinning.

"He's sound asleep," he announced. "How can he sleep like that?"

Angela let Traveler down. She trotted under the wagon.

Barton folded his bulk once more. His fingers closed on the chain to yank the prisoner out by it. Before he could the pup jumped out and licked his face. "Get away!" He put his hands out to ward off her advances and the young man slid out from under the wagon, his tattered shirt splotched with mud and tar from the wagon's undercarriage. Lillian squealed in horror when she saw him. "He looks like a wild man. Oh, oh how awful!"

114

Angela cast a stern look at her sister to no avail; she continued to carry on while Mr. Finch unlocked the chain. He looked up at her and chuckled indulgently.

"Haven't I been telling you about these Indians," he said. He took Lillian's arm and escorted her away. "Have you ever noticed their faces? They don't show emotions, do they?"

Lillian, who until their prisoner had never seen an Indian before, nodded rapidly in agreement. Angela was disgusted with her sister's behavior, but at least it smoothed over Barton Finch's anger.

Angela and Ben followed Lou who was checking on the horses. Luckily they hadn't been too spooked by the storm and were grazing in sight at a half-mile's distance. They lifted their heads at Lou's whistle, but showed no inclination to come.

"May we help catch the horses?" Angela asked.

When he looked at her, sizing her up she added, "I groomed and harnessed our horse for my father before he made rounds."

Lou simply said, "Get Bill there and the boy can get Sam. Watch your toes."

They led the gentle giants back to camp by the lead ropes, which dangled from their halters for that very purpose. When Angela passed the leads to Lou she asked, "Are you familiar... Do you know about Indians and their ways?"

"Known some," he said as he took the horse from her.

"Do they kill and torture?" Ben asked, moving closer.

"Ben, watch you don't get stepped on," his sister warned.

"Same as most folks, some good, some no account."

"Do they have families? Do they have feelings?" Ben asked.

Angela was worried Lou would get impatient with Ben, but he replied without irritation, "Course they have families. Feelin's? You mean like love, hate and carin' 'bout their own? Who's to say 'bout other folks feelin's. I've seen them when one of their own passed on. They holler like they're dyin' themselves. Cut themselves too."

"Cut themselves? Why?" Ben asked.

"Not sure. Maybe to make one hurt take away a worse hurt. Maybe to let the hurt out. Indians I know, have strong feelin's 'bout things."

Lou stopped and spoke directly to Ben. "Just cuz a fellow has hisself under control don't mean he don't feel things. Folks just have

115

different ways." He took the lead rope from the boy. "Now stand back."

Ben tried to continue the conversation at the morning meal saying, "What do you mean Indian's cut themselves? How do they do it?"

Lou just pulled his hat lower and drank his coffee. Turning to Barton, Ben asked, "Prisoner is only half Indian? How can he be half-Indian?

"Fur traders, rough sorts themselves on account of living alone, tending their traps in the middle of nowhere. They mix with Indians and now there's half breeds like him."

"Maybe he's more like us because he is half white?" Ben suggested.

"No, the half breeds are the worse sort. They don't fit anywhere. Makes them kind of crazy."

Angela had many questions, which she kept to herself. She longed for Lou to recount stories and experiences, but it was clear he had his fill of questions at least for today.

She wondered what the young man looked like under all that dirt and hair. His eyes were dark and his hair as well. He had found Ben, easily following signs no one else had seen. Was that a trait he inherited from his Indian side? Where was his family now? Had they given up on him because of what he'd done? She wished she could record these thoughts in her journal, instead she had to record Barton's blustering, all the while biting her tongue to keep from challenging his ideas. Some of his comments he hurled loudly at the prisoner, who unlike the night of the chaining, appeared to take no notice.

Watching Lou and the young man during the day, she was amazed by what a person could withstand. She wondered if infection had set in the bone, if there were any signs of gangrene. Someone should look to his leg. Mr. Finch didn't seem to have any medical knowledge. Did Lou? The lawman would probably not give permission for him to examine it. She doubted the young man himself would let him. She would never have the nerve to ask Lou or Mr. Finch. Would she know what to look for? He balanced on one leg as he slipped the bridle over Toby's long head, his head close to the horse's as if they were exchanging secrets.

On one beautiful July evening, Lou went to the river to try his luck fishing. He let Ben tag along to help. Armed with nets, a spear and a fishing pole, the two fishermen rolled up their pant legs and waded in. Traveler barked from the bank. She didn't like to be left out, but wasn't about to step into the strange moving surface.

When the fishermen returned to the campfire they were mosquito bitten and proud. The nets sagged with fish cleaned and ready for the fire. Ben also lugged new treasures he had found in the water. He presented his findings to his family: pieces of tables and chairs.

"Benjamin what ever did you drag that slimy mess up here for?" Clara said. "Throw it away. Wait, let me see." Examining a table leg she said, "Why this was a lovely piece. It is very fine wood."

Barton was lounging nearby in anticipation of a fresh fish dinner. "Yes, families tried to bring all of their fine things with them. They had no idea how hard this trip would be. They overloaded the wagons. The animals got stuck in bogs and rivers. Many expensive pieces of furniture, gunpowder even food had to be thrown out to lighten the load. We know so much more these days about the trail. And as I said before, it's much safer. You rarely see savages. Except at the forts where they come to trade."

"Why is that Mr. Finch? Why don't we see Indians? Why did they make them move away?" Ben asked.

"I told you; they're being moved so whites can travel safely. Also they follow the buffalo and other game. We don't see many buffalo, so we don't see many Indians." He took the first plate of fish Lou had cooked and Clara passed.

"I'd like to see Indians," Ben said later. They were all sitting with their plates. "Ange and I saw some buffalo one day. They were a long way away. They just looked like black humpy things." He picked fish bones out of his mouth and threw them on the ground.

"Put 'em in here. Later throw em back in the river. Don't want no bears comin' round," Lou warned. He passed him a bucket.

"What would you do if you saw an Indian?" Ben asked Angela later as they carried the bucket of fish bones away.

"I'm not sure. I think I would stand still."

"Lillian would scream."

"Mmm, she probably would," she agreed.

As soon as they returned Barton said to her, "I'd like to dictate more of my ideas."

Angela collected her materials and sat next to him. She didn't dare beg off, after all he hadn't told anyone what she'd done the day Ben was missing. She looked up now and then from her writing to see Barton spitting fish bones from his mouth on to the ground. His voice sounding dully on her ears, her hand wrote the words, but her attention wandered. She saw Ben bringing the prisoner his meal. Barton had chained him to a tree about thirty yards away.

The evening wore on. Angela couldn't see the words on the paper. Traveler was curled next to her. She could make out Ben in the shadowy outskirts of the firelight, sitting a few feet from the prisoner, most likely asking him questions as he did when the others were too busy to notice. Lillian and Clara rose to retire. The air was heavy with night dew. Angela smelled a faint skunkish scent. Where was it coming from?

Lou tipped his hat back, suddenly on his guard. A large furry shape was trundling towards them. It stopped and snuffled around the ground, smelling the remains of the fish. Angela stood up, dropping her papers, pen and ink. At the same time Lillian cried, "What is it?" Then her voice rising, she shrieked, "A bear! Oh my God, a bear!"

"Easy now." Lou reached for his gun.

Traveler began barking ferociously. Angela snatched her up, held her struggling little body tightly and clamped her jaws shut. Lillian and Clara gripped each other's arms. Traveler's barking startled the bear. It stood on its hind legs, rising to its immense height it looked down on the humans.

Across the campfire Ben had been intent on extracting answers from his reluctant, fatigued source. He looked up to see the fearsome beast snuffling into camp.

"Wow!" he stood about to run to them.

The prisoner grabbed his arm. "No," he said hoarsely, louder than any sound he'd made before. He pulled Ben down behind himself. "Stay."

He tugged hard at the chain with one hand the other held Ben. Then he took his hand off the boy to jerk at the chain with both hands. He ceased his futile efforts to free himself and used his arm to keep Ben behind him.

"Bear…" he tried to shout, but ended coughing, his throat unused to speech.

He turned to Ben, "Yell," he croaked between coughs. "Stay behind. Yell."

Ben hesitated. He wanted to run across the camp to his family. The prisoner's hand held him fast. He shouted, "Hey! Hey!"

The prisoner joined in when he could. He waved both arms over his head. "Hey Bear! Here! Come!"

Still standing on its hind legs the bear twisted to see them. The young man pushed Ben further behind him. "Stay. Don't move," he said.

Lou lifted his rifle. "I got him!" Barton said. His shouts turned the bear's attention back on them.

Lillian shrieked again.

"Hey Bear! Here!" The prisoner shouted and Ben added his calls. The animal accepted the challenge, dropped on all fours and lumbered towards them. It stopped a couple of feet before Ben and the prisoner, its body between them and the others.

Lou stared along his rifle barrel.

"Do something!" Clara implored.

Barton readied his gun, but Lou stopped him, his hand on the barrel. "'less you drop him on the spot, which ain't likely, you'll just make him mad. He'll tear 'em to shreds."

"We've got to hit him both at once," Barton said.

"Can't get off a shot without risking the boy and the kid," Lou murmured. The two men moved slowly to position themselves for shots that wouldn't hit the humans.

Lillian sobbed, "My God, my God!"

Angela prayed silently, "Please God don't let it hurt Ben, please."

The bear padded forward and sniffed the prisoner, its nose in his face and hair. It brushed a paw diagonally across his chest and shoulder. The prisoner remained motionless, sitting tall. Ben, sitting behind him felt him tense for a moment. Losing interest, the bear turned and shuffled off into the trees.

Lou lowered his rifle. "Let it be," he said to Barton.

Until it was completely out of sight the prisoner stayed completely still. Then he exhaled slowly and his body relaxed.

"Can I move now?" Ben asked.

119

He nodded once and Ben sprinted to his family.

"Oh Ben, we were so frightened," Lillian cried. "Are you hurt? Look at me I'm shaking so, I don't know how I stayed on my feet without fainting." She sat with a thump.

Clara held him at arm's length to look him over. "I must sit. Here Benjamin sit beside me."

"I'm fine," he shrugged them off, too excited to be restrained, "but the bear scratched Prisoner I think. Did you see the size of him? I think it was some sort of giant bear."

"Yes, Benjamin, it was extremely large. Let's not talk about it any more. Are you certain you are not injured?" Clara asked.

"It never touched me." He continued breathlessly, "I saw its paw. Its paw was as big as my head. And the claws! It had these long claws coming out. It went like this," he swiped his hand across the air. "It wasn't slapping really. It was more like it was just patting Prisoner."

Lillian hid her face in her hands where she sat. "Please let's not talk of it anymore," she wailed.

Ben turned to Angela, "Ange, I think the bear hurt Prisoner." He took her by the hand and pulled her. "Come see."

Ignoring their mother who was calling, "Benjamin, where are you going?" Angela let her brother drag her over to the prisoner.

He was half reclined on an elbow, scanning the edges of the light and dark made by the firelight, weary, but vigilant. He saw Ben's feet and legs coming close, just behind the sight of Angela's skirts made him sit up. Ben bent close. "See? He's got a scratch right there."

He put his finger in a tear in the shirt. The prisoner looked down in surprise at the wound, then back at Ben.

"Look Ange," Ben directed.

Angela came forward, bending her knees to scrunch down and see. The man turned his head away and pushed himself back. He hit the end of the chain and it pulled at his leg, his breath caught.

Ben leaned in again. "It's alright. It's just my sister. Let her look at your cut."

The prisoner shook his head. Angela peeked over Ben's shoulder. She saw a red streak in the shirt. It did not appear to be deep.

"I'll be back in just a minute," she whispered to her brother.

She gathered a towel and some water still warm over the fire. Barton and Lou were scouting the area where the bear had

120

disappeared. Lou was surprised by a touch from Angela. "Could I borrow your flask?" she asked.

"The boy hurt?"

"No, the prisoner."

"Is it bad?"

"No, I don't think so." She followed him back to where he found the flask for her.

Clara was occupied with Lillian. "You must cease this, Lillian. Pull yourself together. Let's prepare for bed."

"I hate this place. It's dangerous. It's miserable!" she sobbed. "I want to go home!"

Barton came back from scouting the bear's whereabouts. He tried to comfort Lillian and assure her of their safety. A worrisome thought crossed his mind. What if these women decided to turn back? Lou might agree. He didn't seem to approve of them anyway. Then how would he get his prisoner to Fort Hall? He'd have to hook up with another party going that way if they turned back. He'd hate to be parted from the lovely company. Although this prisoner got under his skin more than any other, this trip was the most pleasant he'd ever taken. Usually he traveled with men, fur traders or a hunting party. They moved quickly, spoke seldom and were not pretty to look at. On those trips he was always bored and hungry. The criminals were mostly older characters with no fight left in them and resigned to their fate. With this one he could see the defiance in his shining eyes no matter what he did to break him. In many ways the victory of breaking him was satisfying, but there was still a bit of defiance shining through. He anticipated completely breaking the spirit of one so stoical. He had fought them like a mad man, this one, almost making it back to the little cabin.

He cleared his throat. "Nothing to fret about ladies. It's all over now. That bear is long gone."

"It was so large Mr. Finch," Lillian said through her tears.

"Yes, it was a large male. Looking for a bite to eat that's all."

Far from reassured, Lillian again burst into tears.

"No, no, they eat leftover scraps, berries anything they can find. They don't eat humans," he explained.

"Angela, what are you doing?" Clara said. She had spotted her daughter with Lou. "It is time to prepare for sleep." She helped Lillian to her feet.

"Yes mother, Ben and I will be there shortly," she answered, "We're picking up a few things."

Thankful for Lillian being a distraction once again, she walked back to Ben and the young man.

Meanwhile, Ben had been trying to reason with his charge. "My sister knows about stuff. My father was a doctor. She used to help him with sick people. I was too little to remember, but she tells me about it sometimes. She doesn't faint like Lillian and her face doesn't get all funny like Mother's when she sees a hurt."

The young man stayed stretched to the end of his chain. When Angela knelt on the ground before him, he turned away, breathing quickly. Ben moved to his right to look more directly in his face. "It's really alright. Ange fixes me when I hurt myself."

While he talked Angela carefully parted the torn cloth of the shirt. The prisoner shook his head. She and Ben met with their eyes. Her gaze was questioning. Ben shrugged. She poured water on the towel, looked up at the prisoner, then at Ben.

"She's going to wash your cut now," he explained.

The head shook.

"You wouldn't want it to get infected," Angela said. She felt foolish. What did he care if the wound got infected? It was probably the least of his problems. She carefully washed the claw mark. It was not deep. He flinched when she put the towel against his skin.

"Does it hurt?" Ben asked.

He shook his head.

"Are you sure?" he asked.

The young man nodded, still breathing rapidly.

"Ange. He's more afraid of you than the bear," Ben declared.

"Oh, Ben." She almost smiled at this absurdity.

"It's true," he said, not taking his eyes off the man's face.

Her hands were trembling. She picked up the flask. "This may sting a little," she said softly.

"Oh yeah, like the stuff you put on my scrapes," Ben said.

She poured some of the liquid directly on the cut. The prisoner stiffened slightly.

"Blow on it Ange. Like you do mine. It takes the sting away," he explained to him.

At this suggestion the young man tried to pull back more. Angela saw fear in his eyes behind his hair. Ben's right, she thought, he's afraid of me or treatment.

"No, Ben, let's leave him alone to rest. We've bothered him enough for tonight." She collected her things and backed away.

The prisoner's body relaxed when they moved away.

"Did you see him with that bear?" Ben was still worked up from the experience. "He wasn't one bit afraid. He called that old bear right to him. Then he sat up tall, right up to that old bear."

"It was terrible. You could have been hurt."

"No, Prisoner pushed me behind him. He said, don't move. I didn't either. I sat still as a statue."

"That's good Ben. I'm glad you listened." She squeezed his hand. Their mother was standing by the wagon steps about to call when she saw them returning. "Shush, your sister is asleep inside," she said before they climbed into the wagon.

Lying under the blankets Ben whispered, "Do you think the bear will come back?"

"No, it's safe now. Go to sleep," Angela whispered, but she had trouble falling asleep herself.

Images of the bear's massive back as it threatened her brother and the prisoner flashed against her eyelids. The horrible feeling of being helpless to do anything to save her brother, she couldn't shake it off. Then another image intruded; she saw the prisoner defiantly calling the bear from where he sat tall in the flickering nightmarish light.

Before dawn she was awakened by Ben stirring restlessly, mumbling fretfully.

"Angela?" whispered her mother. "Is that Benjamin?"

"Yes," she replied. "I think he's having a nightmare."

Her mother sighed. Ben quieted and Clara fell back to sleep, but Angela lay awake. Her thoughts and emotions wouldn't let her rest. The thin wooden sides of the wagon seemed flimsy protection against the dangers lurking outside in the dark.

In the early morning the world was less formidable. Ben, Angela and Traveler walked through the dewy grass. The dampness clung to their clothing and the air still hung with night's coolness, but Angela

123

felt less fearful. After skimming the surface of the water to clear away frogs, minnows and other creatures, they washed. Individual drops of dew hanging from the tips and edges of leaves caught and held the brightening rays of light.

"The dew drops look like tiny crystals," Angela said. She showed Ben the tiny glistening lights.

"Yeah, like the glass from the chandelier that hung in the dining room at Mother's friend's house. You know the big white house with the bushes in front."

She wondered if he missed their old home, if he regretted this trip. She didn't ask; she didn't want to plant any seeds of regret. For herself, while she knew there were things she missed and more she would come to miss, she tried only to think of the new start awaiting them. She was content to be away from the comments and looks of their old friends who came to realize their changed situation. How the snubs hurt her mother and Lillian though they pretended not to notice. Angela wasn't hurt, the snubs only made her more convinced of the shallowness of those society people. Now they had escaped that life, that world where fashion ruled and you were locked into a position in a little self-enclosed society that believed itself to be all the world. The opinions of one's circle of acquaintances were your lock and key. No matter what you did with your life they would always see you one way. Now we are free, she thought.

"Angela? Do you ever get scared?" Ben asked.

"Oh yes," she answered, surprised that he didn't know.

"What do you do so you don't have scary thoughts?"

"Well, on this trip I try to imagine what our new home will be like. I imagine the building itself, then the rooms. I think of how I would arrange it if it were my own. Do you want to hear?"

"Yes."

"It would be simple, the decor. There would be a large fireplace for heat at one end and a black cook stove for cooking in the kitchen. There'd be braided rugs on the floor and a long table for people to have dinner on or to tell stories or do work, like sewing and canning, any kind of project. Upstairs the beds would have warm colorful quilts and fluffy goose-down pillows. Downstairs in the open space away from the table there would be big stuffed chairs with knit blankets for people to curl up in and read by lanterns on little tables.

Outside there'd be the barns, corrals and further off ... I can just see it ... There'd be rolling pastures speckled with cows and horses grazing."

Ben listened thoughtfully. "It doesn't sound one bit like our Boston home."

"No, I suppose it doesn't."

"I like your house Angela. I think I'll live there too."

She smiled. They would be just fine she knew it in her heart.

Walking in the bright, hot sunshine a few afternoons later, Angela was struck by how changeable the terrain could be. Sometimes gently rolling land opened before them as if it reached to the very edge of the earth. Other times there were ridges and valleys and odd rock formations standing like mythic monsters. There were thickly treed areas, especially along the rivers and around pools and creeks. It was not all dusty dry desert as she had expected. At times they came upon old campsites, which they avoided for fear of sickness. Lou shot a deer and they all ate heartily of the thick venison steaks. Angela's fears diminished, except in the evenings when the light faded. Ben would still sit and ask the prisoner questions in the evening shadows. He was having nightmares about bears. He would stir, whimper and sometimes cry out in his sleep.

One night Angela woke feeling cold. Where Ben's warm body should be there was an empty space. She sat up and felt around: no Ben. She tiptoed outside. The moon was casting its iridescent liquid light on the world. The white canvas of the tent and the wagon cover glowed under its spell. Beyond it the prisoner slept on the damp ground. Something was moving behind him. Cautiously stepping closer to where he lay, she saw Traveler, who lifted her head and wagged her tail from her place behind him. The pup wasn't the only thing with him; there was another blanketed shape behind him.

"Ben?" she whispered.

The prisoner stirred. He did not sleep that deep exhausted sleep now that he was stronger and getting more rest. He pushed himself up on one arm, brushing his hair back with the other.

"Ben?" she tried again. She didn't think she should get too close to Prisoner.

He looked at her for a moment, not understanding. She pointed vaguely over him. He turned to see what she was indicating. He

125

touched the lump on the ground behind him, apparently as surprised as she to find Ben there. Ben murmured, but didn't wake. The prisoner slid himself back down, too tired to fully realize what was happening, but not concerned in the least that Ben was sleeping behind him. Angela remained there for a moment, not wanting to stir the people inside and not sure how the prisoner would react if she pursued the matter. He hadn't been completely awake. She quietly made her way back inside.

In the morning it came to her slowly as sleep dissipated that what she thought she'd been dreaming was real. Her brother was indeed outside sleeping behind the prisoner and worse she had known and let him remain there. She hurried outside. Ben sat up sleepily and saw his sister beckoning vigorously. He carefully stepped over the prisoner, whose head rolled on his arm.

"Go back to sleep. It's just me," Ben whispered as he climbed over the young man's body.

"Ben what are you doing out here?" she asked when they were out of hearing. "You frightened me. I didn't know where you were. That was a dangerous thing to do, he is a criminal after all." Even as she scolded she thought of her own carelessness the day when she gone with him to find Ben.

"I'm sorry Ange. It's just that bears can't get me with Prisoner. He knows what to do," he explained.

"Please don't do it again. Bears won't come into the wagon. Promise me you won't go out at night alone again."

Ben promised, but every so often Angela would wake to find him gone from his place and sleeping behind the chained man.

Chapter 10

"With all respect to civilization, I cannot help regretting this final consummation, and such regret will not be misconstrued by anyone who has tried the prairie and mountain life, who has learned to look with affectionate interest on the rifle that was once his companion and protector, the belt that sustained his knife and pistol, and the pipe which beguiled the tedious hours of his midnight watch, while men and horses lay sunk in sleep around him."

The Oregon Trail by Francis Parkman

"Most trappers were honored to be mistaken for Indians."

The World of the American Indian, National Geographic Society 1974

Continuing toward the next milestone, Fort Laramie, the days were oppressively hot. Angela found her throat and mouth dry after only an hour of walking. Yet, nights were surprisingly cool in contrast. Late afternoons and early evenings were the most pleasant time of the day, but the travelers tired and dirty from the long hot days were irritable. Lou wanted to start earlier in the mornings, take a longer mid daybreak and stop later in the afternoon to save the horses from pulling during the hottest time of the day. He expressed this wish one evening after the meal.

"Got to git going early. 'fore it's too hot," he said.

They all heard him, but weren't sure if this was an order, a suggestion, or if he was making a note to himself. It was hard to tell with Lou.

It was clear the next morning when he wasted no time. Barely pausing to eat and drink, he waited impatiently for Barton to unchain the prisoner. Lillian and Clara, oblivious to Lou's efforts for an earlier start, took their time doing their hair and putting on ointments to protect their skin; they were the last to be ready. Lou had the team all hitched and was grumbling to himself, pacing and casting scowls in their direction.

"Mother, Lillian, I think you'd better get in," Angela urged.

"Oh Angela, we're almost ready. Don't be such a worrywart. Who do you think you are? The trail boss?" Lillian answered.

"It's just better for the horses not to pull in the worst of the heat. It's better for everyone," Angela snapped back. "Why do you think our driver wants to get going? Everyone should not have to wait on you. Can't you try to be accommodating?"

"I think the heat is getting to you. You shouldn't be out walking if it's going to make you nasty," her sister said.

Angela retorted, "Who are you dressing up for anyway. Do you think the birds are impressed with your hair? It would do you a lot better if you washed instead."

Lillian replied loftily, "And who do you think you are? Queen of the frontier? Really Angela, you act more like a boy, lugging buckets, pretending to be some sort of expert frontier's woman. You don't know any more about this than I."

"Girls!" Clara interrupted. "You are not children. This is unbecoming behavior for young ladies. Angela, I do wonder if all this walking in the heat is getting to you. The sun is ruining your complexion; your feet must be hideous from all the walking. You don't want them becoming flat and wide. Perhaps you should ride."

"No, please Mother, the walking does me good in other ways. Besides Ben would drive everyone to distraction if he had to ride inside all day and you wouldn't want him walking alone."

"I suppose," her mother reluctantly concurred.

Angela did not know how she would keep from losing her temper if she was forced to be cooped up with Lillian fussing and fanning and Barton's loud speeches or snoring.

She walked in long angry strides. Lillian had no call to mock her that way. She had made no claims of knowledge of frontier travel. Because she was interested and wanted to help, didn't mean she was

128

unfeminine. She thought of Lillian back in Boston, how she always knew how to act, just what to say, unlike herself. She had so many ideas running around in her head, but couldn't express the simplest statement easily. She didn't have her sister's style and grace or her brother's easy openness. She felt her face all tight with anger. She heard her mother's voice in her head, "Angela you look ugly when you have that sullen expression on your face."

Ugly, she thought, I am ugly. And maybe I am boyish. When I was young I wished sometimes that I were a boy. They seemed to be freer. That wasn't true any more. She didn't want to be a boy, she just wasn't sure she wanted to be herself. Lately she had made an uneasy truce with herself, where she didn't hate herself, she could almost accept herself. Sometimes she thought, well, this is who I am, why fight it? This truce came and went.

When working with her father or engrossed in an interesting book, she could leave herself behind. On this long trip she didn't have time to think about herself. Maybe that was part of why she didn't mind the travel, no time for self-absorption and freedom from the old life, where people were classified like specimens in a naturalist's study. Lillian was charming and pretty, their mother dignified and proper. Then there was plain Angela. Out here she was free. Out here you had to survive, to act, just be … She hoped when they arrived at their new home the frontier community would have this same spirit, not be smaller version of the society from which they had come.

She heard a sound over the wagon's noise. Lou was saying something. The prisoner was holding out a ragged arm and pointing. She saw the sky to the south was hazy.

"What is it?" she shouted up to him.

"Prairie fire. Far away. Won't bother us none."

She wondered if Lou had a wife. If he did what would she look like? She tried to imagine her. First, she saw a tough wrinkled little female version of Lou. Then she saw a large plump woman with pink cheeks, a broad smile and a big soft embrace for everyone who came within reach. Lou spat over the side again and she discounted her own imaginings, most likely he wasn't married.

Much to her surprise she liked, even admired Lou, but she couldn't envision him as a husband, what with the way he made a living driving across the frontier. He didn't shirk from work. He knew how to handle himself that was certain. He could fish, he could hunt; a wife would never go hungry. And what about Barton? She shuddered. He wasn't married she knew that. He'd brought the subject up himself. First he'd asked why Lillian wasn't married, seeing as she was of age. He didn't ask about herself. When Clara explained Lillian was engaged to a most suitable man and he would eventually join them, he said, "I hope he deserves her."

"He is from a very good family," Clara said. "Lillian is fortunate to have made such a good match."

"I'm not surprised, not surprised at all," he said. "He's the fortunate one."

And then he said one thing Angela thought made sense.

"I hope he's adaptable for living outside a city."

A good match? What did it mean? Angela wondered how her mother and father had come to be together. They had entirely different interests. Is that how it always is with married people? Are they two different people sharing the same home? Living their own lives? The woman ran the house and the social obligations. The man attended his work. Did either know what the other did all day? Did they care? As a child she had never questioned these things. They only occurred to her now.

She would never marry. Who would want her for a wife anyway? What did it mean to be married? She thought of Lillian and her fiancé. Except when asked by Barton, she had not mentioned Phillip once this whole trip. Though back in Boston she spent hours discussing the wedding plans with Mother, she didn't talk about him, nor did her engagement seem to be a happier time than any other. Was her marriage just another event for Lillian to sail through in her lovely way? Shouldn't there be more to it?

Didn't marriage vows say something about God bringing two together? If marriage is a special union made by God shouldn't it be more remarkable to the people than a party and a business arrangement? She remembered a pair of geese in her grandparent's pond, they were always together; she never saw one without the other. Then one day the goose was attacked and killed by a dog. The gander spent the rest of its days hovering near the spot where its mate was killed, crying mournfully. Her grandmother explained that geese mate for life. The terrible sadness and the loyalty of the goose stayed with her as something special, something that meant more than just existing side by side, day after day: something much deeper.

In the afternoon they came upon the remains of an old Indian village. The skeletal remnants of homes looked like a child had been playing at building forts in the woods. Ben ran around climbing under cut trees that had framed housing.

"Let's move to another place," Lillian pleaded. "Mother, tell him we can't stay here."

Clara clasped her hands tightly in front of herself. "Mr. Finch, I'm not at all sure this is a good place to stay. Benjamin!"

But Lou was not about to be moved by silly females. He turned a deaf ear and waited for the prisoner to hop down from the bench.

"Do you think the Indians will come back?" Ben asked. "Would they kill us if they found us here?"

"There's no danger of them coming back. They've moved on," Barton Finch said.

Ben, half disappointed, half relieved that there would be no danger of returning Indians, asked, "Are we ever going to see any Indians?"

Barton laughed and grabbed the prisoner by the shoulders. "This is the closest you'll get to an Indian until we get to the fort."

"Will there be many Indians at the fort?" Ben asked.

"Oh yes. They'll be there for trading. Don't be so disappointed about not seeing the savages. Use to be you had to be on guard all the time for them. Natural born thieves, they'd steal your oxen or horses, anything."

"They'd steal stuff? How could people drive the wagons without horses?"

"It was a problem son. Yes sir, Indians can't resist horses." He emphasized this remark by thrusting the prisoner face first into the wagon. Ben looked at the prisoner, who grasped the wagon and leaned against it to stay upright. He scratched the ground with his stick as though he wanted to say something more, then walked away.

"Dig around," Barton Finch called after him, "You might find arrows or pottery."

Angela was walking around the site, her heart skipping with excitement. A people so different from what she knew they may as well have been from another world. This was their home, where they slept, ate, cried and laughed. She felt uncomfortably like an intruder. Ben passed her, his head down.

"Isn't this interesting Ben?"

He didn't answer.

"Is something wrong?" She looked back at the wagon.

Lillian was pleading with their mother to make Lou take them to a different site. Lou summoned the prisoner with a swing of his arm. Barton, with an impatient "Go on," sent him after the driver. Then he found himself a comfortable place to smoke his pipe. She wondered what he'd done this time.

Angela was setting up camp when she saw the prisoner suddenly stop in his work and listen the way he did, seemingly with his entire body. Lou noticed his attentiveness too. He reached up to the driver's seat and grabbed his rifle without questioning.

Through the lengthening shadows and on the cooling air, they heard the rattles, creaks and jangles of a wagon approaching. Voices carried over the noise to them, men shouting to each other. The words were unintelligible, but the tones conversational.

"Benjamin!" Clara called her youngest in the tone that brought him instantly to her side.

Lillian stood by her mother, the color draining from her face.

"Mr. Finch is it Indians?" Ben asked.

Barton put out his pipe and prepared his gun. Around the edge of the trees a team of six mules trotted briskly.

"Whoa, Whoa you!" The driver shouted and stood in his seat to haul on the reins.

Two men on horses rode up beside the mule wagon, another sat with the driver. A third horse was tied to the back of the wagon. The driver himself in a red flannel shirt with dark suspenders held up an arm to signal his companions to halt. "Any of you 'ave da sickness?" he shouted.

The Harrington party stared for a moment.

"Naw," Lou replied.

"What about you people?" Barton asked.

132

"No, we all fine," he answered. "Is good," he said to the riders.

They dismounted and the other passenger got out with the help of a cane.

"Sorry if we seemed rude," he apologized. He held his hat and cane in one hand, the other he held out for a handshake. "It's just that we heard rumors of cholera and measles among the emigrants. My name is Don. Don Masters."

He was thin and fair, his skin almost translucent. He had neat blond hair and his face was smeared with charcoal for protection from the sun.

"This is Tim Warner, Shawn Dawes and that is our fearless guide Pierre."

Pierre was not interested in formalities. A short, barrel chested man, he tended his team with curses and pushes. The others were young men in their early to mid twenties. Their clothes though worn from their travels were of good quality, coats over shirts, vests with ornate buttons that were missing here and there. They wore soft deerskin gloves and hardy boots. Shawn was freckled with sandy hair and merry eyes. He had a more solid frame than his companions. Tim had serious dark blue eyes, long thin limbs and fingers.

"I hope you don't mind," he said. "It seems we'll be staying here as well. Pierre is friendly with the Indians that sometimes camp here. Apparently this is one of his old stomping grounds."

"Don't none of us own it," Lou said. "Can't tell you where to stay or not to." He nodded at the prisoner and they went back to their chores,

"It's the ladies you should ask," Barton Finch said. "They might object."

Clara looked at him to see if he thought she should raise an objection. Lillian had stood close, one hand on her mother's arm, now she dropped the hand.

"We do apologize. Pierre is darn set in his ways," Don said.

"Pierre's the boss," Shawn laughed.

"It is quite alright. We are familiar with the stubborn nature of these guides," Clara said. Her lips were pulled in a thin line.

"We don't have much to spare in the way of meals," Barton said. He narrowed his eyes at their wagon and the stores.

133

Tim said, "We will of course respect your privacy and your wishes."

"Please be assured," Don said, "we are all gentlemen from good families. And meals are not a problem. In fact we would be delighted if you would join us for supper."

"Yes," Shawn said. "We have fresh venison. And I'm not a bad cook if I do say so myself." He was looking at Lillian. The color was returning to her cheeks.

"Thank you, that would be lovely I'm sure," she answered for everyone, flashing her smile.

"I thought you were the Indians coming back," Ben said. "See where their houses were?"

"Yes I do, but it looks like they've moved out." Don said. "Have you found anything they left behind?"

"Not yet."

"We'll have to have a look around after we get settled. Won't we?"

"Eh!" Pierre called. "You gonna stand around and talk all night or you gonna work."

Firewood was gathered, tents pitched and water brought for the pot. The activities gave Angela the happy feeling of holiday preparations. Clara asked her to get the sugar safely stored in India rubber to keep dry. It would be a special treat for the coffee. Ben ran to and fro asking questions and helping gather burnable wood.

The two groups began to congregate in the camp's center for supper. Lou started a fire. The women spread the blankets and brought their contributions for the meal.

"Hey Don," Shawn called to the blond man with the cane, "There's someone more lame than you." The men paused in their activities to watch Barton directing the prisoner. He shoved him down and with great flourish chained him.

"What's that all about?" Shawn asked Lou.

"Takin' him to a territorial judge," was the grumbled answer.

"He is a marshal?" Tim asked.

"Bounty hunter," Lou replied spitting.

Even Pierre stopped his activities to study Finch and his prisoner for a minute.

"Don took a fall from his horse on our first good hunt, sprained his ankle." Shawn explained the "lame" comment.

"I did not fall off my horse," Don defended himself. "My horse fell with me."

"Oh dear were you badly injured," Lillian asked.

"No my ankle got twisted under the horse. It's much better already."

"What's a bounty hunter?" Ben asked.

The young men hesitated.

Pierre answered, "A bounty 'unter 'unts people for money."

Ben scrunched his face. "Mr. Finch isn't a hunter, he's a lawman and I'm his partner."

Tim quickly elaborated on Pierre's definition. "Bounty hunters find people who have broken the law."

Ben's face smoothed at this explanation. To Angela this title of bounty hunter, although she was not familiar with it, had negative connotations. She observed both Lou and Pierre's disdain for the title. Their reactions and Pierre's explanation gave weight to her own wariness of Barton's cryptic descriptions of his occupation.

Delicious smells were carried on the air as the supper cooked.

"Mmm, sure smells good," Ben declared. "I'm hungry."

"How fortunate that you have joined us," Lillian said.

"The pleasure is ours," Tim said sincerely.

"That's the last of our fresh meat," Shawn said. He flipped the meat over the fire.

"Oh, then it is especially generous of you to share it with us," Lillian said.

"Not at all," Don explained, "for us it is a good thing. We are only too happy to take up the hunt again, the sooner the better. After all that is why we are here."

"So you are a hunting party," Barton said. He looked over their clothing deliberately.

"Yes, we're from back East, New York."

"And what made you think you had the skill to hunt here?" Barton asked.

"We have experience hunting," Don said. "Shawn and I have hunted in the wilds of northern New York, that's tough territory I can tell you. And we've all hunted in England, of course that is very different."

"It's not simply the hunt we came for," Tim explained. "We are here to see the West, Indians, buffalo, the prairies.

"Have much luck?" Barton asked. He continued to look at them with a skeptical twist to his mouth.

"With hunting? Not for buffalo, no. I'm afraid we haven't seen many and have shot none," Tim answered.

"Pierre tells us there were hundreds a few years back, but we haven't seen many. Haven't seen many Indians either," Don added.

"Thank goodness for that," Lillian said.

"You tank goodness?" Pierre spoke from across the fire where he sat sharpening a knife. "It is not goodness dat da Indian go, dat da buffalo go. Dey part of dis land and dis land is dem. Now families come," he sneered. "'ave to make da West safe for dem. Chase away da buffalo, chase away da Indian."

"We're not chasing anyone!" Lillian retorted.

Angela tried to signal her sister to shush.

Not observing her sister's warning, Lillian went on. "We are just minding our own business."

"You business. What you business? You don't belong here!" The guide shook his knife in the air.

Lillian gasped and turned her back to him.

"I understand you ladies welcome fewer Indian sightings, but for us it is disappointing to see so few in their element," Tim said diplomatically.

Lillian shuddered. "I cannot understand why you would want to see savages or why would you want to put yourself at such risk."

"We are not sight seeing," Clara broke in, offering coffee around, "only trying to reach our destination. As far as savages are concerned I agree with my daughter. I do not see why you would want to view them any more than you would want to view wild beasts. We've heard only the little that could be spoken in women's hearing and that was more than enough. We do not even want to imagine the full extent of the horrors the savages have inflicted on unfortunate civilized men and women."

"Foolishness!" Pierre said angrily.

136

"Now Pierre," Don interjected, "these ladies are from cities. They haven't your experience. It is different for them."

"Dey should stay in da cities," Pierre muttered.

"I believe the meat is done," Shawn announced. "Let's dine, shall we?"

Hungry and happy for a change of subject, the travelers picked up tin plates and waited while Shawn sliced the meat. The sun was below the horizon, the air refreshingly cool.

"Come on Pierre," Shawn called after everyone else had been served. "I've saved the best piece for you. We'd be lost without Pierre," he said to the Harrington's after the misanthropic guide took his plate to a place apart from all the others. "Both literally and figuratively," he added laughing.

"It's true," said Don, "I had no idea of the value of a good guide, who understands these parts."

"I'm sure you are all quite capable," Lillian said.

The men exchanged sheepish smiles.

Tim said, "Oh no, Miss Harrington. We studied and read all we could about the frontier, before our trip. We thought we could do it ourselves, all we needed was someone's wagon and beasts, but we were like babes out here. Book learning is not enough."

"Uh huh," Barton said.

"We made more mistakes than I care to tell. Our feet and hands were blistered, didn't plan our supplies well, Don got injured. We'd be in serious trouble if not for Pierre."

"What brings you people out here?" Don asked Clara. "Oh," he caught himself. "I apologize if the question was rude. It's none of my business."

"It's quite all right," Clara responded. "My late husband purchased land in the Bear River Valley. We are on our way there."

The hunters all looked at her.

"Pardon me Mrs. Harrington," Shawn said, "but aren't you a little late in the year. Isn't that land in the Oregon territories?"

Clara drew herself up, "Perhaps so, our driver certainly felt that way."

"Hasn't been too bad." To the family's surprise Lou spoke in defense of their decision. "Didn't get stuck nowhere, land's good and dry this time of year."

137

"What is the problem with starting late?" Angela asked.

"I'm no expert, but I believe the weather is the concern. You will run into cold weather by the time you get there, snow possibly," Don answered.

"I've noticed how cold it can be at night on the prairies as opposed to how hot it is in the day," she said.

"Yes. There is a big difference," he agreed.

"You have a home on the land?" Shawn asked.

"Yes. I believe so," Clara said.

"You have not seen it before?" Don asked. "Is someone there now? Readying it for you?"

"No. I am not certain. I will hire a man when we arrive to do whatever needs to be done," Clara answered.

"Is there a township close by?" Shawn asked.

"I really do not know."

Angela saw the hunters exchanged concerned glances.

"I do have a brother- in –law living in the vicinity," Clara added.

There were murmurs of approval at this information.

Lou climbed stiffly to his feet to get himself another cup of coffee. Watching him, Shawn said aside, "Your guide looks as though he's nearing the end of his traveling days."

"Thankfully we have our Mr. Finch too," Lillian said brightly.

"Why thank you Miss Harrington," Barton said. "I do what I can." He hoisted his bulk up and went to smoke his pipe.

Lou went with his coffee mug in his hands to check the horses where they nibbled at grass turned brittle and dry from the hot sun.

Clara sighed. "In spite of the criminal it is a comfort to have Mr. Finch with us."

"Yes. He just happened to be looking for a ride the same as us," Lillian explained. "Aren't we lucky?"

"It is our good fortune to have Pierre," Don said.

"There is no one knows the lay of the land better than a trapper. Eh, Pierre?" Shawn called to their glum companion.

"Da best to be wit out 'ere is a trapper or Indian. You people know nutting," Pierre answered showing that though he was a distance apart he heard every word.

After responding he turned his back again to their bothersome company. He watched Ben bring food and water to the prisoner.

Traveler bounced around the chained man licking his face making it difficult for him to eat, but he never pushed her away.

Angela stood watching also. She was closest to Pierre. "Pris … the prisoner is half Indian," she said.

"Benjamin, come here. It is getting dark," Clara called.

Barton laughed from his smoking place, "Come on boy, before he eats your dog."

Ben scooped Traveler in his arms and hurried back to the fire.

"What did you say Mr. Finch? Prisoner would eat Traveler?"

"Sure, didn't I tell you Indians eat dog? And you know how hungry he is. You've seen him eat."

"Prisoner wouldn't eat Traveler," Ben declared. He hugged her closely and she squirmed. "He's friends with her."

"Sure, he gained her friendship so he can grab her and eat her one of these days," Barton boomed.

To keep herself from retorting Angela quickly picked up the empty plates. Her mother and Lillian stood up and brushed off their skirts. They began to put away the supper things also.

"We'll clean up. Please be our guests," Tim said. "It's the least we can do, crowding you this way."

Ben with his wriggling pup still in his arms walked up to Pierre.

"Do you know about Indians?" he asked.

"Eh?" Pierre turned his head.

"Have you seen many Indians?" he asked.

"I 'ave hunted wit dem. Stayed in dey village…"

"You stayed in their teepees with them?" Ben interrupted. "Do they really eat dogs?"

"Times dey do. You don't worry 'bout dat pup. Dat one, 'ee won't eat 'er."

Pierre stood up and walked towards the prisoner. Ben followed. "Do you have Indian friends?"

Yes, I 'av frens dat are Indian."

"He's kind of afraid of strangers," Ben cautioned when they came within a five feet of the prisoner.

"I be careful," Pierre assured him. "You go first."

Ben stood over the young man who pushed his hair back to see him.

139

"This man has Indian friends," Ben said. He pointed back to Pierre who squatted behind him.

Pierre held his arms out in front of him, palms up in a non - threatening posture.

"Allo," he said.

The prisoner tensed, arms straight on the ground as if to rise and run, though he was chained.

"Who you people?" Pierre asked. "Nez Perce? No, no, no, what I say? Shoshone? Bannock?"

The prisoner nodded at the third name.

"Who Bannock, you pere? You fater?

The prisoner shook his head.

"No, you motter. You fater, 'ee was white. A trapper I tink? How you come to dis?" he pointed to the chain.

"He stole a horse and kidnapped a doctor," Ben said.

"Dat so?" the guide asked.

The prisoner did not take his eyes off Pierre's face or relax his position.

"Where you family?"

He made no response. Then Pierre made a strange sound. The prisoner answered softly with an equally strange sounding word accompanied by a gesture with his hand. Pierre said something else and was answered again. To Ben the whole rest of the world had disappeared until …

"Benjamin!" his mother's sharp cry broke the spell.

The prisoner started.

In the dark Clara could not see her son. She called again, desperation sharpening her tone.

"I'm here," he called standing up.

"You better go," Pierre told him.

Unhappily he walked away. With Ben's departure the young man drew back, turning his head away. The guide looked at Ben's reluctant departing back, then back at the withdrawing prisoner. He stood up slowly. "I don't botter you no more."

He caught up to Ben.

"Mister, will they really hang him?" Ben asked.

"Could be. 'orse stealin' it is very bad. And kidnappin'. I 'spose it depend on who 'ee kidnap."

140

Ben was quietly thinking this over when the guide spoke again. "I don't know what will 'appen. But on dis trip, if dere is trouble, you stay close to 'im. 'ee likes you I tink."

"You speak Indian." Ben was awestruck and not really listening to what the guide had said.

Pierre persisted, "You 'ear what I say?"

"Yes," Ben said. He was a little frightened by the man's insistence, "Yes, stay close Prisoner if there is trouble. I already ..."

"Benjamin!" his mother called again.

"Yes Mother." He slouched to her, Traveler at his heels.

Under the quilts and blankets in the wagon Ben whispered to Angela, "Prisoner speaks Indian. Pierre does too. He said something in Indian and Prisoner answered him. I wish could speak Indian."

"Benjamin, say your prayers and go to sleep," his mother ordered.

A few minutes later he whispered, "His mother is an Indian, his father is a trapper."

Angela wanted to hear more, but Ben was asleep almost as soon as he finished the last statement. Earlier in the evening she had seen them them, Pierre's tree trunk torso and Ben's much smaller frame kneeling before the young man. The three, intent only on each other, appeared from a distance to be old companions making plans in the falling darkness. She felt a funny flip in her stomach. She had been trying to avoid the prisoner and to keep him out of her thoughts because whenever she saw him or thought about him she felt a strange shivery sensation.

The three adventurers who had joined them were pleasant enough company and a welcomed change, but they seemed out of their element, merely playing in a world where they did not belong any more than her own family. They did not hold her fascination, the way this strange, doomed person did.

The next day the hunting party accompanied the family along their route and the day passed like minutes. During supper Ben sat as near Pierre as he dared. Working up his nerve, he asked him, "Mr. Pierre what did you say to Prisoner last night? What were those names you were saying?"

The old fur trader thoughts had been far away. "Eh?" he asked when he realized the boy was speaking to him. "Da names? Oh, dey names of Indian peoples."

141

"You mean like tribes? What tribe is Prisoner from?"

"'ee is Bannock."

"Bannock? What is Bannock?"

"It is 'ees people. 'dey look like da Nez Perce, but dey speak da Shoshone."

"Shoshone, that's what Mr. Finch said he was. Why does he use his hands when he talks?"

"Indians dey make words wit dere 'ands."

Angela listened discretely, hoping no one would try to talk to her.

"Mr. Finch says Indians are all thieves and they don't feel things the way we do."

"Bah," Pierre said, "Dey share whatever dey 'ave wit you. Not like da white man - evertin mine, mine, mine. Da white man more tieves den da Indian."

All too Clara summoned Ben to bed and there was no more discourse for Angela to overhear.

In the morning Angela was talking with Tim over their coffee, biscuits and berries, about what they had expected to see on their travels and the differences between the realities and the myths of the West.

"I was surprised at the wet places, bogs and creeks," she was saying, "I expected the land to be more barren. I did not understand at all what a prairie looked like, even though I've seen pictures."

"Yes," he agreed, "And did you anticipate the tremendous storms?"

"No, nor the insects."

"Yes? You are from the city? Boston your mother said?"

"Yes."

"Ah. That is why you were surprised by the ferocity of the insects. Believe me they are the same in the bush of New York. Speaking of surprises and expectations, I expected to see herds of buffalo every day," he added.

"I had the same idea." Shawn joined them. "It is rather a shame."

"Oh, I see I'm the last one ready for breakfast," Lillian exclaimed.

Lillian was always late because of the care she took in her morning preparations. Her hair was lifted in a smooth sweep, her shoes wiped clean and her dress dusted free of dirt. She was

142

immediately the radiant center of attention. Angela looked down at her scuffed boots, dried mud clung to them and they were nearly worn through in a number of places. She had abandoned gloves. They only wore through the fingers nearly every day. They were not gloves made for labor and she was tired of mending them each night.

"Did you hear those horrid animals howling last night?" Lillian asked. She shivered dramatically.

"No, I sleep right through them now," Shawn said.

"You do? However do you get accustomed to them?" she asked.

Angela felt herself on the outskirts of the circle of conversation, a familiar feeling of estrangement that she hadn't felt since leaving Boston. She didn't mind much from the outside she could observe to her heart's content.

Pierre drained his cup and went to take down his tent. Lou left the breakfast area to break camp as well. "Finch," he called. He wanted him to unchain the prisoner.

Deep in conversation with Clara, the lawman's face showed his displeasure at the interruption, but he excused himself and went to unlock the prisoner's chain. Angela tried not to follow him with her eyes. Ben and Traveler had already woken the prisoner. She knew he was sitting, waiting.

She drifted away from the amiable chatter, her feet and thoughts wandering. Lou crouched beside the wagon with a bucket of grease to paint wherever he thought was wanting. When Barton came back with the prisoner after taking him off to relieve himself, he didn't see Lou. He shoved the prisoner hard at the wagon knocking him into Lou. The old driver growled angry words at the big man and reached a hand up to the young man, who helped him to his feet. Barton said something sour back.

Angela was startled by an exasperated exhale behind her. Turning quickly she saw Pierre watching the same scene.

"Dat one, 'is leg. It is bad," he grumbled.

"Yes," she said though he seemed to be speaking to himself. "It is broken."

"Broken?" He looked hard at her.

"They broke it when they arrested him."

"Why dey do dat?"

"I don't understand exactly. Mr. Finch said something about him getting away."

"Bah," he spat. "It need a splint."

"It should have been splinted months ago."

"I make it."

Pierre went to his wagon, pulled out a piece of cloth and began tearing it into wide strips. He saw Ben and called him, "Boy, you find me two, tree pieces of wood, like dis," In the air he showed with his hands the length and shape of wood he wanted.

Ben, eager to be involved, though in what he didn't know, turned and ran to search beneath the trees.

"Excuse me?" Angela asked.

"Eh?" Pierre turned to face her.

She almost lost her nerve. "Mr. Finch will not allow it." She squirmed under his scrutiny. "I mean I think it's good ... but ..."

"I don't care what dat wind bag allow."

Ben ran to Pierre with the wood held out for inspection.

"Good." Pierre took the branches he liked from the boy's hands. He pulled a large knife from his clothing and split the branches to thinner strips. Scraps flew as he scraped with the knife, shaping and smoothing the strips.

"What are you making?" Ben asked.

"A splint for dat one's leg." Pierre pointed his chin towards the prisoner.

"A splint?"

"You see. You come wit me," he said. When he was satisfied with the wood strips he walked to Lou and said a few words to him.

Angela watched, she couldn't hear the exchange, but she saw Lou look past him in the direction of Barton Finch and say something in return. Inside her stomach whirled. There was going to be trouble. The prisoner wasn't going to like this, Barton Finch wasn't going to like this and there was Ben in the middle. Yet she wouldn't have stopped it if she could. She wanted Pierre to help the prisoner. It was painful to watch him struggle on one leg everyday and though it would only alleviate his misery by an infinitesimal amount, it seemed a small return for the times he'd helped Ben. She hurried after her brother, whatever was going to happen she should be there to extricate him from the situation if need be.

Pierre, Ben and Lou walked to the young man who was holding one of the horses. His head lifted at their approach. Pierre said to Ben, "You talk to 'im. Tell 'im we splint da leg."

"Pierre wants to fix your leg," Ben said. He pointed to Pierre.

The prisoner shook his head. Lou took the horse from him. "He wants to splint it for you, is all. Go on."

He shook his head vehemently. Pierre gave Ben the cloth and strips. He approached the prisoner slowly as he had the night before with his hands up.

"You come sit. I see what I can do."

Angela glanced towards the group at the fire, as she feared Barton had seen the activity involving his captive.

"Mr. Finch is coming," she warned them.

Lou tried to head him off. "Finch don't make no trouble."

"What do you mean? What's going on?" Barton asked. "What's he doing?" He looked around Lou at the prisoner then barged past Lou only to be blocked by the much shorter Pierre.

"'ees not doin' nutting. I splint da leg."

"He doesn't need a splint!" Finch's face was growing red. His fists were clenched. "Stay away from him. It's none of your business."

"I splint da leg. You not going to stop me. It not right." Pierre glared up at Finch like a little Bantam rooster.

"You want to help him run off?" Finch sputtered in the guide's face.

"Ha! You cannot stop a man wit a broken leg?"

Angela was afraid they would come to blows. "Stay back Ben," she warned. On impulse she walked to the men and pretended she believed it was all Finch's idea. "Mr. Finch what a good idea. Maybe now you won't have to hold him up." She hoped he couldn't hear the shakiness in her voice. "How may I help?"

He smiled a false smile that only his mouth made and took one step back from Pierre. "It's a waste of time, but be my guest." He swept an arm out.

The captive and Ben stood together. Ben was talking to him. Ben pulled at his arm when the three men walked back to them. Lou put a hand on his shoulder, "Have a seat son."

He shook his head. Barton circled him. Angela caught Ben's hand and pulled him back. The prisoner twisted, trying to keep his captor in his sights, but the big man got behind him, grabbed both his arms behind his back and yanked them up. He forced him to the ground. The young man struggled, his head down, the foot of his good leg pushing against the ground.

"Hold still!" Finch puffed.

Pierre glared at Finch. "You stand back."

Finch stepped back with an arrogant smile on his face. He was huffing and puffing. Angela wondered if he might indeed have a hard time catching the prisoner if he could run at all. Pierre knelt in front of the prisoner talking softly in words the others could not understand. He did not respond only leaned back, his head turned to the side, his face hidden in his hair. Pierre pushed the tattered strips of buckskin legging up and whistled at the sight of the leg. The prisoner straightened his head to see what Pierre was doing. His eyes were wide, beneath his hair. Lou crouched behind him. "He's not like Finch, Kid."

Pierre motioned with his head for Ben to come closer. Ben knelt next to him. Angela moved to kneel just behind her brother, ready to pull him away.

Ben said, "Don't be scared. Pierre is trying to help your leg. It won't hurt. It won't, will it Pierre?"

"No, just a splint," he answered.

The young man jerked back when he felt Pierre lay the strips of wood along his calf. Barton snorted a laugh at their inapt attempts to control his captive.

"That didn't hurt did it?" Ben asked. "It's to help your leg. Pierre's not trying to hurt you. You need to hold still."

The young man's eyes shone into Ben's eyes.

"You keep talkin' to 'im," Pierre encouraged softly. "Tell 'im what I do. You let im be," he warned Barton.

Barton shrugged.

"He's trying the pieces of wood that he fixed on your leg," Ben began, then he exclaimed, "Whoa, it looks awful! No wonder you don't walk on it."

After this outburst Ben kept a steady stream of explanation flowing. Peeking over his and Pierre's shoulders, Angela saw the calf was purple, red and yellow, and bloated with swelling all the way into the foot. There was a large knot about half way down the shin. That must be the break, she thought. Pierre worked efficiently. He cut the wood shorter and lay the pieces against the calf to size them again.

"Hold 'is leg up..." Pierre started to say to Ben. The prisoner pulled back again. "No you keep talking." He glanced at Angela. She scooted close to reach between him and Ben and put her hands under the leg he held. His hands were free to wrap the cloth around the wood.

"Oops," Ben said when the prisoner winced again. "Did that hurt?"

The young man glanced now and then at his leg and Pierre, but mostly kept his eyes on Ben.

"Now he's wrapping the cloth round and round. Pierre and ... "

Angela caught Ben's eye and shook her head.

"Just Pierre," he said.

The prisoner breathed quickly as if running a race. Angela felt sick for her part in this forced ordeal. She hadn't wanted to add to his misery. Pierre tied off the final strips.

"Dere all finish," he said.

She gently put his leg down. Then she stood and backed a little away.

Pierre held out a hand to prisoner, "It not good, but maybe it protected now, maybe heal."

The prisoner took his eyes off Ben's and stared at the hand in front of him. He would not take it. Ben stood up, took one of the young man's hands and put it in Pierre's. Taking his other hand himself, he helped pull him to his feet. The young man hopped gingerly and nearly fell. He found he could rest his right foot on the ground though the leg couldn't bear weight. He looked over to Lou.

"Let's finish harnessing them horses," Lou said.

He hobbled after the driver.

Angela hurried back to the breakfast area; her heart was pounding. She passed Tim and Shawn carrying her mother's and sister's things back to Lou's wagon.

"Where have you been Angela?" her mother asked.

147

"Yes," Lillian said. "We have decent company after all this time and you disappear."

"What is Benjamin doing?" Clara asked her. "I do not want him near that criminal."

"Ladies is there anything else you need packed?" Shawn asked. Angela was embarrassed that her mother and sister had let the men wait on them.

"No, thank you," Clara said. She shaded her eyes with her fan, trying to see Ben.

"Is anything wrong?" he asked.

"No. I was looking for my son, but I see he is fine. I'm afraid his curiosity about the criminal will lead him astray. We should not be burdened with this; there are enough hardships to bear without having to be concerned about traveling with a dangerous criminal."

"But Mother," Lillian said, "we would not have Mr. Finch if there was no prisoner."

"He doesn't look like he could be much trouble to anyone Ma'am," Shawn assured her.

"Yes, it appears your Mr. Finch has things well in hand," Tim added.

Pierre strode up to them, "We talk all day or we 'unt? You tree like traveling wit old ladies."

"Uh oh, Pierre's getting restless," Shawn said with a teasing smile. "We are sorry to part with you people, but the hunt calls."

They each took turns taking the ladies' hands.

"You are not going the same way? We did so enjoy visiting," Lillian pouted.

"Our paths may cross again," Tim said warmly. "Who knows where the chase takes us."

Each man shook Ben's hand before they rode off waving their hats.

"I wish I was with a hunting party," Ben said when they disappeared from sight. "I'd gallop after those buffalo on my horse." He raised his stick gun and fired at imaginary beasts.

"It is a shame they did not travel with us," Clara said. "They were charming, polite young men."

"Yes, they were delightful," Lillian agreed. "Don't you think so Angela? Don't deny it. I saw you having a tete a tete with Tim before breakfast," she said playfully.

Angela, still shaken from the splint ordeal, was lost in her own thoughts.

"Angela?" Lillian asked again.

"Yes, they were nice I guess," she answered.

"You guess? Mother what are we going to do with her? I only hope that there'll be young men as pleasant in the Bear River valley for suitors, Angela. That is if you don't scare them all off with your serious face."

Chapter 11

"I'm nobody! Who are you?"

Emily Dickinson

Angela had to consciously pick up one foot, then the other. Wasn't Lou going to stop for a midday break? Her stomach ached, the sun was merciless and Ben's energy was grating. Eventually Lou shouted, "Whoa," pulling the horses to a halt. She wanted only to sit in the shade and take off her shoes and stockings, but she waited for her mother and sister to climb out of the wagon to accompany them to a place of privacy. Lou gave her a nod and she glanced up to see the prisoner slumped down in sleep on the bench, his leg resting on the bundle that she passed to them each morning. "Rests easier," he said.

She mindlessly performed her chores before she could rest. The water in her cup was tepid. She skimmed debris off before taking a much-needed swallow.

"Angela I wish you would bring fresh water," said Lillian. She peered into the bucket Angela had poured from the stored water. "More would be nice too, I need to wash my face as well as drink. The heat is dreadfully hard on me."

Angela stared at her sister for a moment then she snapped, "Lillian if you're not happy with the water, you can get some yourself. You have legs!"

"You don't have to be nasty. You and Ben always get it. I thought you enjoyed doing that sort of thing," Lillian retorted.

Angela stormed off to sit by herself. In the shade on the far side of the wagon she pulled her knees up under her skirt and rested her arms and chin on top of them. Her aching stomach felt better in this position. She closed her eyes, shutting out the rest of the world.

"Angela."

She opened her eyes to see her mother standing over her.

"I've been meaning to have a talk with you. Your sister had a point earlier this morning. You must make more of an effort to be

151

polite and friendly even in these barbaric conditions. You never know, as we have just seen, when you might meet a suitable young man. Also, I am afraid you are becoming slovenly. Remember a lady must take care to be a lady both in appearance and manners. You are not a particularly pretty girl, so it's terribly important that you are tidy and pleasant company."

She squinted up at her mother's form blocking out the sun.

"Your mother is right," Barton interjected, suddenly filling the sky next to her mother. "I've noticed you neglecting your appearance myself."

The memory of the night he bumped against her saying in a slurred voice that she should be more friendly, flashed in her head. This was too horrible, her mother saying essentially the same words as him. She got to her feet, feeling the wood of the wagon's side against her back. They blocked her way. She was trapped. She began to quake inside with anger.

"Good men are hard to find in these parts."

He was still talking. Oh God, make him shut his mouth, she prayed.

"Mostly tough old characters, trappers, traders, real rough men," he went on. "You should listen to what your mother says. She is a real lady. You don't want people to get the wrong idea about you."

She gripped the sides of the wagon with both hands behind her. Don't let me start shouting at them, she prayed. If I start I won't be able to stop.

"What is the matter with you? Are you ill?" her mother asked.

She managed to get out through a clenched jaw, "My stomach hurts."

"Well then this is no place to be. Come lie down," her mother said. She steered her to the wagon "There is no need for drama. If you are ill lie down."

Inside the stifling wagon Angela curled on her quilt. Her mother's lecture had been bad enough, renewing painful old feelings of her ugliness, her awkwardness, but then to have Barton join the attack - as if he had the same standards as her mother. Odious man. Brutal and loud. What business of his was it, how she acted? His opinion was not something she valued. She was angry at them and angry at herself for her weakness before them. She should have stood up, calmly said she was fine and walked away.

Her mind took her unwillingly to relive the scene. Outside of her body she saw herself as she'd been, cornered against the wagon, their figures looming over her. She felt again the panic of the helplessness and humiliation, the wanting to lash out blindly. Then in her mind's eye the scene shifted. It wasn't herself at all; it was the prisoner cornered against the wagon. Her eyes that she was squeezing tightly shut, opened at this image. Her feelings, the situation - she had briefly experienced what he endured daily. The shock of this revelation and the discomfort in her stomach drove the anger at her mother and Mr. Finch out of her head.

They were rolling along in the afternoon when low moans from Ben, brought her from sleep.

"Oh, my stomach hurts," he complained.

She sat up. "I know Ben, mine does too. It'll go away soon, I think."

"When?" he whined.

"Try not to think about it. Let's think of something nice."

"Like what?" he sulked. "It's hot in here and my stomach hurts. I can't think of anything nice at all."

"Let's imagine our new home. Do you want to go first?"

"No, you."

"It will be a long way from any town. It will have a beautiful sparkling river running through it. There will be wide fields for the horses and on the borders of the pastures there will be deep woods of whispering pines."

"Angela, does he have a fever?" Clara asked.

Angela put her hand on her brother's forehead, "No, Mother."

"And you? Do you feel feverish?" Her mother's face looked gray, even through the dingy interior.

"Why do you ask?" said Lillian. "Do you think they have the sickness everyone's been talking about? Do you?"

Clara patted her hand.

"Don't frighten yourself Lillian," Angela said. "It's just belly aches, probably from the water."

"My stomach doesn't feel well either," Lillian sniffled. "How do you know it's from the water? How do you know it isn't serious?"

Risking the chance of being mocked, Angela said, "I read documents about frontier travel. They warned about stomach problems from the water."

"Well? What did they say to do about it?" Lillian asked impatiently.

"Boil the water, like we usually do and they say you can put charcoal in the water."

"Charcoal in the water? Yuck," Ben said.

"Also there is quinine," she added. "I wish I knew more about the plants around here. I wonder if there's any that would ease the aches. I wish Rose was here, she'd know."

"Pierre would know too," Ben said. Then after a pause he added, "Prisoner probably knows. Pierre says Indians know about plants and stuff."

Barton, whose head had rolled back in sleep, was jarred awake by a jolt of the wagon.

"What?" he said sleepily.

"I'm afraid we're all afflicted with stomach pains," Clara explained.

"Stomach pains? I had terrible trouble with my belly on my first few trips. Tobacco helps."

Angela turned away. She rubbed Ben's shoulders to comfort him and distract herself. The very sound of Barton's voice irritated her. She didn't want any advice from him.

The family's aching stomachs only got worse by the end of the day. When they stopped to make camp Lillian sniffled pathetically and sat. Ben walked bent over, his arms around his middle. Angela only wanted to curl up somewhere. When Ben sat down instead of his usual exploring and helping, Barton asked, "What are you sitting for? Help set up camp, boy. Fetch some water."

"He doesn't feel well!" Angela said sharply.

Barton looked at her, surprised at her fervor. She grabbed a bucket and tramped off to get water. When she passed Lou unbuckling straps on the harness he said, "Hold on there, Miss. We'll git the water tonight."

"I can do it." She kept walking.

The prisoner was sliding a bridle off one of the horses. Lou nudged him and gestured towards Angela. The young man hesitated, until Lou gestured again. Then he limped over and without looking at her grasped the handle of the bucket. Angela released it. She wished she could control her heart, which raced foolishly. He walked ahead unsteadily.

"No, really I can do it." Her voice sounded loud and high in her ears. She reached for the handle in his hand.

He started and tripped in a dip in the ground and fell.

"Oh your leg? Are you alright?" She reached out a hand to aid him; he turned his head away. Lou walked towards them. "Nothin' like a pretty lady to make a man do foolish things," he said. The prisoner struggled to his feet before Lou reached them. Not wanting to cause him further discomfort, Angela backed away.

"I'd best go with you," Lou said to him. "I suppose you'll keep your feet with no pretty girl to distract you. We can wash up a bit while we're at it. A bit of washing would make you more pleasant company."

He turned his craggy face to Angela and winked. Her heart suddenly felt light. What a dear man, she thought. To think we were all afraid of him. Pretty? He called me pretty. How silly I am to let flattery make me feel so giddy. The prisoner sure doesn't want anything to do with me. I guess I shouldn't take it personally; it's not just me. He doesn't want anyone near him. I wonder if it's because he's Indian or because he just doesn't like people. Maybe it's because of everything he's been through.

"Angela please bring the blankets for sitting," her mother requested when she rejoined her unhappy family.

She obeyed, brought the blankets and spread them on the ground before Clara and Barton Finch. Clara called Lillian and Ben to join them. Angela went to find wood and dry grass. She was feeling decidedly resentful again. There was Barton, fussing over Lillian, bunching blankets to make her more comfortable, doing no real work as usual, while she was the workhorse. She brought her armful of fuel for the campfire and dropped it on the ground just as Lou and the prisoner returned from the river.

"Sit yerself down. Me and him, we can take care of things," Lou said.

She sat on a far corner of the blankets and pulled her legs in tightly.

155

"Angela? That is no way for a young woman to sit," her mother said.

"It feels better like this."

"You're still not feeling well?" her mother asked.

"Not terribly bad," she answered.

"Well why did you not say so. Let our driver do his work that is what I'm paying him for."

Angela felt it was rude and cold of her mother to still be referring to Lou as "our driver."

Supper took longer with Lou preparing it alone, but the family members had no appetites and didn't mind waiting. The prisoner put the hobbles on the horses. Whether it was thanks to the splint or he was simply getting stronger he was more stable on his feet.

Barton was uneasy. He stood nearby smoking his pipe and watching him work. When the young man was finished he shoved him back to camp. He pushed him down by the wagon, roughly attached the iron band to his ankle and gave the chain a hard yank when he fastened it to the wagon. Through the deepening shadows Angela could see the prisoner's hands digging into the earth with pain. She felt quivery with helpless anger.

It was dark and the air was chilly when they put away the supper.

"It is lonely and dull without the gentlemen," Lillian complained. "I feel terrible."

"Me too," Ben said. "Let's tell stories to pass the time."

"I've plenty of stories. Let me think, which would be good to make you forget your bellyaches?" Barton Finch volunteered.

"I'm sure Lou has stories too. Would you tell us of one of your adventures?" Angela asked.

"Not much of a story teller myself." Lou got to his feet. "I'm turnin' in."

"Tell us a story Mr. Finch," Ben said.

"Not tonight. It was very kind of Mr. Finch to offer, but we all should go to bed now," Clara said.

Angela felt Barton's beady eyes on her from across the fire. Something in his expression frightened her. Was it a challenge? Did he sense her dislike of him? Did he resent her deliberate turning aside his offer to regale them?

The pain in her stomach woke Angela before the sun the next morning. She tried to find a position that would ease the discomfort and go back to sleep, but found she could not. If wasn't going to get any better, she might as well start the day.

"Wait for me Ange," Ben whispered. "Brrr, it's cold." He hurried down the steps to join her.

"It'll be hot soon enough," she said. "You should wrap a blanket around yourself for now. You don't want to get sicker. Go get one. I'll wait."

She hugged her shawl around herself. Snoring sounds rumbled from the tent where Lou and Barton slept.

"Oh no, not yet Traveler," she whispered in vain, chasing the pup who had popped out with the reappearance of Ben. She was happily wriggling her way to the crumpled shape on the ground by the wagon. Angela caught her and snatched her up only a foot from the sleeper.

"He must be cold," Ben whispered. "He doesn't have a blanket and his clothes are all ripped."

"Mmm, and the ground's damp," Angela agreed.

She thought he appeared cold; he was sleeping with his body more curled than outstretched as usual.

They returned to the campsite, hastened by the chill and darkness. Ben restrained Traveler, it was early for waking the young man, but they heard murmurs from inside the wagon and Barton clearing his throat in the tent.

"Let her," Angela whispered.

"Go ahead Traveler," Ben said. He set her on the ground.

She bounced over, her little tail beating out her joy and happily licked the prisoner's face wherever she could reach. Before lifting his head or opening his eyes, he put one hand up to guard his face from her advances and touched her with the other.

From a safe distance they were watching him pet Traveler and sit up slowly when Barton Finch's voice broke through the shadows, making all of them jump.

"What is this?" he roared.

Angela gave a little cry of surprise.

He snatched up the pup so hard she yipped. He thrust her at Ben, who held her close. The prisoner half rose on his left knee tense and fully awake.

157

"Didn't I warn you about Indians and dogs boy?"

"Prisoner won't eat Traveler. He likes her. She likes him too," Ben argued.

"That what you think? What do you know about Indians and criminals? You think he can like anything? You know he took a doctor from his office, took him prisoner, a man who helps people? You know squaws grab cute little pups like this, grab them with a big smile and then crush their skulls with a club?"

He swung his arm in a gesture that made Ben flinch away. Angela was not afraid; she was so filled with anger that there was no room for fear. Barely controlling herself, she spoke, "The pup goes where she will. There's no need to frighten Ben or blame him."

There was a rattle of the chain. The young man had managed to get to his feet in spite of it. At the sound Finch spun around to face him. Angela took advantage of this diversion to steer her brother away from the irate lawman, moving themselves out of harm's way left the prisoner to unfairly shoulder Finch's wrath. She sent Ben away, then turned back to see the lawman slowly lighting his pipe. That was a good sign. His anger must be abating, she thought. He casually bent over as if to pick something off the ground, but instead grabbed the chain and yanked it hard, pulling the prisoner to the ground with a thud. Angela's breath caught. Barton blocked her view of the prisoner. He was saying something in an undertone to the captive. He unlocked the iron cuff and straightened up, laughing heartily. He wasn't finished. Finch pulled his boot back and kicked the prisoner already collapsed and rocking in pain over his leg. The kick caught him in the ribs and knocked him on his side. He lay on the ground holding his leg and trying to breathe.

"Mr. Finch!" she blurted in a fury whose black walls closed off everything around except herself and the lawman. "Stop! You stop! You... You're horrible!"

He stared at her. Her arms were at her sides; she couldn't get the words out fast enough to express her indignation. She knew her face was red and distorted hideously. She should stop herself, but there was nothing she could do, the anger had taken over. "You want to kick someone? Kick me! It's my fault!"

"Angela!" Her mother's astonished voice snapped her out of her blind fury.

She ran, her shaking legs seeming to carry her like something mechanically independent of her own will. She sunk down in the brittle grasses, sobbing. She was terribly ashamed of herself for giving in to a childish rage, shouting like some sort of mad woman and for causing Prisoner's pain and she was terribly angry at Finch for his cruelty.

"Ange?"

Ben had found her. Why couldn't he leave her alone? She didn't want anyone to see her like this.

"Ange what's wrong? Are you still angry with Mr. Finch? You sure yelled."

"Go away." She hid her face in her hands; her knees were drawn up under her skirts to ease her stomach.

Ben sat down and put his arm around her. "Mr. Finch makes me angry sometimes too. He sure can be mean. He even hurt Traveler and she's just a pup."

His sweet efforts to comfort her caused a fresh burst of tears.

"Don't cry Ange. I didn't mean to make you sad."

She tried to smile. "You remind me of Father sometimes," she said.

"I do?"

"Yes, you have an easy way with people," she wiped her face with the ends of her skirt, "and you don't like to see anyone suffer needlessly."

"I wish I could remember him better."

They heard a rustling of the grass and saw their mother approaching like a warship parting the seas. Her pale face was stony. Neither they nor she said anything. They simply followed her back. She stopped when they came close to camp and turned abruptly to face Angela, her skirts twirling about her ankles. Lillian ran to them, her arms around her middle.

"Please don't leave me alone like that," she pleaded before her mother could speak. "You all went off somewhere without telling me. I was frightened. Angela?" she said seeing her sister's face. "You are a mess. What is wrong?"

"She yelled at Mr. Finch," Ben explained, "for being mean to Prisoner."

"Benjamin, go rest by the wagon," Clara ordered.

"I feel much better. I don't need to rest," Ben said.

"Go."

"You shouted at Mr. Finch?" Lillian was shocked. "Why? Oh Angela you know how your face gets all ugly when you're angry." She pulled out a handkerchief and wiped her sister's cheeks.

"Angela." Clara's voice sounded tight with restraint. "You were not raised to behave this way. You will apologize to Mr. Finch. You will stay away from him and that criminal from now on. Is that clear?"

"Ange can't help it Mother." Ben had not obeyed his mother instead he lingered near. "She can't bear to see anyone hurt."

"It's true," Lillian agreed. "You know how she is, Mother. She was always bringing home injured creatures. And remember how she would beg Father to take her with him to his office."

Angela was too miserable to appreciate her sister's support.

"There is no excuse for her behavior," Clara said. "She can and will behave herself. Benjamin, I told you to remove yourself."

The weariness in Clara's voice drew Angela out of her own unhappiness. How old her mother looked and sounded. This trip must be difficult for her, yet she never gives in to ugly displays of emotion. "I am sorry Mother," she said.

"Don't apologize to me. Come and speak to Mr. Finch." Her mother turned and walked straight-backed towards the campfire where Lou was cooking the breakfast.

When they neared he swallowed the last of his coffee and walked away from the fire. He signaled to the prisoner, who struggled to his feet and followed him. Barton was drinking his coffee and eating a biscuit between sips. He seemed to be the only one of the party to have any appetite. He hauled his bulk to his feet as the ladies neared. Angela stood in front of him.

"I apologize for losing my temper." She forced each word.

"Well we all get short at times," he returned. "This long journey wears people down. I've done it so many times I've forgotten what it's like for first timers."

He leaned his smiling red face towards her. She thought, if he comes any closer I'll run. She could feel his breath on her face. His eyes were boring into hers and they had a strange gleam. Again she had the disconcerting feeling that his words and what he truly felt were opposites.

"Yes," Clara agreed. "I am certain the difficulties of travel and not feeling well have contributed to Angela's ill mannered outburst."

"You're not feeling well? Here sit down and rest." Barton took her elbow and seated her.

His grasp was hard. She suspected it was a warning, meant only for her. They all sat unhappily while Lou and the prisoner broke camp and hitched the team.

The next few days continued tediously the same. While Ben professed to feel better, his mother made him ride in the wagon and sit quietly when at camp. All this confinement made him fidgety and wearisome to everyone else's patience. Lillian's whimpering inspired solicitous attention from Barton, Ben's inspired reprimands. Angela watched Barton Finch with her sister uneasily. Although their mother made no complaint, her furrowed brow and the lines on either side of her mouth showed Angela that she too felt ill. Lou and the prisoner worked incessantly. The young man helped during the midday break now instead of sleeping.

Angela thought about what could be the source of the stomach pains and what possible treatments she could try. They were being careful to drink only boiled water. The Platte River was mostly wide and shallow. Its water would be healthier if it were swift moving. But worse were the few places where the trail had turned away from the river and the only source was murky pools. It could be the water. But could it also be the insect bites? Biting flies pestered their faces when the sun shone and when it set whining mosquitoes descended. Or could it be their food? They were down to dried meat and vegetables, which they mixed with flour. They needed fresh food. Lou hadn't shot any game in a while. She wished she were more familiar with the local plant life. The quinine wasn't causing any noticeable improvement in their conditions.

Angela was beginning to believe that she would be afflicted for the rest of this eternal journey. Frustrated, worn down and feeling guilty about feeling poorly (after all she was a New Englander, you just kept going, ill or not), she tried to push through it. Working and ignoring the discomfort didn't help, neither did resting. Finally, whether it was the quinine or simply time, the stomachaches slipped away before the sufferers were fully aware they were gone.

She and Ben resumed their regular chores, helping Lou and the prisoner, who had borne the full burden of the work. She was amazed to see that even during this time of illness Barton Finch did nothing to ease the workload. Did he not see how much needed to be done? Or did he feel it was beneath him to help? The prisoner would sleep whenever he was not helping Lou. Injured as he was he must be exhausted from the work. Angela tried not to think about him because of confusing emotions she could not shake off. Then too, she would remember how he was going to die; this made her shudder inwardly. Was it like not naming the livestock in your barn because they were going to be slaughtered? If you named the sheep or chicken, then you had a connection; they were real individuals. Oh how awful, now she was trying to think like Barton or her mother. No, she could not think of him in an inhuman way. She tried not to think of him at all.

Chapter 12

"I've just seen a face.
I can't forget the time or place."

"I've Just Seen a Face" Lennon /
McCartney

One afternoon Angela stole a moment. They had stopped for the night and instead of accompanying her mother, brother and sister she held back. She gazed across the endless space, letting its beauty refresh her weary body and spirit. She relished the peace, a respite from Ben's chatter and fidgeting and the wagon's creaking and jouncing. She could see Lou and the prisoner working without speaking. Indeed, except for an occasional word to the horses from Lou, they seemed to communicate thoroughly with just a look or nod. She stood in the shade of the wagon, one hand grasping its solid sides because she felt as if her body would float off into the open blue space if she let go. Tomorrow she would walk in the sun out of the dark cramped wagon.

"Whoa. Where you going?"

Angela saw the prisoner's legs folding under himself. Lou caught him and helped him to the wagon where he sat with his back against it.

"Damn," Lou cursed, then seeing Angela he apologized, "Sorry Miss."

She hurried to them, not in the least offended. She saw a tremor in Lou's hands as he took off his hat, wiped his brow and put his hat back on. He was getting old for this kind of work. He climbed up to his seat and pulled a canteen from under it. He bent over the young man, "Here."

The prisoner didn't respond until Lou put it to his mouth.

"Drink," Lou tipped it into his mouth.

He took a swallow without much interest. Then leaned his head back against the wagon.

163

Lou scratched his head under his hat. "You eat this mornin'? I don't mean what I give you while we was drivin'. I mean breakfast."

The young man gazed at him blankly.

"Damn," Lou cursed again forgetting Angela's presence. "Bet you haven't eaten nothin' but what I give you since the boy's been feelin' poorly. Finch is too busy feedin' hisself. I should've known."

Lou spotted Ben and waved him over.

"What's wrong with Prisoner?" Ben asked.

"You been givin' him meals lately?" Lou squinted at the boy.

"N... no," Ben said slowly. "Is he hungry like before?"

Lou made a noise in his throat. "Git him somethin'. Hurry up."

Angela went with her brother to search in the stores. While they were getting food Ben told her, "I forgot. My belly hurt and I forgot. Didn't Mr. Finch give him any food?"

"He probably thought you were doing it. Anyway, you know he doesn't give him enough."

"I never forget to feed Traveler, even when I was sick."

Angela was disappointed with Ben. Was this how he saw him? As a pet? She told herself she shouldn't be judgmental. It could be worse he could see the prisoner as something to wield power over, to make himself feel bigger, like Barton Finch.

Together they prepared a plate of food. She watched for her mother and sister, remembering her mother's orders for her to stay clear of the prisoner. Ben ran with the plate and sat before the prisoner. "Here I brought you some supper."

He was too groggy to notice. Ben took a biscuit from the plate and put it in his hand. "You're getting sick like before. Better eat." He put it in his hand.

The prisoner shoved it in his mouth. Ben shook his head, "You sure have bad eating manners."

Lou gave a short, "Ha!"

As soon as he finished the prisoner tried to get to his feet, but his good leg buckled under him and he sat heavily.

Lou pushed back his hat again. Angela met his eyes.

"It's more than bein' hungry," he said. "Think he's got a fever. Been sweatin' and talkin' to hisself. Got too many hurts, the leg, who knows what else. Now the ankle's all messed up from that damn chain."

Without a thought for the trouble it might raise, Angela bent down to look at the ankle. The prisoner was too dazed to mind her. There were streaks of dried blood tracing down from a fiery red band encircling his ankle. Grit was imbedded in the band. What was worse was pus mingled with the red and grit, sure signs of infection.

"It has got to be soaked and cleaned," Angela said to Lou.

"Yep. Boy help me git him on his feet."

Ben and Lou hoisted the prisoner. Before they could get far Barton Finch looked over.

"Where are you going?"

"I'm takin' him to the river. Leg's infected," Lou said.

"Leave him. Doesn't matter."

"He's no good to me like this. You gonna help with the horses in his place when my back freezes up again?"

"Very well. Move away boy. I'll take him." He lumbered towards them.

Before he could grab the prisoner Angela spoke, "Mr. Finch, Ben and I going for water. You know how Mother and Lillian like fresh water. I'm afraid they will be frightened if they return to the wagon and no one is there. Would you like to get the water and I'll wait for them?"

"I'll wait for them," he quickly volunteered. "Lou, I'm holding you responsible. Make sure it's not a trick of his."

Lou spat.

Angela grabbed the buckets and followed Ben and Lou, who supported the young man between them. They eased him down at the edge of the river.

"Soak that leg real good," Lou said. "Tell him boy," he said to Ben. "I've got to relieve myself. Only be a minute."

The brother and sister watched him walk off, then turned their attention back to the man slouched on the ground.

"Put your leg in the water," Ben said. He pulled off his own shoes and stockings and waded in. "It feels good. See? Look at me."

Ben's voice reached him through his stupor. His eyes found the water. He rolled over on his stomach and worked himself head first down the slope of the bank. He reached back to pull his bad leg along as he went until his head and shoulders were over the water. He

165

pushed away the filmy green algae floating on the surface then cupped his hands and drank handful after handful.

Angela tried to busy herself. She pulled off her own shoes and stockings, washed her hot face and neck and then wiggled her toes in the water. Ben sighed impatiently as the prisoner continued to drink. She shook her head at him as a warning not to interrupt the prisoner.

Finally satisfied, he stopped drinking and ducked his whole head under. He seemed to be staying beneath the surface interminably. Ben and Angela looked at each other worriedly. Just as they were about to take action, he pushed off from the earth with his arms and lifted his head out. He took a deep breath. Bending his elbows he slipped under again, all the way to his shoulders this time. Angela got to her feet. Should they pull him out? Finally he pushed himself up again. This time he shook his head vigorously, his hair flinging out like a shaggy dog's, sprayed water all around. Angela laughed in surprise.

"Hey!" Ben protested at being splashed. Oblivious, the young man slowly worked himself to a sitting position and adjusted his splinted leg. He pulled his wet hair back behind his head and down his shoulders sleekly. The top half of his ragged shirt was dark with the water it had absorbed.

"Tell him to soak his ankle," Angela whispered.

"Put your leg in. Go on put it in the water." Ben walked out of the water and sat next to him.

He hesitated then swung his left foot easily into the water. He picked up his right leg with one hand behind the knee and the other under the calf and placed it in the water. Angela saw his foot and ankle again as he swung it over the bank. The foot was purple and swollen, the ankle raw and oozing. When the open sore hit the water, he inhaled sharply between his teeth and sank down on the bank.

"He's fainted Ange!" Ben exclaimed.

"Are you sure? Make certain he's breathing." Her heart was beating a rapid tattoo.

Ben leaned over his face. "Yep. He's breathing."

She sat on the edge of the water next to him and pulled his leg out. Lou was filling his canteen downstream. "He alright?"

"Yep, he's just fainted," Ben reported.

166

Angela looked the ankle over. "It must have stung terribly." She put his leg back in the water. After the initial shock she didn't think it would hurt him more, and it really must be soaked well.

"What a mess. How is he Ben?"

"He's waking up."

Lou watched them.

The prisoner's head moved, he opened his eyes and rose to his elbows quickly.

"You fainted," Ben said matter-of-factly.

The young man saw Angela leaning over his leg, lifting it out of the water and patting his ankle dry with the ends of her skirt.

"I'm sorry," she said. "We should have warned you the water would sting …" She stopped and stared at him suddenly speechless. His hair slicked wet and pulled back, she could see his face fully for the first time. She was held in surprise by the clear lines and angles of his features. He had a fine straight nose, distinctly shaped narrow dark eyebrows. His skin was discolored with bruises. His eyes large, dark and solemn were framed by thick black lashes. He turned his face away, sat straighter, turned to stared at Angela's hands still holding his foot and looked away again. His breath caught.

"It's alright." Ben put his hand on the man's shoulder. "Don't be embarrassed for fainting. It must hurt. I probably would have done the same. Ange will fix you."

The prisoner looked at Angela, his eyes wide and anxious.

"Ben hand me one of my stockings," she said.

When Ben put it in her hands he whispered, "He's afraid of you. I told you." Then he saw his sister's face was flushed and her hands shaky. "Ange, you act as funny as he does."

She wrapped the stocking around his ankle and tightened the ties around the splint.

"You … should soak your ankle whenever you can," she said quickly and moved away.

. . .

For so long pain was all his mind and body knew, pain or nothing. The nothing, the numbness was easy. Now other sensations. The

167

cushioning bundle that the girl gave him to rest his leg on ... the leg throbbed more softly. No more flashes of pain when the wagon rocked over rough spots. He stopped bracing himself in anticipation. The hunger wasn't as sharp. His mouth and throat worked, didn't burn as much.

The numbing fog in his head was lifting. He didn't want it to. Wanted to stay in the fog. Couldn't ignore the wriggling life touch of the pup every morning like a memory of a kindness. ...the boy, pulling him out of the fog with food, water and questions. ... the warmth, the scent of the horses. ...The old man, why did he help? Why doesn't he hate?

The watery world had closed around him like a soft summer night. Didn't want to come out of that world. The boy said, put his feet in the water. He did, following orders. He just did. One breath at a time his stubborn body wouldn't give up. He was a ghost. His body didn't know it yet.

The right ankle stung from the chain all the time. He ignored it. When the water hit the raw circle, it seared.

Next he saw the boy's bright blue eyes looking into his. What? What happened? The girl. She was touching him.

"Please?" His mind asked, "Back away. Don't be so close."

She was clean and soft. She must be disgusted. This was like when the bear scratched him. The scratch was nothing, her closeness was excruciating. She smelled fresh like the air on a fall day.

Please, please don't touch me.

He wished he could get away; his body was heavy, not responsive to his own mind. She was saying something. What? Her voice was soft and low. It floated on its own gentle current. Then mercifully she was done, she moved away; he could breathe now.

Finch and the loud bright one were coming. Finch was making angry sounds, not at him. They were at the boy and her this time. Had to get to his feet. Had to protect them. He struggled. His slow weak body angered him. Finch would do what he liked to him. It didn't matter; he was dead, but as long as he was earthbound nothing would harm these two kind ones, especially Finch. He knew what the man was capable of.

Barton escorted Lillian to the river.

"Thank you, Mr. Finch," Lillian said. "I can manage from here." Then she caught his arm. "Ooh. Don't take me near that criminal."

"No, no. Here you are." Barton led her upstream and released her arm. "You all done with him?" he asked Lou.

The driver shrugged.

"You shouldn't be that far away. What with the family near." He walked to the prisoner, looked closer and saw the stocking tied around his ankle. "What's that?" His face changed from merry red to an angry red.

"I hope you don't mind Mr. Finch. His ankle had to be cleaned." Angela quickly stepped up to him. "I thought that was why you brought him to the river."

"You did this. You messed with him?"

"He … his ankle is badly infected. It should be soaked or … or maybe you should leave the chain off," she babbled. "Infection is serious. It could get inside and who knows what is happening in the broken bone …"

His eyes narrowed. He stared at her.

"Oh that's Angela," Lillian piped in, "she can't resist playing doctor. You'll have to excuse her audacity. She just acts without thinking when there is a chance to play doctor to some wounded stray."

"Who told you to stand?" Finch roared at the prisoner and shoved him down. Angela opened her mouth to yell at him when Lillian mincing towards the water was startled by his shout. Her feet peddled back and forth as though on ice. "Woo," she shrieked, her arms circled like windmills. Whump! She fell on her backside, her legs straight out in front, and slid into the river.

"Oh help! Help me!" she wailed. "Oh!"

Traveler barked at her along the shore.

The poetic justice of it struck Angela and she burst out laughing. At the sight of their disheveled sister sitting in the water Ben laughed so hard he had to sit. Barton hurried in, boots and all to pull her out and help her wipe the mud and grass from her skirt. Lou took the prisoner back to camp. Realizing she shouldn't be laughing, but unable to stop, Angela grabbed Ben's arm and started back as well.

She immediately prepared for supper, knowing guiltily there would be repercussions. Sure enough, when Lillian came indignantly

169

back to camp she marched straight to her mother, where Angela could see her gesturing and tearfully telling her tale of woe. Barton joined the two to add his complaints. Delaying facing her mother for as long as possible, but not wanting a reprimand in front of the others, Angela waited until Clara was alone and went to face the music.

"Angela you are behaving foolishly and what is worse, dangerously. You forget that man is a criminal, a dangerous half savage, though I do not see how you can overlook the obvious. You are interfering with Mr. Finch's work, endangering yourself and your brother. I cannot imagine what goes through your head. I know how fond you were of your father, but you are not a doctor. You cannot bring him back by playing at one. You will conduct yourself with more sense and caution for the duration of this trip or you will have to remain by my side at all times."

Angela turned away.

"Where are you going?" Clara demanded.

"I have to ... the supper ... I ... thought you were finished speaking."

She had to get away before the crying, which was building up, came to the surface. Half running, she hurried away; the tears erupted. Sinking to the ground just out of earshot of the camp, she couldn't control the sobs, which came one pushing another, starting from the hurt inside and finishing out of her mouth. How could her mother misunderstand her so? She wasn't playing. She never thought she was a doctor. It was perfectly natural to want to help people. There were no underlying reasons for what she did. She couldn't do nothing when she could be of help. People are supposed to help each other; it's in us to do. "Feed my sheep." Wasn't that Jesus' last instruction? Didn't it mean more than to teach? To take care of each other?

When the sobs ceased, she wiped her face and headed back before anyone could find her crying. The tears kept coming, but now they were tears of anger at the injustice of her mother's remarks. She brushed them away and kept her face averted as she passed Lou resting against the wagon.

"Some folks do what needs to be done. You got good sense. Trust it," he said into the air.

She hesitated mid stride and glanced back at him. He nodded. She felt a warmth like the soft rays of sun coming through a window on a winter's day. Though her eyes burned she smiled at this kind affirmation. When she closed her eyes that night images from the day raced in her head. She saw her sister sliding into the river and her mother's condemning expression, but the image that kept intruding through all the others was the face of the prisoner.

Chapter 13

"All the world is blowing away.
It is almost daylight.
Are you warm?"

"Before the Big Storm" by William
Stafford

The world always seemed a more promising place in the early morning. The mist rising from the river suggested new adventures, mysteriously inviting. The birds celebrated, and the biting flies didn't dare come out and disturb the new creation yet. Ben and Traveler went with Angela. They passed the prisoner waking on his own. Angela suddenly didn't know where to look or what to do with her hands.

During the morning's work she tried to avoid him, but found her eyes often drawn to him. He was helping Lou, his hair partly pulled back as it had been yesterday, his face partly visible. She saw him turn and look Ben quietly in the eyes when the youngster held out a handful of berries. He looked at Ben's hands then nodded. Ben shoved the berries in his mouth and smiled.

The horse behind the prisoner shifted its weight, pushing him off balance. He hopped, nearly falling, but Ben put an arm out to steady him. The prisoner put his hand on the offered arm, removing it quickly when his balance was secured. Then turning away he continued his work with the horses and Ben went cheerfully off to look for more sweet berries.

Lillian came unexpectedly alongside Angela. "What are you staring at?" she asked. Before Angela could turn her eyes away, Lillian shivered. "Oh, him. Frightening isn't he?"

"No, not really." Angela answered slowly.

Lillian studied the prisoner with an expression of disgust. "He looks different."

"Yes, he washed in the river yesterday."

173

"Well those clothes just need to be burned. I'm sure he didn't use soap. He's still filthy. He stinks."

"Who wouldn't be in his circumstances," Angela retorted. "None of us are especially clean. Even your Phillip would stink. Or doesn't he get dirty? He wouldn't have lasted for a week under the same conditions."

Lillian responded equally sharp, "None of us are criminals. You can't put Phillip in his place. There is no comparison. What a horrid thing to say Angela."

What was she saying? Lillian was correct of course, any reasonable person would agree. The words that came out of her, she didn't know where they came from, but still she felt there was truth in them, sensible or not.

"I'm sorry. Lillian," Angela softened her tone, "if you were stuck out here, if something happened and it was just you and one other person ... If there were no supplies left, no shelter, bears and coyotes all around ... Who would you feel safest with?"

"Mr. Finch of course. I do not want to think about that Angela. We are in capable company with our driver, unpleasant as he is, and of course there's Mr. Finch. What is going on in that head of yours? You say the oddest things."

Not responding to the question, Angela continued speaking more to herself than her sister. "Have you seen his face? Did you see how young he is? He can't be much older than you or I, if he is older."

"No, I don't look that closely. You shouldn't either. Are you feeling well, Angela? I'm going to get Mother."

"No," Angela stopped her sister. "I'm fine. Don't say anything to Mother. She's worried enough."

Lillian puckered her delicate forehead and hurried away.

"Hey, where is he going?' Ben asked his sister. It was early afternoon, too early to be stopping for the day, but Lou was veering off the trail. Shading her eyes, Angela could see the driver and the young man studying the direction they had been facing and talking. Lou drove the horses over hilly terrain and down into a sheltered area between softly rolling hills. Ben and Angela followed. He pulled them up and climbed down from his seat.

"What's going on? Why are we stopping?" Barton asked sticking his head out through the flap.

Lou was quickly going about the business of unhitching. "He thinks a storm's comin'," was all he said.

Barton scanned the horizon. The family stood together, puzzled.

"I don't see anything," Barton fumed. "Doesn't that old fool know we can't be wasting time sitting still?" He stomped over to Lou.

"Yep, storm comin'. Kid's right," Lou said.

Normally slow and steady, Lou was working quickly. This alarmed Angela. She grabbed a bucket to look for water.

"No time, Miss," he warned her.

After both hobbling and tying the horses, something he did not normally do, he began securing the wagon, putting blocks of wood behind the wheels. He and the prisoner tossed extra ropes across the canvas.

Clara asked Barton, "Mr. Finch do you think there is any need for all this?"

"No, a nonsense and waste of time," he said. "A little rain shouldn't hold us up."

Angela felt a stream of cool air. It didn't feel threatening, just a subtle change of direction and temperature.

"Ange, should we get out supper things?" Ben asked.

"I don't think so. We'd better wait," she answered.

Passing them standing around, Lou said, "Go do what you gotta and git back quick."

A few minutes later the light had changed. Angela could see no clouds. The air was hot as it had been all day, but there was an eerie feel to the atmosphere. A distant rumbling could be heard for the first time. The family members cast nervous glances at the sky. Ben seemed charged by the air. He leapt and shouted, "There's a storm coming! I heard thunder!" Traveler barked at the rumbling.

The sky darkened quickly. Lou finished a last knot and motioned everyone to the opening. "Inside. Come on."

They clustered around the step. Large drops of rain began falling and the sky lit up in the distance.

"Sorry ladies, looks like we'll have to sit this one out all together," Barton said. He offered Clara his arm.

175

She looked around uneasily, searching for an alternate plan. "How long do you think it will last?"

"Who can say. It may blow through quickly. May pass us by."

The wind gusted hard, causing them to reach for their hats.

"Not him," Lillian exclaimed. She pointed past Barton to the prisoner who was standing with Lou.

"No, you don't have to suffer him," Barton laughed.

He helped her up the steps. Angela slipped by him to go inside without his help. Lou climbed in after her and sat near the front. She heard Ben ask, "Mr. Finch where is Prisoner going to be?"

"Benjamin!" His mother called. "Come in out of the weather."

He backed in. Angela put her hand on his arm.

"He's chaining Prisoner to the wagon," he answered her unspoken question. "I think he'll go under like before."

The rain began pummeling the canvas and Barton came in dripping.

"Poor Mr. Finch," Lillian sympathized. "Here let me get you a towel.

"Shall we have some dinner?" Clara asked. Her voice wavered. "Benjamin, will you please climb among the supplies for the food?"

A flash of lightening and a great crash of thunder made Lillian shriek and Clara gasp.

They passed around simple food and made themselves as comfortable as possible.

"Mr. Finch It's a bad storm. Shouldn't Prisoner come inside?" Ben asked.

"Benjamin!" Lillian exclaimed. "It's uncomfortable enough in here. How can you even suggest such a thing? Imagine him in here with us."

"He use to ride in here," Angela pointed out.

"Yes. Things were different then," Barton Finch said. He looked at her and lowered his eyebrows.

"What do you mean?" she asked.

"My methods had him passive. You wanted him to have more food and water. Well now you see. He's stronger, has to be restrained and watched more carefully."

Angela turned away.

"What are you worried about boy?" he asked Ben. "He might get sick, have a sore throat for when they put a rope around it?" He laughed.

"Shut up Finch," Lou mumbled.

The pounding rain found its way in through holes and seams, stole down the canvas and slithered on the floorboards. The wind gusted in bursts, swaying the wagon like a ship on a choppy sea. Lillian gasped and whimpered. White faced, Clara gripped the sides of the wagon. Ben whooped with excitement every time the lightening brightened the interior through the thick covering.

"Ben, stop that!" Lillian shrieked and covered her ears.

Angela sat tensely. She tried to keep her fears under control and her anger at Mr. Finch. They heard snores from Lou, who had fallen asleep where he sat. Barton's snores soon joined his.

"How can they sleep?" Lillian cried.

"Lou and Mr. Finch aren't worried Lillian. Why are you?" Ben asked.

He was soon asleep too, cocooned in his blankets. Angela sat, trying to breathe evenly and not jump when the thunder crashed. She prayed for the storm to move on.

"Aren't you frightened?" her sister asked, "or are you such a rugged frontier woman now, that nothing scares you?"

Lillian 's derision hurt. Angela blinked back tears.

"This is miserable. I wish we were home in Boston. Why did we have to leave? I'll never understand," Lillian whined.

Through a flash of white light Angela saw her mother's face. She looked gaunt her face was thinner than it had been when they started. There were dark marks under her eyes and deepening lines in her face. She edged closer to her sister.

"Sh," she pointed to their mother and whispered, "How can you be so insensitive Lillian."

Lillian peered through the dark trying to see what it was about her mother she should observe.

"I'm not insensitive," she whispered back. "No one has ever accused me of being insensitive. It's just that this horrible experience has been so hard on me."

"It's hard on all of us. Don't you see how hard it is on Mother?"

"Don't you talk to me about Mother. I'm the one by her side, helping her. You are always off somewhere being a pioneer woman. You, Angela, cause Mother the most anxiety, getting mixed up with that outlaw, being rude to Mr. Finch. I swear Angela when we get to a civilized place you won't know how to behave."

The sisters turned their backs to each other, alone in their unhappiness.

The lightening and thunder gradually moved away, but the rain continued to batter their little ark and the wind pushed against the canvas like invaders trying to break through the thin barricade. Angela held herself in a tight ball away from her sister and the damp floor. She was too tired to argue and she was not at all sure Lillian was wrong. She behaved badly and maybe her sympathy for the prisoner was wrong. On the other hand, she was the one helping with the labor of this trip, she and Ben. At least she wasn't acting as though this were some luxury tour where she should be waited on. As for civilization, she wasn't convinced that Lillian would know how to behave in small territorial settlements either. Would she act as if everything was a formal dinner party? Would that not offend people accustomed to a working life? She closed her eyes to sleep, but felt dampness seeping through her clothing; the rain puddling on the floor was spreading to her little island of dryness. Traveler kicked her little legs in her sleep and curled tighter against Ben.

Damp and uncomfortable, Angela thought of the young man chained under the wagon. How much worse off he must be. The rain surely had run under the wagon. She remembered his eyes, shining and serious. She wondered if what he'd done was so terrible to justify the length and depth of the misery he endured. To relieve her own stormy emotions, she tried to imagine his transgressions from the victim's viewpoint. She imagined the doctor, working in his office, the door bursting open, a gun being held to him by a wild man. She attempted to picture her own father as the doctor, how frightening it would be for him, but she could not imagine her father fearful before this man. She could only see him smiling gently, putting a hand on the intruder and trying to calm him. Then she tried to see the prisoner with desperation in his eyes and violence in his movements, but she saw only his quiet expression. Did he deliberately seek out a physician? It suddenly occurred to her that someone must have been hurt or sick. Why else would he need a doctor? But why did he take him by force?

Angela was suddenly awake. In the cold, wet wagon she was surprised that she'd slept at all. She thought she heard noises, light tapping sounds. Everyone appeared to be sleeping, but she heard it again. Then she heard Ben whispering. She inched closer. He was rapping the floorboards with his knuckles. "Tap back," he whispered through the floorboards.

All was quiet.

"Maybe he's asleep," Angela suggested quickly, deducing that he was communicating with the young man under the wagon.

"I'll try one more time." Using his stick this time, Ben tapped three times. "Knock back if you can hear," he whispered.

This time there was a muffled knock.

"Are you alright? Knock two times for yes and one time for no."

There were two knocks in answer.

"Is it wet under there?"

There were two more knocks. Someone in the wagon stirred.

"You'd better stop," Angela warned.

"I have to stop talking," Ben whispered.

"Shush, now," Angela said, "you'll only get yourself and him in trouble."

"Yeah. Do you think he's cold Ange? He says it's wet under there."

"Of course he's cold."

"Mr. Finch says Indians are different. They don't feel things like we do."

Someone mumbled in their sleep.

"Shush," Angela said, "Go to sleep, Ben."

He fell asleep quite quickly, for her it took much longer.

A cool breeze left behind by the storm blew playfully at daybreak. Angela wrapped a shawl tightly around herself and she paused at the foot of the steps. Traveler had felt her get up and would be waking Ben. Lou was already up and out, to see how the horses fared in the storm. Ben stepped down, his hair now grown quite shaggy, was rumpled with sleep. Traveler bounced down the steps and sniffed around the wagon. Wiggling with delight, the puppy followed the chain underneath. A few seconds later the prisoner dragged himself out. Positioning his leg he sat up, squinting in the morning sun. His clothes were smeared with mud from the ground and tar from the wagon. When he brushed his hair out of his face with a sleeve, he smudged mud across his face. Ben put his hands on his knees and leaned over him. "Boy are you a mess. Are you cold?" he asked.

Angela looked over from where she had picked up a bucket. She saw he was indeed shivering. At the same time she heard Barton's heavy tread on the stairs. "Ben," she warned.

But Barton came to them and leaned over to look more closely at the prisoner. He laughed heartily. "What's this? War paint?" He reached a hand towards the prisoner, who turned his head away. "Look at that," he nudged Ben. "He's got war paint on. Who does he think he's going to fight? The hangman?"

He scooped up mud and slapped it across the side of his face. Laughing harder, he put a glob in Ben's hand and motioned for him to do the same. Ben imitated Barton's motion, not actually touching the prisoner's face.

"Here boy, here's some for you."

Barton scraped up more mud into his fingers and stroked a line across each of Ben's cheeks. "Now you're a wild Indian like him."

"Really?" Ben asked.

"No. Doesn't look very wild now does he?"

Lou walked from the other side of the wagon surveying for damage. "Loose 'im Finch. Got work to do."

"Sure, sure." Barton, all good humor pulled the key out of his vest pocket and unlocked the cuff.

"He's really shivering Mr. Finch," Ben pointed out. "He's kinda wet too."

"Don't worry about him boy. He'll survive long enough, just long enough." He patted Ben on the head.

"Good morning. Isn't it lovely to hear cheerful voices," Lillian said. She and Clara were emerging from the wagon.

"What are you doing over there? Come away Ben," Clara ordered. "Have you two been off yet?" she asked Angela. The crease between her eyebrows deepened.

"No Mother."

180

"Well then? Take your brother. There's a breeze, do not let him get wet. You know better than to be standing around..." She flapped her hand, "there."

Angela was disgusted with Ben for the way he had mimicked Barton's taunting of the prisoner. She ignored him and walked away. He followed, caught up with his own game of pretending to be an Indian. He shot imaginary arrows from invisible bows. A sound like a low growl startled her; she froze. Carefully parting grasses as tall as herself she saw Barton and his captive also on their way back to camp. They were higher where the land leveled out above the river.

The lawman stood facing the prisoner, speaking in tones so menacing that Angela shuddered at the ugliness of the sound. His face, open earlier, was furrowed and dark. Words came over the air to her, horrible curses the like of which she had never heard. Though she knew people used such language, the actual hearing of each hideous word felt like a blow. She glanced behind. Ben was out of hearing and facing the other way. His arms up, one elbow pulled back on the imaginary bow.

Finch questioned the prisoner, thumping him in the chest with a fist. The questions were unanswerable ugly threats. He was asking him to choose between the horrible things he threatened to do to him. She felt as though her breath had stopped and only her heart pounded. The young man turned his face aside, refusing to answer. Finch lashed out, punching him on the right cheekbone. He staggered back and fell. Angela gasped and Barton spun around in her direction. She ducked down, hidden in the long grasses. Peeking out when she dared, she saw them continuing on their way. Finch now walking behind, punctuated their progress with blows to the back of his charge with his walking stick.

The breeze was gone and the ground was already drying when it was time to start. The horses, still jumpy from the night's storm, were restless and inattentive. Lou was trying to push them into their places. The prisoner limped away from Finch, moved to their heads, and backed each pair quietly back into place.

When Lou was ready to leave he impatiently cleared his throat. The prisoner stood by the step to the driver's seat waiting for orders.

181

Angela, pausing for her family, unintentionally caught his eye. He looked away quickly. She did likewise, but not before observing the large red blotch over his right cheek.

As he strolled to the wagon the lawman casually rested his beefy hand on Ben's shoulder. He was boasting of some adventure and Ben was beaming up at him. Angela, knowing what violence that hand was capable of and still hearing the horrible things that had come from his mouth, wanted to knock it off her brother. She heard a soft sigh near her ear. "I'm grateful Mr. Finch has taken Ben under his wing," Clara said.

Angela looked in undisguised horror at her.

"Really Angela, that is a most dreadful expression! What is wrong?" Lillian giggled.

Clara looked more closely at her younger daughter. "Is there something wrong Angela?"

She hesitated, searching her mother's eyes for some possibility of understanding if she tried to explain. "No Mother," she said, but she resolved to keep a close watch on that man especially if he was near her brother, mother or sister.

Chapter 14

"There are birds in the clouds even as there are angels above human distress, but what can they do for him?

"He yields to despair; worn out, he seeks death, no longer resists, gives up, lets go, tumbles into the mournful depths of the abyss..."

<u>*Les Miserables*</u> *by Victor Hugo*

Angela marveled at the colors brought out by the rain. Midsummer blossoms opened themselves joyfully across the rolling prairie. The day was hot already. The horses' hooves soon puffed up the little clouds of powdery dust as if it hadn't rained. After a while the beauty of the land only deepened Angela's sadness. Out of sorts with everyone, she felt alone. Tired and discouraged, for the first time she doubted this journey to their new home as a fresh start. What if they found only cruel hard men and sullen faced women for companionship? Or rich pretentious young men playing adventurer? Oh, what did she care? She had no particular interest in companionship. People only made her feel ugly and awkward.

Even Ben, who understood her at times or at least accepted her the way she was, seemed a stranger today. His admiration for Barton made her skin crawl as if a snake had slithered across her path. She wished she could show her mother the real Barton Finch. She felt the sharp pang for her father's missing presence. He was a keen observer of people. He would have believed her about Finch and seen it for himself. Her mother quickly formed opinions of people and had no qualms about stating them, but Angela always felt they lacked insight and were based on flimsy outward impressions.

Ben came whooping around her suddenly, his face still streaked with mud. "I'm an Indian on the war path!" he shouted, pretending to shoot her with a bow and arrow. "Be scared! I could scalp you!"

"Get away from me!" she snapped. "I don't even want to see you!"

He stopped short, then dropped back pretending to shoot the wagon and its occupants, but he glanced over his shoulder at her now and then.

After an hour or so Angela heard a noise. Voices? The wind? No, it was rushing water. Then the river itself came into sight. The rivers they had seen thus far had been sleepily calm. Now it was threatening; emboldened by the rain it bubbled and swirled sinisterly.

"Wow, look at that!" Ben shouted over the noise. He dashed to the very edge. Angela ran after him, caught his arm and gave it a shake. "Ben, have you no sense at all? Can't you see how deep and fast the water is?"

"I only want to float a stick in it."

"If you don't behave you can ride in the wagon," she scolded. "I'm tired of having to watch over you like a baby."

"I'm not a baby, and I don't need you to watch over me! I can take care of myself." He walked away. During the rest of the morning's trek he sulked, but his eyes were often on the river.

During the midday break, Ben continued his game of Indian. Barton Finch rigged up a stick and string for him, a facsimile of a bow. Circling the wagon he pretended to shoot at the prisoner who slept on the driver's bench. Angela saw with growing horror that as Barton became more friendly with him and his influence grew, Ben was growing less sympathetic towards the prisoner.

The adults sat in the shade watching him play. Lillian giggled, "I'm afraid if we do not reach civilization soon our Ben will be completely wild."

"Just being a boy," Barton chuckled. He hoisted himself up. "Here boy." He cut a small stick for Ben to use as an arrow and helped him fit it into the toy bow. "Try a shot." He stood behind and helped him hold the bow and arrow.

When Ben fired his imaginary bow, Barton slipped the arrow out of the bow, dropped it behind him and threw a small stone with his other hand. The stone struck the sleeping man on the side of his face. He started. Barton clapped him on the shoulder. "Good shot."

Ben's mouth dropped open. Lillian giggled and Clara's face softened. The captive put his hand to his face. Angela got up and walked away. As she fumed she had a terrible vision of Ben grown to be a pompous cruel younger version of Finch. Please don't let it be, she pleaded prayerfully.

She tried to reach him during the afternoon's trek. "Ben, what would you like to be when you're grown?"

"A lawman!" he answered quickly, then added, "maybe an explorer."

"Mmm, an explorer, that would be exciting," she said thoughtfully. "What about a doctor like Father?"

"Yes a doctor!" he said with equal enthusiasm.

She wanted to hear his thoughts to soothe her own fears. Trying to articulate her inner doubts she continued, "To be a doctor, like Father, a good doctor, you have to care about people. You have to study hard of course, but you must also have sympathy, empathy and understanding of each person as a ... a human with feelings like yourself, but unique to themselves."

Ben was looking at her blankly. She tried to dig deeper, pointing him in directions she wished he would consider. "Do you want to be like Father or Mr. Finch?"

"I don't know," he said carelessly. Then more thoughtfully he said, "I don't remember Father. Why can't I be like both? I know! I'll be a lawman and a doctor, a doctor lawman." Something caught his eye. He ran ahead. "Look at these! Are they bones?" he shouted. He picked up ribs, bleached by the sun.

Angry with herself for not being able to honestly express her thoughts, and angry with Ben for not caring to listen, Angela groaned.

"Do you think they are horse bones? Do you think Lou's horses will die? Do human bones look like that only smaller? Ange why won't you talk?"

"Ben hush, I was trying to talk to you." She felt tears starting.

"Ange why are you upset?" he asked.

"How could you?" She finally got what she really wanted to say out.

He stared at her.

185

"How could you play cruel games like… like Finch. He never hurt you. Why would you hurt him?"

"I'm sorry," he said.

"Don't apologize to me. Just… just … don't be like him." She spun away.

He stared after her for a moment then walked off sadly kicking at the dirt until a new distraction caught his interest.

When they stopped for the day the sun was still hot. The river rippled and sparkled dangerously. Angela went about her chores and toiletries by herself. She didn't ask her brother to help or to go with her. Lillian was fretting about the discomforts as she and her mother returned from their place of privacy.

"This heat is beastly. There is not a breath of air moving. Look at me I'm covered in dirt. I must have water to wash my face and a cool cloth for my head."

"Take it from the barrels," Clara said. "Do not go near the river. See how fast it's moving?"

"The barrels? The water in the barrels is nasty. I'm sure I'll be sick if I put it near my face. Won't there be fresh water? Can a bucket be lowered into the water? Ask the driver, won't you Mother?"

She complained until Angela thought she would scream with irritation. She grabbed a bucket and marched determinedly, risking the water was better than listening to Lillian's incessant whining. The prisoner noticed her as he and Lou secured the horses' hobbles. He stopped his work, bringing Lou's attention to her.

"Plucky, that one," he remarked. "You think she's gonna fall in or somethin'? She'll be careful. She's got a good head."

Angela reached over and dipped the bucket in by the handle, the ends of her skirts dragged in the flow. She saw Ben further upstream. He stayed back from the edge, but his eyes were on the seductive water. She watched him with her hands on her hips until he felt her eyes on him. He glowered at her and guiltily moved further from the river.

When the prisoner was finished helping Lou, Barton pointed to where he wanted him to be for the night, near a tree for chaining. Ben brought the captive's food to him. Angela watched from where she was serving the stew.

186

"Hold on there, partner," Barton said. "I haven't got him secured yet. I'll let you chain him up."

Ben shook his head. "Come on," Barton said and he followed.

"Set the plate down," Barton said. "Here you are." When he did as told, Barton handed him the end of the chain and reached for the key. "You, help the boy put it on," he said to the prisoner.

The young man looked up at Ben, his expression calm.

Ben stared back at him.

Barton cuffed the prisoner on the back of his head. "Go on. Hold out your leg for him. Put this part around his ankle," he said to Ben.

Ben shook his head and backed away.

He sought out his sister. She was sitting by herself, her plate in her lap. "Ange I was just playing. I didn't mean to hurt Prisoner."

She looked at him questioningly.

"His face, he has a big mark on his face."

She said nothing, not a word to soothe the anguish she heard in his voice.

Neither Ben nor Angela had an appetite that evening. He stood apart, drawing in the dirt with his stick gun. She picked at her food, feeling miserable for letting him believe he caused the bruise on the young man's face.

Later in the evening when shadows eased the heat and a breeze blessed the tired bodies and spirits of the weary group, they heard a cry for help that brought everyone to their feet. It was the kind of cry that strikes horror deep in a person before it truly registers in the conscious mind. It was Ben. Pulled by the terror in his cries they ran to the river. Angela tripped over her skirts and fell. Everything blurred, she picked herself up and ran on. She was vaguely aware of the prisoner yanking fiercely with both hands on the chain as she passed.

Don't let him be in the water. Please, don't let him be in the water, she prayed with each stride.

The first to reach the river, she scanned without seeing in her terror. Traveler was barking frantically along the bank. Finally her eyes found Ben's head in the water. He was clinging to large boulder.

"Ange!" he cried. "I can't let go. I'm too scared!"

187

"Stay there! I'm coming." She ran down the bank into the water.

Lou caught her arm. "Can't do it in that skirt. We'll git him." He stepped into the river. Barton Finch held out an arm to support him. Then he waded in as well.

"Help!" Ben yelled. He clawed the rock for a better grip.

"Can you stand?" Barton shouted to him.

"The water is too fast. It pulls me!" he replied. "Help!"

Lou tried to move forward over the slippery rock-covered bottom. The little stones rolled under his feet, the larger ones were slime covered and the rushing water pulled at his legs. He continued slow step by slow step supported by Barton's arm. Barton inched forward, established a foothold, helped Lou move forward and inched forward again. Their progress was slow, too slow.

Ben was panicking, his hands slipping off the rock.

"I can't hold on!" he cried.

"Do something!" Clara shouted from the shore. "Oh Benjamin!"

"Stay calm. Hold on!" Angela shouted. "We're coming!" Their progress was too slow. She hiked her skirt up in one hand and splashed her way farther into the river. Using Barton Finch's back for balance she would have passed him, but he caught her with his free hand. He held her tightly by the wrist. She tried to shake free of his grip, precariously keeping her balance. The water was wrapping her skirts around her legs and the rocks underfoot were slick.

"No, I've got to get to him!" she yelled.

"We'll git him!" Lou shouted."

Still trying to shake free, she felt a hand on her shoulder.

The prisoner used Barton's back as she had. He moved past herself to Lou, using each of them for balance.

"Hey!" Barton yelled.

"Let him help!" Lou said. "We can make a chain!"

The prisoner steadily worked himself deeper. The chain still attached to his ankle dragged over the stones on the bottom.

"Hurry!" Ben pleaded.

"Ben, hold on! We're coming," Angela called again.

Lou and Barton inched farther out, legs apart and braced, the water rising up to their hips. The young man reached the end of Lou's outstretched arm.

"Wait 'til we work ourselves out more," Lou said.

Instead he let go of Lou's hand and moved on determinedly securing balance on his left leg, arms out. The water rose past his waist, he had to forcibly pick up his injured leg, weighed down by the chain and water, in order to move it. Ben was quiet now.

"Watch out," he said. "It's real deep right before this rock."

Angela wanted to go forward, but Barton Finch maintained his grip on her wrist and Lou held out an arm to keep her back. The ground dipped and the water was up to the prisoner's chest. He caught the rock and pulled himself next to Ben. He paused for a few moments then put one arm around the boy. He pulled him from the rock. Ben clung to him. His progress was slower with Ben's added weight. The rushing water pushed against them. He established footing, moved a step, established footing again.

"Ben!" Angela called. Her voice was shaking. "Put your feet down. You can do it! Put your feet down and help!"

Ben gained control of his fear and supported his own weight. Angela waded as far as Lou would let her. Holding his hand she stretched out her other arm. The prisoner braced his legs and guided Ben with outstretched arms. Ben reached the ends of his arms and staggered through the water to his sister. Lou caught them both and passed them to Barton, who brought them to shore. Clara and Lillian reached to pull Ben up the banking. Angela climbed out, her skirts dragging heavily.

"I'm sorry," the drenched boy sobbed.

Clara looked over him at Angela her eyes were like stones. "You were to watch him. He could have drowned."

Angela stared, too stunned to believe what she'd heard. This was her fault? Lillian's eyes were wide, her face white.

"Come, you must put on dry clothes before you take ill," Clara said. "You too, Angela."

They started to walk to camp, silent except for Ben's sniffles.

"Get out of there! Now!"

Barton's bellow stopped them in their tracks. Looking back, Angela saw the young man standing in the river not any closer to shore then when he had stopped to pass Ben to safety.

"Come here!" Barton roared, signaling with his arm.

The prisoner stood unmoving in water to his waist. What was he doing? Oh no, was he thinking of escaping?" The void from the shock of her mother's words was quickly filling with fear.

"What?" Ben twisted to see about the shouting. He tried to move closer, but Clara grabbed him. "Benjamin if you take one step towards that river I will whip you myself. Come with me."

Ben wouldn't stir from the spot.

"Lillian, Angela, help me with your brother."

Like Ben Angela was held by the scene in the river. The prisoner stood out of Barton's reach. When the big man stepped closer he backed away. Barton nearly fell. Because of his heavy tread, he did not dare risk trying to get to him. He pulled out his gun from his belt.

"Come son." Unsteady himself Lou reached an arm to him.

The prisoner hesitated for a moment or so more, then took a step toward Lou with his left foot, the right stayed in place. He reached down to pull at his right leg and fell under with a splash. His head emerged above the water. He half rose on his left leg and his left arm pushed off the bottom, but the leg went out from under him and he fell beneath again. His head and shoulders surfaced once more. It was clear from his motions he was pulling at something under the water.

"The chain, the chain is caught!" Angela tried to shout.

She wasn't loud enough for the men in the water to hear, but Ben standing next to her heard.

He ignored the commands and the pull of his mother and Lillian and shouted, "His chain is stuck! It's stuck Mr. Finch! Help him!"

His shouts started him coughing and crying. Angela slid down the bank. She saw the young man stop fighting with the chain and slip under the water. There were no signs of struggle; he did not rise for air. Panic closed her throat.

"Damn!" Barton cursed. He pushed through the water towards his charge.

Angela saw Prisoner's back floating.

"Get him out of there. Please," she whispered.

Barton lifted him under his arms. Lou made it to them and reached below to tug at the chain, nearly slipping under himself with the effort. It took several tries before it pulled free. He and Barton dragged the prisoner to the shore where Angela stood. She could hear Ben shouting as his mother and sister forced him back to the wagon.

190

Barton cursed and dropped the unconscious body. Lou bent over it, hands on his thighs. He shook his head sadly.

"Damn! Wake up! Wake up you!" Barton shook his shoulder, but the body only jostled limply.

Angela, scarcely breathing herself knelt by his head. His eyelids and lips were blue lined, his mouth was open, his face white.

"He's not breathing," she said. Her stomach flipped.

"I'll get him breathing." Barton straddled the prisoner. He shook him harshly by the shoulders, banging his head against the ground.

"Breathe! You're not going to get away from me, damn you! You're not getting off this easy!" He stopped to catch his breath.

Angela couldn't bear the way the prisoner looked. She wanted to reposition his head. She put one hand on his forehead, the other under his neck and tilted his head up and back. Her simple action opened his airway. He gulped in air, his chest rising. Then he began to gag and cough. Angela rolled him over on his side so he wouldn't choke to death. He leaned on his right elbow his left palm flat on the ground, coughing up water and gasping for breath, his head barely off the ground.

"Ha!" Lou slapped his hand on his leg happily.

After the prisoner stopped bringing up water he lay taking gasping breaths.

Barton and Lou carried him back to camp. It was dark and cold now. Ben was wrapped in blankets by the fire. When he saw them coming he jumped up and ran to them, not heeding his mother calling him. The young man's head hung down. They laid him by the fire.

"Is he drowned?" Ben asked desperately circling, trying to get a closer look.

"He's alive," Angela reassured him.

"Are you sure? He doesn't look so good."

"He'll be fine I think, as long as he doesn't get sick. He's got to be kept warm." She directed this remark to Barton.

"Let's get some blankets Ange."

"I'll get them, you go back to your blankets. We can't have you getting sick either. Go," she ordered firmly when he didn't move.

Clara came, took his elbow and led him back to the other side of the fire.

"Get these wet rags off 'im," Angela heard Lou say as she went for blankets.

She brought back a blanket of her own and laid it down discreetly. Lou and Barton were tossing aside the remains of his clothes. They had already been in tatters; they were now mostly disintegrated from the rocks and water.

"Angela," her mother called through the flickering firelight. The family walked to the wagon together to turn in.

"Honestly Angela, you're paying more attention to that criminal than you own poor brother," Lillian chided her.

Angela, shaky and hollow from the whole experience, turned in shock and anger.

"I'm fine, Lillian," Ben said quickly. "Ange didn't do anything wrong. Prisoner almost drowned. Didn't he Ange? He almost drowned because of me. I'm sorry," he said starting to cry again.

"Inside the wagon now. We will say our prayers and go to sleep. We've been through a terrible ordeal," Clara said.

When Angela lay under her blankets she thanked God for sparing her brother and the prisoner. She saw her brother looking so little and helpless, clinging to the rock. She hadn't wanted to be near him that day. Everything he did had annoyed her. Now she could not imagine feeling angry at him. Why did she expect him to want the same things she did? To be the exact person she wished him to be? He was his own person after all. What kind of person was she to reject him for not fulfilling her own images of what he should be? She reached over to touch him where he slept, blankets rolled around him. Tears slipped out from under her closed lids; her stomach knotted uncomfortably.

She saw again the blue tinged face of the young man lying on the ground. He looked dead. He'd been dead; he wasn't breathing. Her father had always sheltered her from the dead and dying. This was the closest she'd come to seeing an actual dead person. How still he'd been, his handsome face open to the world, his hair streaming out on the ground, his arms lay out, palms up, fingers slightly curled. He looked so … exposed, helpless to any cruelty. Even now thinking of him, she felt oddly protective.

How frighteningly fragile life is, she thought. We go through each day with such casual forgetfulness of the frailty of life. How quickly and easily it can be taken away. She felt fearful of everything and snuggled closer to her brother.

. . .

He was coming out of the darkness. The darkness was safe, pain free. He didn't want to leave it, but his eyes opened. Slowly it came to him that he was looking into a pair of bright eyes directly trained into his. The boy.

"You're awake! I thought you were going to sleep all day!"

Something was different. Taking his eyes from the boy's he saw the sun was fully above the horizon. Rising to his elbows, he saw the fire busily burning. He felt an unexpected coolness on his shoulders. Looking down, he saw his shirt was gone. A dark wool blanket lay across him. Panic started in his gut. Where were his clothes? This can't be, he thought desperately. Boy? His eyes silently asked the eyes beaming back into them.

The boy's forehead furrowed, then smoothed. "Oh, you want your clothes? They're drying I think."

Please, he pleaded silently, please.

"Don't worry, you'll get them back. Here drink this."

A steaming cup was thrust in his face.

No, the clothes, just get my clothes, he thought, trying to see around the steam to the boy.

"You'll get your clothes. Drink this first. My sister said, make sure he drinks every bit. I had some already. It's supposed to be good for you. It tastes kind of strange. Not bad, just different."

If it'll get my clothes I'll drink anything, he thought.

Sitting up to take the mug, the air touched his back; he wrapped the blanket more tightly around himself and reached for the drink.

"Be careful, it's hot."

He made himself drink slowly. The steam touched his face, the warmth slid down his throat and chest. He was feeling things. This boy, why did he keep breaking through? It hurt to feel. Why did the boy keep bringing him back?

"Hey, drink it all," the boy warned, noticing he had stopped.

193

He finished the drink and set the mug down. The boy was sitting in front of him with a blanket draped over his own shoulders.

"Try this," the ever-busy voice said. Then the boy put his head back, heaved in a long draft of air and motioned for him to do the same. Blindly obedient as ever he took a deep breath, but as soon as his lungs filled the air burst out of him in uncontrollable coughing. His eyes filled, his throat itched, he couldn't stop. Through bleary vision he saw the boy coughing too and laughing at the same time, not at him just laughing happily.

Getting his breath back the boy explained, "It's from swallowing too much river."

"Ben! That wasn't nice."

The voice was soft, but it jolted him like he'd been stuck with something sharp. He saw the skirts in front of him, next to the boy. He pulled the blanket all the way up his chest and clung to it with a fist.

"Sorry," the boy was saying.

The river, the boy was in the river. The chain, it caught on the rocks. He remembered.

"I suppose it probably helps to clear your lungs."

She was talking; her voice carried her feelings for the boy, her brother. There was the sound of a smile in her voice.

"Are you cold?"

"Are you?" The boy was talking to him. Her question was for him? He stared at the ground.

Please go away, he pleaded voicelessly, but he shook his head.

"No, he's upset about his clothes." The boy was speaking for him.

Yes, my clothes, please give them to me. He glanced at the boy gratefully. She was speaking again.

"You two eat. I'll find clothes."

The skirts didn't move.

"Eat, before it gets cold," the soft voice ordering, a kind order.

Though it was meant for the brother, the sound of kindness gave him a pain. It hurt more than any ugly words Finch spat out. Accidentally he found himself in those soft gray eyes. He looked away quickly. Trying to slide back moved the leg and it cried out over its everyday aching. He didn't dare move to reposition it. What if the blanket slipped? What if he frightened her? He was paralyzed with

194

panic. It was hard to breathe; he felt the warning itch of a coughing spell about to start.

"Why are you scared of Ange? She's just a girl." The boy was talking.

The skirts at his feet had disappeared.

"She's nice really."

The words were coming to him clearly. The boy was talking about his gray-eyed sister. He had no sense that he shouldn't be talking about someone like her to someone like himself. He slid forward and reached for the leg, which was burning. Wishing the boy's words would stop, he carefully bent the knee with his hands and rested his calf on top of the other leg.

"It still hurts bad?"

In the beginning the voice had been a sharp intrusion, then a background noise, not unpleasant, like birds. Sometimes a word or two would come clear and he would understand the boy was asking him something. Now he was beginning to think the boy could read his thoughts.

"One good thing," the boy was saying, "at least you're clean now. I am too. You better eat."

He saw a bowl on the ground next to him, like the mug it was steaming. He picked it up and ate the contents. There was a gentle swish.

"Did you two finally finish?"

It was her again. He looked down at the blanket.

"Your clothes fell apart from the water," she was saying.

He looked up at her in alarm. His throat tightened, it was hard to breathe again.

"But here are some of Lou's things," she leaned over to put a bundle at his feet. "They're spares, so they're nicely fresh."

She stopped abruptly. He realized that he'd been staring at her in amazement and fear, then stunned relief. Dropping his head he closed his fists on the blanket.

"You're clean and you'll have clean clothes," the boy said.

He wanted to disappear, if only he could burrow inside the earth like a ground dog. He turned away, the heel of one hand on his face, his fingers in his hair.

"Well none of us can brag about being particularly clean, Ben."

195

He heard her words and the gentleness struck him again, making him swallow the lump in his throat. She didn't sound disgusted by him at all. What kind of person was this? Different from what he'd come to expect from all others, different from any white he'd ever known. Watching under his hand he saw her look over her shoulder. Turning back she said in a whisper, "You might want to dress, now." Then with a swish like a breeze moving through fir trees, she was gone.

Not wanting to move, held by the feeling of her presence, he sat still until Finch's voice from across the fire jarred him. Got to dress before that figure loomed over him. He picked up the shirt and slipped his arms through, letting the blanket fall to his waist. How was he going to get the pants on? His leg was like a dead tree and he wasn't about to let the blanket drop, not with all these white women around. He picked the pants up by the waist, put them down by his feet and under the blanket. The thing the trapper had put on his leg was destroyed. The cloths had slipped down around his ankle, the pieces of wood were gone. He slipped the cloths off, worked the leg of the pants over the bad leg up to the knee, and then slid his other leg through. He found he could lay back on the ground with the blanket over him and pull the pants up the rest of the way. He struggled with the buttons his fingers were not working well. The boy had left; he could hear him over by the wagon. He was buttoning the shirt when he saw a pair of moccasins and a strip of cloth on the ground. He slipped the moccasins on his feet; the right was tight over his swollen foot. What was the piece of cloth meant for? He picked it up, brushing back his hair to see it. He tried it around his waist. Good, it would hold up the loose pants. He tore off the extra that dangled down. As he tipped his head and was tying his hair back, Finch's wide legs appeared over him.

Clara had been fretting about Ben, his whereabouts and health. Angela had made excuses for him as long as possible, though she knew where he was.

"Is that him over there, by the criminal?" Clara said. Her face stiffened.

Angela said, "Mother, he's fine. That criminal is the one who saved him."

Her mother looked at her sharply, she felt her face burn.

196

"We are grateful that Ben is safe, but both you and Ben must keep it clearly in your minds that is a dangerous criminal, not a decent person or some unfortunate sort that needs saving."

"Well said Ma'am. I couldn't have said it better myself," commented Barton. He had been listening while he lounged with his pipe. "None of us should let our guard down. He cannot be changed into a respectable person. No, there's only one way to deal with his type. If you'll excuse me…" He walked off to reclaim his captive.

Ben ran across the campsite, which set off a bout of coughing.

"Benjamin, I told you to remain quiet for a while," Clara said. She tried to comb down his hair.

"Ooo," shuddered Lillian, "it was so frightening. You won't scare us like that again, will you Ben?"

He shook his head seriously.

"And stay away from that awful person."

"He's not awful. He saved me!" Ben snapped back at her.

"Let us not talk about this now," Clara said. "Lillian, do not upset your brother."

Lillian looked hurt that her mother did not take up her point. Then noticing Lou leading the horses to the wagon she exclaimed, "Oh no, the driver's bringing the horses to the wagon. I'm not ready at all. Angela, will you help me find my things? Where did I set them down? My nerves are all topsy - turvy."

Angela was collecting her sister's toiletry items and sewing supplies when she was surprised by Lillian, who squeezed her arm.

"Angela, you were so brave yesterday. I never could have done what you did," she said.

Angela looked into her sister's bright blue eyes, the whites red from crying and was too touched to respond for a moment. Then she said, "You're braver than I am Lillian. You can walk into a crowded room of strangers and be perfectly at ease."

Lillian laughed, "That's not the same at all. Oh look, Angela. Is that your blanket on the ground?"

The blanket she had brought for the prisoner lay crumpled on the ground. He was holding two of the horses for Lou.

"I'll get it later," she said. They took Lillian's things to the wagon.

"You don't have to help kid," Lou said to the prisoner, who shook his head and reached around a horse's belly for a strap to buckle.

197

"Suit yerself," Lou said.

When the young man turned to adjust the harness on the back pair of horses, he faced the wagon where Angela had just exited. His tied hair lay smoothly down his back. His features struck her once more: the clean angles and lines of his Indian heritage. Her breath caught, she turned away to pass more things through the opening in the wagon. Stealing a glance again she saw him reach over the horse's broad back to pull the reins through the brass circles. This movement set off a bout of coughing that forced him hold the harness for support until it stopped.

"Go sit," Lou said from the other side of the horses.

The young man, his forearm across his mouth, shook his head and continued working. Lou mumbled something about him being a stubborn Indian.

When he grabbed for the harness Angela had instinctively stepped forward to help him. She caught herself before he noticed. She blushed. This is ridiculous, she thought. All she had been told about him was bad. She didn't know him at all to have such disquieting feelings. But that was just it, he wasn't like anyone she'd ever known. He just acted. Quietly, calmly, without any fear for himself, he stepped into dangerous situations. He seemed to have no fear of anything, yet at the same time he appeared so defenseless. He invaded her thoughts all during her waking hours. She found herself wondering as Ben had about his family. Where were they? Why had he done the things Barton Finch said he'd done? She saw his face when she shut her eyes. Her legs felt quivery when she was near him. She'd never reacted to anyone this way before, but then this whole journey … everything about it was a new experience.

"I'm fine Mother. I don't want to ride in that old wagon!"

Ben's protests brought her from her unsettling thoughts.

Everyone had gathered to enter the wagon. Clara directed Ben ahead of her and up the steps. Barton stood alongside to offer a helping hand. The prisoner usually waited for Lou to tell him to climb up. This time he turned and limped away from the wagon. Angela's heart stopped a moment. What was he doing? She looked to see if Barton noticed. She looked back. The prisoner picked up the blanket she'd forgotten, from the ground. He limped back just as the lawman turned his head. The prisoner held out the blanket to Lou. "Not mine. It's the girl's," Lou said. "Give it to her."

He hesitated then held the blanket out to her, looking down.

"You keep it," she said.

"Nooo, we don't want it back after he's touched it," Lillian said. She was standing before the steps waiting for Barton's assistance.

Angela gently pushed the blanket towards him, "You can have it. It's cold at night."

He ducked his head.

"Come on," Lou called him.

She watched him limp to the steps for the driver's bench, the blanket bundled in his arms. He hesitated before the steps; he needed his arms free to pull himself up. After a moment's thought he draped the blanket over his shoulders like a cloak and hopped up the steps.

He positioned the bad leg over the bundle that they routinely placed there at the girl's insistence. The blanket remained over his shoulders.

"Ha, another thank you," Lou said. "Think she likes you kid." His face crinkled in a smile. "Don't stare at me like I'm crazy. Saved her brother, didn't you?"

. . .

What was he talking about? A thanks? No, she didn't want it after he'd used it. Couldn't blame her. He scanned the land ahead as they moved off. No trouble that he could see; the sky looked peaceful too.

199

Marty Young Stratton

Chapter 15

*"I stood for sometime in silent
admiration of the resources of Nature
and the littleness of man; and when I
was obliged to leave that enchanting
solitude, I exclaimed with sadness…"*

Alex de Tocqueville

Safe, together, Angela was nearly content in spite of riding
inside the stuffy canvas. If only Barton wouldn't be in such a
close conversation with her mother. She was confiding in him. He
listened solicitously. Angela tried to hear what she was saying without
appearing obvious. It was difficult over Ben's shifting and
complaining.

"I don't see why I have to ride inside. I feel fine. I'll be careful."

Over the wagon's noises she caught phrases… "Can't handle, …
he's too much." Barton's responses were, "… needs a man, … firm
hand… glad to help."

"Can I walk this afternoon?" Ben whined for the thousandth time.

"Young man!" Barton's cutting tone made Angela start. "Haven't
you learned a lesson, after yesterday? What will it take to make you
behave? You put yourself and others in danger. You delayed our
journey at a time when every hour counts. Most importantly, you have
given your mother a terrible shock. Have you learned a lesson or
not?"

Angela's blood quickened, her chest tightened. Her mother was
nodding in agreement with Barton, so she held her tongue. Ben bent
his head.

"Well?" Barton demanded.

"Yes," Ben answered meekly.

"What is the lesson?"

"To obey my elders, to behave." he said meekly.

"You owe everyone here an apology. To start you will apologize
to your mother."

Now this is enough, Angela thought. A prickle of sweat broke out on her forehead. Their mother was perfectly capable of demanding what she wanted from her children. Ben had been terribly frightened by yesterday's adventure that was punishment enough.

"Enough," she whispered.

Lillian heard her and whispered, "Angela, don't interfere. Mr. Finch is trying to help. Mother just can't bear much more."

Angela peered past Barton. Her mother's normally impeccably arranged hair had loose strands and she clenched her hands together, the nails digging into her own flesh. Angela bit her lip and held back her words.

"We're waiting," Barton spoke again.

"Sorry," Ben said sadly.

"I hope you mean that. From now on you are going to be more of a help to your mother. Where I come from boys who disobey their elders are whipped."

"Oh dear." This time it was Lillian who protested.

"I'm sure that won't be necessary," Barton added quickly. "The boy is going to behave from now on. Aren't you boy?"

"Yes sir."

Angela passed the time looking through the opening in the canvas. It kept her calm. She wanted desperately to be out in the sunshine. She imagined the feel of the soft warm dust between her toes and the grasses off the sides of the wheel ruts tickling her legs.

Because they had started late they didn't stop until evening. Before coming back into camp to help with supper Angela couldn't resist flopping down in the grasses like a child making angels in the snow. She felt wonderfully alone. The sky was all she could see above her. The birds sang, the insects trilled and hummed in their hidden world. Completely surrounded by nature like this she could feel God's presence palpably. She whispered a prayer of thankfulness. "Thank you God for all this beauty. What a precious gift it is to be alive. You are indeed great."

The grasses played with the evening breeze and whispered to her, but she had work to do. Her shoes in her hands, grass caught in her hair and clothing, she walked back to camp. With her eyes on the blue immensity she whispered another prayer of thankfulness for Ben's and the prisoner's lives being spared and for Finch to stop striking him.

Camp was subdued that night. There was only an occasional word between people and coughing from Ben and the prisoner. Ben sat by his mother, who was too tired to do anything but sit. Angela cleared plates and food.

"How can you be so lively?" Lillian asked.

"I don't know. I guess it's relief," she answered.

"I'm beginning to think you're half wild, Angela. Look at you. I'm worried you are growing quite mad."

Angela paused, her arms were full of supper things; she was not at all annoyed by her sister's remark. "Don't you think it's beautiful?" She turned a slow pirouette, her eyes on the sky.

"Beautiful? What do you find beautiful? The heat? The dust? I'm completely bruised from being knocked about in that horrible contraption. I can't sleep for the howling animals. I need a bath and new clothes. Conditions are primitive. Civilized humans were not meant to live like this, Angela." Lillian was working herself up to a real fuss.

"Come with me," Angela said. She set down her burden. "Mother, we're going off a bit. We won't be far," she called.

"Can I come?" Ben jumped up, but his mother shook her head and he slumped down.

Angela took her sister to her magical place amongst the grasses. Lillian sat reluctantly, smoothing her skirts.

"Lillian, it's like we're birds in our own little nest. Isn't it?"

The brown, brittle forest of grass blocked everything but the twilight sky above.

"Isn't a summer evening a wondrous thing?" Angela said. She strove to absorb the beauty through her very skin.

"Angela how can you stand these insects? Ow, they're biting me."

"Insects? They're not so bad tonight. Maybe it's like looking out a window. Some people see the dust on the glass; others see the lovely view outside. I don't even notice them."

"I can't stand it," Lillian whined, slapping at a bug. "I'm going back. Are you coming?"

"In a minute. You go on."

"It's getting dark, you had better come."

"I will, just go on."

Though disappointed about being unable to share the experience with her sister, the spell was not long broken for Angela. It reclaimed her. The sky was showing shades of rose, red and orange as the sun set. The air was as soft and warm as bath water. She turned her eyes away from the sky and lying back on her elbows studied the vegetation. Each stalk was like a tree in its own tiny realm. Little insects climbed here and there, hurrying to finish the day's work.

As if the beauty of her surroundings was too much, tears filled her eyes. Her body felt light, euphoric. It came to her that she hadn't experienced anything this intensely since her father's death. To smile, to laugh, seemed a betrayal. How could she be ecstatic over the hush of a snowstorm turning the dirty city into a fairyland or experience the joyous freedom of a summer's day when he could not? There was a secret recrimination - it wasn't right to enjoy life without him.

There was also a deep unspoken guilt. If only she'd noticed he wasn't well sooner. If only she'd done more for him. This guilt was too frightening to think about, like a monster hiding in the dark corner of a child's bedroom at night. Just then a single bird's song rang out, the same bird's song that had called to her in Boston. Only it wasn't a song so much as a call. What was it? A phoebe? It couldn't be a coincidence. The message went straight to her heart again. She couldn't interpret the exact meaning, but it was a bittersweet comfort. The sun's light disappeared. The evening star made its appearance. She wished on the star that her father might know she loved him and hurried back to camp.

Her mother was standing with Lillian looking for her when she returned. Lou was preparing to enter the tent. The prisoner chained, was sitting watchfully. She could see his eyes shining through the shadows. Was he looking for her as well?

"There mother, I told you she wasn't far," Lillian was saying.

"Where's Ben?" Angela asked.

"He's inside," her mother said curtly. "It has been very difficult convincing him to sleep with you off somewhere."

She turned and climbed the steps, her straight back serving as a reprimand.

"Angela you are as much trouble to Mother as Ben," Lillian accused. "She doesn't know what to do about your strange behavior, and frankly neither do I."

"Good night ladies," Barton called. He went to the tent with his bedroll.

From the step Angela looked over to see the prisoner slide down to rest, pulling the blanket over himself.

"Will you go in Angela? I'm cold," Lillian complained from behind her.

* * *

The sense of reprieve and security was shaken again for Angela when they passed several graves over the next few days. Some were marked with piles of rocks, others with weatherworn crosses.

One night Ben asked, "Mr. Finch, today we saw places where the ground sinks in. There's not anything growing on top. They're about this long and this big." He traced the dimensions in the ground with his stick gun.

Barton answered nonchalantly, "Those are graves."

Faces turned to him.

"Graves?" Ben asked. "But why are they sunk down?

"Didn't put enough soil over or they've been dug up. Robbed."

"Robbed?" This was interesting to Ben. He sat down next to Mr. Finch.

"Coyotes dig them up sometimes, but mostly Indians rob the graves."

"Why would they rob dead people?"

"To get their clothes," Barton replied.

"To get dead people's clothes? Don't they have their own?"

"Sure they do, but Indians having such thieving natures will steal anything."

Clara had paused in her sewing when the conversation began, she cleared her throat, a hint to discontinue this subject, but as it took a new direction she resumed her work.

"Natural born thieves," Barton spoke loudly over Ben's head. "They steal emigrant's animals all the time. Why I've heard stories of them stealing blankets right off people while they slept. That is if they didn't scalp them."

Lillian froze in mid stitch at this information.

"Mr. Finch," Clara warned.

"Sorry ma'am. Don't you worry Miss," he said to Lillian. "Me and Lou sleep in shifts. Don't we Lou?"

Lou looked out from under his hat and grunted.

"They're mostly nuisances. Just cowardly thieves, Indians are." He projected these words across the campfire.

He was loud ordinarily, but Angela realized he was sending these insults across the campfire to the prisoner as he had on the night when he first chained him. This time the prisoner was reclining chained, showing no reaction. He could have been asleep. She couldn't tell from where she sat, but she had a strong feeling that he was not.

The next morning Angela awoke shivering. Nights were getting colder. She slipped out quietly. Greedy for time to herself, she walked away through the wet grass. On her return to camp she saw a narrow gray figure at the steps of the wagon. Too tall to be Ben, she soon made out her mother.

"Angela?" Clara asked. "Isn't Benjamin with you?"

"No Mother, he's sleeping."

"He is not," her Mother told her. "He is not inside."

Before they could worry, they heard a familiar cough from the end of the wagon. They followed the sound through the early morning mist to the vague shape of the prisoner wrapped in the blanket. Clara caught Angela's arm when she tried to lean over him to look for Ben. "What are you doing? Get away from here," she hissed.

Traveler wiggled out from behind the sleeping prisoner.

"Ben," Angela whispered.

"What?" Clara's voice rose. "Where is your brother?"

A blanketed bump moved behind the prisoner. It grew and turned towards them. The blanket slipped down; Ben's tousled head revealed itself.

"Benjamin! What are you doing here!" his mother blurted.

Her shouts startled the sleeping prisoner, who bolted upright.

"Mother?" Ben was too disoriented with sleep to understand what was going on. Hearing Ben's voice, the prisoner twisted to look behind himself. Half asleep himself, he put an arm out shielding the boy from the confusion of noise and shadowy shapes before them.

"Get away from there now!" Clara's screech carried to the men in the tent.

"What's going on? What's the matter?" Barton came out of the tent pulling up his suspenders.

"Benjamin... Get him away," Clara stammered. She pointed a long finger at the prisoner.

"What?"

Barton bent over and peered where she pointed. Making out the boy in the shadows, he reached out to grab him.

The prisoner was between the lawman and the boy he kept his arm up. Ben pushed it down.

"It's just my mother," he said.

He carefully stepped around his protector. Clara snatched him and pulled him away.

"What were you doing out here by that savage?" she demanded. "Benjamin he could have killed you!" She shook him by the shoulders.

"No he wouldn't... I don't know..." Ben was flustered.

"What do you mean? You don't know? You expect us to believe you don't know how you got out here?" Barton joined the interrogation.

He spun around and yanked the prisoner's chain where it was attached to the wagon, causing the young man to grunt softly and clench his fists.

Finch turned back to Ben. "You were with a criminal and you don't know how you got here? You don't know how you left the wagon in the night?" His fury was barely suppressed. "Tell the truth!"

"I don't remember. Honest I don't," Ben pleaded. He started to cry.

"That's it boy! You've had your last chance!" Barton took him by the shoulders and was about to lead him away.

"No! It's true!" Angela cried. She caught her brother and pulled him from Finch's hands. "You keep your hands off my brother!"

They all stared at her. She held Ben in front of herself, her arms wrapped around him.

"After the bear, sometimes Ben would come out here and sleep behind the prisoner. He ... he felt safer. He didn't know he was doing it. He was sleepwalking."

"He ... has ... done this ... before?" Clara spoke one word at a time, which could only mean trouble.

The prisoner climbed to his feet causing the chain to rattle. Finch turned on him and drawing a booted foot back he kicked the young man's supporting leg out from under him. When he went down his captor swung his leg back to kick again.

"No!" Ben tore out of his sister's arms and jumped between them before the kick could land. "Don't kick him! He didn't do nothing! It was my fault!" He stood with his legs spread and his arms out. Tears streamed down his face.

Lou cleared his throat, "Finch. Let's git a move on. Time's wastin'."

"Benjamin cease this at once. Come here," Clara ordered. Her voice lacked its usual authority.

Lillian was standing behind her mother and Mr. Finch making little nervous noises like sighs, she suddenly went limp. Her mother and Barton hurried to lift her from the earth. They sat her up and fanned her. Ben remained standing stubbornly before the prisoner, legs apart, cheeks puffed defiantly.

"Benjamin!" his mother called when she straightened up from attending Lillian. "You are frightening your sister. Come here."

"Not if he's going to beat him, I won't," he shouted.

"Angela, get your brother," Clara said.

Angela tried to take his hand.

"No Ange, not 'til he promises not to hurt Prisoner."

The young man on the ground was breathing hard from the pain of the kick. He put a hand on the back of Ben's leg and tried to gently send him away. When Ben ignored his efforts he attempted to get to his feet. Ben placed his hands on his shoulders and said, "You don't have to get up." Then he faced forward defiantly.

"He just doesn't want the prisoner to take the blame for what he did," Angela pleaded. "He doesn't mean to be disobedient." She wasn't going to force her brother from his stand, but she stayed between him and the lawman.

Finch took a step closer. "I'm not going to punish him."

208

"You swear?" Ben asked doubtfully.

"Yeah, yeah I swear."

Angela took her brother's hand, but he stayed put until Barton Finch unchained the prisoner and walked away. Then he let her lead him away. He kept watch over his shoulder though.

Worried over possible punishments on Ben and the prisoner, Angela found a time to approach Mr. Finch when he was not with her mother.

"Please, I know it appeared as bad manners, but Ben didn't mean to interfere. He was not really awake and the whole experience confused and startled him. He admires you, truly. It's just that Pris ... your prisoner saved him only recently, he feels grateful. He won't behave like that again. I'll keep a closer watch over him."

Barton smiled down at her magnanimously. "It's difficult for your mother raising a son alone. The boy needs a firm hand to keep him in the right direction; he's a bit confused. You have an influence on him, you'd best use it for his benefit, not to confuse him more." He put his hand on her shoulder and rubbed it as he talked.

"I'll try," she said. She slipped out from under his touch and hurried away.

She nearly bumped into her mother, who was waiting to interrogate her.

"You knew your brother was sleeping beside that criminal and you never told anyone. How could you leave him unprotected? What is wrong with you?"

Miserably Angela tried to explain, "He was safe Mother. That's why he went. Even in his sleep he knew where he'd be safest."

Her mother was staring at her in disbelief. "Safe?"

Angela plowed on, "I didn't hear him get up. I would have stopped him. I just found him there one morning. Prisoner didn't know he was there. He didn't this time either. You saw. He was as surprised as you and I find Ben there."

"You found your brother there another time and never spoke one word of it? You saw your little brother curled up with that ... that serpent. Who are you protecting Angela? Not your brother."

She raised her hand as if to strike. Angela couldn't move, but Clara lowered her arm. Angela felt as though she'd been slapped just the same. It was not out of character for Clara to strike her children,

209

but it had been years since she'd done so. Angela's face burned with anger and shame.

She trembled with anger as she went about her morning routine; her mind raced. I didn't endanger Ben, she argued silently. He was safe. He was! Who saved him? Not you, you slug, she thought, directing her anger toward Finch. Her mother was wrong. Ben knew innately where he was secure from bears, real or imagined. What was it her grandmother use to say? Animals know who to trust. Traveler knew, didn't she? And Ben did also. Children sometimes had the pure instincts of animals.

"Angela, you will ride inside today," her mother spoke stonily. She paused next to her then marched away.

Inside that box? Trapped with everyone? Angela thought she would go mad if she had to spend all day riding with these people. That violent lump of a man, sitting next to her mother, engaged in more friendly conversation than she'd ever had with her own daughter, her mother, cold, hard, ever disapproving, Lillian, silly and irritating. Ben, thoughts of him made her tired. When would he learn not to be so reckless?

Rocking along in the wagon, she shut her eyes and leaned her head back. Behind her eyes she saw Ben standing before the prisoner, legs apart, arms out, determined expression. She couldn't help but smile at the memory and opening her eyes she met Ben's. Seeing her smile, his face lit up. He slid closer to her.

"Ange, I'm sorry for the trouble," he whispered. "Honest, I don't remember going out in the night. Ange?" He paused. She waited.

"If I don't remember doing it how can I stop?"

"You sleep on the inside of me. Then you'll have to climb over me and wake me."

When the wagon finally stopped at midday Angela was surprised. She had dozed. Stiff and sleepy, it was a relief to be outside though the sun blazed brutally. She didn't know if her mother would allow her the freedom of walking the rest of the afternoon. The women set up the blanket on the shaded side of the wagon with plates and mugs neatly laid out. Angela filled the mugs with water. This resting place had been frequented by other travelers. The remains of old fires and discarded camp equipment were strewn here and there. While they rested and ate, Ben asked if he could explore as long as he stayed within sight. Clara nodded her consent, which confounded Angela. After the experience in the river and then last night… she thought her mother would never let him out of sight again. She glanced at her mother, not knowing if she was expected to follow him or not. Barton Finch heaved himself up off the ground and slowly meandered after Ben.

"Angela, please get the last of the apples," Clara requested at the same time. There was her answer. She was not expected to watch Ben. She went to the wagon bewildered by this and the request. The fruit was something usually saved for supper. They would boil any fruit that was starting to go bad, but only at night when there was time. Before she climbed into the wagon Angela saw the prisoner out of the corner of her eye. For the most part she avoided looking at him since it caused such chaotic emotions, but the way he was watching something intently made her stop and look. She followed the channel of his attention to see Ben with Barton Finch in deep discussion. She had witnessed enough of the lawman's behavior when he thought he was out of sight to be deeply concerned for her brother. She glanced at Prisoner. His lunch biscuit lay in his hand; there was tension in his back.

Nervously she hurried into the wagon, felt around until she found the barrel of apples and scooped the last few into her skirt. She went straight to Barton and Ben.

"Would you like an apple? Mother thought people might like them," she rushed through the words.

They both looked at her as if she had spoken a foreign tongue. She held out her skirt to show them apples. Then she saw they were standing near a plank stuck in the earth.

"Thank you Miss." Barton Finch took an apple. "The boy and I were talking about why he needs to mind his elders and darned if we didn't come across the best testament of what happens to careless children out here. Look yourself."

She stepped forward and saw there was an inscribed message on the battered piece of wood. It said, "Buried here son Horace. Fell off wagon tongue."

She looked beyond it at the desolate immensity. How awful for the family to have to leave their child in this lonely spot, she thought. Her eyes filled.

211

"We'd better go back Ben. Mother will worry."

"Your mother won't worry, she knows he's with me, but I suppose we better move along. The sooner we get to Fort Laramie the better," Barton said.

Angela couldn't argue with Finch's point. It was dangerous to make mistakes out here. Ben had put himself in life threatening situations more than once. What if he had died? She felt cold in the hot sun. She couldn't have left him out here in this lonely place, alone. As if this thought weren't bad enough, another more immediate worry nagged at her. Her mother knew Barton Finch had taken Ben apart. She must have deliberately sent her after the apples to divert her. And she wouldn't have noticed if not for Prisoner. Why was it only he and she were alarmed by this? It occurred to her that her mother was now in a partnership of sorts with Mr. Finch. A partnership she felt she must guard against. She wished she could express her concerns to her mother, her feelings regarding Finch. If only she could open her mother's eyes to see the real man hidden beneath his slick mannerisms. Even Ben sensed something amiss about Finch; he stayed close to her these days.

To her great disappointment she was ordered to ride inside again that afternoon. Bumping along for an hour or two with everyone's voices humming in the background of her thoughts, she heard Lillian ask, "Are we nearly to the fort, Mr. Finch?"

"Yes, I'd say we'll be there in a few short days," he answered.

"Will there be many people there?" Lillian continued.

"Sure, the Fort is a busy place. There'll be families, soldiers, trappers, all types. You'll be able to stock up on provisions, visit with other emigrants and rest up."

"Thank goodness," Clara said.

Angela noticed the "you" in his statement. He had brought no food and he sure partook of a good portion of theirs.

"Is it difficult to get supplies?" Clara asked, "are they plentiful?"

"No, there's enough, but it can be tricky bargaining if you don't know what you're doing. There'll be plenty of Indians around wanting to trade."

"Indians!" said Clara. "I am certainly not dealing with any Indians."

"I can intercede on your behalf ma'am. Make sure you don't get cheated."

"Lou did very well setting us up, Mother. We should leave it up to him to re- supply," Angela said.

"Did very well? Angela, I had to argue with him for hours. He was terribly difficult."

Barton chuckled at this.

"Indians in the Fort?" Ben could no longer keep still.

"Oh yes, they come to the Fort to barter. Some live there. They're pests, but you can get fresh provisions cheaply from them."

"Indians live at the Fort? I thought we were coming to civilization," Lillian said.

"No need to worry Miss," Barton said with a laugh. "The soldiers keep the place in order."

"If there are soldiers there, couldn't they take charge of your prisoner?" Clara asked hopefully. "Surely a man of rank could try him and carry out the sentence?"

"They may be legal to do that ma'am, I'm not certain, but there's fellows that would be mighty disappointed. They're the fellows helped catch him and they want to see him tried and hung as much as I, the man whose horse he stole in particular. He is paying me the reward, plus a bonus for the chance to see his end with his own eyes."

"Oh." Clara was disappointed.

"Soldiers and Indians?" Ben whispered. He was too excited by these subjects to hear any other part of the discussion.

Angela was greatly relieved by Barton's reply to her mother. It meant a delay at least for Prisoner. She had all but forgotten his destination and what fate awaited the young man quietly riding with Lou until her mother brought up the subject just now. Happy anticipation of the Fort as a break from this seemingly eternal traveling and a milestone bringing them closer to the destination was mixed with dark thoughts of what the end meant for him. There would be a trial, she reasoned. Of course there would have to be a trial, after all this was a right of all people. Maybe they wouldn't find him guilty. If they saw him the jurors would see this was not a vicious person who should be put to death to keep the world safe.

"Angela?" Lillian whispered, "Mother and Mr. Finch are both napping, but I'm too excited to sleep. Can you just imagine how wonderful it will be to sleep in a real bed? To have a bath? Do you think the Fort will have rooms?"

Angela's head ached with swirling thoughts. "It is not a hotel Lillian. To sleep in a room without wheels would be a luxury though."

Lillian squeezed her hand and they giggled. Ben heard their whispering. He slid closer. "What kind of Indians do you think will be at the fort? Do you think they'll speak English? Will there be any my age?"

This last question made him stop. He hadn't thought of Indian children until it came out of his mouth. Boys and girls his age, dressed in Indian clothes? Would they play with him? Would they have real bows and arrows?

"Let's not talk about Indians," Lillian said. "Let's think only of the good things, like people to talk too, clean clothes, solid ground. Oo I can't wait."

"And soldiers," Ben added.

Angela felt less disconnected for once, not that she couldn't be happy by herself, but at times it was nice not to feel apart and different.

Chapter 16

*"The captured mouse was very puny,
but the cat exults over even a lean
mouse."*

<u>*Les Miserables*</u> *by Victor Hugo*

During the night Angela woke from a nightmare. She couldn't
remember it perfectly, only images. Barton had grown to the
size of a giant, laughing at the prisoner lying on the ground. In the
dream figures shifted and became clearer; she saw it was not the
young man at all, but Ben in the chains.

She tried to shake off the images later when she went out, only to
find the sky covered with heavy clouds as if it were confirming the
ominous unease the dream left with her. A gust of air billowed her
skirts.

The travelers rushed through the morning preparations, eating as
they worked. Lou didn't take the time to eat. He gathered the horses
two at a time. The prisoner held their heads as they looked around,
their eyes showing white, their hooves restless. Just as she finished
her chores, Angela felt a sharp sting on her head, then another on her
cheek. She pulled her bonnet up and looked around in surprise. Lillian
shrieked, pulled her shawl over her head and ran for the shelter of the
wagon with her mother. The wind came up fiercely.

"Go!" Barton shouted over it, pointing Ben and Angela to the
steps. The air filled with small white balls.

"What is it?" Ben asked once safely inside.

"Hail," Barton answered.

"Ow it hurts." He rubbed his face.

"It can pack quite a sting. You ladies get stung?"

"A bit, thank you for asking," Clara answered.

"I've never seen hail that big," Lillian whimpered. "It hurt right
through my clothes."

They had to shout to be heard over the pelting on the canvas. The
wagon lurched off under the assault. The ride was more rough than

215

usual. Angela held on to the wood on either side of her. The higher rate of speed set her nerves on edge. The horses were agitated by the hail. Could Lou and Prisoner keep them under control? Would they panic under the sharp pings of hail? She hoped her mother and sister wouldn't notice the irregular speed and become frightened.

The pelting noises gradually gave way to gusting rain and the wagon's motion steadied. The air was damp and biting cold. The passengers wrapped themselves in their blankets.

"Maybe we should pass blankets to Lou," Angela suggested.

"Yeah, he and Prisoner must be getting stung from that hail," Ben added.

Ben started to crawl towards the back, but Barton stopped him. "Don't bother son. He'd ask if he needed anything. I believe he has an overcoat stowed under his seat. That old hardtack knows how to handle a little rain. As for the criminal, seems to me someone gave him a blanket. Next you'll be wanting to give him a featherbed."

He looked in Angela's direction when he said this, grinning with his teeth; showing her that he did not miss anything in regard to his captive. Lillian laughed lightly at his humor, unaware of the underlying message. Angela held her tongue.

"Tell us more about the Fort, Mr. Finch," Ben requested and general conversation resumed distracting them from their present discomforts.

As before, when it rained the water leaked through the holes and seams in the canvas and made the floorboards damp and downright wet in places. Little bubbles of condensation clung to the inside of the canvas. The wagon lurched to a stop without warning. They heard Lou shouting. They sat in silent surprise for a moment.

"What's going on?" Barton shouted. "Pull back that flap boy, so he can hear me."

Ben crawled to the front of the wagon, but as he reached for the canvas it rolled forward and he was rocked back. Angela slid forward to help, but Ben crawled forward again and succeeded in pulling back the canvas behind the driver's seat.

He shouted, "Lou!"

The driver looked down through the opening, his face red from the cold.

216

Barton cupped his hands around his mouth. "What's the shouting for?"

"Other folks!" Lou returned then his face disappeared as he turned forward. They were terribly curious, but it was impossible to ask further questions of him. They had to be content to ponder amongst themselves.

Lou stopped only briefly that day. The rain was coming down hard. Covering their heads the family ran out quickly. They glanced around for signs of the others Lou had mentioned, but saw no one. The horses stood with their heads hanging low, ears back. The prisoner on the bench had the blanket over his head and shoulders. Lou climbed down and circled the wagon, eyeballing it for any problems. Then he joined the others inside for a cold lunch of dried meat and water. Water dripped from his hat brim and made his coat dark. He cradled the meal in one arm and reached the other towards the back of the wagon. "Pass two of them blankets."

Clara being the farthest back pulled the blankets out from behind her and passed them forward. Lou took them without a word and left.

The traveling was rough that afternoon. The wagon jerked and bucked through what must have been low muddy places or streams. The passengers held their breath each time, hoping it wouldn't get stuck.

Lou pulled the team up after only a couple of hours. The rain filled the air softly now. The fire had to be made and the cooking done, rain or not. Lillian scurried back into the wagon as soon as she could without offering to help. Ben tried to help, but Clara ordered him undercover, concerned about his cough.

"Mother, you should go inside too," Angela suggested. "There's nothing one person can't do. Lou has put the pot over the fire. I can make sure the stew doesn't burn."

Clara hesitated.

"Really Mother. Ben won't stay inside if we are both out here."

"Yes. I suppose so." Clara went under cover.

Angela squinted through the misty air. She loved the rich heavy smell of the rain and the feel of it on her face. She lifted her face to it. Her shawl slipped off her head. She didn't mind the rain flattening her hair to her scalp.

Barton returned with the prisoner, shoved him down to the ground near the wagon and went inside to get the makeshift leg iron and chain. The prisoner folded his legs, the bad over the good. He wore two blankets over his shoulders. Lou stood by and waited while the lawman put the chain on. Then he walked to the fire where Angela stirred the stew. He held his rough reddened hands over the heat.

Angela ladled a bowl of stew and passed it to him.

"I'll take another one," he said. He went to the prisoner with both bowls.

"Give me one of those." Barton reached for one of the bowls of stew.

"Git your own," Lou said. He passed one to the man on the ground. "Slide under when you're finished. Outta the rain," he advised.

Barton came to the fire for his supper. After she gave him his, Angela brought her family their stew.

Over steaming plates they chatted. Barton Finch, like the lord of the manor, answered questions and smiled indulgently at their inexperience. Lou went out when he finished eating and returned with a pot of coffee.

"Hey Lou," Barton said. "What happened to those others you saw? Who was it? Soldiers?"

Lou paused over his mug, "Other wagons."

"Where'd they go? They ahead or did we leave them behind?" Barton asked.

"We haven't seen anyone in so long," Lillian sighed. "It would have been lovely to have company."

"Kid thought it better to head north. They was stayin' on their path. Told 'em we thought it looked low. They're liable to get into soft goin'"

He sipped his coffee. The others all sat soberly. Then Lou added, "May meet up with 'em tomorrow. If they don't git stuck. They've gone ahead." He set his mug on the floor and leaned back to rest.

'The Kid,' Angela wondered? Barton apparently had the same thought for he said, "What do you mean, 'he thought'? You mean to say you let that half breed pick the direction?" He leaned forward.

"Hasn't steered me wrong yet," Lou mumbled with his eyes shut.

218

"What?" Barton was incredulous. "He'll take us out of the way. He's in no hurry to get to the end."

"Mr. Lou, please explain yourself," Clara said.

"Awe, he's not pickin' the route. He's got a good eye for the land. 'Sides who do you think helped keep these horses under control today, when they was hard to hold and the reins all slippery?"

Finch's breathing filled the wagon.

Lou turned to calmly look at him. "I've ridden with a lot worse characters than that half dead kid."

Barton Finch rose to a crouch. "He may look bad now, but you don't know him like I do. These Indians are very subtle. Watch out, he only looks weak. You didn't see how desperately he fought four grown men. Four of us couldn't hold him. I'm telling you, you don't understand how wild he really is. You think I don't know what I'm saying?"

Angela had a terrible fear he would strike Lou at that moment. Then Clara spoke, smoothly interceding, "It is a credit to your methods Mr. Finch, the criminal is so manageable."

She lay a hand on his arm. Having said this she turned stern-faced to Lou, "You must not take chances with our lives. I am extremely disturbed to hear of my family being placed in the hands of a criminal. If you are not more careful we will be forced to find another driver when we reach the fort."

Lou murmured, "Suit yerself," and closed his eyes.

"Do you think he would?" Ben whispered to Angela.

"Would what?"

"Take us in the wrong way?"

"No, don't be silly. Lou wouldn't let him."

"But Mr. Finch is right. Why would he want to go where he's going to get punished."

"What are you two whispering about?" Lillian asked.

"Ben was a little concerned. I told him not to worry. Besides, Lou knows what he's doing. And the prisoner really doesn't have the strength to cause us any trouble," Angela whispered.

"I think you may be right Angela. He can barely get around. He scares me just the same," Lillian said.

"Yeah he sleeps a lot. And he seems kind of confused most the time," Ben agreed.

219

"All part of my plan," Barton said, relaxing back against the sides. "You're starting to understand."

"Yes, we have great faith in you Mr. Finch," Lillian said.

"A medical person would be able to explain it in more scientific terms. I'm just a simple man," he continued with false modesty. "It's a matter of controlling the animal, the body. The first step is restraint, for obvious reasons, then physical deprivation. Only then does the mind, the will, become submissive. Any living creature's first instinct is to stay alive. When they realize they only live because you allow it, that they only get relief from suffering when you dole out the relief, then they're yours whether they want to be or not, survival instinct takes over."

He was explaining all this directly to Angela. Her face ached from forcing an interested expression. She'd heard his theories many times before. There was no one to free her from this conversation. Ben had lost interest and was playing with Traveler. Clara and Lillian were talking quietly. Eventually Finch grew drowsy, his chin dropped on his chest. Only then did Angela dare move to make herself comfortable.

The sun came out gloriously the next day as if it were the first day of creation. Bonnet down her back, Angela let the warmth bathe her face as she walked. They hadn't been underway for more than two hours when Lou stopped the horses. She walked forward to where she could look up to see him for an explanation. He was scanning ahead, shading his eyes with one hand. The prisoner was pointing southwest.

Oh no, she thought, looking anxiously at the canvas doorway, I hope he's not letting Prisoner pick the way again.

Staring in the same direction she thought there was something moving a long way away. It looked like a lone leafless tree on a rise, blowing in the wind, only there was no wind.

"Why are you stopping?" Ben called to Lou.

"Someone over there," Lou returned, not changing the direction of his gaze.

"Now what's wrong?" Barton lumbered out.

"Someone out there," Lou pointed.

"Person? On foot?" Barton squinted his eyes.

"Yep, looks that way. Want to get a closer look. Could be the folks we saw yesterday."

Barton shook his head. "Can't tell from here. We'd best keep a safe distance."

"Is something wrong?" Clara asked. She and Lillian tiptoed out and stood behind him.

"There's someone out there," he explained.

"Lou thinks it could be a person from yesterday's wagon," Angela said.

"He thinks? He's not certain?" Clara asked.

"No ma'am," Barton answered. "Too far to tell. There's no sign of any wagon. I think we'd best avoid any trouble."

Clearly of a different opinion, Lou pointed the horses to walk in the direction of the figure. The family followed nervously. He stopped again to observe the distant figure and confer with the prisoner.

"He's wavin' for help," he said.

"Could be a trap," Barton said. He climbed the steps and reached to bring out his rifle.

"Is it an Indian?" Ben asked.

"Better eyes than mine say no," Lou answered. "I'm goin' to see what he wants. Either stay put or git in."

Lou's tone did not invite argument. The family climbed the steps and entered the wagon rather than be left behind.

Barton sat by the opening, rifle in hand.

"Oh dear, I hope this is not dangerous. Why can't we just go on our way? Mother, won't you insist?" Lillian prattled. "Can we change drivers at the fort?"

Angela so wanted her mother to tell her sister to hush.

The wagon stopped and the passengers heard a voice hailing them. Barton sternly cautioned the family to wait inside then went out. Ben spied through the door flap. He declared, "It's just a boy, a skinny boy."

Barton's head reappeared through the doorway. "Don't worry yourselves ladies. It is a boy from the wagon Lou saw yesterday."

Lillian sighed loudly. They went out and saw a boy of eleven or twelve, covered in mud from his toes to his head.

"Please," he appealed, "our wagon's stuck. Been stuck since yesterday. The rest of our train went on ahead. We can't budge it."

221

He pointed about a half a mile down an incline where they saw a Conestoga wagon tilting precariously like a ship run aground. People were moving around it.

Then the boy led the Harrington party to three women in mud-caked dresses who greeted them. The eldest, evidently the mother, stepped forward, "Thank God Jonathan found you. The oxen can't get us out. My husband and sons have tried all night. They're about done in. They've got it braced up, but I'm terrible afeared it'll tip over when it starts to move."

Lou thoughtfully surveyed the situation while she was speaking. He said, "Looks like yer in a real fix."

The stuck family's possessions lay forlornly on the ground. Two males were digging out the sunken wheels. Their clothes entirely covered with mud, so the cloth and colors were unidentifiable and their hair was thick with mud. The boy who'd hailed the Harrington's touched one of the men on the shoulder. "Pa, there's folks come to help."

The father stabbed his shovel into the soft earth, straightened up and walked to them. "Thanks for comin'," he said. He wiped his hand on his pants before offering it, not that the action made it any cleaner. He looked at Lou, then at his wagon with recognition in his eyes. "You're the ones we passed. You took the higher country."

Lou nodded.

"Have any trouble?"

"None to speak of," Lou answered, studying their wagon.

"Sure wish we'd gone that way too. All the wagons got stuck. Ours worse than the others. Thought we could get it out and be right along. Glad you're here, we could use the extra hands."

"I don't know what we can do," Barton said. "Lou here is pretty old and stiff. Myself, I got a bad back and knees. The ladies, of course can't help."

Angela looked from Lou's face to Barton's. Why were they just talking? What were they waiting for? They made no move to help.

"I see," the father said. "We wouldn't want to trouble anyone. What about your team? Could hitch them to the oxen for help pullin'."

Barton shook his head slowly, "We can't risk the horses. Where would we be if one or more got hurt?"

222

Angela couldn't believe what she was hearing. Weren't they going to help?

"I'll help. What can I do?" she volunteered.

"Me too," Ben said. "I'm strong."

The father's face softened beneath the mask of mud and fatigue.

"That's mighty nice of you. What I need is good strong backs. It could go over. Wouldn't want you youngsters to get hurt."

"We can send help back once we reach the fort," Barton said. He smiled. "It's only a day or so's ride from here."

"Our folks will most likely do that if we don't show. Or they might turn back theirselves," the father said.

Angela saw tears starting in the eyes of the two girls. Her stomach felt uncomfortably light.

"Could we give them a ride to the fort?" she asked her mother.

"Where ever would we put them, Angela?" she replied as if surprised at the outrageousness of the proposal.

Lillian had been studying the family with disdain. She stared at her sister with disbelief.

"I can't leave the wagon and all our things," the father said thoughtfully, "it'd be good to get the women safely to the Fort, though. You could wait for us there," he said to his wife.

"No," she objected. "I won't leave you and the boys out here."

Lacking the strength to argue, the husband shrugged his shoulders.

"What about him?" The young son who'd flagged them down pointed to the prisoner, who was watching from his place on the driver's bench, hands closed on the sides ready to hop down at the first indication.

"No, no, that's a special situation," Barton said. He shook his head.

"Whatever you think best," the father said resignedly He turned back to his work, his sons following. Their shoulders slumped with fatigue.

"Please, can't you help?" The smallest of the daughters beseeched, tears were making trails down the mud on her face.

"Caroline!" Her mother took her by the arm and led her away. The family returned to their work without looking back. The daughters and mother carried away mud in buckets, fetched ropes and boards; the men shoveled.

The exhaustion and disappointment in their backs made Angela fight tears herself. "We can't leave them like this," she said. They couldn't. They couldn't just drive away.

"Don't be foolish Angela," her mother warned. "We're doing what we can by moving on to the Fort and sending help."

"Your mother's right. You have to take care of yourself out here," Finch added. "This side trip has delayed us as it is. And young lady, what if Lou or I were to get hurt? Where would you people be then? Tell me."

"Oh no. You mustn't get hurt. What would we do?" Lillian shuddered.

"There must be something we can do." Angela looked from one person in her party to the next. "What if we were the ones stranded here?"

"It's not as though we're doing nothing, Angela," Clara said. "We came and saw their situation. We'll get them help at the Fort. Your carrying on will not be of use to anyone."

Angela saw the young girl glance back at them. Her mother spoke and she turned back to her work. The despondence in the child's face and the pride Angela read in the mother's back wouldn't let her walk away.

"We can't just leave!"

"Don't get excited there, Miss," Barton said. "It isn't us. Now is it? We used better judgement."

His words ringing in her head and delivered in his insufferable tone were the final straw for Angela, she burst out, "Better judgement? Better judgement? Whose judgement? Only because of him," she pointed to the prisoner. "It's only because of him, we're not in the same situation!"

"Angela!" her mother's order stopped her.

Ben and Lillian were staring at her. Lou, who was walking back to their wagon stopped and looked in her direction. The prisoner was braced on his arms at Lou's approach as if to jump down. Angela wanted to run and hide herself, but fleeing now would make as much of spectacle as her shouting had. She stood paralyzed.

"Ange is right," Ben said. He spoke slowly, carefully thinking over her words. "It was Prisoner's idea to go this way. What about the Golden Rule Mother?"

224

His mother and Barton glared at him.

"Come on down. Let's see what we can do." Lou directed the prisoner. He hopped down quickly his expression was determined. He and Lou went to the horses and began to unhitch them.

"What?" Fury prevented Clara from saying more. She grasped Ben's wrist tightly to keep him from joining Lou and the prisoner. They unhitched the horses and led them still in harness, down to the Conestoga.

"That man! He's suppose to be working for me, yet I seem to have no say in what he does," Clara complained.

Angela was watching Lou and the prisoner. Thank you, thank you, she said silently to Lou. She was surprised to hear Barton say, "Might as well make yourself comfortable ma'am. I don't blame you for being upset. These old guides like Lou, they're always independent characters. At least this one is honest. I'll say that much for him."

"That's very charitable of you, Mr. Finch," Clara said. Her anger modulated to resignation.

"Get your mother some blankets to relax on. This may take a while," he said to Angela.

Normally she would have resented taking orders from him, but she happily ran to the wagon. After smoothing the blankets in a shady spot she strode to the mired wagon, hoping Clara wouldn't call her back.

The father, older son and prisoner braced themselves on the low side. Securing their feet for a base of support, they wedged their shoulders against the boards. The youngest son stood by the oxen's shoulders with a long stick. The horses were hitched in an improvised fashion to the front of the oxen team and Lou held the bridle of the lead animal.

Angela went to the higher side where the mother and daughters held thick ropes, the other ends of which were attached to the wagon.

"How may I help?" she asked.

"Take hold of the end of Caroline's rope," the mother said.

She pulled off her shoes and stockings, tucked the ends of her skirts up in her waist. It still drooped down modestly, but now her legs were free from the knees down. She grabbed the rope behind the little girl.

225

"Thank you for helping," the girl said. She smiled at Angela over her shoulder. "I knew you wouldn't leave us."

"Yeah, thank you," the older daughter said. She looked down at the rope in her hands.

Angela smiled at them, her eyes blurring at the child's faith nearly betrayed. Lou came around from the front to be where they could see him.

"Hold on tight now," he prepared them to begin.

He disappeared around the front of the animals. They heard shouting, Lou and the boy urging the oxen and horses.

"Here you!"

"Come, come."

"Git up!"

The wagon creaked and tilted more. Angela tightened her grip on the rope and planted her feet in the mud.

"Hold tight girls. Don't let it go over," the mother shouted.

The wagon groaned and rocked. They joined the shouts of encouragement, trying to will the wagon to move.

"Go, go, go!"

Angela heard her own voice with the others. The wheels strained against the ground. The rope burned her hands. She didn't care. Slowly, slowly the animals pushed their chests against the harnesses; the leather stretched, the wagon tilted more.

"Pull girls!" the mother shouted.

Through the concentration on their immediate tasks the women felt the wagon inching forward, righting itself, tiny inch by inch. Encouraged, they shouted with renewed vigor. The wagon painstakingly straightened and Lou came around.

"Let go now!" he shouted to the women. "Stand back!"

They dropped their ropes and stepped back as the men and animals labored to pull and push the wagon out of the sinking earth. Slowly, slowly the wheels progressed to firmer ground. When they heard Lou shout, "Whoa, whoa!" the women threw their arms around each other rejoicing; one body bonded by their efforts and victory. They heard whoops from the other side and went around.

"Ange! Ange!" Ben waved both arms over his head from where he stood on higher ground. "Come get a drink of water. I got the water ready."

226

Her throat was so parched she couldn't swallow or speak. She trudged to where Ben had set up water with mugs to dip into it. It was Clara's suggestion, her only way of keeping him involved, yet not in the midst. The muscles in Angela's arms and legs quivered. She took a mug from her brother and offered it to the girls. The father and mother gathered round, drinking thirstily and catching their breaths.

"Thank you," the father said. He grasped Lou's free hand after they both drained their mugs.

"Didn't do much of anythin'," Lou mumbled.

"Where's the other fellow? I want to thank him." He turned to look for the prisoner. The older daughter touched Angela on the shoulder, "Your husband got hurt."

"Who...?" Angela asked. What was she talking about?

The girl took her arm. "He got hurt. Down here."

She led her down to the wagon. The sons were crouching over the prisoner. He lay on his left side gripping his left leg.

"He went down when the wagon pulled free," the older of the boys explained. "We thought he just slipped, but he's hurt. He won't let us help him."

"I'll get Ma," their sister said. She hurried to where her mother stood, tapped her on the shoulder and said a word or two in her ear.

Angela knelt on the ground next to the prisoner. His leg was drawn up he leaned over it, head down, his fingers digging into his thigh. His shoulders heaved with his breathing though he didn't make a sound.

"Let me take a look here," said the mother. She pushed her way through her children. She removed his clenched hand and kneaded his leg. He shook his head in protest.

"Melissa bring me water and the rags," she said.

Angela didn't know what to do. She went back to the wagon and got a blanket. She bunched it under his knees. The mother soaked the rags in the water then she laid them across the place on his thigh where he gripped. "Right there?" He stared into her face with wide eyes. Then he glanced quickly at the people crowded around. Shaking his head and trying push back started a bout of coughing and he had to lean back on his elbows. Ben ran down the slope.

"What's wrong? What happened to Prisoner?" he said.

"He got hurt," Angela said softly.

"He'll be fine in a few days," the mother said. She replaced the rags with newly soaked ones. "Nothin' broken. Got a good knot in the muscle. Not lastin', but sure can hurt. Can't it?" She put her hand on the prisoner's shoulder and stood up, not noticing in her fatigue his fearful stare.

"You hurt your other leg?" Ben asked. He leaned in, close to the prisoner's face. "How did you do that?"

The prisoner looked seriously at Ben, too tired to protest further about the unwanted attention. Angela saw his breathing was slowing. He sat up, his fists unclenched and the leg began to relax.

"What now?" Barton's voice broke in. "What is the trouble with you now?" he demanded of the prisoner.

"Pulled something in his leg," the mother said.

Barton flapped his arms at his sides in disgust. "Aah. The least of his problems." He went back to where food was now being served. The two brothers followed.

"He was helping us," little Caroline said. She shook her head sympathetically.

"I'm sorry," the mother said to Angela. "We didn't want no one to get hurt."

Her face was marked with the lines of a person accustomed to hard outdoor work.

"It's not your fault. He... he hasn't been well," Angela responded, "I'm sure he wanted to help."

"A pity just the same. Have him soak it with cool rags; he should be better real soon. Melissa, bring the man water to drink."

She watched him with concern as her daughter went on her mission. Angela took the mug from the oldest sister when she returned and gave it to Ben to pass to the prisoner.

"Better already," the mother noted.

Angela admired the woman's fortitude. She had to be tired and thirsty herself, but she didn't hesitate to assist a stranger. She must have felt desperate at her family's situation, but she wouldn't beg for help. Angela was thankful they were able to help this proud family. They would have done the same if it had been someone else in their place.

They shared a meal. The father spoke to his family.

"Have to let these people move on. We've held them up long enough."

"You comin' along?" Lou asked.

"No, not just yet. I want to give the wagon a bit of a look see, make sure it's in working order," the father explained. "Thank you for the help. Couldn't have done it without you folks."

"Want us to wait in case you need help with repairs?" Lou asked.

"Nope, we can handle it from here. You've done enough. God bless you."

Angela and the girls found themselves suddenly shy now that the work that bound them together was over. They shook hands and smiled temerariously.

"I'm sorry your husband got hurt," Melissa said.

Angela blushed at the misunderstanding. It wasn't the time to go into a long disclaimer. She simply said, "Thank you."

The sons, one on each side got the prisoner to the wagon, where Lou helped him to the bench.

"Sorry the young man got hurt," the father said. "Hope it heals fast. Tell him to rest. Those things take their own time to heal."

He shook hands with Lou and Barton, though Barton had not lifted a finger to help.

Angela pulled her hat on her head to continue the day's walk, doing so she saw for the first time her skinned, red hands. They stung. She dropped them self-consciously.

"Angela." Her mother spoke icily and gestured toward the wagon.

She was to ride inside, she'd forgotten about her earlier outburst; her mother had not.

Once underway Clara said, "Angela you owe Mr. Finch an apology for your rude behavior."

It was difficult to apologize to him, the memory of his smug indifference still strong. Physically and emotionally depleted, she gave in and said, "I'm sorry." Then she slid tightly against the side of the wagon and closed her eyes to shut herself away.

Chapter 17

"Trust I seek and I find in you."
"Nothing Else Matters" Metallic

"How the people used to meet!
starved, intense, the old
Christmas gifts saved up till spring,
And old plain words.
And each with his God-given secret,"

"Face to Face" by Adrienne Rich

They arrived at Fort Laramie late afternoon two days after helping the stuck family. When it came into sight Lou halted the wagon in order for the passengers to get out and enjoy the sight of a building and fellow humans. Barton Finch supported Clara's arm gallantly. Lillian clasped Angela's hand in eager anticipation. They could see connected buildings of various shapes and heights. There were children playing in and along the river. People were engaged in various activities along its banks, some wore brightly colored shirts.

"Oh look," Lillian pointed, "It's so nice to be amongst people again."

Upon closer observation Angela saw the people in the calico colors were Indians. Lillian eventually noticed this too and tightened her grip on her sister's hand. Indeed it was mostly Indian children splashing and shouting in the water. Ben longed to run to them, but he maintained self-control, though he stared so hard he tripped and nearly fell.

The Harrington family, having been a small group in the wilderness, now found themselves daunted by the noisy activity in and around the fort. The buildings seemed to loom terribly large. Many people bustled about. Uniformed soldiers stood here and there, dogs barked and ran under foot. Traveler barked right along. Indians holding goods to trade approached them, but Barton waved them away.

231

Lou halted the horses and tied them to a hitching post outside the walls. He went inside and came out shortly with a man in a military uniform, who looked the emigrants over as he greeted them. He was a solidly built officer, not tall but with wide shoulders and bowed legs. He shook Barton's hand and greeted the ladies politely. "We have a room inside for folks if you prefer that to camping outside. You can stay down there, in the fourth place on the right. If you have any questions be sure to ask."

They nodded their thanks mutely overcome by the people and animals inside and outside the fort.

"You! Come down!" Barton ordered the prisoner.

The officer watched with a frown as Lou helped him slowly work his way down the steps. Barton grabbed his arms behind his back and tied them with a piece of rope.

"What's this about?" the soldier asked.

"This? My prisoner. I'm taking him to Fort Hall to wait for the circuit judge to try him."

"We've got a stockade for prisoners. You can put him in there."

"No, no thanks, I'd rather keep him close by," Barton said.

"I can't allow that. We've got families camped around here. If he's a criminal he's got to be kept under lock and key."

"He's a criminal, no question. I'm authorized. Here I'll show you my papers."

"That's all well and good; he has to be locked up just the same. I assure you it's secure. You're welcome to check in on him any time day or night. Follow me."

Barton Finch complied though his face was dark with anger. He jerked the prisoner after the officer.

The Harringtons followed Lou. He led the horses to a small cabin like others built along the wall of the fort. They passed through an open doorway into the simple one room space. There was only a small fireplace for cooking. The floor was hard packed dirt, neatly swept.

"Is this the only room," Lillian cried. "Where are the beds? Are there no chairs? Do we sleep on the dirt?"

Angela was surprised herself to find it so stark and small, but it was cool out of the sun.

Clara surveyed the space distastefully. "Well let's get the bedding from the wagon."

232

"You want to camp outside the fort?" Lou asked. "Most folks do 'less they have the cash."

"No. This will do," Clara sighed. "Can we at least get our bedding from the wagon?"

Ben and Angela got what they needed from the wagon, including a chair for Clara that was quite difficult to access as it was tied tightly behind trunks. They also brought out some of the plates, spoons, cups and pots for cooking. Lou led the horses to where there was open space for the wagon then he took them to a common grazing area.

Barton Finch found the room just as the Harrington's finished setting up. "Isn't this cozy," he remarked, "Very homey."

"Where's Prisoner? Is there a jail with bars? Can I see him?" Ben asked.

"We'd better see about supplies," Barton said to Clara, ignoring the boy.

"Yes," Clara said, "I suppose I ought to get it over with. I hate the thought of bartering like some trader. Would you assist me Mr. Finch? I'm sure I do not know where to begin."

"Certainly ma'am. I'd be glad to."

"One thing I want to make clear, I do not wish to do business with savages."

"The truth is ma'am they are the best source of fresh fish, meat and such, if you know how to deal with them. Let me do the bartering for you. You can stand back. You don't have to be near them."

"If you think it best. I'll trust your judgement," Clara agreed reluctantly.

"What kind of Indians are they Mr. Finch?" Ben asked. He was following Barton and his mother to the doorway.

"Mostly Sioux and Cheyenne," he answered.

Lillian sat heavily in the chair her legs splayed out in front of her in a most un - Lillian position. Angela stood, arms at her sides, at a loss what to do, rather missing being out in the open air of the prairies and knowing the routine.

"Hello!" A bonneted head peeked through the doorway.

"Hello," Angela greeted the speaker.

A wisp of a girl not much younger than herself entered the room. "You all just git here? Know where to fetch water and fuel and

233

whatnot? I can show you. I have to fetch water myself fer supper," she said in response to Angela's negative shake of her head.

"Thank you." Angela picked up a bucket by the little hearth. "This is my sister Lillian," she said.

Lillian wiggled her fingers at the girl.

"How'd you do. I'm Pauline. We're stayin' right next door to you people. Been here 'bout four days. Ma's awful weak after the baby. How long you stayin'?"

"I'm not sure," Angela replied. They talked as they went out the door. "I think only for a night or two."

The girl's thin blond hair hung down her back, her dress was too small, revealing long thin legs and bare feet. Sensing someone following Angela turned to see two dirty little children, a boy and girl. They stared at her, eyes large in their thin faces, grimy fingers in their mouths.

"You can come along. Only stay close," Pauline told them. "That's my little brother and sister," she explained. "My big brother is with Pa talkin' to the men."

They wound their way through bushy bearded men in garb like Lou and Barton's or in buckskins with long rifles resting beside them, riders, children running, small groups of Indians and whites bartering and groups of young people talking and laughing. There was a whole village of tents and animals set up outside the walls of the fort. Staring like Ben had, Angela found herself falling behind and had to hurry after Pauline. They followed a smooth worn path to the river, where Pauline turned to her brother and sister and said, "Go on in. Watch you don't drown or nothin'. I don't want no whoppin' from Pa."

The two little ones looked at each other. One put a foot in then the other did.

"No further than your knees. You hear?"

Once in the water they smiled mischievously at each other and began to splash playfully.

Somehow amongst the smells of many people Angela felt more dirty than she usually did from the dust and dirt of the trail. "Do you mind if I take the time to wash?"

"Nope. Might as well wash a bit myself," Pauline said.

They sat on the edge of the river. Angela rubbed her face, neck and arms, feet and legs with water. She wished she'd brought some soap.

"It's nice here. I wish we could stay put right here," Pauline said.

"You mean here at the fort?" Angela asked.

"Yep, have everything we need here. Feels real safe."

"It's awfully crowded and noisy," Angela said. She watched the children play.

"It don't seem noisy to me. I guess that's cuz our wagon train was pretty noisy. What with little ones squallin' and folks shoutin' and the men arguin' every night about which way to go, where to camp and whatnot."

They sat for a moment enjoying the coolness of evening air coming off the water. Then Pauline asked, "How many you lost?"

"Lost? What do you mean?"

"Died, how many folks from your wagon train died?"

She was pretty though her chin was sharp, her face drawn and dirty.

"No one," Angela said. "We're a small group, one wagon."

"Only one?" The girl was amazed. "Is that safe? Don't you feel kinda scared all alone?"

"Sometimes, but it hasn't been bad. We've been lucky. I think I'd better be getting back."

"Yeah, I better git supper started before Pa and Junior git back. Hey," she called her brother and sister, "don't make me have to come git you."

They dutifully followed her.

The smells of many suppers cooking over open fires wafted throughout the grounds.

"Have you had any of the fish from here yet? It's the most delicious I've ever et. And some folks have hens, you can git eggs and milk. Our cow dried up and folks in our train don't like to share."

Angela's memory of the last time she had fish was overshadowed by the image of the threatening bear. They paused outside her door.

"Will you be comin' out after supper?" Pauline asked. "Most nights there's music and dancin'. It's a real good time."

"Sounds nice," Angela said before slipping into the cool room.

235

Tired as she was, she couldn't imagine dancing. Her mother and
Barton Finch were back with supplies. Lou came in behind her,
loaded down with fresh fish and moss and wood for building a fire.

"Where were you all this time?" Lillian complained to her.

"I'm hungry," Ben said. "Angela did you see the Indians? And the
men dressed like Indians? You went to the river? Will you take me
next time?"

Lou built the fire. The small room filled with smoke. It was
difficult to do anything without bumping into each other. Barton stood
in the door with his pipe. Lillian sat in a corner on some bedding,
fanning herself. Crouching before the hearth, Lou cooked the fish.
The room soon filled with the crackling sounds and the delicious
smell.

"We'll all smell of fish," Lillian commented. She moved to the
doorway. "There isn't any door?" she announced. "What will we do at
night?"

"You want a door Miss?" Barton said. "Someone can tack a
blanket over the opening there."

Pauline was right, Angela thought. The salmon was fit for royalty.
The skin was crispy and the meat faintly pink. She believed nothing
on earth could taste better. It's a good thing to be without for a while.
How much more the wanting makes you appreciate things. Would
they have fish at their new home? Fish from the ocean might be
another thing that she would miss from the east. They had stewed
apples and berries to finish the meal.

There was the steady sound of footsteps passing by the open
doorway as they ate, accompanied often by conversational voices.
Occasionally a shout or a passerby looking in the door would startle
the family. Lou would nod, Barton waved halfheartedly, but Clara
started and Lillian gasped at each intrusion. Angela couldn't keep her
eyes off the activity outside the doorway. She caught glimpses of
Indians lightly passing by, singly or as a family. One young male
stopped, entered the room and silently helped himself to a piece of
fish before leaving. This was too much for Lillian, who was
disappointed with the accommodations to begin with, never mind
these encroachments. She burst into tears, "I can't stand it! Why do

these people think they can walk right in! Why isn't there a door? Hasn't anyone here any manners? Savages can walk right in?"

Ben had gone to the door to watch the departing Indian.

"Benjamin, come inside," Clara commanded.

Angela tried to console Lillian, "It's not what I imagined, but I'm sure it's safe here."

Lillian refused to be comforted, she pushed Angela's arm away and wailed all the harder. Lou put on his hat and went out. Barton cleared his throat and asked, "Ma'am, do you mind if the boy comes along with me for a bit of fresh air?"

Clara looked up from where she had gone to her daughter. "Thank you Mr. Finch, I'm certain that Ben would enjoy that."

After she had emptied the room, Lillian continued to carry on loudly. "It's horrible here! People are rude. It's dirty!"

Angela was afraid she would offend people nearby.

By the time Barton and Ben returned, Lillian had exhausted herself and her sobs had faded to hiccups. Clara had settled her in the chair. Angela was cleaning up after the supper. They were carrying a large wooden tub between them

"Look what we borrowed!" Ben declared. "Now you can have a real bath, Lilly. Look!"

Lillian examined the tub placed before her with her upper lip pulled up and her eyebrows arched in disgust.

"Thank you Mr. Finch," Clara said. She eyed the old tub warily, but said, "This was very thoughtful of you."

"Yes, thank you," Angela added. She had been silenced by surprise.

"Glad to help. Now if you'll excuse me, I'm going to get caught up on the news and see if I can't find any old acquaintances."

Ben started to follow him out, but his mother caught his arm.

"You stay here for a bath." She looked at the pot of water over the fire. "I'm afraid there is not nearly enough water."

"I'll get it," Angela said. "I know where to go."

"Take Ben with you, neither of you are to go anywhere alone. There are many disreputable looking people about. Hurry I'm concerned about the unhealthy night air."

In the softening evening light the atmosphere of the camp was becoming more tranquil: voices were quieter, families were finishing their evening meals, babies were being put to bed. People were beginning to gather in small groups. A harmonica and fiddle could be heard playing.

Her shoulders ached and her arms felt as if they were being stretched by the heavy buckets on the long walk to the little room. Ben lugged his bucket manfully. Clara was tapping a blanket over the doorway with a rock for a hammer.

The hot water from the pot over the fire was poured into the tub and refilled. The room filled with fuzzy, warm steam that touched Angela's face like gentle kisses. Ben stood guard outside, at Lillian's insistence. She stepped into the tub with reluctance and much coaxing, but her cheeks soon glowed and her discouragement dissipated like the rising steam.

"I'd almost forgotten what a bath is like," she said. "I must thank Mr. Finch. It really was kind of him to find this for us."

"I'm glad you are remembering yourself," her mother said as a quiet reprimand.

"Oh dear, I behaved horribly didn't I? I'll apologize to him the minute I see him."

When she finished, Lillian left the tub as reluctantly as she'd entered it.

"Mother?" Angela invited.

"No, you go next," Clara said.

The tepid water soaked her skin, washing away miles of soil that felt as if it had worked its way under her skin and was part of her life's blood. Pouring water over her head she was taken back to Saturday night baths.

Ah, Saturday night baths, lovely preparations for Sundays. They would spend the morning in church. Angela would stare up at the vaulted ceiling. Words, fragments would reach her from the preacher high above as if from heaven itself. Wonderful words, words that made her think that encouraged her spirit to reach out to God's. Then Sunday afternoons unless there was an emergency her father would be home. The house smelled of good things cooking in preparation for the big dinner, perhaps a chicken roasting with potatoes and onions, pies or pudding for dessert. The Grandparents joined them. On Sundays disagreements were put away. Mother didn't snap, her face wasn't tight with annoyance at Father's long hours and not having the money she wanted. Grandmother hugged and exclaimed over her and Lillian. Grandfather let them climb in his lap, his eyes beaming love on them.

She dried her hair next to the fire with Lillian. Her scalp felt light. Lillian appeared nearly content herself. Angela hugged Ben when he was drying himself after his bath. "Thank you Ben. I feel wonderful."

The three women were brushing out their hair when they heard Pauline's high voice outside the blanket. "Hello there?"

"Come in," Angela called. "It's the girl from next door," she explained.

"Are you comin' to hear the music? Whew, it's steamy in here. Folks'll be dancin' and singin'. It's great fun. They've already started. Comin'?"

"Dancing?" Lillian's spirits brightened more, but Clara hesitated. "You've only just got out of the water. Your hair is damp." She frowned and she felt her daughters' heads.

"Oh please, do let's go," Lillian pleaded.

"I suppose it would do your heart good," her mother conceded. "Put kerchiefs over your heads."

In the evening shadows and flickering campfires the Fort seemed almost enchanting. Groups gathered around fires sharing stories, smoking and laughing. The largest crowd formed a horseshoe, clapping their hands and tapping their feet to the music of three fiddlers and two harmonica players. In the open space of the horseshoe people danced. Pauline led Angela, Lillian and Ben to a group of their peers. They shouted introductions over the music and babble of voices. When the next song started they joined the dancers.

Lillian, forgetting her troubles, was soon the center of the happy cluster. She grabbed Angela's hands when she hung back shyly and pulled her into the dance. The music carried Angela, smiling eyes and laughing mouths spun past her. The tired dark circles under eyes disappeared; callused hands grasped other rough hands and then moved on. Skipping by, Angela saw her mother in conversation with other women. Ben ran, danced and played with other children, Traveler chasing after his heels.

One by one the winded dancers wavered out of the spinning world and collapsed happily on solid ground. The musicians shifted to slower, more plaintive songs. Older couples waltzed amongst the

239

younger. Angela admired how the older couples moved together. They seemed to know their partner's steps as well as their own, one's moves answering the other's. They flowed, looking into each other's eyes, dancing as one.

Clara touched her shoulder. "Your sister and I are returning to the room. Please bring Benjamin and come directly. Do not go alone. Pauline has agreed to accompany you."

Pauline stood by her when her mother and Lillian walked back to the cabin. Leaving the dancing circle, they searched until they found Ben sitting on the outskirts of a group of men who were talking and smoking.

"Thank you Pauline. I'm fine. I'm sure you want to get back to your family," Angela said.

"Yeah I best be gettin' back."

Angela listened to the conversations. She caught phrases, bits of dialogue. A man standing with one foot on a crate declared, "The only good Indian is a dead Indian! I'm gonna shoot one first chance I get!" His voice was thick in his mouth.

"There'll be no shooting anyone in this fort," a soldier said.

"Naw, not here, but just as soon's I get the chance," the man continued.

"That so?" A new speaker interjected. He was dressed in deerskin clothes. He took his pipe out of his mouth to speak.

"Yeah, you have a problem with it?" the would- be- killer challenged.

All eyes turned to the deerskin man, who shrugged. "It's your affair. Only I knew a man like you. Braggin' all the time 'bout how he was gonna shoot the first Indian he came across." He took a draw from his pipe. "Did too. He shot an Indian, like he said he would. It was a woman getting water from a river."

There were murmurs. Angela felt a chill.

"She should have kept out of sight better," the other countered.

"Maybe so, with the likes of you around," the pipe smoker said slowly. "Her people didn't take kindly to her murder. They massacred the shooter's whole wagon train to avenge her death."

There were more murmured responses.

Angela took her brother by the hand. "Come Ben."

240

Passing Indian families with their children sleeping wrapped in blankets on the open ground, she wondered how they saw people like herself. Did they think all whites were like that man with the gun? Did they fear for their children?

"Do you think that man's story was true?" Ben asked.

"Which man?"

"Both I guess."

"Could be. I don't know, let's hope not."

Back in their room they settled in their bedding for the night. Lou had set up his tent near the wagon to guard against thievery. Barton joined him after bidding the family good night. Though it was good to be on solid ground, the sounds of people all around kept Angela awake. She wondered if Prisoner was alright. Her mother sat up at every sound. When she did sleep, Angela dreamed they were in the wagon rocking along.

Angela rolled over and that was good enough for Traveler, who greeted her wriggling joyfully in her face. Clara was sitting in the chair by the fire. Ben was holding back the blanket to look out the door, letting in a bright beam of light. She rolled her bedding and put it to the side.

"Your brother is waiting," her mother said.

"Do you want to come?" Angela asked her.

"No, I will wait for Lillian to wake. You may go."

Angela paused outside, waiting for her eyes to adjust to the light. The early morning sounds of the fort were muted, activity quiet. They passed the building where Barton Finch and the soldier had taken Prisoner yesterday. She wondered again how he was. At least he was inside, not sleeping out on the damp cold ground. Maybe he was better off. Ben caught her looking at the building.

"Can we go see Prisoner in the jail? It's in there isn't it? Do you think it has bars? Can we go in?"

She blushed as if he had read her mind and didn't answer while she considered how to go about arranging for Ben at least to see him.

They returned to the room, all smoky with breakfast cooking. Barton Finch was waiting placidly to be served. Lou had brought a pail of milk and Lillian was ladling it into their mugs.

"Benjamin be sure to drink plenty of milk while we have it," Clara instructed. "What more do you think we should obtain by way of supplies?" she asked Barton.

"Let me see. Yesterday we got soap, matches, sugar, vegetables and flour," he paused.

"I'd like more apples," Clara said. "What other fruit is available?"

"You should be able to get apples, plums and such."

"More quinine, Mother," Angela suggested.

Ben finished his meal and went to the door where he fussed with the blanket covering until it came partly down.

"Angela will you take your brother outside?" Clara asked.

She was interested in the conversation about the supplies, but obeyed.

Once outside, Ben started with the subject on his mind. "Let's go see the jail. Please Ange."

She hesitated, wanting to, but uncomfortable at the idea.

"I don't know. It may not be allowed." What possible excuse could they give, she wondered. She could say her brother was curious about seeing a jail. What about seeing Prisoner? How could she explain? They strolled towards the entrance of the fort, past the two-story building where Lou had met the officer and Barton had followed him with the prisoner.

"The jail is in there," Ben pointed back.

"Yes," she answered. She saw their wagon amongst others, its wheels blocked, Lou's tent next to it. Something on the driver's bench caught her eye.

"Wait here." She jogged to the wagon and climbed to the bench. There was the blanket she'd given Prisoner. She gathered it up and hurried back to Ben. More people were moving about now, the place would soon be buzzing as busily as a hive. They returned to the door of the official building. Angela held back, but Ben knocked. It wasn't latched and swung open under his knuckles. Inside was a large desk, but no one attended it. The room was spacious and simple; there was a door in the back. Angela opened her mouth to propose leaving when that door was flung open by a plump, little gray haired woman with a towel over one arm and a basin in her hands.

"Oh," she said, "I didn't know anyone was here. Can I help you children?"

242

"We came to see Prisoner. He's in the jail." Ben said.

The little lady looked from one to the other. "I beg your pardon?"

"Please pardon my brother," Angela said. "I'm Angela Harrington and this is Benjamin. The person, in the jail, he is traveling with our family," she tried to explain. "Mr. Finch is in charge of him. He… that is the prisoner and Ben, well he …"

"He saved me from the river," Ben blurted, "Can we see him?"

"He's not dangerous," Angela said. She blushed and wished she hadn't come at all.

"No, no, I didn't think he was dangerous, the poor dear." The woman shook her gray curls and set down her basin. "I was just going to get my husband, the doctor, to have a look at him."

She sized them up with quick, blue eyes. "Come with me. I could use the help."

They followed her through a hallway to a bolted door. She pulled a key from her apron pocket and turned to face them. "I brought him one of my nice meals this morning, like I always do when there's someone in here, but he didn't move. I thought to myself something doesn't look right. I went over close. What do you think I found? His hands were tied behind his back. He must have been like that all night, the poor dear. His hands were black. I cut the rope off. Can you imagine leaving him like that all night? The Captain wouldn't have left him like that. He doesn't even tie the rowdy drunk ones when they're in here for the night. And how some of them carry on." She clicked her tongue. Unlocking the bolt she pulled back the heavy door with both her little arms.

"Friends to see you dear," she announced.

The room had no windows. It was empty except for a cot with a thin straw mattress. After a moment they could discern the prisoner slumped on the floor, his back against the cot.

"Here we are," the doctor's wife said brightly. Angela heard his breath catch and saw his head lift then drop again. They followed her to him.

She bent over him. "It's a shame you were left all night tied. We'll set you to rights. Here," she said to Ben, "Rub his arm and hand like this." She vigorously massaged up and down his left arm. Ben took his right and imitated the lady's movements.

243

"That's right. Every once in a while open and shut his fingers." She demonstrated.

The prisoner bent his left knee up, pulled his arms away and tried to cross them in front of himself.

"Pins and needles?" the little lady asked. She peered into his face. "Good. Means you're getting the feeling back. Keep rubbing," she reminded Ben.

"I hate that prickly feeling when my leg goes to sleep. Your hand looks strange," Ben said. He held up the prisoner's hand and studied it curiously.

"Keep opening and closing his fingers for him 'til he can move them himself. That's the way," the lady encouraged. After more rubbing she said to the prisoner, "Make a fist. Go on."

He tried to get his fingers to obey. They curled, but did not close in a fist.

"Getting better. Least you can move them. Try to eat your breakfast."

His head tilted down, his eyes were half shut.

"Come dear, you need to eat." She picked up the plate from the floor. "I know you're tuckered out, but you need your strength."

Ben took the plate. "They have good food here at the fort," he said. "We had fish last night and meat this morning. It's much better than that dry stuff we've been having. The fish was real good. Lou got it from some Indians. Remember when we had fish before? When the bear came? Remember?"

He held the plate before the prisoner, who took no notice of it.

"You better drink first, so you can swallow." He held a mug of water up. The young man took it; his fingers did not work properly. He pressed it between his palms and Ben helped him hold it and lift it.

"There's lots of Indians here. Maybe you know some," Ben rambled on naturally, taking pieces of bread and meat from the plate and handing it to the prisoner, who ate slowly watching Ben's face with his solemn eyes.

The little woman laid her hand on Angela's arm, "He has a way with folks, your little brother. I'll see if the doctor is free." She paused before opening the door, "You'll be fine here?"

"Yes," Angela said softly.

The door shut and the bolt slid behind her. The room was dark.

"This isn't what I thought a jail would look like," Ben was saying. "Here, have some more of this bread. It's fresh and soft, not like the hard stuff we've been eating. And you don't have to pick off the bad spots. Your hands look different. They're kind of swelled up and red. I can still see the lines where the rope was."

A strange tingling sensation ran down Angela's arms and into her palms. She tried to breathe quietly to not disturb them with her presence. She didn't know what moved her more, Ben's sweet attentiveness or the young man's quiet dignity even in his helpless state.

There were voices outside the door. Then the little woman bustled in holding a leather case. A round-faced man with a big, bushy gray mustache that was curled on the ends followed her. He wore spectacles.

"Here we are," she said.

The doctor, short and plump like his wife, cleared his throat. At the sound the prisoner got to his feet, using the cot behind him to hoist himself up. He tried push back, but the cot impeded his way and he sat heavily on to it. The doctor took the leather bag from his wife, set it on the floor and opened it, watching the patient with a scowl under thick brows.

"Can't see a darn thing. Martha, open the door and let some light in."

Martha hustled to the door and opened it.

He pulled a stethoscope from the bag and came to the cot. "Let's have a look at you. Martha says you don't look good."

The prisoner sat with his legs over the edge of the cot. He gripped its edge with both hands. He shook his head. His hair was half tied back the rest fell across his face. He began to breathe rapidly.

"He's a doctor. It's alright." Ben tugged at his sleeve.

"Take it easy. I'm just going to have a look at you. What's the problem? You hurt or sick?"

The uncooperative patient only shook his head and leaned back.

"Can he speak?" the doctor asked.

"Sure he can talk. He's just doesn't like too," Ben explained.

"He's not dangerous is he? I'm not going to have a fight on my hands. I won't bother risking it. I'll just be on my way. I've got others to see you know."

"No, he's not dangerous," Angela said. She stepped out of the shadows. "He just doesn't trust people he doesn't know. He's ... he's been hurt. He trusts Ben; he'll listen to Ben. Just tell my brother what you need him to do and he'll tell him."

"Hmm." The doctor frowned. He put his stethoscope around his neck.

"What's wrong with him, medically?" he asked her.

"He has an old break in his right lower leg. It was never set. Also a few days ago he hurt his left."

"Come dear, let the doctor look at you," Martha encouraged the prisoner. He drew back from her. The doctor tried to put his stethoscope to the prisoner's chest, but he jerked away.

"It doesn't hurt," Ben explained. "You sure can be scared about the silliest things."

"I don't like this. Have him lie down," the doctor grumbled.

Ben pushed against his chest. "Lie down, so the doctor can look at you. He only wants to listen to you with the stethoscope. Didn't you ever have a doctor before?"

He shook his head, his eyes large. The quick lady took advantage of his preoccupation with Ben to lift his legs up on the cot. He braced on his elbows, breathing irregularly, unwilling to lie the rest of the way down, not strong enough to flee.

Angela's own throat was closing with an irrational panic. It wasn't that she feared he would harm anyone. It was as if she were being held against her will. She knew it wasn't pain he feared; it was others so close, closing in on him. It was being trapped. She wanted to shout at them to leave him alone. The doctor was becoming more impatient with each passing minute. No, he should be looked at by the doctor, she resolved.

She moved next to Ben at the cot. "Move to the other side. Keep talking to him," she whispered.

Ben moved to the far side of the cot. He stood at his shoulder. She lay the blanket across the young man. He glanced at her quickly, breathing in short gasps.

"Say something Ben," she whispered.

"Let the doctor look at your leg," Ben said. "Like Pierre did. You remember? It helped didn't it? Don't be such a baby."

The doctor put one hand under his right knee for support and slid the baggy pant leg up all the while watching the prisoner suspiciously. The young man watched him equally suspiciously. He'd turn his eyes momentarily to Ben, to Angela then to the doctor.

"Mrs. Mullins," the doctor said to his wife, "Get me the brace. You know where it is in my office."

She hurried out of the room, her little feet drumming.

"Our father was a doctor," Ben said.

"Is that a fact?" he responded, scowling at the leg.

He swung it gently from the knee. When he reached down to the foot he was surprised by the abrasion from the chain. "What's this?"

"Mr. Finch... he ... chains him," Angela tried to explain. "It was infected. Well, it looked infected," she continued hoping the doctor didn't think she was being presumptuous.

He looked at her from under his shaggy brows then studied the ring around the ankle.

"Hmm, should be kept clean." Next, still supporting the knee he tried to move the foot slightly from side to side. The prisoner's breath caught and he sat up higher.

"Mmm, that bothers does it?" Doctor Mullins said. Then he tried to flex the foot. The young man stiffened straight up on his arms, rising off the cot.

" Mmm, I won't try any more," the doctor assured him. "Not much I can do about it after all this time. Should be broken and reset I suppose, but I'm sure it won't get proper attention and rest. Give it some support is all I can do."

Mrs. Mullins returned. "How are we doing?" She set something made of leather pieces on the end of the cot and slipped a bolster under the prisoner's leg.

"Why did it hurt when you moved his ankle? Is it injured too?" Angela couldn't resist asking.

"No, not the ankle. He's just feeling it up the leg. Both bones were broken and didn't heal in place. Everything's a bit frozen up on him. A nasty break."

"Will it get better with time?"

"Some, but the leg will never be as strong. Will always give him trouble."

The young man dropped back down to his elbows. He tried to watch each face, his chest rising and falling, but his eyes were shutting against his will.

A voice was heard growing louder as it came nearer. He sat up.

"What is all that fussing?" Mrs. Mullins asked.

Barton Finch charged through the open door. "Who gave permission? Who gave you permission?" he roared.

The captain from the day before hurried in behind him.

"Easy now, I didn't let you in to cause trouble. The doctor and his Missus routinely check on whoever is locked up."

"This is my prisoner! My responsibility. I must be notified," Barton blustered. "The door wasn't even locked."

Mrs. Mullins stared at him, her mouth opened in an "o".

"Now you listen," the doctor said. He was not one bit impressed. "Don't you come in here carrying on. You're responsible are you? This prisoner is in deplorable condition. You've done a lousy job of your responsibility. Now you wait outside until I've completed my work. You want me to report you?" The little man punctuated each of his words with a poke of his finger in Barton's chest, backing him up until he was out the door.

"Better come with me. The doc can get real peckish if he's bothered when he's working," the captain said to Barton. Winking at the people in the room, he shut the door behind himself and Barton Finch.

If she hadn't been so nervous Angela would have laughed at the sight of the little doctor backing the big man out the door.

"Let's get this brace on," he said turning back to his patient.

At Barton's interruption the prisoner had swung his legs over and gripped the sides of the cot to push off, but lacked the strength.

"Lie back down there. Here you go." The doctor put his legs back up on the cot and he fell back on his elbows. "Pass me the brace Martha." He held up the leather contraption she placed in his hands.

The prisoner tried to pull away. Ben put a hand on his chest. "He's helping your leg, like Pierre. Remember? It was much better after."

The only response was a quick look at Ben then back at the doctor.

248

"It buckles on like this." The doctor put the brace around his right calf and adjusted the buckles. "There. That's all I can do about the leg," he said grimly. "Can't undo the damage or neglect."

"Doctor would you look at his other leg?" Angela asked. She was sorry to extend the patient's torment.

"Hmm?"

"When he was pushing a wagon out of the mud he collapsed. He was holding his thigh," she explained. "It was all pulled." All the while she spoke softly for only the doctor's hearing.

The doctor pushed the other pant leg up, but it would only go as far as the knee, where it bunched. He put his hand on the young man's thigh and kneaded it carefully. The prisoner pulled the leg back.

"Hold still," Ben reprimanded him. "He only wants to find where you hurt yourself the other day. If it scares you don't look, just look at me."

He stared at Ben then back at the doctor. The doctor watched him cautiously as he felt for an injury.

"Hmm?" he said thoughtfully. "He must have damaged the muscle here. It's no wonder with the leg doing all the work for both. You say he was pushing a wagon? Here, feel right here," he indicated the spot to Angela. Without thinking, she put her hand where he showed her.

"Feel that raised band?"

She nodded. She also felt the young man shaking under her hand and heard him breathing. She pulled her hand away, her face burning. The doctor seemed to think nothing of involving her in his work. She stepped back and glanced at Prisoner from behind Mrs. Mullins. He held the blanket with both hands, where it lay across his lap. Her eyes stung. He looked more like a child holding a blanket for protection or comfort than the vicious criminal Finch portrayed him as.

Mrs. Mullins pulled the pant legs down and patted his foot lightly. "Rest and good food is what you need now," she said. The doctor gathered his bag and left the room.

Exhausted from the anxiety and the long night, the young man leaned back on his elbows, when they moved away he fell completely back, his eyes closed, his breathing was irregular. Angela hesitated, then walked quietly back to him on her toes, she pulled the blanket up to his chest.

"Poor dear," Mrs. Mullins whispered. She escorted them out the door after her husband.

"Where is that pushy fellow?" Doctor Mullins asked He looked around the front room like an angry rooster.

"I calmed him down and sent him off," the captain said. He was writing at the desk. "Had to assure him you all weren't conspiring to help the prisoner escape. The way your Missus spoils them all I don't know why they would want to leave," he winked at the little lady.

She laughed and waved a hand at him. "I just give them decent meals, that's all."

"If he's so concerned, why didn't he stick around," the doctor grumbled. "I have a thing or two I'd like to tell him."

"We'd better be going," Angela said, "Mother will be worried and Mr. Finch will be angry if he thinks we've had anything to do with interfering with his prisoner."

"Finch? That's his name?" the doctor growled.

"Be on your way now," his wife hushed him. He went out the front door grumbling to himself.

"Wait one moment children. I'd like to come with you. First let me get a little something for your family."

She disappeared back through the door to the hallway, her little feet tapping along the floor. The man she called Captain chuckled to himself. Mrs. Mullins soon popped back in with a basket full of eggs.

"I bet it's been a long time since you've had fresh eggs," she said smiling.

"It sure has," Ben said happily.

Angela's nervousness increased by degree the closer they got to the door of their building. When she held back before entering, Mrs. Mullins asked, "Is this it?"

She nodded mutely and the little lady barged in with a cheery, "Hello dears."

Mrs. Mullins, all energy, took charge of the road weary travelers and the room.

"Don't get up dear," she said to Lillian. She put her hand on Clara's shoulder. "I apologize for startling you. Are you the mother of these remarkable children? So bright they are, and kind too. This must be another." She patted Lillian's cheek. "Any more? I had to meet the parents of these children."

Clara said, "No there are only three."

"Their father?"

"He passed away."

"Oh, I'm sorry. What a shame, what a shame. He's looking down proudly. You can be sure." She emptied the eggs as she talked. "Are you finding all you need here at Fort Laramie?"

"Yes," Clara said. "Mr. Finch has been a great help to my family."

Barton stood in a corner, quiet for once.

"That so?" Mrs. Mullins turned and glowered at him, both hands on her rounded hips.

She turned away from him. "How are you set for medicinal supplies?"

"I am sure we are fine," Clara said.

"I'll set you up. You come with me," she directed Angela before anyone could protest.

Clara stopped them as they headed out the door; her little drawstring purse was in her hands. "We can pay for what we need," she said, opening it.

"Oh no dear, I'll trade for your daughter's assistance on my visits today."

Angela's and Ben's transgressions never surfaced. Although Angela waited for Barton's wrath, the little lady never gave him a chance. She took her by the arm and pulled her out.

In a cool room in the building joining the one that housed the captain's office, Mrs. Mullins showed Angela herbs, roots and powders, some hanging to dry, some in jars or tied up in cloth.

"Let's see. Here take some willow, it's good for fevers and here's some snakeroot. Oh yes, Indian tobacco is good for hunger pains and stomach ailments. Take some peppermint too. I'll get you some quinine. Opium for severe situations." She wrapped everything in neat parcels and put them all in a satchel. "Make sure you store these some place where they won't get wet. I believe you're all set up now. Do you mind accompanying me on my visits?"

"No, not at all."

Angela followed the vivacious woman as she went about spreading advice and comfort. She was appalled by the condition of many of the emigrants. There were pale, thin children in rags, hollow eyed men and women, including Pauline's mother who lay

251

apathetically under quilts, new baby squalling beside her. Mrs. Mullins gave food from her baskets and advice.

"Poor dears," she said as they left the last room, "I hope they make the wise decision to winter here. They'd be taking an awful chance trying to make it to the end of the trail. I suppose they might make it to Fort Hall, but after that I'm told the trail gets quite rough."

She left Angela with a soft kiss at her own door. "You take care now dear. Thank you for your help. I must do my baking, the day is getting on."

Angela didn't see how the hardy woman needed any help from anyone. She had been hard pressed to keep up with her.

Later in the afternoon Angela, Lillian and Pauline went to wash clothes. They met some of the people they had danced with the night before and the washing was delayed for happy visiting. Angela was more interested in the variety of characters passing back and forth, than the conversation of her peers. A particularly unusual young woman suddenly wholly seized her attention. She walked between a soldier and a severe looking woman dressed in dark wool, who held tightly to the younger woman's wrist. The young woman's hair hung loose and snarled down her back and over her shoulders. An oversized dress draped her wiry frame. Her feet were bare, her arms, face and legs tanned. Locked between the two people, she was scanning in every direction. When her face turned in her direction, Angela was struck by the wild blue eyes filled with frenzied desperation. She touched Pauline.

"Who is that?"

Pauline turned from the group to see. "Who? Oh her?" Her voice took on a hushed tone. "She was captured by Indians when she was a kid. Her family was killed or somethin', no one knows for sure." She paused dramatically. "Anyway she had to live with the Indians ever since."

"What did she do? Why is she with those people?"

"Soldiers rescued her from the Indians and brought her here. They put a missionary woman in charge of her."

"She sure seems unhappy."

"Yeah, she keeps runnin' away. They say she has an Indian husband and she keeps tryin' to get back to him."

Angela turned to watch the person being led away. She heard one of the other girls say with a horrified whisper, "It's better to be killed than be kidnapped by Indians."

"I know I'd kill myself," another said.

"How do you know?" Angela asked. "If it was so horrible, why would she keep trying to go back?"

The speaker was aghast at Angela's remark. She replied, "Anyone can see she's not right in the head."

"Bein' with the Indians all those years made her crazy," Pauline agreed.

Those geese in her grandmother's story suddenly popped into Angela's head. She wondered if it was life with the Indians that caused the girl's craziness, or the separation from that life. Throughout the rest of their stay at the fort, she hoped for another glimpse of the sad young woman, but she didn't see her again.

Angela, Lillian and Ben went out amongst the people after supper. Clara fretted about them being out in the damp night air, but decided they were starved for human interaction and let them visit. Lou and Barton had left on their own business as soon as they finished eating. Lillian joined the dancers and Ben found boys to play with. Angela was free to wander about and pause outside circles to listen to the stories. She heard a familiar laugh and saw Barton Finch with a group whose members seemed exaggeratedly animated. She felt a nervous twinge, recalling the night with Rose's family when he had been drinking. Last night he had said good night unsteadily. She avoided this group.

She watched an Indian woman with four children across the space. They sat around a fire. The mother paused in her cooking to wrap a blanket around one and speak sharply to another who was reaching for something on the fire. The mother's sharp eyes caught her observing them. Embarrassed by her invasion of their privacy Angela moved on.

She stopped outside a cluster of men and women. She recognized the man in buckskins from the night before. She thought as she listened that evening shadows made people bolder to speak their inner thoughts, good or bad. Tonight they were telling stories of people leaving messages along the trail for others coming after them. One tale told by a bearded man wearing suspenders and pants patched at

253

the knees, held her with horrible fascination. "Yep, a piece of cloth tied to branch," he was saying, "Gingham, I believe."

"A woman's dress," said a grim-faced woman. "They say to leave signs if you're kidnapped."

"Could have been, but we couldn't take the chance. Could have just as likely been a trap. We mighta started a rescue and ended up the one's in need of rescuing," he said.

"You mean you just left the poor woman to the savages?" another woman asked. Her face blanched in the starlight.

"We don't even know if it was a woman," the man's wife defended him. "We couldn't take the chance. It sounds terrible, but you wouldn't have done differently if it were you. None of you."

There were quiet affirmative murmurs in response to her argument.

Angela was appalled by the indifference of these people. She thought of her own party nearly ignoring the family with the stuck wagon in a situation more certain than the one in this story.

"Yeah," the husband continued, "the trail still isn't safe from Indian trickery. That family just a few weeks back, the father and son were killed just for sport."

Here the man with the pipe who'd spoke up to the man bragging about shooting an Indian the night before interrupted, "The way I heard it, some Indian women and children come up to the wagon train to trade, and some fool panicked and shot at them. They froze where they stood, except one youngster, who took off for home. The braves follow him back to find their women and children being held at gunpoint. The way I heard it, they figure they're being held for ransom and try to trade to get them back, but the man don't understand and shoots at 'em again when they try to get near."

"Well who wouldn't?" a woman said indignantly.

The speaker ignored her. "They waited for hours. Indians can be very patient. But was gettin' dark, the man's jumpy ways finally drove them to action."

"Oh yeah?" said the first man. "I heard they left and came back later in a sneak attack."

"Folks from one of the other wagons said they did go off for a bit," said the man with the pipe. "It's Indian's way to go off and discuss a thing before acting. They agreed on a plan, came back to

254

save their folks. The white man had backed himself into a corner, afraid if he didn't keep them as protection the braves would come back for revenge. Too bad, just a matter of folks misunderstanding each other."

Some of the listeners eyed this man with hostility.

"You one of them fellows that's lived with savages? Think we're intruding on their ways, so they can do anything they like to whites?" a man asked

"I'm not saying that exactly. Indians are just people. They can be as cruel as any white, worse than some, better'n others. I'm only saying it's misunderstandings and ignorance that cause most problems." He took up his pipe, finished with the matter.

A cold breeze on her face reminded Angela that it was getting late. She hurried back to the dancers to find her brother and sister, the man's word ringing in her head, "Misunderstandings."

In the gloom of the early morning they packed their things in the wagon. Lillian tearfully hugged the few new acquaintances that came to see them off. Clara's rigid posture belied her apprehension.

The captain brought the prisoner out. The blanket draped over his shoulders, his hair tied back, he stood looking out at the sky, giving Angela that strange erratic increase in her pulse. Only she observed Mrs. Mullins touch his arm and slip a parcel of wrapped food into his hand. A muscle in his jaw moved. Lou directed him to the bench before Barton had a chance to reestablish his authority with some rough gesture.

As they progressed the sun began to lighten the sky behind them. They would continue to follow the North Platte River. Ahead lay Independence Rock, the Bear River Valley, their Uncle and their land, the final leg of the journey. This time instead of the prickle of excited anticipation tickling her skin, Angela's head was heavy and dull and her stomach queasy. They had been lucky on the first half of the trip, no injuries, no life threatening illnesses. Now they were well into August. Would their luck hold out or were they due for a double dose of trouble?

Marty Young Stratton

Part 2

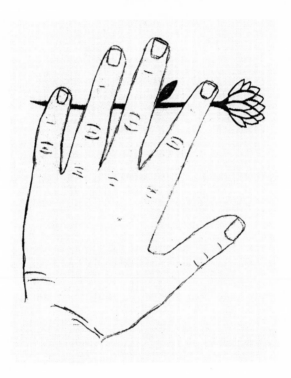

Chapter 18

*"The River spreading flows,-and spends
your dream.
What are you, lost within this tideless
spell?"*

"The River" by Hart Crane

With the warm sun and security of the fort at their backs, they faced resolutely forward. Riders trotted past them. Ben walked backwards to watch the fort getting smaller and smaller behind them, but Angela wouldn't let herself look back. She faced the cool shadowy land ahead. She couldn't shake clear the heaviness in her head. Ben chattered away, seemingly unfettered by the misgivings of the rest of his family.

"Wasn't the fort great? And the soldiers. I'd like to be a soldier and live at the fort. The next fort, what is it called?"

She realized he was talking to her. "Fort Hall," she said.

"I wonder if Fort Hall is close enough to our new home to visit it any time we want? I could be a soldier there. Is it close to our place, Ange?"

"I don't think so. I believe the land is days away maybe weeks, down the Bear River," she answered vaguely.

"The Bear River?" This gave him pause.

Angela noticed his pensiveness and added, "I'm sure it doesn't have an especially large amount of bears. It's just a name."

He nodded. In her brother's silence Angela remembered that in spite of his childlike enthusiasm he had his own fears. She wondered how well she really knew him. She thought of the man with the pipe and his simple word, "misunderstandings." Not such a simple word after all was it? How many authors used misunderstandings for the comedic heart of a story or play? The deliberate use of miss-communication, a pun, a play on words, people found entertaining. Purposes misconstrued, doubts cast, missed messages, hidden truths, loved ones not truly understood; authors used these for the heart of tragedies as well as comedies.

What was the answer? A logical mind might say knowledge was the key. If those emigrants on that wagon train had understood Indian ways, could their deaths have been prevented? She wasn't sure. Logic and knowledge certainly couldn't unlock all the complexities of the human heart. She herself was ruled more by her emotions than logic. She said a little prayer for understanding and courage.

The rising sun warmed her shoulders and neck. The steady solid clop of the horses' hooves had been a reassuring sound to her now the hoof beats seemed a relentless march carrying her inexorably along. She lifted her head to see Lou and the prisoner. Lou leaned forward, his elbows resting on his knees, reins loosely held. The younger man sat straight and attentive, his eyes taking in all that lay ahead and around them. Angela wished they would slow down, hesitate in this dreary march. Why were there no traces of dread or regret in the prisoner's face? Didn't he care that they were moving closer and closer to his terrible end? She shivered. Maybe he didn't care, maybe he wanted to die. Or perhaps he did care. It could be simply that she couldn't read his face. Wasn't that what they said about Indians; they are stone faced? No that wasn't true, his face showed reactions, emotions. The monotonous hum of the insects only deepened her growing gloominess.

Lou grumbled to his passengers when he stopped the team, "Don't git too settled. "Got to move along."

Angela looked at him. Why was he in such a hurry? She thought he liked Prisoner. Lou, his eyes quick under the brim of his hat caught her expression of inquiry mixed with resentment.

"Be gettin' more 'n' more into bad weather as the season goes," he explained. "Got to move along."

She nodded. Of course, she knew he was right, but the strange regret was strong. The young man himself, limped briskly about helping Lou feed and water the horses with sure movements. He was much stronger now, having benefited from a brief respite from Barton Finch's abuse. He shifted easily to his left leg for balance. His coloring less pale and yellow tinted had a healthy touch of gold. Lou's clothes hung loosely on him.

"Angela are you coming?" Lillian called.

Angela blushed, caught again watching him.

Clara noticed only her color. "Are you getting too much sun, Angela?" she asked.

"I would think she would be with all that walking," Lillian declared. "Don't you have a parasol? You look terribly coarse. Your nose is red your cheeks are also. You don't keep your bonnet on. I know these are not very attractive, but it's better than having your face ruined." She fussed with her sister's bonnet.

"Well come," Clara insisted. Angela joined them to look for a private spot. Her mother frowned at her as they walked, but she bent her head and hurried along to prevent closer examination.

They passed around a bit of food and water before starting off again.

"Angela, perhaps you should ride inside," her mother suggested.

"I'll keep my bonnet on, Mother. I'll be fine." She tried to sound calm though her heart was beginning to race at the idea.

Clara said nothing more. And when she lifted her hem and climbed the step Angela took it as permission to stay out. Strolling back to the wagon, Barton saw everyone ready to depart and hurried over his face shining with sweat from the effort.

"Go on Kid." Lou tapped the prisoner's shoulder and he pulled himself up the ladder.

They have to give him a trial Angela thought that afternoon. She trudged one step after another. The dry grass crunched under foot. At the trial the judge and jury will see that he's not vicious by any means. Ben and I, we could testify on his behalf. We could tell of the times he saved Ben and he kept the whole wagon of us out of trouble. That should count for something. I wonder where they'll try him? At Fort Hall? At the nearest town? Will we be there to testify? Will Mother allow us? What kind of law do they have out here in the territories? Do they even hold court with juries and a judge presiding? They must, they have to. They won't hang him; reasonable people wouldn't do such a thing. They have to be fair they have to.

Each rhythmical step of the horses' hooves seemed to repeat this chant, "They have to they have to."

The cold dropped in quickly at night. Lou would start the fire each evening, leaving the young man to finish with the horses' care. The

261

little group clustered around the warmth for their meal and coffee. Barton as always was very attentive to Lillian and Clara. Angela grudgingly told herself to be grateful.

"Put on extra shawls ladies. Hope you have warm clothes," he said. "Get your mother and sister some blankets," he called over his shoulder to Angela. She moved slowly to comply. Her mind was lost in the stars she gazed up at. There were stars that looked blue, some white and wispy blurs of clouds that weren't clouds at all, but clusters of stars. She went out of the security of the firelight into the shadows to the wagon. The shape of the young man sitting by it with his blanket over his shoulders emboldened her. If there were something to be afraid of he would know. Fishing around in the dark of the wagon, she found the blankets. She wanted to speak to him as she passed by, but the very thought started nervous vibrations running through her and she hurried back to the fire.

"Mr. Finch, I forgot to ask," her mother was saying, "Did you receive word from your acquaintances while we were at the fort?"

"Yes ma'am, thank you for asking. The fellow I'm working for will be waiting at Fort Hall."

"I see," she said politely. "It must be a great relief to your mind knowing we are on the last of this journey."

"Yes ma'am, it's been a long trial for me and it's not over yet, not by a long shot." He glared through the darkness in the direction of the prisoner.

Lou rose rustily to his feet and walked off to check the horses one last time. Noticing his pointed departure, Barton commented, "Lou may not think he's much trouble. I know this criminal considerably better than he does. Besides, I'm the one in most danger from him."

"Really Mr. Finch? Do you think he'd dare do anything to you?" Lillian asked.

"Sure I do. He'd kill me in the blink of an eye if he got the chance."

"Kill you?" Lillian squealed.

"Why would he want to kill you, Mr. Finch?" Ben asked and then added with a child's bluntness, "because you hurt him?"

"I only do what is necessary, boy. You remember that. You see how he looks at me? He hates me."

"Not me," Lillian said dramatically. "I won't look at him, not if I can help it. Oh yes, I do recall one night when he was staring at you in a frightful way."

"Well take my word for it. He would do me harm given half a chance."

"Mr. Finch are you ever frightened transporting dangerous outlaws over long distances?" Lillian asked.

Ben slid closer to him.

"No, when I started I was too young and brash to think there was possible danger to myself. First I went along as an assistant to others in the business. I watched, learned from their experience and mistakes. I formed my own ideas of how I'd do things pretty quick. Had to, out of necessity for my own protection. I'm getting too old for this kind of work." He heaved a sigh.

"Oh no, not at all," Clara murmured.

He smiled broadly. "Not that I'm not perfectly capable. It's only that I want to settle down. I'm not getting any younger. You reach an age you start to think of the things you've missed, traveling all the time. Living like this can make a man forget he's civilized. You've seen some of these characters at the fort and men like that Pierre. It comes from living out here too long."

"We certainly have," Clara agreed.

"Mr. Finch," Angela began. She cleared her throat, annoyed at her nervous hoarseness. "What is law like in the territories? I mean who conducts trials and presides?"

"Let's see, there's the federal marshals appointed by the President himself. They're hard to come by because they have to cover thousands of miles of territory. Then there are local marshals and sheriffs for more local law enforcement. For court there are district judges or justices of the peace. They can try petty criminals. This one here is up on serious charges; that is why I've had to chase down a district judge. Now for courthouses, there aren't fancy pillared places like you'd find in Boston. The building itself is not important, now is it? It's the law that counts. Any place with enough space will do, a meeting house, a saloon."

"A saloon!" Ben exclaimed.

"The judges, I suppose they get educated in a city in the East?" Angela asked. Through the flickering firelight she could see Lillian's eyelids drooping, but her mother watched her disapprovingly.

Barton continued, "Some are educated in law, but not always. Out here men have to wear more than one hat. Often it's a regular working man." He saw her eyes widen. "You don't need someone whose head is filled with fancy philosophy, just someone who can read and has good sense of right and wrong."

Angela stared at him. She did not know what to say to this. How could he think any person pulled off the prairie could be a judge?

"We must go inside before the night air makes us ill," Clara said rising.

Barton boosted himself up to escort them. After taking Lillian and Clara up the steps, he grasped Angela's elbow. "You don't have to worry about your mercy case here. His situation is cut and dry; it won't take any genius to figure it out. It'll be over and done quickly."

He grinned at her in the dark and squeezed her elbow.

Finch's confidence pulled down the fragile reassurance she had built up for herself during the day. She lay for a long time while the others slept around her, their easy sleep mocking her turbulence. Was life really so simple? Good and bad so clear? It seemed to be for everyone but herself. How nice it must be to see all matters as clearly as her mother, sister and Finch saw them. No wonder her mother stood so straight and tall, all was straight lines inside her. But Angela was plagued with doubts, questions and barely checked emotions.

Snoring, it must be one of the loneliest sounds on earth. If only someone would wake and talk to her. What could they say? There was no one here with whom she could share these feelings, these ideas. She was alone.

With the new day the sun glinted harshly off another slow brown river. Angela vowed to be more decisive concerning right and wrong. Ben went along as merrily as ever judging no one, questioning everyone. He was a child; it was understandable. She was a young woman, not a child to be swayed by free-floating emotions. And the prisoner, who seemed to set sail to her emotions, he was not a child either. He knew right from wrong and he chose the wrong. Now he must face the consequences. Indeed he appeared to accept his fate.

One of the horses blew his nostrils startling her out of her tangled thoughts. She tripped.

Lou chuckled from above, "Watch your step there."

She looked up at him. She'd been caught daydreaming again. The young man sitting straight backed beside him looked straight ahead.

Though mornings began with a chill left over from the night's visits, by midday Angela's blouse stuck to her back and shoulders. Sweat dripped down her neck, gathered along her collarbones in the front and more trickled down her spine. Dust and dirt drew lines in the creases of her elbows. Ben's face was red and his hair stuck to his forehead. She pushed through the heat knowing the cool night air would bring relief.

At the midday break she took a moment to rest, leaning against the side of the wagon. She resented her skirt's length and heaviness and fluffed it out to feel the air on her legs. She pulled the material of her blouse away from her skin. There was a thump thumping sensation reverberating against the back of her shoulders. It took her a moment to realize it was her own heart. A strange sensation, it didn't frighten her, only made her marvel at the amazing workings of the human body. She lifted her hem and rubbed her face, hoping her mother and sister wouldn't see the effects of the heat and command her to ride inside the stifling canvas. Wouldn't they be horrified if they caught her with her skirt up and wiping her face with it. Someone cleared his throat and she dropped the material. Lou and the prisoner were walking by.

"Water?"

Flustered, she didn't understand Lou. She saw a canteen thrust at her and took it. The water was warm, but it wet her dust-lined mouth and throat. She handed it back to him. He pretended to examine the underside of the wagon. She straightened her clothes and smoothed her hair back. The prisoner waited for Lou. The shirt that had belonged to Lou was baggy on his thin frame. It slipped down on one side revealing a shoulder defined by muscle and sinew. The delicate composure she had barely regained was lost.

* * *

Checking her journal by the fickle light of fire that night Angela read in her notes that the trip from Missouri to Oregon generally took four months. She calculated they had been on the trail for about 71 days. She'd been lax in keeping records. She could be off by a day or two. Sometimes their start in Missouri seemed another lifetime away, at other times like yesterday. Out here her sense of time was as stretched as the endless space. Their journey however would not be as long as most, as they were leaving the trail to follow the Bear River rather than going deeper into the Oregon Territories. She found a quote she had copied from one of her research documents. It described the Bear River Valley as being lush and green. She felt as though she had found a little treasure. "Mother," she said excitedly, "I have here in my notes a description from a man who visited the valley where our home is located."

Clara looked at her with no change of expression.

Her look dashed Angela's enthusiasm.

Clara said bitterly, "It doesn't matter what it resembles, does it? Since we have no choice. Don't get your expectations too high Angela. It cannot be all that wonderful or we would have had people banging at our door to purchase it at a price that would allow us to stay in our home." She sipped her coffee.

Angela opened her eyes widely to dry their sudden wetness.

"What else does it say?" Ben asked.

She studied her paper waiting for her vision to clear. "It says the Oregon Trail was called the Great Medicine Trail by the Indians."

"The Great Medicine Trail? Why did they call it that? Was there medicine on it?"

Though his sister had spoken softly, Ben's noisy questions caught Barton Finch's ear.

Angela saw his eyes turn in their direction. She tried to ignore the dread she felt at his oncoming participation. She went on, "Could be. You know many medicines come from plants."

"Possibly," Barton broke in, "that could be part of it, but mostly it was a hunting and trade route."

"Angela," their mother spoke, "you'll ruin your eyes reading in this poor light. Put away those papers."

A thought occurred to Angela as she went to the wagon that night. Didn't "good medicine" mean good luck to Indians? If this were true it was a good sign for the trail. Would this journey bring great medicine to them?

One afternoon Clara was able to get Lou to stop early. She didn't ask herself, of course, but sent the request through Barton Finch. Though he wanted no time wasted to finish the trip, he agreed to speak to Lou.

They had time to do some washing before the air turned chilly. Angela went to the river before everyone else. The sun sparkled off the thousands upon thousands of facets on the surface and gave the ordinarily dull brown water brilliant beauty. She pulled off her boots and peeled the stockings from her legs. The water was mild on her tired hot skin, not shocking like ocean. She stepped from rock to rock, her hem trailing in the river. A large smooth rock on the bottom made an underwater seat. When she sat on it the water level was at her chest. The coolness seeped into her sweat stale clothes. Her skirt floated around like a flower blossom. She ducked her head and shoulders into the muffled underwater world and her sun-chafed face was soothed.

She scrubbed her scalp and hair with the soap she'd brought then put her head under again to rinse. Her hair swirling about her brought to mind the old mermaid myths told by sailors. She could understand how from a distance someone could imagine a beautiful water maiden. What a lovely kind softening of truth distance had. Up close the observer would be disappointed to find only plain Angela.

Hypnotized by the flashing surface and the drone of insects, she sat half in the water half out, knowing she ought to climb out and let her clothes dry. She rubbed the soap absently on her dress. If she didn't get out and let her clothes dry soon her mother would be dreadfully put out with her for wearing wet clothes into the evening. Still, the quiet beauty held her. Four young ducks floated near, feeding as they came. Probably this spring's hatchlings now grown independent of their mother, they stay together for safety and companionship. They paddled silently leaving a miniature v shaped wake. One paused and tipped its tail feathers straight up in the air to nibble delicacies beneath the surface. The three others did likewise and there they were, tails pointing skyward. "Bottoms up," Angela whispered, trying not to laugh and spoil the moment. When they floated past she stood up and picked her way to shore.

267

On the river's edge she sat with her skirts fanned out to dry, her eyes closed to the sedating warmth of the sun's rays.

Your family will soon be here, better move, a little voice warned, but she couldn't. She dozed briefly and woke to voices. A few yards upstream Lillian was picking her way to the water. Carefully she placed her shoes and stockings on the earth, unbuttoned her bodice, and leaned awkwardly over the water splashing her neck face and arms. Angela almost laughed out loud at how comical her sister looked flapping little bits of water on herself. Ben crashed into the water near Lillian.

"Don't splash Ben," she protested.

He stopped when the water reached his knees. He had more respect for rivers now.

"Hey Ange!" he waved. "Do you think it's deep?"

"No. Be careful."

Clara picked up a dress from a bundle of clothes she'd brought. Angela got to her feet to help.

She took articles of clothing from her mother and moved further down the river to prevent notice of her wet dress. She flopped each piece one at time in the water, scrubbed hard with the soap, swished vigorously and repeated the procedure. Then she passed the clothes back to Ben, who handed them off to their mother. Lillian was dabbing at a blouse. She laughed. "Lillian what are you doing?"

"I'm washing of course."

"Girls do not be too particular," Clara called. "Work quickly so there will be time to dry the things before the sun goes down."

"Yes Mother," Angela said. "I'm nearly finished. Should we ask the gentlemen if they would like us to do any washing for them?"

Clara stared at her for a moment, then she said, "Certainly not. We are not washerwomen to be washing the clothes of single men. Ben come out of that water and dress before the air changes."

Angela was stunned. Yet another of her simple ideas was greeted with severe negation. Now what had she said?

"What an inappropriate suggestion Angela," Lillian said. "I can't believe you asked such a thing."

Angela felt stupid for not understanding what was wrong with her suggestion.

"I'm sure Mr. Finch is accustomed to doing his own washing," Lillian continued, "he is a working man. I doubt our driver troubles himself much about cleanliness. He hardly seems the type."

Ah, it was a matter of stations. Now she understood, her mother and Lillian saw themselves as being of a higher rank then their fellow travelers. She didn't see how Lillian could think herself as better than the others. She kept her clothes in good repair and did her hair up, but she hadn't washed, really washed except for the one bath in weeks.

Barton Finch came to the water pushing the prisoner in front of him. "Good evening ladies," he called. "Getting the washing done I see. I think I'll do a little myself." He began unbuttoning his shirt.

"Oh dear. Children let's return to the wagon," Clara said.

The prisoner bent his left knee and put his hand on the ground to sit on the water's edge. It was still difficult for him to get up or down. He positioned his right leg.

Barton pulled off his shirt exposing his soft white flesh.

"Oh dear. Children," Clara called more adamantly.

"Mother, I'll finish laying the clothing out to dry," Angela offered.

"Yes, well come right along. We can get it later after it dries," Clara said. She and Lillian started back to the wagon. "Benjamin!"

"I'll stay and help Ange," he offered.

"Escort your mother. Be a gentleman," Barton Finch ordered him.

The prisoner rolled on to his stomach and drank water cupped in his hands. When he finished he put his face into his hands full of water and rubbed it. Then he lowered his head under the water as Angela and Ben had seen him do before. Barton Finch was watching Clara, Lillian and Ben walking away. He turned to see the prisoner with his head under water. He grabbed him by the hair and yanked his head up. "What do you think you're doing? You bastard. Trying to drown yourself again? Huh?"

The prisoner fought to support himself, his arms seeking the ground.

"You think you can get away from me that easily? Damn you!" Finch shoved his head back under the water. "Think this is a good way to go? You'll go when I …"

"Mr. Finch!" Angela shouted. From his surprised look she knew he hadn't known she was there. She felt quivery nervous. Don't make him angrier, she said to herself. "It's alright. He does that. He's not trying to drown. Please let him up."

He stopped pushing against the young man's head and untangled his fingers from his hair. The prisoner pushed himself up. He didn't cough or gasp; he just shook his head like he had before.

"Oh, it's alright is it?" Finch said to Angela. Then he made a sweeping motion to the prisoner. "Go right ahead. Whatever you want to do. You think you know better than me?" he said to Angela. "Do you?"

The prisoner got to his feet and faced Finch. Finch swung his fist as hard as he could into his mid section. He doubled over and would have fallen if his captor hadn't grabbed him. Finch stared directly at Angela. She had made things worse. What should she do now? Then she spotted a bit of cloth floating down the river.

"Mr. Finch. Your shirt." Her voice broke a little.

He went after the shirt. Angela waited. He pulled it out of the water.

"Your mother won't be too happy to hear about this!" he shouted.

"I don't think she would approve if she knew just how much of a brute you are," she shot back. He stared at her. She thought for a moment he would like to punch her. She made a point of letting him know she was watching him over her shoulder as he dragged the prisoner back to camp.

She bumped into her sister nearly knocking her over. Lillian reached out to steady herself and touched Angela's blouse.

"Angela! Your clothing is damp! Did you fall in?"

Clara looked over sharply.

"No, I … I wasn't paying attention how deep I waded. I didn't fall," she protested. "It was just that the water felt so good."

With a tight jaw Clara spoke deliberately, "Angela, do I need to keep you in my sight at all times, like a young child? You are careless as well as foolish. Find a dry dress to put on."

"No mother. Yes mother," she mumbled. "It's nearly dry."

"She washed her dress with it on," Ben laughed.

"This is not a joke Benjamin. Would you find it amusing if Angela became ill?"

"No ma'am."

How quickly things could change. From the idyllic time in the river to Finch's violence, now the very air seemed sullen. Lou had the fire started. He groused at their slowness. "Thought you people wanted an early night. Be dark by the time we eat."

He was further displeased when Finch returned with the prisoner unable to stand straight and unsteady on his feet. He muttered a curse.

"I will not tolerate profanity," Clara said.

Lou ignored her. He watched until the Prisoner had his meal and no further violence was done towards him. Then the old driver turned his back on all to eat his meal.

"Kind of quiet around here," Barton blurted, looking around with a big grin. He seemed even more pleased with himself than usual, Angela thought with disgust. She looked over at the prisoner, who sat calmly as ever, his bad leg loosely crossed over the other, his back resting against a small tree, the chain trailing from his ankle to another tree.

"I believe we are all tired," Clara said. She rose to prepare for sleep.

"You'll excuse me if I finish my meal," Barton said with his cheeks full. "Must keep up my strength," he added gesturing towards the captive significantly. "I want to keep you people safe. Makes it especially hard, what with a certain girl who thinks she knows everything."

Clara turned, her face changing instantly to a taut mask. "Angela? I do apologize for her Mr. Finch. Come Angela."

"But, I haven't put away the supper things," she protested.

Clara grabbed her wrist. "Benjamin, Lillian clear the supper things please. Then come directly to the wagon."

Ben and Lillian stared after their mother and sister.

Over by the wagon Clara dug her nails into Angela's forearm. She told her daughter. "From now on you will remain close to me. You will do nothing without my permission. You behave like an unruly child, you will be treated like one."

The next morning Clara pinned Angela's hair up so tightly it pulled painfully at the roots. Angela tucked her hands in the folds of her skirt and was thankful the morning shadows hid her sun freckled face. She was ordered to ride inside.

271

On the miserable day's ride she felt the terrible trapped feeling she'd experienced when her mother and Finch had stood over her. She tried to concentrate on the scene passing by her hole in the canvas to keep down the desperate anger while her mother lectured her on decorum and etiquette. Lillian joined in with her concerns for her sister.

"Really Angela you do not want to reflect badly on me. You know I must maintain a good image for Phillip and his family. What if they were to see you or if word got back to them?"

Though Angela strove to open her mind to their opinions, the words coming to her sounded foreign. White skin, soft hands, demure steps, tranquil expressions, manners for their own sake; these things were incompatible with the world they were now in. Images of ladies and gentleman in evening attire, trying to dance stiffly stylized steps in slippers on the rough prairie grass floated through her mind as the voices droned on and on. She saw herself laughing at the dancers trying to execute the slow steps tripping, shaking grass from their clothing and swatting insects. At her laughter, cold faces turned to her then turned away, backs shutting out the sun. Doing and saying the wrong things in that world condemned a person to the scorned life of an outcaste. Whispers aside and down turned eyelids and the rolling of the eyes could hurt as much as a cruel name. In this wild world a mistake could cost you your life. Both places were dangerous she supposed, but she preferred the honesty of the latter.

Angela heard murmuring. She must have slept. Now her mother's and Barton's voices became recognizable to her.

"Yes," he was saying, "you are taking her in hand not a moment too soon. Not my place to say of course, but I've been concerned, deeply concerned."

She couldn't hear her mother's words, only the hum of her voice responding. She awoke fully and realized her mother was discussing her with that man. She curled against the wall, covering her ears, trying to slip away in sleep, but the hardening hurt inside wouldn't let her.

Would the wonderful freedom she'd discovered on this trail be taken away? Would she be constantly inspected and judged? Not a moment to be herself? Back in Boston the only time she felt she could breathe easily was when helping her father. He took her out of the house to his office and on calls. He let her roll bandages, fold towels, help with minor injuries, organize and list medicines. He conversed with her as though she were an intelligent adult. When she helped him she forgot to worry about making mistakes, about saying something stupid.

As she feared, her freedom was lost. Clara kept her close, grabbing her wrist now and then as a reminder not to stray. She was not even allowed to perform the chores she had taken on as her own. She could help with meals, under her mother's supervision.

Clara tried to reintroduce proper manners at suppertime. With everyone seated and Angela serving, she would guide the conversation in polite subject areas. Barton remarked every evening how nice this all was, but would forget to wait to be served and come to the pot for seconds or worse start some wild tale about animal attacks or Indians. Lou simply refused to participate. He took his plate and had his meal off by himself. Angela ate only after the others were served and then she would have to get up frequently when a nudge from her mother told her to offer refills of cups or plates. Normally a hearty eater, she was hungry all the time now because she wasn't able to finish her meals.

Supper was dreary, the days' rides miserable and days no longer started pleasantly. Her hair was done, her clothing inspected, her posture criticized. Then one morning Clara did not fail to notice the condition of her daughter's skin. She stopped her inspection, rubbed at Angela's face with her thumb and exclaimed loudly, "Angela! I had no idea how far things had gone! Look at you! You look like a dirty savage!"

The prisoner happened to be passing on a mission for Lou; he froze. Angela saw him and lowered her head at her mother's hateful words, so like something Finch would say. She peeked up to see him hesitating, flustered. He thought the words were for him. Clara had her back to him at that moment she turned and saw him.

"What is he doing alone? Get away!" She flapped her hands at him. "Mr. Finch!" Her shouting frightened Lillian who stood nearby attending her own coiffure. She shrieked and ran to her mother.

Their noise brought Lou and Barton hurrying from different directions. Seeing Clara pointing, Finch charged the object of her fear, pushing him until he crashed against the boards of the wagon. Finch pinned him with his forearm across his neck.

"Get him away!" Clara cried.

"What'd you do? What'd you do?" Finch demanded, thumping him against the boards. "Are you alright Ma'am?"

"Yes, yes," Clara sobbed. "Just get him away."

In that moment Angela was struck by the similarity between her mother and Lillian. They both appeared poised and sophisticated in their own safe circles, but take them out of their element and just look what they became, silly hysterical creatures.

"Now Finch," she heard Lou.

The big man had raised the puffy fist of his free arm.

"He didn't do anything!" Angela got out. Her voice sounded like someone else's. "He was just walking by!"

She looked to her mother for support of the truth. "Mother this time it is our business. You caused the fuss. Tell him."

Clara drew in a shaky breath and patted Lillian's hand, while everyone looked to her for a response. "It may have been an accident of timing," she said. "All the same he should not be near us. Why was he alone?"

"Yes, Ma'am. I've been remiss. When he's with Lou I let down my guard thinking he's being supervised." He cast an accusing eye at Lou, who spit. "I have been keeping a closer eye on him lately. I have to watch all the time now."

"Yes, I have noticed your vigilance and I do appreciate it," Clara sighed. "I'm not blaming you."

"Thank you ma'am I appreciate that. I'm sorry you had a scare. Are you sure you're not faint? How about Miss Lillian?"

Finch released the prisoner inadvertently while he sought assurances from Clara that they were recovered and not angry at him. Lou took the opportunity to lead young man away.

At the end of the day's ride Angela paused near the front of the wagon. She was to be getting camp supplies from it; no one was watching her at the moment. She loosened the sash on her dress that Lillian had tightened. Foolish thing, she could barely move for fear of tearing it. She rubbed her temples, aching from her severely combed hair. Would it never end? It had been another day of her mother picking at her and her sister's endless prattle. Please, she prayed, an hour to myself. Two would be heavenly, but one, just one would keep me from going mad. I'm barely holding on. I'm afraid I will burst into tiny pieces. How can it be that in this enormous space I feel like I'm shut in a wardrobe? Her fists clenched. Her mind searched frantically for relief. Perhaps when everyone is asleep I can slip out by the fire, rekindle it and write in my journal. If they found me, sitting by myself in the night, what a scene there would be and I would feel like such a fool. Her teeth gritted with desperation; there was a nagging twitch beneath her left eyebrow. How could she keep the screaming inside?

She leaned against the reassuring solidity of the wooden sides of the wagon watching Lou and the prisoner going about their labors. How she missed the mind-clearing physical chores she use to do. She almost envied them. Lou would grunt a direction now and then, but mostly they carried on without a word. He would pause, smooth his gray hair back and spit while he waited for a strap to be handed or a bucket passed to him. His shirtsleeves rolled up, his clothes faded, he worked with the flawlessly timed pace of experience. His young partner, balancing adeptly on his good leg unbuckled harness pieces, slid bridles off and passed the horses all without any wasted movement. His shirt was showing signs of hard wear, a few buttons were missing and the fraying sleeves dangled around his hands. The pant legs he had rolled up to prevent them from dragging over his feet were colored with dried mud. His hair was pulled back, but some dark strands always escaped and fell towards his face.

Angela watched him quietly going on and on with never an expression of resentment, never a refusal. How does he do it? He silently takes Finch's punishments day after day. He works through pain. Where does he find the strength, physical and the inner, not to just explode? He is healthier now, stronger, which Finch doesn't like. He punishes him for having a little strength. A new black eye or bruise appears nearly every day. How does he take it? And here she was, thinking she could not endure her own small restrictions.

"Now, look at this. Look at this." Barton Finch suddenly blocked her vision. "What a remarkable change. Who can this young woman be?"

He walked back and forth appraising her up and down. She wrapped her arms around herself and wouldn't look at him.

"Quite a difference." He continued evaluating her, one hand under his chin, feigning thoughtfulness. "Turn around and let me see this transformation."

She was shocked at his rudeness. Her annoyance was rapidly changing to apprehension. Her heart beat faster, but she refused to play mouse to his cat. She longed for her mother and sister to appear around the side of the wagon. Looking past him for a way out, she saw the prisoner stop his work, tense and motionless he watched her and Finch. Once again his intense watchful attitude projected a warning to her. She was right to feel threatened; he knew it and so did she. Her heart raced faster, her breathing as well. Over her examiner's shoulder she saw Lou come to his partner to see what held his attention. He looked over at her and Finch then he put a hand on the prisoner's shoulder and said a few words to him. He tried to turn him away, but he would not be diverted. Lou did not distrust Finch as much as she and Prisoner did. He leaned toward her and put his hands on the wagon, arms on either side of her head. Lou cleared his throat, but Finch either didn't hear or didn't care. The prisoner started to walk in their direction. Lou held him back, his face close to the prisoner's he was saying words of caution to no avail. He called, "Finch what are you doing?"

"What's it to you?" the big man twisted to see Lou and Angela slipped out from under his arm. She ran to her mother and sister. Her heart was in a race with itself; the dampness of a fear sweat had broken out under her hairline.

"Angela, slow down. A child rushes about, a young woman does not," her mother said. "Where are the supper things?"

Their faces pointed at her curiously, she took a breath to tell them what had just happened. She stopped. How could she explain? They would not believe her if she did manage to get the words out clearly. What had he done? He'd only complimented her. She knew she would not be able to convey the threat lying beneath his words and body language. No matter what words she used, she would come out of the story sounding ridiculous, Finch innocent. She went slowly back to get the supplies, looking for him, but he had gone off.

276

Chapter 19

"There are among those dwarfish natures, which if they happen to be heated by some sullen fire, easily become monstrous."

<u>*Les Miserables*</u> *by Victor Hugo*

Rocking along on yet another tedious day, Angela realized it was September. Back in Massachusetts the leaves would soon be turning. By October they would glow as if lit from within. The sky, not willing to be outdone, would take on its most vivid blue. The wind would flow in conflicting currents of warm and crisp air, swirling fallen leaves up and around in whirlpools of exuberance. She remembered raising her arms and twirling joyfully, feeling she was flying on the wind with the leaves.

"Ben!" Lillian's shout brought her back to her miserable present.

"Sit still boy!" Barton roared, silencing everyone.

The boy had been crawling about the cramped wagon in search of entertainment. Angela's confinement was hard on him. Without her supervision his freedom was limited also. He grew more restless by the day. He sat glowering, arms crossed, scowling at Angela.

Angela lay waiting, the next morning. She had to wait until her mother and Lillian awoke each morning. Lillian slept the longest. The sleep of an unburdened mind, Angela believed. She bided her time, trying to conjure the image of her new home. The pictures wouldn't come.

"Ange, let's go," Ben said irritably.

"We may not. Please be patient."

"Why? Why do we have to wait? Lillian takes too long. I have to go. Traveler is already out there. What if she gets lost?" He drummed his heels on the floor.

"Angela, take your brother out." Clara spoke through her blankets.

They took their time, though the air was cold. This was not to be the brief escape Angela so desired. Ben hounded her with questions. "Why are things different? What did you do?"

Please, she prayed silently, just a bit of solitude. There must be a safe place somewhere, a place where I can breathe, where no one looks at me with shock or disgust or makes demands.

"Why do you have to stay with Mother all the time? Is it because you have to be a lady now?"

She looked all around, trying to ignore the torment of questions like relentless insects. Now what was that Barton Finch doing? She stopped to watch him. He had just unchained the prisoner, who was getting to his feet. The bulky lawman made a show of scraping his boots on the ground. Then he reached down to pick up something from under his feet, the corner of the blanket. He wiped his boots with it, his face towards the young man. When he stepped away, the prisoner draped it muddy and damp over his shoulders where it normally rested if it wasn't tossed on to the driver's bench.

Later, staring through her tiny canvas window hole Angela saw not the scenery passing before her, but the stoic young man with his muddied mantle. How selfish I am. I greedily long for self-indulgent moments. Like a spoiled child begging for treats I plead to God for frivolous pastimes. Weak, that's what I am, weak and selfish. Here I am wanting so to escape in a journal or imaginings of my own frontier home. Of what use are these to anyone? I'm not different from everyone else; there's nothing special about me. They all must feel the same things, the same frustrations as me. She peered through the shadowy interior trying to see the faces of her mother and sister. These thoughts were no consolation; they were her accusers. She pulled her knees up to her chest her body in a tight ball.

Into her unhappy musings floated thoughts of her father. She pushed them away. Whether she feared the pain of remembered loss or the idea that he was watching in disappointment, she didn't dare consider. It was too hard. She wanted to keep him with her, but in the dark recesses of her mind, not quite conscious enough to hurt.

Angela tried to adopt the ways of her mother and sister, believing if she did not conform she would go mad. Still, her mind rebelled. She fidgeted waiting for them, lost herself in daydreams while they lectured her or drifted off to watch the scenery or Lou and the prisoner at their work. Her mother soon tired of correcting her and left the job to Lillian, who quickly grew bored and forgot.

All the travelers were irritable. Lou complained about everyone riding inside. "Too much weight for the horses," he said. Ben was a trial to his mother, who didn't understand him or boyish ways. He became careless again, wandering out of sight, getting too close to the horses' hooves and spilling things at meals. More than once a day Barton Finch bellowed at him, making the ladies quake and Lou and the prisoner stop short. Angela had to restrain her anger from bursting. Lillian's face went whiter than usual and Clara dug her nails into Angela's forearm as a warning not to interfere.

Once again this morning they were startled by an enraged roar. Finch's fury rang out across the prairie. "Who did this? Who? Did you do this? Look at what you did! Come here and look!"

Angela ran around from behind the wagon to the fire. She saw the ponderous man towering over her brother, his arms flailing, his mean little eyes nearly disappearing in his face.

"Angela, get your brother," her mother called. Apparently this time she shared Angela's fear that the man would momentarily strike the boy in his rage. Angela grabbed Ben by the hand and started to pull him back to the family.

"Stop right there. See what he did?" Finch bellowed at her like a mad bull. He was pointing at the ground. "See? The boy is irresponsible! He can fix this mess! Fix it!"

She glanced down where he indicated and saw overturned cups and plates, their contents mingling with the dirt. She opened her mouth to yell at Finch, but Ben's sad face stopped her. "I'm sorry Ange. I was running and I forgot. I ran right over."

"I'll fix it later. He's coming with me," was all she said. She led her brother to the far side of the wagon.

Ben slumped to the ground with a despairing thump. He stared blankly at the earth. Tears ran down his cheeks, his arms hung in front of him.

"What happened?" Angela asked him. She tried to sound calm.

"I wanted to go see the big bird flying across the sky. I was running under it like I was a bird too," he answered dully. "I was going to pick up the things I spilled."

"He didn't give you a chance did he?" Angela said.

279

He nodded meekly.

"Benjamin when will you be more careful?" Clara asked, but it really wasn't a question.

"That's it," Angela mumbled. Turning to confront the man, she was held up by her mother.

"Angela, where do you think you are going? There is no sense in you losing your temper," Clara said. "We must all get along."

"Yes, please Angela don't cause a scene. It only makes things worse," Lillian pleaded.

"You can't let that man scream at him! Frightening him like that! You can't! Someone has to let him know he can't treat Ben this way! I won't stand by and let him!"

"Calm yourself. I will speak to him. You control yourself."

Clara walked primly to speak to Barton Finch. Angela and Lillian followed her around the wagon then waited as she told them to.

"Really Angela, what did you think you were going to do?" Lillian asked.

"Lillian didn't you think he was going to strike Ben? Didn't you hear him? He is out of control. Aren't you angry at him?"

"He does have a terrible shout. It is frightening, I admit. Men do have loud shouts and quick tempers. That's just how they are. He wouldn't have struck Benjamin."

Angela was stunned by her indifferent acceptance. She went to her brother and sat with an arm around him.

When Clara came back Angela went to her and stood facing her, waiting. Clara started to tidy up and then decided to respond to her daughter's unasked question.

"I told Mr. Finch he was much too rough to address Benjamin in that manner."

Angela waited.

Clara sighed and continued, "Benjamin is not without fault either, Angela. He made a mess that could have attracted animals, never mind the waste."

Angela sputtered, "Mother, the man is violent. He nearly struck Ben!"

"That's enough Angela. We must all abide together as best we can. You exaggerate. Now take your brother to clean up the mess and wash his face," she said. She resumed picking up her things. Furious, Angela didn't move until her mother snapped, "Go on!"

Her fists closed, her eyes and mouth tightened in determination, she looked for Finch while she and Ben went about picking up the remnants of breakfast. Determined to confront the bully herself, she was disappointed when he stayed out of her sight. She prepared all the things she would tell him next time they were face to face.

Doing chores together again cheered Ben. Being young and easygoing he did not remember a hurt long.

"Don't worry Ange. I won't make Mr. Finch angry any more," he said. He was more concerned with her than any offense done to himself.

The only good that came out of the incident was that Angela regained some of her freedom. She was allowed to do chores because the work kept Ben occupied, out of everyone's hair and supervised. Still she longed to confront the horrible man, but he kept his distance from her over the next few days. His ingratiating cordiality to her mother and sister sickened her with its falseness whenever she spied them together. She glared at him openly, but he appeared not to notice.

Emboldened by Clara's forgiveness, he began to pick at Ben and her. One evening he remarked offhandedly there wasn't as much water as they needed, on another he wasn't satisfied with the supper service. Couldn't Angela have put more on his plate? She was too impatient dishing it out and it wasn't hot yet, or she wasn't careful and some spilled on him.

Beautiful bright days followed. Although Angela's body tightened whenever she saw Finch, she enjoyed the work and its freedom. Lou, however was stiffer than ever. He rested more while the prisoner did most of the work involving the horses and wagon. The young man's growing strength continued to surprised her. Though he limped badly, when he was at a standstill she believed a person would not be able to detect anything wrong. He lifted and tossed heavy things into the wagon, moved the horses firmly, hammered boards and repaired wheel spokes. His expression was almost serene, she thought. She watched him furtively in spite of the shivery feeling she got. If he turned in her direction she slipped away, her cheeks warming.

281

Men sound that way when they're angry, that's what Lillian had said. Not all men, Angela thought. Yes, most people, men and women shouted, snapped even swore at times. She recalled a few of the many times she'd lost her temper. How she hated that side of herself. No, not all men are like Finch. Lou doesn't rant and rave. Was he too old and tired? The only expression she could recall on her father's face when it came to her was a merry one. And what of Prisoner? He barely makes a sound, never mind an outburst. He may have been too weak and ill before; he is stronger now and still never an expression of anger, no matter what degradation Finch inflicts. No, Lillian is wrong. Men are not that way. Finch is different. He's not happy in his own skin; a meanness keeps bubbling out. What makes him think he has the right to lash out at everyone else?

. . .

Moving, lifting, reaching, his body doing what he told it to, was good. The heaviness and slowness frustrated him, but the dragging weight on his shoulders, arms and legs was lighter. Yeah, the leg hummed, throbbed and yelled some. He could handle it. The simple solid truth of real things was all he needed. He could see clearly now and think. No, don't think. Don't remember. See that horse? Back it up. Feel it move under your hand. Buckle that strap. The leather smells good. Stay outside your own head. The simple, the real.

Angela's desire to confront Barton Finch did not diminish. She did not act on this desire, prevented both by her mother's controlling presence and his avoidance of her. She waited and watched for the opportunity to find him alone and apart, where she could tell him in no uncertain terms where he stood with her and what she would not allow him to say or do. She wasn't intimidated. A determined ball of strength was building inside her gradually, but steadily. It wasn't an agitating anger or a hardness of heart, but a new strength. "Vengeance is not mine," she told herself. "It belongs to God."

And it was not vengeance she wanted. It was clarity, not lines drawn in the sand as a dare. Lines that said this is me and mine and you may not abuse us. Keep your meanness in check.

She sought to know Finch's whereabouts at all times and when she saw him she pulled herself up straighter and taller and looked directly at him.

Finch's tirades were growing more frequent and he was loosing his customary restraint in front of Clara and Lillian. Angela found she could detect the signs of an oncoming rage. From this particular morning's beginnings she believed it was only a matter of time before the storm broke. Nature's weather itself was cold and the sky moodily gray. Finch stood wrapped in a blanket, speaking sulkily to no one in particular. "Weather is going to get rougher and rougher. Got to make time. That coffee should be ready first thing, first thing."

"The water is boiling. Go make it yourself," Angela shot tersely at him.

"Angela," her mother warned.

Here we go, Angela thought. This is how it starts. He begins with general complaints in a voice trying too obviously to sound reasonable. Then he'll begin repeating himself, until he finally lashes out at someone. She saw him turn his attention to Lou and the prisoner tending the horses.

"Should be underway sooner. Old timer is too slow for this work. Rain's coming. People that have jobs to do need to start sooner. Rain's coming."

"Oh no, it's pure misery when it rains," Lillian complained hugging herself and looking skyward.

"Here Mr. Finch," Clara handed him a mug of coffee. She no longer asked Angela to serve him, sensing it wise to keep them apart. He was temporarily appeased, but Angela knew once he began the outcome was inevitable.

The wind gusted, bringing on it the first patter of rain.

"Got to get started. People shouldn't be standing in the rain," Finch growled in Lou's direction. From an ever so slight lift of Lou's head Angela could tell he had heard. It appeared the more the big man complained, the slower Lou worked. She smiled and sipped from her cup, taking on the driver's contrary slowness.

Closer to the time of departure Finch barked at Ben, "Boy you do sloppy work. I don't think you put that fire out completely. If it starts up it'll sweep across this land. Nothing to stop it. Go do a proper job and fetch me a new walking stick."

283

Ben started to run to the ashes. Angela caught his arm she spoke to her brother, but she looked directly at Finch. "Leave it Ben. I'm sure we put it out completely and there are no trees for walking sticks."

"Better to be safe than sorry," Clara said. "Go on Benjamin."

Finch nodded smugly at Angela. She glared at him. How she wanted to tell him what she thought of him. She would wait until her mother was not close by.

Well maybe her mother's indulgence was soothing away his temper this time, she reasoned. But she was wrong.

They gathered near the wagon to start.

"Let's go!" Finch shouted. Lillian started for the steps. Lou and the prisoner stood looking at the sky. They exchanged a few words about it. What little patience Barton Finch had gave out. He grabbed the prisoner and shoved him face first into the ladder. "Get up there!"

Ben happened to be standing closest; he was knocked to the ground. "Hey!" he shouted. Lillian had just lifted her foot to place it on the step. She shrieked and fell back. Angela caught her and they both landed in a heap on the ground. Finch blind in his fury took no notice. He was shoving the prisoner against the wagon. "Damn you! Get up there!"

"Finch!" Lou grabbed his arm, but he shook him off.

"Help me in, hurry," Lillian whispered to her sister.

"Mr. Finch! This is entirely unnecessary!" Clara declared.

Angela saw the surprise in his face - he was stopped cold by Clara's reprimand.

Angela took some comfort that evening from Finch's reserved behavior. He pouted; his sloping shoulders sagged more than usual. The rain had passed quickly in the morning, but the damp air lingered all day and reddened fingers and noses. Lillian huddled under blankets as close to the fire as she dared. Angela found the chill and Finch's silence invigorating. He rubbed his knuckles and his knees. Finally he addressed Clara. "I suppose ma'am you found my actions rough this morning?"

Clara regarded him sternly.

He continued before she could reply, "It's hard. That's all. This work, it's hard on me," he shook his head pitifully. "The weather... my back and knees plague me. I can't sleep at night for the aching."

284

He peered into Clara's eyes, then Lillian's, his expression sorrowful. He avoided Angela though she stared at him with open disbelief.

"I apologize for upsetting you people. Not fit for this work anymore. Too old."

"You're not so very old Mr. Finch," Lillian said. She reached over and patted his hand.

"That's nice of you to say. It's tricky transporting vicious criminals, having folks around complicates things. I've tried to accommodate you all. I've kept you all safe. It's a rough business."

"Mmm, I have no doubt," Clara sympathized.

Disgusted by Finch's woebegone expression and her mother and sister being taken in by it, Angela tried to shut out their conversation. She watched Ben carry food to the young man sitting outside the circle of firelight.

"Yes," Finch went on. "It's more difficult than usual. I enjoy your company. In my work I don't often have company. I'm sorry this has made your trip more difficult. I didn't want that, not at all. It was going well I thought. I relaxed my methods to satisfy some of you and… Look for yourself," He indicated the prisoner. "He's strong enough to work. He's plenty strong. Remember how he was before. No one had to worry did they? I could rest a bit. Not now."

"Benjamin, come away from there," Clara called.

"He is chained though," Lillian said. She looked from Finch to the prisoner. "You can rest when he's chained. Can't you?"

The lawman shook his head, "I can't rest until I'm done with him."

"You have things very well under control," Clara said. "I admit, I had my doubts in the beginning. I simply request you moderate your temper around us. Benjamin, come here at once!" she called again.

"He's fine mother. He does this every night," Angela said.

Clara's eyes flashed at her.

"What is it?" Ben asked coming to her.

"Nothing. I want you here, away from that Indian."

"Why?"

"Because he's dangerous."

"He's not dangerous," Ben protested.

"You see?" Finch glared at Angela. The firelight flickered across his face. "This is your influence!"

285

She took a deep breath to respond, but he went on. "You may have some silly notion because of a couple of situations with your brother. Silly notions of the noble savage, that some idiot who never saw an Indian wrote in some book that foolish women read. Don't think for a moment he didn't have ideas other than saving your brother. You can be sure he had some crafty plan for escaping!"

Ben interrupted, "He didn't try to escape. He saved me! He did!"

"Benjamin!" Clara stopped him.

"Ha," Finch gave a snort of disdain. "You don't know what you're talking about."

" Escape? How ridiculous. He nearly drowned," Angela said.

"Oh he nearly drowned," Finch mocked. "That shows your ignorance. He wants to die! He thinks he can escape me by dying. You think he cares about you boy?" he asked Ben. "No, he wanted to die to spite me. And you," he turned to Angela his, face puffed with anger, "you listen. I'll tell you about him."

"Savages do not have romantic notions about women or children. Get that out of your head. Why do you think the women are called squaws? What do you think the word means? A love term? No, it means … well, you figure it out. Sure it's a white word, but it reflects how the males see women. Women are slaves to them to use any way they please. And I mean any."

Lillian gasped, but he went on.

"You've heard that decent white women kill themselves rather than be captured by Indians. I'm sure you women have discussed this among yourselves. There's good reason for that practice. You think that one over there is quiet and harmless? You didn't see him before. Were you there when he kidnapped the good doctor, took him on horseback all the way out of town? It took five men to bring him down.

We only found out about him and the kidnapping because the horse he was riding was stolen. Stole it from his nearest neighbor after the neighbor wouldn't let him borrow it. The neighbor hotfooted it after him. Got to town in time to see him riding away with the doc and ran next door where I happened to be visiting with some fellows. We took up chase on our mounts and surrounded him half way back to where he was headed. He didn't care about our guns, wasn't going to stop for nothing. The doc managed to pull him down off the horse

286

and when they fell we all jumped him. Fight? He fought like a wild animal using everything he had. He banged us up some, I tell you. The fellow whose horse he stole wouldn't let us shoot him. Wanted him taken alive.

Try as we might to drag him along, he kept fighting and getting away. Stunned him a couple of times, but he'd revive and get away, running toward the shack he lived in. Came within sight of it too. He was saying some Indian gibberish. We didn't think much on it at first, didn't have the time. Almost made it back there too; we were about to give out. That's when one fellow came up with the idea to hobble him so to speak. He was too slick for us to keep a hold on. We held him down one last time and the doc, he smacked the leg good. That held him for a while. Then, when he came to he started struggling again, tried to crawl with us just standing there watching. We weren't worried though couldn't get far. The fellow whose horse he took rode up to the cabin out of curiosity to see what he was so determined to get back to. He came back and told us there was some dead squaw lying stiff on a bed. Well, this bit of information finally stopped him. He gave up, passed out and stayed out for a while. Made it easier to drag his carcass back to town. All that fuss over some dead squaw! Heard she wasn't even a looker, just some leathery old squaw. These Indians don't care. Like I told you, they don't see women like decent folks do. Squaws aren't human to them! Isn't that right?"

No one moved or spoke during this story. Ben stared open-mouthed. Lillian's face was white, her hands clasped together under her chin. Only Lou was oblivious to the exciting tale. He dozed until the shout startled him.

"All for some squaw! I hope she was worth it! Was she? Disgusting old squaw! Probably been with every man for miles around!" he shouted across the smoke of the fire.

"Really, Mr. Finch. I do not approve of this kind of talk," Clara said.

"I thought you said they didn't care about women?" Angela said.

They heard a rattling. The prisoner was yanking at the chain with both hands. Though he was across the fire his eyes shone like lights, fixed on Finch.

"Mr. Finch." The hand that Clara pointed shook in the air. Lillian shrieked and held her hands to her mouth.

287

The Lawman hoisted himself to his feet and marched over, intent only on his nemesis. Undeterred, the prisoner continued to fight with the chain that held him, never faltering in his gaze. Finch crouched next to him, "All for some old squaw. Some old dead squaw! The stiff is probably lying there still unless dogs or coyotes dragged her off."

As the family stared in horror, the captive lunged and grabbed Finch by the throat. He hung on, staring into his eyes. Finch fell to his knees. He struggled to peel the fingers from his neck. His eyes bulged, his face growing redder and redder. While one hand dug at the fingers, he reached with the other spasmodically under his vest. He pulled out his pistol and pressed it against his foe's temple. His face dripped with sweat. "Let go," he rasped thinly. The prisoner did not loosen his grip.

"Let go. I'll kill you."

Lou moved carefully alongside. "Let him go Kid."

The prisoner shook his head, his eyes locked on Finch's. "Do it," he said.

The hammer of the gun clicked back.

"Oh God," Angela whispered.

The prisoner seemed to smile with satisfaction.

"No, please, no!" Ben ran to them before Angela could stop him.

"Please stop! Mr. Finch don't shoot!" He stood close, his arms out in a plea to both. "Prisoner, please!"

"Easy now. Everyone be easy," Lou said. Angela was moving to get Ben. She stopped.

"Let go," Lou said to the prisoner. "Think of the boy. You want him spattered with your blood an' brains? You don't want him to see this."

The young man's eyes flashed from Finch to Ben. His arms fell, and when they did Finch lashed out with the pistol and bashed him across the forehead, hurling him to the ground.

Chapter 20

"Angels answer me
Are you near if rain should fall?"

"Angeles" Enya

"Brought from the wreckage of your
silent reveries,
You're in the arms of the angel,
May you find some comfort there."

"Angel" Sarah McLachlan

He lay splayed on his side, motionless. Barton had thumped back on his haunches gasping and gagging, his hands to his neck. Angela and Ben were the first to react. They knelt at the prisoner's head. A jagged little river ran along his right temple and into his eyebrow. As they watched the red stream increased, overflowing its banks and dripping down his face. The skin stretched and swelled.

"Is he dead?" Ben sobbed. "Ange?"

Lou unfastened the chain from his ankle, then moved to his head. He shook him gently. "Wake up Kid. Come on, open your eyes."

Getting no reaction, he stood, using Ben's shoulder for support. "It don't look good," he said. "You really did it this time Finch."

"Ange?" Ben cried.

"He's not dead Ben," she said, shaking off her own shock.

"Hold on Miss," Lou said and he hobbled away.

Angela was wiping the blood with the hem of her skirt. It wouldn't stop. She pressed the material against the gash.

Finch lumbered to his feet. "What about me?" he began. But Clara came to them instead of sympathizing she turned on him. "This is too much! Just too much Mr. Finch!"

He trudged away, his head down, his step unsteady.

289

Lou came back and knelt beside Angela. He helped her wrap a bandage tightly around the prisoner's head.

"Mother, what are you doing?" Lillian demanded. She circled around, not wanting to come too close. "Get away from there," she pleaded.

"We must try to keep him alive, Lillian. Do you want to ride with a body?"

"No, he wouldn't... Mr. Finch?" She looked to have him discount her mother's horrific suggestion, but he disappeared around the wagon.

"Please mother, you wouldn't let him..." she whined.

"Can we move him inside?" Angela asked Lou.

"Yep. You go ahead Miss. Clear a space, git some blankets ready. Boy, you an' I'll lift him."

In the wagon Angela rolled out blankets to make a bed. Then she hurried to help Lou lift his head and shoulders up the steps and through the doorway. She slid a folded blanket carefully under his head and lifted his injured leg over another. Ben in his worry was everywhere at once, bumping into her and crowding her. She gave him a job. "Ben, bring water. And then go find the blanket he uses. It's outside somewhere. Take Traveler. I don't want her licking his face."

The boy nearly fell out in his hurry.

"Here Ange, I've got everything," he panted. "Is he awake?"

"No." She spread the blanket over him.

"What can I do? I want to help."

"Wet a cloth then keep it here on his forehead. When it starts to feel warm dip it back in the water, wring it out and put it on again. It shouldn't be dripping wet. Don't push hard, just press like this," she demonstrated.

"I can do it, let me."

They sat quietly in the darkness.

Lou stuck his head in.

"No change," Angela said and he withdrew.

By the light of a lantern Clara and Lillian entered. Clara placed the lantern next to Angela. She and Lillian carefully stepped around them to arrange their own bedding.

290

"Benjamin, mind the lantern there," Clara cautioned before lying down.

Neither Ben nor Angela slept all night.

The early morning light revealed the results of the blow more clearly. The right side of his face was swollen and the eyelid puffed shut. Angela carefully pushed his hair back and held a cool rag to his head in hopes of keeping down further swelling. The bandage tied around his head was red and damp though the blood no longer ran out from under. She changed it and they sat on either side of him. Clara and Lillian awoke, and picked their way over his feet. "Come Benjamin," his mother ordered.

"I don't want to leave him," he said.

"Go. I'll be here," Angela reassured him. "When you are finished, you can stay while I go out."

"I'll be back in three shakes of a lamb's tail."

When Ben relieved her she tried to avoid detection, but her mother saw her returning from behind the wagon. "Angela, come eat."

She wanted to run into the wagon, but she joined the others around the fire. Barton Finch stood apart, picking at his food.

"How is he?" Lou asked.

"No change," she answered. She took a plate from her mother.

"Hurry and eat Angela," Clara said. "It is late."

"No sense hurryin'," Lou said. "We're stayin' put for today."

"Staying?" Clara asked.

Barton Finch's head jerked in Lou's direction.

"Yup," Lou said. "I'll give him a day, see what happens. Don't want his head bangin' 'round."

To Angela's surprise there was no further protest.

She rushed back to Ben as soon as she could. "Are you hungry? Go get more to eat. Take your time. Lou says we're not moving today."

"He does?"

"Yes. When you come back bring fresh water."

Angela wrung a new cloth over the water and carefully laid it on the side of his face. Alone in the shadows, she dared to study his face. On the undamaged side she saw his delicately formed eyebrow, thick dark lashes, mouth…

"Any change?" Clara startled her.

"No," she answered. Her mother didn't linger.

Shortly afterward Lou climbed in. He sat down and peered into the young man's face with a frown. He gently felt his forehead with crooked arthritic fingers, grunted and climbed out.

Ben dozed in the afternoon. Angela, her own eyelids heavy, rested her head back against the side.

Something woke her. The day had slipped into early evening. She could smell supper cooking outside.

"Ange, he's moving." Ben was poking her.

His head moved from side to side, his left leg bent then straightened and his fingers opened and closed on the blanket. His mouth moved as if he was talking, but no sound came out. Angela washed his face and neck. He was sweating. What should she do? She had to keep her nervousness under control, but it was difficult.

"Get some fresh water, please," she requested.

Clara accompanied Ben when he climbed back into the shaded interior.

"Mother, he's terribly hot and agitated," Angela said.

Clara felt his forehead, "Yes, he has a fever."

"Why would he have a fever? I don't understand how a blow to the head would cause a fever."

"Perhaps it's not the blow by itself, Clara said, "but a combination of things, the blow and an infection."

"There was one from the chain, a while back. I'll check." Angela pulled the blanket back and pushed his pant leg up.

"Here," Clara handed her a wet cloth while she washed his face with another. "Clean it out well while there is the opportunity."

"It looks infected again. There's some nasty looking proud flesh," Angela said. She dabbed at the raw ring.

"You need a knife to scrape away the bad," her mother said. "Benjamin go ask one of the men for a knife."

When Ben passed Angela the knife she hesitated.

"Better to do it now while he's unconscious," Clara recommended.

She gingerly scraped.

"Yuck," Ben commented

"No." The prisoner murmured and turned his head on the blanket.

Angela stopped.

"He's not talking to you. He does not know we are here," Clara said. "He's got to drink. Has he drank at all?" she asked. Then she added, "Do not look so surprised Angela. I do have three children and they did have the common childhood illness and injuries. I do know a little. Continue to clean up the leg, I will try to get him to take some water."

The patient murmured.

Clara lifted his head and held a cup to his mouth. She tried to pour a trickle between his lips. It dripped down his chin.

"Please," he said more clearly.

Clara still supported his head, he moved restlessly in her hands. "Trying … please… don't die."

"Sh," Angela tried to quiet him. These almost incoherent words were scaring her. He was in another world.

"Coming … trying," he said. He drew his left knee up, his arms moved vaguely.

Clara gasped, and Angela saw his one eye that was not swollen shut was open. He stared at Clara. One hand reached weakly towards her face, "Deer Mother… tried. They… my leg…" His chest heaved up and down. "Sorry, sorry."

"Sh," Angela said. She moved alongside her mother.

His eye shut and he lay unconscious again.

"What was he saying?" Ben asked.

Angela looked at Clara, whose eyes met hers for a moment.

"Nothing. He is delirious," Clara responded.

"Do you think he'll die, Mother?" Ben was studying the prisoner's swollen countenance.

"I do not know." Clara shook her head doubtfully. "All you can do is try to keep the fever and swelling down," she told Angela and she left the wagon.

Occupied entirely with the urgency of the young man's condition, Angela didn't wonder at her mother's assistance and her allowing them to stay with him. She hardly noticed Clara leaving a lit lantern for her again that night.

Sometime during the night the prisoner's movements woke her. Ben was asleep on the other side of him. The lantern threw a soft glow against the canvas. She cooled his hot face; his head rolled and

293

his lips moved to speak without a sound. She lifted his head and brought a cup to his mouth. "Drink," she whispered.

His eye opened into hers.

"Please, you should drink." She pressed the cup against his mouth and let a little water trickle in. He swallowed once, staring with confusion and concern. Instead of taking more water he whispered, "Who?" and brushed her face with the back of his hand.

"Angela," she answered back.

"Angel?"

"No, Angela. Drink some more."

"Angel," he said. His chest began to rise and fall as if he were running. "Angel?" Both arms reached towards her.

"Sh, lie quiet." She looked over and saw her mother sitting in her blankets watching.

"Help her... help her, please. Angel ... she's ... sick," he pushed weakly against the floor as if to sit up. "I couldn't. Help her," he pleaded. "Deer Mother."

The significance of his desperate words and frantic movements struck Angela like a flash in her brain; the dead woman that Finch had so callously maligned was his mother. In his delirium he still struggled to get to her. She was the reason he wanted the doctor.

"Help her, Angel." He tossed and turned, trying to get up.

"Sh, it's over. She's at peace. She's not sick any more." She babbled anything she thought would calm him. "I'll take care of her. You need to rest and drink. She wants you to." Still holding his head, she lifted the cup again.

"Please, she's..."

Reasoning with a delirious person didn't work. "I'll take her with me." Angela decided to enter his world. "Sh, the angel will take her with me to heaven," she whispered. "She wants you to be easy."

His eye closed at these words, but he swallowed some of the water.

Whenever he moved during the night she coaxed him to drink. He said nothing more and remained calm.

Leaving Ben on duty, in the morning Angela ventured out. Lou and her mother were talking.

"Of course I do not want a corpse," she heard her mother say. "I also understand that we cannot delay indefinitely."

Barton Finch hung back, subdued and silent.

"How's he this mornin'?" Lou asked Angela.

"Not much different. He is taking water though."

"Hate to move him. Think you could cushion his head? Keep him from bangin' around?"

"I'm not sure how well we can protect his head," she answered doubtfully. "Do we have to move on today?"

"We'd best," Lou said. "You go set him up. I'll stop now and then, see how he's doin'."

Lou followed Angela back inside the wagon. She rolled blankets to pillow his head. "Ben, you'll sit on one side, right up against him. We'll keep his head steady between us."

"Sure," Ben said easily. "When's he going to wake up?" he asked Lou, who was feeling the prisoner's forehead once more with callused finger tips. He left scowling without giving the boy an answer.

The wagon lurched and bounced along. Angela didn't need to tell Ben to take extra precautions when the ride was particularly rough. Serious and attentive, he took no notice of anyone or anything except his task. He put both hands against the blanket, held the young man's head steady and scolded Traveler to stay away. The prisoner lay quiet except to mumble a word or two during the trip.

Lillian chattered and complained. Back in the shadowy recesses Barton Finch made no noise except for snoring when he slept. When they stopped Clara said, "Come Angela. Benjamin, there is no sense in you sitting in here. There is nothing you can do. If the bouncing of this contraption did not wake him I very much doubt there will be any change soon."

Lou cut the day's travel short at this first stop. No one knew his plans until they saw him unhitching the horses. Angela and Ben cast concerned glances at the wagon while they made camp. She was resolved to wait only so long, then she would return to it no matter what her mother said.

Ben was able to get away unnoticed first. Sitting cross-legged he replaced the cloth on the young man's forehead. A hand reached to pull away the cloth.

"No don't touch," Ben warned moving his hand away. "You shouldn't touch it. Your head's hurt. Don't you remember?"

295

The prisoner tried to sit up, fell back, rested a moment, and then tried again.

"Don't move. I'll get Ange."

"Angel?" He paused in his struggle. He tried again to push himself up.

"No. Lie still. I'll get my sister."

"Lou."

"Lou? You want Lou?"

"Lou."

"I'll get him. You lie still and I'll get him."

Dashing out of the wagon and running around until he found him, Ben pulled Lou by the hand.

Inside Lou leaned over the prisoner. "Decided to wake up?"

The young man pushed himself up on one elbow.

"Where do you think you're goin'?"

"Out…"

"Don't know if that's such a good idea."

"Out," he struggled to sit up.

"Stubborn. Take it slow now. Let me help. Move out of the way boy," Lou said to Ben.

Heads turned to see them coming out of the wagon. Lou held Prisoner with one arm wrapped behind him. He placed the young man's arm around his own neck and slowly they made their way off.

"Well that is a good sign," Clara remarked. "If you exercise moderation we may be able to complete this journey without a dead body after all," she said to Barton. He was crouched by the fire lighting his pipe.

A short while later they all watched when the two made their way back. They stopped before the wagon's steps. Prisoner's arm reached the other way. They heard Lou say, "Naw, you rest inside."

"Better git some food into him," he said to Angela and Ben after helping his companion inside.

"I'll get it," Ben said.

"Make it something easy on the gut," Lou recommended.

They brought a bowl of broth and a biscuit to soften in it. He appeared to be asleep, but opened his eye when they raised his head and shoulders.

296

"We brought you something to eat," Ben said. He held the bowl up.

Prisoner looked blankly at the boy.

"You haven't eaten for two days. You must be hungry."

"Here," Angela said nervously. Now that he was conscious her shyness was nearly disabling. She brought the spoon to his mouth. Seeing her, his chin lifted in a small sharp gesture of half recognition. He shut his eye tightly then opened it as if to clear his vision. He put his own hand on hers that held the spoon, taking it himself. The touch sent an odd little jolt up through her arm.

"Does your head hurt?" Ben asked.

He turned to Ben questioningly.

"I thought you were dead. It was scary. Don't you remember? Mr. Finch hit you. You choked him and he hit you. Remember?"

He gazed at Ben silently.

"Ben, he needs to eat. Here." Angela moved the bowl into his line of vision.

"Yup, eat," Ben encouraged. He took his hand that still held the spoon and put it into the bowl.

He ate a few spoonfuls from the bowl then lay back.

In the morning Lou helped the prisoner out of the wagon and off, returning a short time later to help him to the ground. He sat listlessly near the wagon. Ben, bowl and cup in hand, parked himself alongside and coaxed him to eat a little. Angela watched guardedly for Barton Finch to awake from his chastened passivity.

"Here, let's git you in," Lou said to the prisoner when it was time to depart.

He and Ben helped him to his feet. The prisoner looked up to his usual place.

"Think you can manage?" Lou asked.

He nodded and swallowed, his jaw clenched.

"Your stomick feelin' poorly?"

He nodded again.

"Generally does when you git a good bump on the head."

The prisoner tightened his grip on the wagon. With his head down he took a deep breath and blew it out.

"Here," Lou helped him turn around and put his hands on the upper rung to push himself one hop at a time.

297

"You said it was rough up there," Angela said.

"True enough, just the same be best for him out in the air. Looks kinda green around the gills, better he's with me outside if he's gonna be upchuckin'."

"Certainly," Clara agreed quickly. "Do as you think best. Come Lillian. Angela keep a close watch on your brother."

That night Lou helped the injured man down from the wagon and situated him for the night. He stretched out wearily, cushioning his head on his arm for a pillow. Lou pulled his blanket over him. Angela blinked. Rough, gruff old Lou's tenderness and Prisoner's sad head caused an ache in her.

Walking a few days later, Angela wondered, were these early Fall days particularly beautiful? Or was it because the nights were so cold they only seemed so by contrast? On the days when it didn't rain the grasses glowed golden under the sun. The rolling landscape and graceful animals gifted her with their presence. Sometimes she'd stretch out her arms to feel the space. But there was also a cruelty in the swift passing of days. She tried to hold them back by enjoying each moment. Too soon the light would subtly fade, the sky would whisper faint hues, then gradually intensify the rose and orange colors. Lou would pull over the team, another day gone.

Even on one unpleasant night when sleet mixed with rain, Angela stood by the fire praying for God to slow the rush of days.

"It's nearly snowing," Lillian sniffled. She was warming her hands. "We'll freeze to death before we reach our land. Mother I'm so cold!"

"Yes Lillian, we are all cold. Get another wrap. It is only a matter of a few weeks before we arrive," Clara said.

"At our home? We won't have to stay at another fort will we?"

"Hopefully not for long. I wrote your Uncle. We may stay with him. We will see when we arrive."

"What if he didn't get your letter? What if we don't make it?"

"Of course we'll make it. Don't exaggerate Lillian."

A coyote howled and Lillian shrieked, just as Angela was about to say some words of cheer about the majesty of the land. It was just as well that she didn't. Her words would have only produced hostile stares.

In spite of the cold mornings that made leaving her warm blankets an effort of sheer will, Angela wished she could hold back time. When this was over would she ever see Lou again? And Prisoner? Now that she knew his story, what he went through trying to save his mother, the pain and guilt he carried, she wondered more than ever how he endured day after day. Somehow he did. He was once more Lou's assistant, though he didn't always remember what to do. He stood near the horses until Lou gave him instruction. He was slower and didn't to know what to do with himself when finished. Ben or Lou would lead him to some place to rest for the night.

Chapter 21

"Turn around
"Every now and then I get a little bit
terrified and then I see the look in your
eyes."

"Total Eclipse of the Heart" Bonnie
Tyler

Another afternoon, another day gone, the sun still shone, but
the goose bumps on her arms warned Angela of the night's
air stealing the warmth. She learned to put on more layers at the first
sensation otherwise the cold would slowly seep inside before she
knew it and she would shiver all night no matter how many blankets
she wrapped around herself. She went to the wagon for a wrap,
passing Ben and Prisoner sitting on the ground at the far end. For the
first time since the blow to his head, Finch had chained him. He did it
quickly and without looking at him. Every person in camp turned to
watch. Clara was the first to turn away with a terse command to
prepare for supper, making Angela wonder if she had suggested the
restraint to Finch.

Inside the wagon she found her woolen leggings and pulled them
on under her skirt. She slipped her arms through the sleeves of a large
sweater and went out the steps. Ben was talking to Prisoner. "Can you
teach me Indian words? How do you start a fire without kerosene or
oil? How do you say fire? Why do you use your hands to talk
Indian?"

She wanted to sit with them, not to say anything, just to sit with
them and listen. Her heart fluttered at the thought. Maybe she could
sit at a bit of a distance so as not to disturb them or be noticed. No,
she must sit by the lonely fire where Lillian would whimper and
whine, Finch glower sulkily at his meal and Lou would sit on the
farthest side.

"Ow!" Ben exclaimed. He had taken his boots off and was slowly peeling the sock off one foot that was crossed over the other leg. "Ow, my toes are bleeding!"

Angela didn't have to think twice, she went to them. Prisoner leaned over to look closely at the foot Ben was waving in the air.

"See? These darn shoes hurt," he said.

Prisoner held Ben's foot and ripped a piece of cloth from his own shirt with his free hand.

"Ben what happened?" Angela asked.

"My toes, Ange. Look." He wiggled them.

She sat to see for herself. His toes were covered in dried blood from broken blisters. She picked up one of his shoes and held it to his foot. "You've outgrown these. Why didn't you tell anyone?"

"I was afraid Mother wouldn't let me walk outside," he shrugged. He pulled off the other sock. "Traveler, don't lick my toes."

"I'll get some water to wash them off. No, don't," she stopped Prisoner from ripping another piece of his shirt. "We have cloth for bandages."

"It stings," Ben complained when he stuck his toes in the water Angela brought.

"I know Ben. You must soak them just the same."

Ben soaked one foot, while Angela tore tiny strips from the cloth. Prisoner wrapped the dried toes individually.

"Do you have any bigger boots Ben?"

"I don't think so, not boots. There are some shoes that were Father's. Prisoner, show Ange how to say boots in Indian words. Fire, show her fire."

Angela peeked at the young man, who only bent his head further over his task. His eye was no longer swollen shut.

Intent on their project they were unaware of the developments around them. Angela wondered later how they could have been so unaware. Prisoner was still not entirely clear-headed because of the blow, Ben was concentrating on his toes, even Traveler didn't bark a warning.

Prisoner's body suddenly went rigid. Angela looked up to see Lou coming slowly from where he'd been checking the horses. There was something odd about the way he moved. In breath-stopping horror she realized there was a man behind him, holding a gun to his head and

302

trailing a saddled horse. At the same time twenty yards to the right another came holding Barton similarly. "Oh God," she whispered.

"What?" Ben began loudly.

Prisoner grabbed his arm. "Under," he said. "Under now," he pushed Ben beneath the wagon. "No sound, no moving, a rock," he said sternly.

"Please Ben," Angela pleaded, "Do what he says."

"You," he nodded to Angela.

She got on her knees to crawl under, but was frozen by a scream. Three more men riding out of the nearby grove, galloped to Clara and Lillian. Two climbed off their mounts. One tried to cover Lillian's mouth with his hand. The other wrapped an arm tightly around Clara. "Is that everyone?" the third shouted as he whirled his horse. He jumped down and squinted in the direction of Angela and Prisoner.

Too late to hide, he had seen her.

"Oh God," Angela whispered again.

A strong hand gripped her wrist.

"Sit, don't move," he said calmly.

"I've got to go to..." She was caught in an undertow of panic. She couldn't see, couldn't sit still.

"Don't move," he said softly. He pulled the blanket off his shoulders and wrapped it around the front of himself, covering his body entirely except for his head and neck.

"Here," he pulled her tightly next to himself never taking his eyes off the men. He stretched the blanket to cover his feet and the chain. He did all this smoothly without appearing to move.

"Stick," he said to Ben. "Stick," he repeated louder, reaching a hand behind.

Ben slid out his gun stick, which Prisoner slid under the blanket across his lap. The man who had seen them first was walking carefully in their direction, knees bent in a half crouch, his gun pointing ahead.

"Behind," Prisoner motioned for Ben to slide deeper under the wagon, behind himself and Angela.

Lillian screamed. The man approaching Angela and Prisoner stopped and looked back. The companions circled the two women, laughing and poking them with their guns. One lifted the hem of Lillian's skirt with his.

"Leave us alone!" Clara screeched. "Leave us alone you…" Her protest was drowned out by the men laughing. The one toying with Lillian put his face in Clara's. Like the others he had shaggy hair bushing out from under a floppy brimmed hat and a long beard. Angela started to get up. Ben stirred behind her.

"Don't move," Prisoner cautioned again.

The man in front of Clara stepped back and snatched the chain of her sapphire necklace. Yanking hard, he nearly pulled her over. The chain broke and he held it dangling through his fingers.

"Give it back!" Clara sobbed.

"Want to trade something for this?" he taunted waving it in her face.

Lillian and Clara clung to each other. The thief who was paused halfway between the women and Angela squinted through the dusk. "Who's over there? Don't move." He snarled over his shoulder, "Make 'em shut up or I will!"

Ben scraped along the ground under the wagon.

"No," Prisoner said. Then he shut his eyes, tipped his head back and leaned against the wagon as if asleep. He seemed scarcely to breathe. Angela watched him afraid if she turned her eyes to the menace coming closer and closer she would scream. She wished she could stop the shaking. Her breathing sounded so loud to herself she was sure this man could hear it. He stopped, his boots to the left of Prisoner. What was Prisoner doing? Sleeping? Leaving her to fend for herself? One boot nudged his leg. "What have we got here?" the man said. He bent over them. "Make them stop that wailing!" he shouted once more to the others.

Angela saw one shake Lillian like a rag doll. She gasped and the man over her grinned and lay a finger across his lips.

"You," he nudged Prisoner with his rifle. He didn't move. The intruder swung his rifle back to strike him with it.

"Please don't," Angela blurted. Her voice quavered.

"Why not?" he sneered leaning closer.

"He… isn't well. He can't be any trouble."

"Is that so?" He bent down on one knee. "Real sick is he?"

She nodded.

He reached across Prisoner. Angela leaned back.

Afraid to look up into his face, afraid to move, she saw with down turned eyes that he held his rifle in his right hand, fingers on the trigger.

"Your husband real sick?"

"Yes," she breathed shakily. "And injured."

"I can see. Then he won't mind if I have some fun with his wife."

He lifted the barrel to Prisoner's head and reached across him to put his hand on Angela's shoulder. His hand started to move down her shoulder. She tried to twist away. The hand suddenly stopped.

"Don't -Touch - My - Wife," Prisoner spoke each word with grim emphasis. He hadn't appeared to move. His eyes were staring into the offender's, who slowly pulled his hand off Angela with fingers spread.

"Don't move," Prisoner said in a low threatening voice.

"Easy now, what good do you think that's gonna do?" The man glanced down.

Angela saw Prisoner had Ben's play gun under the blanket shoved into the man's lower belly. The man gritted his teeth. "I've got my rifle to your head. I can kill you in a second."

"Yeah," Prisoner answered calmly, "or I could shoot you first. If I don't…" he shrugged lazily. "You know what happens when you get shot? You seize up. Nothin' you can do to stop it. My hand will close up on the trigger soon as the bullet hits my brain. Close up so tight the fingers can't be pried off. Alive or dead, I get my shot."

Was the intruder buying this story? She feared he wouldn't. It really didn't matter to Prisoner, that's what chilled her. She searched frantically for a way to reinforce the charade.

"Please, dear," she put a shaking hand on his arm, "not again. Don't gamble with your life. I want you around for the little time we have left."

For an instant Prisoner's eyes met hers in a flash of surprise, then returned to the menace before him. "Sides," he continued, "I'll die quick. You'll go slow and painful." He drove the stick slightly deeper.

The man hesitated.

"Please leave." Angela tried to sound light. "It always ends up worse for the other. And such a mess."

Their foe shifted his weight back, but Prisoner pushed the stick into him. "Don't move. Here's what you do. Call your men off. Tell

305

'em there's nothing here. Tell 'em get on the horses and get. Don't move! Just call over your shoulder."

"I don't see how they'll believe me. They'll think somethin' funny's up if we leave empty handed," he grinned, showing gaping spaces between blackened teeth

Angela's bubble of panic started to rise again. Without turning his head Prisoner said to her, "Do you know where our money is?"

"Yes," she whispered.

"Go get it. Wait 'til I say, then go quick. Make sure no one sees you go or come back."

His eyes passed over the entire scene. The two men holding Lou and Barton were poking them with their guns and asking questions.

Their companion shouted. "I'll get what there is and join you."

Prisoner tightened his grip on the stick. After a minute or two he said to Angela, "Go."

Angela frantically searched the wagon for her mother's hidden moneybox. She grasped it and stumbled back to the opening. An impulse seized her just before leaving. She opened the box and shoved fistfuls of bills in her pockets, then peeked out. The men guarding Lou and Barton were talking to each other and the two with the women had their backs to the wagon. How her legs carried her she didn't know, but she made it back beside Prisoner.

"Now do what I told you," Prisoner said to him.

"How do I know it's not empty?"

Angela felt Prisoner's body tense, ready for trouble.

"You callin' my wife a liar?" The fierceness in his tone and his bruised face made him look to be a foe even the toughest character would not like to challenge. Angela was a bit intimidated herself.

"Here," she snapped the lid open and shut.

"Don't get excited. I'm not insultin' her. That all you got?"

"Do we look rich?" Angela said.

"Now," Prisoner said in a hard voice, "No mistakes."

Angela held her breath. The thief shouted, "I got the stuff! Get the horses and meet me where we started from this mornin'!"

"What? What do you mean nothin'? I got good stuff here," the captor of Lillian hollered back.

"Leave em! I got everythin'. Let's get before others come along!"

306

The other thieves looked at each other, then the two holding the Lou and Barton nodded. They tied them back to back then swung up on their stirrups, maintaining aim with their rifles until they whirled the horses around and galloped off. One of the men with Clara and Lillian did the same. The fourth lingered, spinning his horse in the center, rifle in his hands.

"Drop the rifle," Prisoner said to the man he held at stick point.

"You can't take my gun. My man will think somethin's up."

"Empty it and you can keep it. Slow and easy."

Angela saw Prisoner's eyes flick to the man's horse grazing between them and the wagon. The other started to ride closer. Prisoner nudged the thief with his stick and nodded at the rider.

"I said I'm comin'. Get a start, I'll catch up!" the thief called. He kept his back to his companion and emptied his gun, then paused, bullets in his hand.

"Put em in my wife's hands," Prisoner directed. "Count em," he said to her. "All there?"

"Yes," she answered.

"Tell your friend to go," Prisoner said.

"How'm I suppose to git away. You can shoot me."

"When your friend is out of sight grab your horse. Keep your back to me and I won't shoot."

"I don't know," the man said.

"It's true. He's never shot a man in the back," Angela said.

"Well don't see what choice I have. I'm gonna wave my hat to my fellow. It's a signal he knows."

Prisoner nodded.

The thief flapped his hat once through the air. His compatriot galloped off.

"Go!" Prisoner jabbed him with the stick.

The man ran to his horse, grabbed the pommel and pulled himself onto the saddle.

Barton and Lou managed to get through Clara's panic and convince her to help them. She pulled a knife from Lou's pocket and struggled with shaking hands to cut the rope. Once free he cut Barton loose. They ran for their rifles. Lou was unable to get a shot off. Barton was a little faster; he fired into the thief's departing dust.

307

Angela clasped her hands together to stop their shaking. Not trusting her legs to stand, she stayed where she was and leaned weakly against the wheel spokes behind her back. She turned to stare at Prisoner. He stared back.

"You were wonderful," she said.

He dropped his eyes and shook his head. "No, you. You alright?"

"Yes, thank you."

"Can I come out now?" Ben called.

"Oh yes, come out. It's safe," she said. "Is it?" she asked Prisoner.

"Yeah."

"Wow, you sure tricked that robber." Ben crouched before them.

"You heard?" Angela asked.

"Yeah, it was like you were in a story or something. How did you know what to say?"

"I didn't. I just followed Pr… his lead," Angela smiled. "It was your stick gun Ben," her smile widened.

"Really?"

"Yes, your stick gun and my husband," she said laughing.

"I've got to tell everyone," Ben said. He bounced to his feet and ran.

Laughing uncontrollably Angela faced Prisoner. He smiled back, his eyes shining, strong white teeth showing for a moment. Angela's giddiness faded to wonder as she looked at him.

He dropped his gaze. "Your people," he said solemnly.

She saw the rest of their party gathered under the starlight and went to them, her legs supporting her uncertainly.

Finch and Lou were arguing about giving chase. Lillian was a sobbing heap of dress material on the ground. Lou stopped arguing and brought water, set it down, scrutinizing the surroundings through his squint. Barton paced back and forth, his hands clenched in fists. "I'll have them caught. They'll pay for this. I have many friends who can take care of the likes of them. They won't get away with this."

"It's safe now, Lillian. The robbers are gone." Ben patted her back. "They won't come back."

Angela scooped some water in a ladle and let her shaky legs fold under her, plopping next to her sister.

"Sh, Lillian. It's over," she said.

308

"They won't dare come back," Barton boasted. He was sufficiently recovered to support Clara's elbow and sit her on the grass. "You saw how they took off. Didn't take much either. They bit off more than they could chew with us, knew it too."

"I'm wonderin' why they left so sudden like?" Lou's question caused attention to turn his way. "What happened over there?"

"I can tell you," Ben began excitedly. "Prisoner said, 'Get under' and I hid under the wagon. Then it was real quiet. I could hear big boots coming. I wanted to see, but Prisoner said, 'Don't move.' I hear the robber say something and Angela says something about Prisoner being sick and for him to leave. Then it was kind of quiet again, then Prisoner says, 'Don't touch my wife.' Prisoner tells the robber not to move and they talk about who is going to die first. That kind of scared me until Prisoner tells Ange to get the money and tells the robber what to tell the other robbers. Then he left." Ben told the story all in one breath. He had to catch his breath on finishing. No one said a word for a moment.

"What was the box the fella was carryin' when he lit out?" Lou asked.

"The moneybox," Angela said in a subdued voice.

"The moneybox? Our money?" Clara pronounced each syllable emphatically. "You let those animals take our money!" She got to her feet. Her eyes were hard on Angela, her hair hung down her face. She clutched the front of her torn dress.

"My sapphire! Our money! How could you?"

"It was the only way to get him to go," Angela pleaded.

"Don't you see what you've done? You let that criminal give our money to those, those criminals who abused us!" She shrieked.

"Not all," Angela tried feebly. "I saved some, most really." She showed the money to her mother. Clara did not look. She shrieked, "How could you! How could you!" She put her hands to her face and sobbed.

"Now, now, no one is hurt," Barton said. He stooped beside Clara. "They didn't get it all."

"Yeah they won't come back after what Prisoner said." Ben began to tell the story again.

Angela got to her feet and stumbled off sobbing. She ran back to Prisoner. He was resting, his eyes opened at the sound of her running feet. She flopped down beside him, wiping her tears with her sleeve like a little girl.

"Alright?" He sat straight, looking for trouble.

"No, it's fine," she got out. "I just wanted to … sit here."

He returned her gaze.

"No, I'll not have it!" Clara was bearing down on them. Suddenly above them, she struck Prisoner across the face. "Wife! How dare you!" She raised her arm to strike again.

"No!" Angela jumped to her feet.

"I won't have it, I won't," Clara ranted.

Barton caught her arm. "There, it's all over. Come rest." He led her away.

Angela stared at their backs. She looked down at Prisoner. He turned away, his head and shoulder against the wagon. "I'm sorry. She shouldn't have. I'm…" she tried to apologize.

"No, she's right. Shouldn't have said…"

"No. You saved us. She's not right." Angela reached towards him, but he stayed turned away, defensively withdrawn. The connection was gone.

Lou appeared next to her. He spat and cleared his throat. "You best go in now."

She wiped her face before climbing the stairs. He cleared his throat again. "Good thinkin' to keep some," he said to her back. "Yep, they won't be comin' back if they think they got all there is."

310

Chapter 22

"Nothing I can do
Total eclipse of the heart."
"Total Eclipse of the Heart"

Bonnie Tyler

Angela woke; her heart was pounding though the sun was fighting off the darkness and birds were singing. She forced herself to stay in her blankets in spite of the disturbing scenes passing through her mind. The thief leaned across her once more, his hot breath touching her face while the violence of the others holding Clara and Lillian worsened. She could see them struggling over his shoulder. Pinned, she was helpless to aid them. What if the thieves had not stopped when they did, not left as they did? People died out here. She'd known that. She had been foolishly, falsely confident.

Though they may have been mostly thwarted, the thieves had succeeded in damaging the family. They had been uncomfortable, ill equipped and nervous from the start, now they were violated, vulnerable prey in a predatory world. Lillian clung trembling to her mother's arm when outside the wagon. Clara, disheveled and haggard, waited until Finch emerged from behind the wagon.

He stood over Prisoner, who was tying back his hair. That trouble –making girl and the brother were out of sight.

"Ha!" Finch poked him with his rifle, which he now kept close. "Ha, she showed you didn't she? Did you think you fooled them? Did you think they cared about the likes of you?" He rattled the chain roughly before unlocking it. "Slapped you back in place. She did. Good morning ladies." Then seeing their trepidation he said, "There's no danger. Here, I'll be happy to go ahead."

"Thank you," Clara said. She took his offered arm. "Wait for my daughter please. Angela!"

Angela was horrified at the idea of having Finch along for morning rituals. She held back and was relieved when her mother did not insist she come along.

311

In the evening every little sound seemed increased by tenfold, the crackling fire, the grasses rustling, animal sounds. Angela stirred the stew, straining to hear any out of place noise. Lillian wrapped her arms around herself and stared at the ground. Only Ben carried on as usual. Sitting cross-legged next to Prisoner he leaned forward, talking, but even in the waning light Angela could tell his efforts were futile. Prisoner held himself as far away as the chain allowed, his face averted. He was like one of those people she'd read about, called untouchables. They keep themselves away and warn others to stay their distance. Giving up, Ben came to the fire. He pulled his pup into his lap.

Traveler suddenly barked, shattering the thin ice of composure. Lillian gave a short scream. Angela felt as though her body and spirit had jolted apart and lingered somewhere in the air. Clara dropped the bowls she was carrying, her arms swung wildly. "Benjamin control that animal!" She looked from Lou to Barton. "Isn't someone going to see if anything is out there?"

Lou had glanced around, apparently unconcerned. Angela noticed he peered first at Prisoner, who rested against the wagon, showing no signs of alert warning. Lillian was sobbing.

"Now, now," Barton said, hoisting himself to his feet. "It's nothing. I'll take a look for your peace of mind. I'm happy to." He went off whistling.

In opposite proportion to everyone else's emotional frailty, Finch grew more and more dominant. He boisterously reclaimed his authority over Prisoner and his self appointed rank as protector of the women. Returning from the outskirts of camp, he paused in front of his charge, pointing and mocking. "They know. You're no hero." Angela was occupied in conversation with Ben, who wanted to scout for robbers.

"A coward, trying to take the coward's way out. You're not getting out of facing your punishment." He held his rifle under Prisoner's chin then he lowered his voice and told him how he would desecrate his body when he was dead. He glanced over at Angela and Ben and marched back to sit with a groan next to Lillian. "Now, now, there's nothing out there."

312

"Why?" she sobbed. "Why did they treat us like that? Why? What did we ever do to them?"

"There's just folks who aren't fit. I know it's a shock to someone like you. It's a shame you had to experience it first hand, a real shame. Men like them are why people like me are necessary."

"They're not human," she sobbed.

"I know, I know," he commiserated, stroking her arm.

Don't let him touch you, Angela thought. To stop herself from saying this out loud she picked up the bowls her mother had dropped. Clara left Lillian's side and snatched them out of her hands.

Though Angela's body registered the physical sensation of the sharp thin shoulder's jab as Clara shoved past, she did not feel the familiar sting of hurt and humiliation, nor did defensive tears well. When she saw in her mind's eye her mother's hand flashing out to strike Prisoner, her teeth set hard. She felt anger for him. For herself she felt nothing, not the desperate need to explain, nor for some sign of softening, some signal that she was acceptable. Go ahead, continue the cold messages, she dared in her mind. You can't hurt me any more than that horrible man can intimidate me. It only makes me stronger. See? I feel nothing. I'm empty. You can't hurt me.

Then she wondered if there wasn't something wrong in this void. Am I a bad person to feel nothing? Am I hateful? No, this isn't hate. Different from hate, this void of emotion is more truly the opposite of love. It cannot be a good thing. Just the same, it was a relief not to feel.

Since leaving Fort Laramie the terrain was rougher than any they had experienced thus far. There was little time to be concerned with one's own state of mind when the horses were climbing painstakingly up or tentatively down steep passes. Some days the weather was raw with biting wind and rain mixing with sleet. Lou stopped the wagon before a steep incline to put on chains for braking. Finch glanced out to see what the stoppage was for.

"You wanna lend a hand here," Lou asked.

"The ladies are much too fearful for me to leave their sides," he said and he disappeared back inside. Lou let Ben assist. The youngster passed chains through the wheels to him while Prisoner held the horses' heads.

313

Angela noted with bittersweet surprise how seriously Ben listened to Lou's instructions and how capably he worked. Who was this person? Where was the child who bounced around wanting to be involved, usually more of a hindrance than help?

She felt safer walking with Ben behind the wagon when it swayed down precarious descents. She swallowed the building fear that it would careen out of control taking her mother and sister over a cliff. Concentrating on where she placed her feet kept her fears under control.

Not only was traveling arduous, but supplies were getting low. The bad spots could be cut out of the potatoes and they had dried meat as well as dried pumpkins and other vegetables. Clara guarded the preserved fruit from their old home, fearing there would be few supplies when they reached their destination.

In the evening when Angela and Ben were walking into camp he complained, "I'm so hungry. Can't we have different food tonight?"

"Shush Ben, everyone is hungry and tired of the same things." Angela was embarrassed by his whining within earshot of Prisoner, who had even less to eat, though she did sympathize with his complaints. Her own stomach swirled hollowly. Prisoner stopped, stooped and after parting the dry stalks, picked from the undergrowth.

"Hey, what did you find?" Ben joined him.

He held out a handful of greens.

"Are these for eating?" the boy asked.

He nodded. Ben shoved them all into his mouth without hesitation. "Thanks. Show me where you find these."

Prisoner pointed and Ben pushed aside dead plants. He picked a leaf and held it up.

"Can I eat this? It looks like what you gave me."

Prisoner nodded and showed Ben where to find more. Angela joined them and picked the last of the year's currant berries that weren't completely withered. She nibbled one of the leaves that Ben and Prisoner were picking. It tasted like spinach. She hoped it would help ward off problems from lack of fresh vegetables. She'd been wondering if they could get scurvy like sailors. Prisoner was such a rich source of information, she wished they could use his knowledge more, but her mother and sister wouldn't touch anything if they knew it came from him. Finch wouldn't allow it And Prisoner himself, though stronger, would it be fair to ask more of him?

The wind howled for the third night in a row. Scruffy trees permanently bent in one direction gave Angela to believe it never relented here. She wrapped a blanket over her head and shoulders. She wanted to put her hands over her ears to shut out the noise. Lillian whimpered by the fire, which was all she did these days.

"It won't be long now," Finch said. "It may be rough traveling, but that's a sign we're getting closer to Fort Hall."

Clara looked up quickly.

"Is that true?" Lillian said. It was her first full sentence that wasn't a complaint since the attack.

"Yes indeed. This here river is the Sweetwater. We'll come to desert land then for your place you go towards the Bear River Range, then the river itself. Soon enough you'll be in the settlement with family. I believe you said you had a brother?" He addressed this question to Clara.

"Brother-in-law," she answered.

Lillian wiped her tears.

"There, now that's better," Finch said. "We'll all be happy then. Hey, maybe there will be a work for me, so I can settle down. I'll be happy to be free of my burden and be done with this kind of work. This one has done me in."

"Yes Mr. Finch. I do not know where you find the strength. We are fortunate to have you with us even if it meant traveling with that creature," Clara said.

"If you can't find a judge," Angela began, forgetting her resolve not to engage him and pushing aside her anger at their words, "Would you keep him in a jail until one could be found?"

"Not likely," he said. "First, I don't believe they keep long term prisoners there. Second, I don't know if I can take the strain of waiting any longer to be done with him. I'm not getting any younger. I only hope the man has tracked down a circuit judge and they will be waiting for me. If not I can't wait and there are those who could help me if necessary."

"Who?" Ben asked.

"There are men who roam the territories of their own free will, carrying out justice. As you see out here justice is slow and hard to find. Criminals get off sometimes. These folks take it upon themselves to protect decent folks."

"You mean men like you?" Ben asked.

"No, not quite like me. These men are less ... official."

Lou stood up and walked away. Angela's stomach tightened. What was he talking about?

"Now before anyone gets worked up, I know there are those who don't approve of the work these fellows do. You ladies have seen for yourselves how wild men can be out here, thinking there's no law to stop them. The territories are too big and spread out for our government to handle just yet. These men that I'm referring to are self-appointed sentries of order. They put an end to the mad dogs out here."

Ben watched Finch curiously. Clara nodded approvingly.

"Where were they when those animals attacked us?" Lillian said. She started to cry again.

"They might have already caught them somewhere out there, if not, don't you worry, they will. Word gets around, even in the territories. Descriptions left at settlements, stories passed among emigrants. You've seen the notes left along the trail, carved into the rock."

"That is satisfying to hear," Clara said.

Angela wrapped her blanket more tightly, picked up her plate and went to the fire.

Ben followed. "Prisoner is not a mad dog. Does Mr. Finch mean those men would shoot him like they do a mad dog?"

"I don't know," she replied. "If they are anything like him I wouldn't be surprised."

"They can't do that!"

"Sh," she glanced at the others. "I will make certain he stays within the law and Prisoner gets a fair trial." She put a biscuit and the dried meat they had boiled with peppermint on her plate. It wasn't very appetizing, but it was edible. Her words to her brother assured him, but she was anxious. Through the darkness she made her way to where Prisoner sat.

"Here," she shyly offered the plate.

Ben plunked himself down next to him. "Go ahead, eat."

"Thanks," he said barely above a whisper.

"Are you cold?" Ben asked.

"Would you like another blanket?" Angela asked.

He looked into her eyes for a moment, his swallowing hers in their soft light.

Then he looked down, shutting her out. Being in his eyes was painful in an odd pleasant way. Being shut out of them hurt with a dull thud like a slammed door. She wasn't empty of feeling after all.

Marty Young Stratton

Chapter 23

*"She's a friend of my mind. She gather
me, man. The pieces I am. She gather
them back to me all in the right order."*

Beloved by Toni Morrison

Before crossing the desert. Lou extended their stay by the
Sweetwater River.

"Be 'bout eighteen miles before we see any water or much else,"
he growled by way of warning. "We'll stay put a day to stock up, git
ready and such."

In the morning they washed clothes and began the all day process
of getting water, boiling it, adding quinine and storing it in containers.
Though there was much work to do Angela welcomed this delay.
Hearing the familiar clink of the hammer on iron as Lou and Prisoner
reshod the horses she could almost imagine that they were a family
tending to the daily chores. Voices called to each other, repairs were
being made on the wagon, clothes being washed; it seemed natural. If
only it were as she imagined, Lou the crotchety grandfather, her
mother and siblings working together, the shiftless boarder resting in
the shade and the handsome young man … She shook her head and
blushed at her thoughts.

The sun was brutally unyielding for the first day's trek into the
desert. A dry breeze stirred sweet scents and dust particles, providing
no cooling relief, but, the stark desert had its own beauty and Angela
drank it in. By afternoon mountains could be seen in the distance.
When the stars came out hanging thick and low over the expanse
Angela thanked God for allowing her to see this beauty and she
wondered regretfully if she would ever see the like again.

Angela started the morning meal on what would be their last
dreary trudge through the desert. Finch stopped Ben on his way to
Prisoner with food and water.

"What do you think you're doing? Got to ration water until we're out of the desert. Save it for deserving folks." He took the tin mug and downed it himself.

Angela gripped the ladle in her hand more tightly. She stood poised on her toes, ready to take action, but her anger at Finch was quickly pushed back by Prisoner's unsettling behavior. He had barely noticed Ben or the food. Usually calm, today he was looking quickly in all directions.

Later, when working with the horses his attention seemed to be everywhere at once. He conferred with Lou for a moment. Shadowy fears crisscrossing through Angela's thoughts made it difficult to keep her mind calmly on her chores.

The horses were hitched and ready, everyone gathered to depart when the giant hooves began to dance up and down like marionettes. Their heads lifted on tense necks, eyes rolling, showing white, coiled springs of nerves.

"Hold 'em! Hold 'em! Whoa! Easy!" Lou shouted.

A cloud of dust was coming closer and closer. Prisoner grabbed the bridles of the two lead horses to help control them. Riders suddenly descended on them from the cloud, their horses stirred the dust as they reined them back. Seven Indian men leapt lightly off their animals' backs. They handed the rawhide reins to one and stalked around the camp lithe as cats. Lou left the jumpy horses in Prisoner's hands and walked slowly to the family. Lillian and Clara cowered against the wagon. Angela and Ben were across from them where the campfire had been.

"Quiet," Lou ordered. "Don't make no sudden moves. Stay easy like. They just want to see if we have anythin' of interest."

An Indian searched him and took his pistol and knife. Another did the same to Finch. A fierce looking Indian with a scar across his cheek stationed himself in the center of all the action. A sixth poked his head inside the wagon. Angela grabbed Ben's hand and gave it a little yank as a warning not to move or speak.

Two braves strolled easily, yet with caution to Clara and Lillian. They ignored Traveler's yapping. The one in the center barked a word at them. They stopped, peered at the two women and said something back to him. Lillian whimpered like a puppy. They inspected the women precociously, pinching the flesh on their ribs and feeling their

320

hair. Contrary to Lou's warning, Clara slapped a hand away. Angela gasped, but the slapped man and his companion laughed. They examined the women's hands and commented to each other.

"They're looking for women," Finch said.

Lillian's whimpering modulated to a thin wail.

"Shut up Finch," Lou said, "These are braves they don't have no problem findin' agreeable women on their own. Probably got a handful of wives each."

Holding Ben's arm tightly Angela tried to inch forward to close the gap between themselves and her mother and sister. One of the Indians covered his ears then made a gesture to his companion in Lillian's direction.

The horses lowered their necks and ears, calm now. Prisoner left them. The Indians stopped what they were doing to watch him limp then dismissed him. Three entered the wagon, climbing the steps one at a time and crouching through the opening. They could be heard banging, tossing and searching the contents. Prisoner carefully placed himself in front of Angela and Ben.

The braves came out carrying blankets, pots and other cooking implements. They rejoined their companions and carried on a discussion. The eyes of one flashed in Angela's direction a few times. Now he spoke to the Indian with the scar and they strode to her. The speaker tipped his head trying to see her behind Prisoner.

Before they could come within arm's length Prisoner put up his hands and spoke in words Angela had never heard. The Indians stopped. He repeated his words, thrusting his hands in a warning to keep back. They stood their ground, but shook their heads and talked to each other. They did not understand him.

Angela heard Prisoner make a growl of frustration in his throat. He spoke again, this time with accompanying hand gestures. They responded with gestures of their own. The second tried to step around Prisoner to get a closer look at the brother and sister, but Prisoner moved keeping himself a wall between them. The leader signed at Angela. Prisoner made a different sign in her direction and shook his head insistently. The brave made a sound of surprise and question. Prisoner repeated his sign at Angela and made one towards himself. The second Indian pointed to Prisoner's injured leg and said something that sounded disdainful.

321

Ben was getting harder to restrain. He moved to Prisoner's side asking, "What are you saying?"

His answer was a gentle push back to his sister. The Indians signed towards Ben. Prisoner signed back. The conversation continued, the language of the three men growing more emphatic, both spoken and unspoken.

The other Indians watched the proceedings. One stood before Clara and Lillian and the others padded around Barton and Lou.

Finch made a sudden move and an Indian flashed a hatchet blade to his throat.

"Don't be stupid," Lou said in a low quiet voice. Then he asked Prisoner, "What do they want son?"

Prisoner exhaled slowly. "Many women and children died of white sickness. They want help in camp to replace the lost. Can't agree. Some don't want to bring whites into the village."

"They want slaves?" Barton asked loudly. His voice had a quaver and sounded high. An Indian thumped him on the head with the handle of the hatchet. He went to the ground with a thud, his hand to his head.

Lillian screamed.

"Quiet," Lou warned. "What do you think they're gonna do?" he asked Prisoner.

"They say one's too loud, the other too old."

"What about them?" Lou asked. He indicated Angela and Ben.

"They want them."

"Oh no, oh no, …" Clara began to chant mindlessly. Lillian crumbled to the ground and wailed.

Angela's insides went hollow.

"Go on," Lou said over the noise.

"Told them the boy has fits."

"What about her?"

"Told them she is my wife. Sorry," he ducked his head.

"Good," Lou said evenly.

"They won't take me?" Angela whispered.

He took a slow breath. "He says I'm not a fit husband. Not strong enough. You'd be better off with his people."

"You're plenty strong!" Ben blurted. He pulled out of Angela's grasp and stepped forward. "You took on that huge bear." He made his hands in the shape of claws and waved them in the air as he spoke.

The Indian who had taken particular interest in Angela looked quizzically at Ben. He signed a question. Prisoner signed an explanation.

"Tell them," Ben insisted, "tell them you are strong."

"They don't believe," Prisoner said.

"Don't believe? Show him where the bear clawed you." Ben pulled at the collar of Prisoner's shirt until the small scar was visible. "There," he pointed. "See? The bear did like this," he jumped up slashing his hand at Prisoner as though he were the bear.

The Indians seemed to consider this. Then the second reached around and grabbed Angela by the arm.

"No." Prisoner caught his arm and pulled it off. The leader put his free hand on Lou's knife at his waist. Prisoner began to sign rapidly, aggressively, speaking in English at the same time.

"Can't take my wife. I may look not strong. I provide. For your honor and mine you can't take what's not yours. That's a white way."

The others watching the proceedings murmured. The two talking to Prisoner turned back to consult with their companions. After a brief discussion the leader approached Prisoner once more, knife in his hand. He and Prisoner exchanged adamant signs until Prisoner finally dropped his head in acquiescence. He turned to face Angela, his eyes sorrowful.

"We have to go with them. Can't stop them. If I fight they will win and take only you. Sorry."

Angela couldn't breathe, couldn't think, couldn't see. He looked into her eyes until she was able to focus on them.

"I won't let anything happen to you."

She exhaled a long shaky breath. Before she realized what was happening the Indians leapt to their horses' backs and surrounded her, Prisoner and Ben.

"No, you can't take my sister!" Ben yelled. He threw wild punches and grabbed at their feet and legs. They kicked him away. He came back at them. They began to lose patience, leaning over their horses to strike at him.

"You can't take her!" he shouted furiously.

323

The significance of his words penetrating through her own panic, Clara began to scream.

Prisoner caught Ben, held both his arms at his sides and he said, "I'll take care of her. You take care of your mother and sister. Hear your mother? Go to her."

Ben wavered. He looked at Angela, his was face covered with wet dirt from his tears, his eyes were glassy.

"Go," she whispered, "I'll be fine." Her eyes were dry. She was in a state of disbelief.

Prisoner pushed him out of the throng of horses and Indians. Angela could see only the horses' bodies and the dangling legs of the riders. A high pitch sound cut through the dusty confusion. It was Clara wailing. The anguish in the sound paralyzed Angela. A horse's shoulder shoved her forward she would have fallen, but she bumped into Prisoner's back. He turned and looked into her eyes before they were pressed forward. She could hardly see through the tears now falling and her body shook. She stumbled against Prisoner's back, made out the familiar colors of the blanket he wore and was guided by it.

Chapter 24

*"When love has dissolved and mingled
two beings into an angelic sacred unity,
the secret of life is found for them."*
*"The day a woman walking past sheds a
light on you as she goes you are lost,
you love."*

<u>*Les Miserables*</u> *by Victor Hugo*

After a while she could no longer hear her mother's wails.
Prisoner's back was a blockade in front of her. She peeked
sideways. The Indians rode quietly, their moccasin-covered feet
hanging loosely. She could see intricate bead and quill work on the
footwear and leggings. They all wore bows and quivers of arrows
hanging down their backs as well as rifles. They wore no shirts, only
blankets they had taken, as well as some of their own. Pouches hung
from long straps over their shoulders. Prisoner felt her looking around
and glanced back at her.

The march went on and on. Prisoner stumbled once, then twice.
Angela winced to see of how difficult all the walking must be for him.
When he stumbled a third time she stepped alongside him, linking her
arm in his. He tightened for a moment then accepted her help. They
stopped to make camp only after the moon had risen and then set. The
Indians gave them water from skin containers and strips of dried
meat. Angela shivered, her teeth chattering more from fear than the
cold. Prisoner took the blanket from his shoulders and draped it over
her. "Eat," he said. She tried to gnaw the meat he handed her,
wrapped the blanket around herself and curled on the ground, too
tired to hold her head up, too scared to sleep or eat. The blanket
smelled faintly of earth, tangy of horses and sweetly of him.

She sat up when the sky began to lighten. Prisoner sat still as a
stone, his arms and chin leaning on his left knee, his right leg
awkwardly bent, resting on his left foot. He had been like that all

325

night. He held out water and meat for her. He didn't say anything, but he kept them before her until she gave in and took the offering.

Her legs felt heavy, the joints stiff. She was accustomed to walking distances, but yesterday's march had been longer than she had ever done. Prisoner's gait was rougher and slower on this day. She glanced at him from time to time. He caught her looking at him and questioned her with a lift of one brow. She gave him a small smile of reassurance and walked alongside, hooking her arm through his. His breath caught, he stared straight ahead.

Tired as he was, that afternoon she felt his head lift to scan the horizon. She saw nothing, but knew to trust his senses. An hour later she caught the scent of smoke in the air. After a few miles more she saw trails of smoke rising. A variety of scents filled the air, wood burning, meat cooking and animal skins drying.

Suddenly the air filled with cries of glee. Children seemed to come out of the rolling earth to meet them. They dashed through the horses' legs and stopped to stare at herself and Prisoner, impeding their progress. Some simply stared, others touched her dress, even lifting and tugging at it. She leaned over, letting them examine her hair and buttons. She in turn touched a beautiful cheek or braid. She laughed at their reactions to her shoes. They pointed, touched, stepped back and walked with high steps pretending to feel the weight of such ponderous footwear. She glanced up and caught Prisoner looking at her his face registering surprise, his eyes smiling. He signed in response to the children's questions.

Introductions and explanations were interrupted when a few women appeared. They snatched up and pulled away the children. Then they stood at a distance eyeing Angela with mistrust.

Angela and Prisoner were herded down a path into a busy village of lodges, fires and activity. The inhabitants gathered to watch them pass. The children ran ahead proudly proclaiming the information they had already gleaned.

They were led to a dwelling before which stood a stately man, his face creased and bronzed, his arms crossed before him. He and several elderly men and women watched their approach. After exchanging a few words with the lead captor he entered the dwelling. The others who had stood with him followed then the leader of the captors. Angela and Prisoner were pushed inside by the remaining

326

captors. Sitting cross-legged in a central position the elder waited for all to be seated before speaking.

Angela sat partially hidden behind Prisoner. While the scarred man and the one who'd tried to grab her talked to the leader she looked around in fascination at the construction of shelter made of skins and trees, at the tools and the furs on the ground. The leader addressed Prisoner directly, snapping Angela's attention back, for he spoke in English.

"My braves tell me you do not speak our tongue. Do you speak this tongue?"

Prisoner nodded. "I hear you."

"They tell me you know the signs. You are?" He signed, drawing two fingers from his wrist to his knuckles.

"My mother."

"What tribe?"

"Bannock."

"Your father?"

"White."

How did he stay so calm? Angela wondered. Was he familiar with Indian homes like this? Had he been in places like this?

"We have lost many old ones, children and women to white man's sickness. Others have moved to camps far away for safety. I myself have lost two wives. This man has lost his wives." The old leader nodded at the Indian who had wanted to take Angela. "He has no one to tend his fire and children. You say this woman is your wife," he did not pause for Prisoner to confirm. "This man believes you are not strong to provide for a wife. My eyes tell me he speaks true." Here he paused.

"I am sorry for your losses. It's true I have been wounded," Prisoner spoke quietly. "I grow stronger every day. I can provide for this woman."

The old man translated Prisoner's words.

His competitor for Angela snorted at Prisoner's words.

"You see for yourself she is well," Prisoner said.

The leader craned his neck to see Angela better. He waved his palms up.

"Stand," Prisoner said softly. She shook her head and shifted closer to him. All eyes were on her. She couldn't possibly stand and

327

have all these people inspect her like a horse for sale, she wasn't even sure her legs would cooperate. He turned, taking one of her hands he said again, "Stand."

She stood on weak legs. He let go of her hand and stared at the ground. She was offended by the examination and her irritation gave her strength.

The elder nodded and she sat quickly. "She looks well for a white woman," he said. "You are lame. You are young; a brave with a lame leg does not live to be an elder. What of her old age and children?"

"Your words are true for a brave, but it is different in the white world. Weak and lame white men can live to be old. But I am here. I'm willing to prove myself in this world."

The leader considered his words then translated for the others. The challenger spoke impatiently. His elder listened then translated for Prisoner. "This brave believes it would not be honorable for him to defeat one weak as yourself. He believes the decision is clear. The woman should be his."

"No." Angela was unable to keep silent, "He is strong."

Prisoner reached out and gripped her arm, his eyes pleading.

She rushed on, "He has endured terrible abuse and survived. He saved us. He fought a bear. We showed these men the scar." She had to stop to gain control of herself.

Everyone stared; disapproval was stamped on their faces.

"You see how white women speak out," Prisoner said. "They do not make good wives or helpers for others unless they are adopted young." He took her hands and flipped them over, showing the palms. "See her hands? They are not good for hard work."

The people in the shelter leaned closer, studying her hands.

Angela thought she should be insulted, but was too bewildered.

Prisoner continued speaking and signing, "I came willingly. This brave and I made an agreement that I could prove myself. It would not be honorable if he breaks the agreement now. If he wants this woman there must be a challenge to answer. True, a running race would not bring honor."

The people in the lodge laughed when the leader translated. Prisoner smiled slightly, the edges of his mouth turning up and his eyes brightened.

How can he joke? Angela thought.

328

"There are different kinds of strength. There's strength of the mind, there's endurance," he said.

The Indians counseled amongst each other. Finally the leader said to Prisoner, "There will be a contest. In the morning I will tell the nature of the contest. Now we eat."

Large amounts of boiled meat were placed in the center of the gathering.

A smiling woman thrust a bowl of water at Angela. She looked at it blankly until Prisoner took it and held it for her to drink from. A piece of meat was dropped into her hands. She could not possibly eat.

"Eat," Prisoner whispered. "It's an insult to refuse."

The people in the room chattered and ate, studied her and Prisoner and discussed them freely. Peeking around Angela noticed some of the people had cut their hair raggedly. Many looked thin. The woman who served the food had cut marks up her arms.

The elder stood, signifying the end of the evening. Rising, Prisoner said to him, "Thank you for your thoughts."

He smiled, "Rest well Bear Fighter."

Prisoner bowed his head, embarrassed.

They were led to a smaller dwelling and directed to enter. Like the other, a low fire glowed inside. There was food and water and furs covering the ground. They were alone. Angela stood uncomfortably for a minute or two. "I need ... to go out." Prisoner went to the hide door flap and held it back for her. She hesitated. "It's safe," he said. They went out into the dark. She saw no one, but Prisoner who stood at a distance with his back to her, guarding her privacy as he had on the long walk.

Back inside they sat silently. He adjusted his leg and drank water.

"What do they mean, a contest?" she asked shyly.

"A game."

"What kind of game?"

"Skill, endurance, it will be decided."

"Endurance?"

"Who lasts longest wins."

He poured water into another bowl and offered it to her. She declined. He turned his back to her. She watched him curiously. He opened his shirt and washed his hands, face, neck and lastly his feet.

329

Watching him calmly washing, she felt another twinge of pain for him.

"These contests, are they like Mr. Finch said? Are they dangerous? They won't hurt you will they?"

He didn't answer.

"If you win we leave?"

"Yeah."

"There was no one guarding us."

"No, we're guests."

She leaned closer, "Then we can leave? Please, let's go now."

"Won't make it. They'd catch us, then we would be prisoners."

"What's the difference?" she asked bitterly.

"They don't keep prisoners."

"Oh?" She thought for a moment that this was a good thing. Why had he said it so gravely? Then she realized what it meant. Her heart sunk. She reached around him, took some water and rinsed her grimy face and sore feet.

"What can we do?" she asked.

"I won't let anything happen to you." His voice had the same determination it had when he talked to the thief.

"What will you do? What about you?"

"Doesn't matter. You will be alright."

"It does! It does matter! I couldn't stand it if anything happened to you. If it was my fault…"

His head jerked in her direction.

"I'm sorry," she started crying.

"Don't…" He spun around to face her, his arms moving as if to reach for her then dropping to his sides. "Don't … I'm not important. I'm gone."

"No. You've been so good to us. You don't have to do this for me. It's not your responsibility. I'm afraid they'll hurt you and I couldn't stand to see you suffer anymore."

"You are…" he stumbled over the words, "kind … gentle."

With tears on her face, she laughed in surprise and awkwardness and put her hand on his forehead. "You must have a fever again. I am not any of those things. I'm impatient, bumbling…"

"No."

She'd never seen him flustered before, never imagined he could be flustered.

"You... see past the ugly. You're small and pretty to look at, but strong. You see through the dark, like an owl." He cut off his words abruptly.

No one had ever talked to her this way. Her pulse raced. "No, I'm ugly and mousy."

"No. You are ... beautiful. And your spirit carries fresh air of good medicine."

"I thought you didn't like me," she whispered. Did he really say those words?

He looked at her in astonishment then looked away. "Isn't right... for me to think ... speak of you."

"I think of you. I can't stop. Do you know when I first knew how I felt about you?" she asked.

"Don't," he whispered.

There was fear on his face. She thought nothing could scare him. He looked away, but she continued, "I thought there was something special about you almost from the beginning. But, when you stuck your head all the way under the water and then pulled it out, shaking your hair all around like a great wet dog..." She stopped, hoping he couldn't see the red of her burning cheeks in the dim light. It was her turn to look away. She continued, "You aren't like anyone else. You're brave, the bravest person I've ever known. You never complain. You are so strong, I mean outside and inside, your spirit ..." She peeked at his face and her breath stopped at the sight of a tear running down his face. She wiped it with her fingertips. "I'm sorry. I've upset you. I didn't mean to hurt you. Please don't be upset."

He turned his face away. "Don't say these words. Not to me. It's you who is good. How can *you* ... say these words? Don't ..."

She could hear him breathing unevenly. She fingered the furs beneath her. Was this real? Any of this? God only knows what is going to happen to him tomorrow and she'd carelessly hurt him. She wanted badly to soothe him, to protect him. "Please, rest," she patted the furs, her own face wet.

"You."

"I can't. I'm too scared. What will we do? Talk to me?"

He took a deep breath, "Will you rest?"

331

"Yes. Your mother was an Indian?"

He didn't answer. Lou was right he was stubborn. She curled on the thick furs and pulled another over herself.

"Yeah."

"Have you ever been in a building or village like this?"

"Summers with my Grandmother's people."

"And your father? What was he like?"

There was silence for a moment, then he spoke, "He came, went."

"Did you miss him?"

"No."

"I'm sorry about your mother." She felt him start. "You talked about her when your head … when you were sick," she explained apologetically. "I lost my father. It scares me to think about him being gone. It's like a huge black place, like a night sky with no stars." She sat up. "You're not resting. I can't if you won't. Am I bothering you?"

"No."

"Lie down please."

He slid down gingerly, his back to her. She lay down again.

"Do you have a girl?"

"A girl?"

"A special girl, who you like above all others?"

"No."

"Maybe there is someone, but you don't know. Sometimes men are kind of dense about things like that. They don't notice when a girl is fond of them."

He said nothing.

"I'm sorry, that was a rude of me. I'm saying too much."

"I'm a half breed. Whites, Indians… don't want me around."

"That's not true. I do. I want to be with you. I feel safe with you, safer than I've ever felt. Ben does too. You know he does."

She heard his breath catch.

"You should sleep." She popped up and sat over him for a few moments. Then she whispered, "What is your name?"

He took a deep breath. Had he a name? Of course he had, but not for a long time. "Rory. Rory Fletcher."

"Rory Bear Fighter Fletcher."

He gave a little laugh under his breath, "Didn't fight any bear."

"Not exactly, but isn't it the spirit the name suggests that's important? Please try to sleep."

. . .

He had to keep his thoughts straight. He knew with every inch of himself no harm would come to her. He must stay clear-headed, but her words; it was like a dream. His heart that he thought was safely dead was giving him pain. He must be dreaming. She'd asked his name and when she spoke it he became real again. He had to rest, had to be strong for tomorrow. The feelings were tangled, wearing him down. The good darkness of the sleep world was closing over him. He thought he heard his name whispered, "Rory," and felt a blanket laid over him.

Angela opened her eyes to the skin and stick walls. The furs were soft and warm. It was almost pleasant being there, just her and him in a cozy nest. She sat up slowly. He wasn't there. She felt around the furs, as if he could have disappeared into the earth beneath them. He couldn't be gone. "Rory," she whispered. "Rory." She tried to call to him, but it came out as a whisper- croak, like the sound a terrified child makes, trying to summon parents to save her from the monster under the bed. The child wants to shout but is afraid of alerting the beast. "Rory," she cried to the air. "Rory!" He rushed through the opening to her side.

"You alright?"

"I thought you were gone," she panted. "I thought they had taken you."

"No, I just…" he waved an arm. "I didn't want to wake you. You alright?"

"I'm fine. Sorry for the fuss."

"Don't be sorry. Want to come?"

She jumped to her feet and followed him to the outskirts of camp. People who saw them paused briefly in their activities to watch them pass. He led her to a river where trees and brush grew thickly along its banks. He walked away from her. She watched him furtively; he unbuckled and slid off his leg brace. Then he took off Lou's shirt and waded waist deep into the water. He stretched across the water. Angela watched the muscles move across his shoulders as he swam. Then she lay her blouse, skirt, shoes and socks on the bank and walked in with her chemise on. The cold water stung her feet and legs. She couldn't help but gasp when she sat in it. After she swam and soaked her hair she sat on the bank and rubbed her hair between her hands. She saw him wade to the edge of the river where he sat and rubbed the shirt in the water with a rock.

She cleaned her own clothes similarly and spied on him. He tied his hair back and cleaned his teeth with a twig. She found a twig for herself and followed his example. She heard Finch's voice saying Indians were dirty. Given the chance he was much more particular than either Finch or Lou or members of her own family for that matter.

While they were out someone had left more food inside their shelter.

"Eat," Rory said.

"I can't. You should. You'll need your strength for..." She stopped short, trying to cut off a sob before it could surface. Her body was tight with of fear. "Please, be careful." She was afraid to look at him; her feelings were too strong. "Don't do anything that will harm you. Promise, Rory." She touched his hand.

He looked at her hand on his and swallowed. His eyes were large. "Whatever happens... you? your words ... your kindness, this... thanks."

Chapter 25

"What love begins can only be finished by God."

<u>*Les Miserables*</u> *by Victor Hugo*

"... She smiled upon my soul as I lay dying."
... wipin' out the traces of the people
and the places that I've been
teachin' me that yesterday was
somethin that I never thought of tryin
Talkin of tomorrow..."

"Loving Her Was Easier" Kris
Kristofferson

She took his hand and kept it as they walked through the crowd to take their places in the meeting circle. The leader sat, the central figure, his body held naturally erect with inborn nobility. Angela sat behind and a little to the left of Rory as she had the night before. He carefully positioned his bad leg and she ached in sympathy for him. The leader nodded at them. He spoke to the people in his own language then to Rory he said, "There will be a contest for this woman. It will be between Bear Fighter and Wolf." He paused.

"May I speak?" Rory asked.

The leader nodded.

"I am not arguing your decision. I have something to ask you to consider. This woman is a white woman. She would not make a good wife for this man, her hands are soft, she argues. Myself I am half-white with a white's weaknesses. I ask this: if I compete honorably and bravely, if I have done my best to overcome my weakness, whether I win, lose, or die, you will allow her to return to her people."

The leader translated his words. There were murmurs. The challenger protested, but was stopped by an upheld hand.

"You speak well. I will think on your words," the leader said. "Now the game will begin."

A large pot was placed before them.

"Each brave will eat of the unpleasant plants cooked in here," he indicated the pot. "When one can no longer eat the game will end."

"They're poison?" Angela asked Rory. She put a hand on his back. He only gave her an up turn of the corners of his mouth.

Rory's challenger waved his arms at the pot and shrugged his shoulders. He said something and the others around laughed. Rory looked at the leader who signaled his permission. He reached into the pot first and pulled out a handful of soggy greens. Staring at his opponent he put the mass into his mouth, chewed rapidly and swallowed. Angela strained to see what he held. She needed to know what they were to help if he got sick. As soon as the brave grabbed his handful Rory caught up another, not waiting for the other to finish. What was he doing? Angela wondered. Why hurry? Wouldn't it be better to go slow? He did not break his stare at the other or slow the pace. She recognized the stare that he challenged Finch with.

After a while she felt his back grow hot then wet under her hand. The other pointed out Rory's face and spoke in a taunting manner. He and his friends laughed. Angela looked around to see Rory's face flushed and wet. Rory ignored them. The leader translated, "He says you are weakening quickly."

"My white side may look weaker to him, but I'm not the one slowing down to talk, hiding weakness," he said even as he grasped another handful of the green slop. The elder translated and his opponent's face became serious once more.

As the game went on Angela felt his body tense under her hand. He leaned forward. The Indian noted his posture and commented. "You're delaying," Rory retorted tersely, not waiting for a translation. He threw a fistful into his mouth. Angela felt the muscles across his back contract and he bent lower.

"Please slow down," she whispered. He only took another handful. Was he trying to die? Whether here or with Finch, he was a prisoner. She knew with horrible certainty that he'd rather die here as a guest and by his own will, than at Finch's hands. Was that what he meant when he said it didn't matter about him and he was already gone? She studied Wolf; his face was flushed and shining; veins stood out on his forehead. He tried to disguise his discomfort by leaning over to chat with his companions.

Rory swallowed with effort and doubled over even as his hand reached into the pot. Wouldn't it ever run out? He forced himself to swallow and doubled over again.

"Stop Rory, please," she leaned forward and around to see into his eyes; they stared without seeing.

"Rory?" He didn't appear to hear her, still his hand reached. It might be too late. Why had she let this go on? On her knees she worked her way to face him, stopping his arm as he reached once more.

"No more Rory! Stop!" Holding his arm, she turned to the leader. "Stop this! You can't do this! People who are married are joined together by God. You can't separate them by a contest. They are still joined in spirit even if they are separated by space."

The challenger sat crookedly with glazed eyes, not joking now, not saying anything or moving. The elder gazed at her.

"He has proven himself! He won't stop until he dies! Can't you see?" she continued her desperate appeal. She grabbed a handful of the soupy mixture herself. "I'll take it for him!"

The old man raised his hands. There was silence. "I hear your words. I see that Bear Fighter and this woman are one. The contest is over. You may go."

There was much murmuring and then open conversation. Their opponent still did not speak or move. Then his body moved as if in a hiccup. Two of his companions helped him to his feet and carried him away.

"Rory, we can leave," Angela said. She was frightened that he had taken too much poison for her to reach him. "Rory? We can go. Can you walk?"

"Get – me - clear - of - camp," he got out between clenched teeth. He leaned heavily on her as they made their way out. She had no idea where to go. She followed the sun, heading west, staying where there was a good growth of trees for hiding. It took all her strength to hold him. Finally he collapsed, writhing on the ground.

"Rory, please. Lie still. You'll hurt yourself." She couldn't get near him; he rolled and twisted violently. She looked around, ran a ways off, looking for something - she didn't know what, came back.

337

"Go," he moaned. "Leave."

"No, I won't leave you. Help! Someone help!" She ran this way and that calling. She thought she heard something. Yes, she did. "Help over here!" she shouted.

"Hello! Hello!" men's voices called.

"Here! We're here!" she called back.

Three men came through the brush.

"Over here!" She ran to Rory, waving them on.

"Please help, he's poisoned!" She knelt by him.

"We'll take him back to Ma. She'll know what to do," someone said.

They crouched to pick him up. He thrashed all the more and struck out at them.

"Rory, they're trying to help. Let them," she begged.

"No, leave me," came out in an anguished moan.

"He don't know what he's sayin'. Come on boys," a man with salt and pepper hair said.

He fought them, but they were strong and carried him for two miles until they came to some rough cabins with a cow, some oxen in front and odd wagons that seemed familiar.

Dark-haired women hurried to meet them. Not quite believing her eyes, Angela recognized a woman.

"Angela?"

It was Rose.

"It's Rory. The Indians made him eat poison plants."

"In here," Rose called the men to a building. "Poison?" she asked Angela.

"Yes a lot."

The men lay him still fighting on a bed.

"Hold him boys," Rose ordered. "He's going to do himself harm."

"They're hurting him! Don't!" Angela cried.

"You get a look at the plants?" Rose asked. She was searching through satchels and dried herbs hanging on the wall.

"No, they were all mixed together, green and brown. There were leaves, bark. I don't know."

Rose quickly stirred water and some herbs in a bowl. She moved to the bed with the mixture, a mean looking tube and a funnel.

"Hold him tight boys."

338

"What are you doing to him? Stop!" Angela cried.

Rose looked at her severely. "We've got to get the poison out. If I can get this sassafras into him it'll make him vomit it up. It's our best hope. Calm down and help. Go around there and hold his head."

Angela went to the head of the bed and put both her hands on either side of his head. "Rory, hold still. They're trying to help you. Rory, it's me, Angela. Listen to me. Rose is here."

His eyes found hers and he ceased his struggle briefly. That was all Rose needed, she forced the funnel into his mouth and poured the liquid down it. His eyes went wild; he choked and fought. Angela nearly released him. She had betrayed him, helping them to force him against his will.

"There. I think we got most of it in him," Rose said standing back.

He choked and coughed then lay gasping, his eyes shut.

"We can take it from here. Thank you boys," Rose said. "Tell Rosita to come with a bucket of water and an empty one."

As Angela watched his face grew paler, his breathing came faster and faster. Before she could say a word of concern, Rose hoisted his shoulders and supported his head over the bucket Rosita had placed next to the bed just in time; he vomited. Angela cried, frightened by the violence and duration of his vomiting; it seemed he would never stop. To her relief he finally stopped, by passing out. Then to her horror Rose patted his face briskly. "Wake up. Don't pass out yet."

"Let him be. Let him rest!" Angela cried trying to stop her.

Rose held her off with one arm, the other still holding Rory. "He could choke to death while he's out. He can't faint away 'til he's empty." She shook him.

His head rolled, he moaned, "Let me die. No…"

Rose supported him over the bucket as he vomited again. The misery in his voice was too much for Angela.

"I'm sorry, I'm sorry," she sobbed.

When he stopped Rose lay him down. She shook Angela to reach her through her crying.

"Wet this towel. Wash his face and down the front of him," she directed.

Angela did as she was told, then sat on the side of the bed stroking his face and hair. He lay on blankets folded behind his head and shoulders to keep his upper body high, breathing shallowly, his eyes shut. Rose wet his dry, cracked lips and wiped the inside of his mouth with a dripping cloth.

"Got to get water into him as soon as he stops throwing up," she advised.

"No," Rory moaned.

"I got you," Rose said lifting him again.

"No…" he moaned.

"Don't fight it," she said. "Just give in."

"No," he said as another bout took him.

When he passed out from the exertion, Rose lay him on his side, his head tilted forward. Angela wiped his face, her hands shaking.

"He can't take any more. Make it stop."

"We've got to get the poison out," Rose explained. "Whatever it is, it's eating him up. Gave him elderberry bark and sassafras to make him bring it up. I know it's rough on him, but it's best." She unbuttoned his shirt and slid it off.

"It's not fair. He's been through so much. I can't ask him to keep suffering. He wants to die. He can't, he just can't."

"He doesn't want to die. He's just saying that because he's hurting."

"No. You don't understand; he never complains if he's hurt, so he must really be in pain. He wants to die. Finch is right; he wants to escape from him from pain, everything, but I can't be without him. Please don't let him die. I'm sorry Rory." The sobs overtook Angela again.

"Rosita," Rose called through the doorway. "Take her."

Rosita took Angela by the arm and steered her out of the cabin.

"No. I won't leave him!" she cried.

"I'll take care of him," Rose said. "You're no good to him like this. Get rest and food. You can come back when you're calm."

. . .

Everything hurt. No, it was happening again. Someone lifted him. When it was over someone was washing his face and wetting the inside of his mouth. He tried to turn his head away. Couldn't move. His arms were floating in the air. His throat burned all the way down his chest. His ribs ached like he'd been kicked by a horse. Across his back the muscles screamed.

"Swirl this around your mouth and then spit it out," a woman said. He couldn't stop her from lifting his head, but he wouldn't open his mouth. She pried it open with her fingers. He felt something against his lips and cool water in his mouth. Why wouldn't she let him die?

His eyes opened again. He breathed long surface breaths trying to keep his gut calm. The woman was there - he could feel her presence. She held a cup to his mouth.

"Drink."

She wouldn't let him be? He was not going to let anything set off his gut, not even water.

"Just a swallow," she persisted.

"Let me die," he moaned.

"I can't do that."

"Please." It took all his strength to get the words out.

"I know it hurts. You're a real sick kid, but you're not going to die if I can help it."

"Going . . . to die . . . anyway. Please."

She dripped water into his mouth. "You can't up and leave that girl. I'm afraid of what she'll do without you. You got more than yourself to think about now. What about Angela? Isn't she worth staying for?"

What? He saw two brown eyes. This woman? Why was she familiar? Angel? She'd said Angel? He had to stay alive for her? She didn't understand. He rolled his head and his gut flipped. "No. Angel."

"Yes, Angel. Angela," she spoke more gently. "Think of the poor girl. She loves you."

She had it wrong. He had to explain. "No. Angel... she's ... her heart ... is ..."

"Her heart belongs to you. Don't tell me no," she scolded. "I know what I know. You two belong together. What's more, she knows. Hush don't get riled. It's a good thing. Don't you remember? I told you your love line is clear and deep? You take your time and get well. Don't be afraid of love."

341

...

As long as he didn't move it was alright. If he stirred at all his insides turned inside out. Oh no, here it goes again. His eyes watered, his hair stuck to his face and sweat coated his body. It was shorter this time. He didn't black out. Lying exhausted, he recalled what the woman had said about Angel. It couldn't be true. He tried not to think about it. It got his gut contracting.

"I can't keep her away any more. She's fit to be tied. If I don't let her in here she's liable to hurt someone." The woman was talking to him.

"Angel? No. Don't let her... see me. I'm..."

"You think I can keep her away? We'll make you presentable first."

The woman washed his hair, tied it back then washed his face and neck and slipped clean clothes on him. He slipped in and out of blackness. He was so weak any movement sent him back into unconsciousness.

"There," he heard her voice through the swirling in his head. "Now she'll be pleased."

Rosita could not delay Angela any longer. She had helped wash her face though the tears kept coming. She washed and combed her hair, put a simple clean frock on her and had tried to make her eat.

"If you eat a good meal and calm down, Mama says you can see him."

Angela's eyes flashed angrily, she nearly pushed Rosita aside to rush out of the cabin they were in.

"You can't keep me away."

She ran to the cabin where Rory lay. His head was turned to the side, nearly off the bed, his arm hanging over. She touched his face.

"He's cold," she whispered, jumping to her feet and searching for blankets. She covered him with two she took from the other bed in the cabin.

"You're going to make him too hot," Rose cautioned. "He feels cold to your hands. He's not."

342

Angela put his arm back on the bed. She sat on the dirt floor, her face close to his. He opened his lids halfway.

"Rory," she whispered. "Please don't leave me. I'm sorry. I know it's not what you want. I'm selfish to ask. Please stay with me." She kissed his forehead and he shut his eyes.

When Rose came to check on them Angela was asleep on the floor next to his bed. She covered her with a blanket.

Angela woke and sat up to watch Rory sleeping. Rose handed her tea and bread spread with preserves. She set them on the floor beside her and felt his face.

"He still feels cold," she told Rose.

"He's not. You eat. We've got to get food and water into him when he wakes," Rose said.

"I hate to ask. He may not keep it down. It's terrible for him when it comes back up."

"It may not. We have to try; he is getting weaker by the minute. If we must, the boys and I can force it, but I'm afraid it'd be too much for him." She looked at Angela with narrowed eyes.

"No," Angela said quickly. "I'll try to convince him."

"He's probably strained his back and the muscles around his ribs. We can bind them for support."

Angela sat attentively until Rory opened his eyes again. His face softened when he saw her. Rose wrapped his ribs with cloth, moving him as little as possible; lifting his head was enough to make him pass out.

"Rory, please try to drink this," Angela asked when he came to.

"Can't."

"Just a little and I won't ask for another hour. Try. I'll help."

She slipped a hand behind his head and he took two sips of weak tea with honey. His gut contracted after. He lay breathing shallowly, keeping it down. Every hour she'd cajole him into taking a few sips more. The next day Rose tried to give him bread soaked in milk. He turned away from it.

"Don't ask," he said.

She looked at Angela. "Tell him," she mouthed.

"Only a little," Angela pleaded. She hated pressuring him. His eyes looked so large and pained in his face.

"He's got to," Rose encouraged her.

343

"Please Rory," Angela begged.

He couldn't refuse her he ate a small piece, shortly after a change in his breathing made her regret insisting. He pulled his left knee closer to his chest, inhaled hard and let the air out slowly. His face was strained. He curled in on himself, the spasms squeezing his middle. The veins in his neck grew more pronounced. Angela put a hand on his damp forehead and cast a pleading look to Rose. She came to them and held him over the bucket, saying, "I've got you. Let it go."

After he passed out Angela wept, "It's my fault."

"Sh," Rose reprimanded her. "Take care of him." She took the bucket and left the building.

Angela leaned over the bed and watched him. Little moans came out each time he exhaled. "Uh," he breathed. A pain hardened in her own abdomen. Hearing his unconscious complaints was too much; tears started again. Before she could wipe them one dropped on his face. His eyes opened. "Angel?" He searched her face anxiously. "Alright?" He reached to touch her face. She took his hand.

"Me? It's you who's not alright. I wish I could take it away from you." She brushed his hair back.

"You do." His eyes shut.

"It's not fair, you of all people. You didn't have to come. It should have been me," she whispered.

"No." His eyes opened. "Won't let anything happen to you."

"I believe you," she said.

His mouth turned up and he smiled and closed his eyes again. She lay her palm on his forehead. He shivered.

"You're cold." She pulled the blanket higher on his chest.

"No, not cold."

"Here," she put one hand behind his head and gave him a sip of water. "You don't mind me here with you? Near?"

He bit his lower lip. "No."

She sighed. "Oh good. I can't bear to be away from you, but I don't want to make you feel worse. You use to not want me near." She couldn't speak. She felt a huge dark hole was eating up the space behind her and she would tumble into it at any moment. What she felt for him was frightening. What if he didn't feel the same? Why would he? Why should he? He was incredible. She was just ...

He rolled his head slightly from side to side "No." He squeezed his eyes shut. "I was … filthy … you are clean … beautiful."

"You are beautiful. Even before I saw your face. I thought … Rory you are the most special person there is. There is no one else like you."

He blinked and stared widely at her. Was she real? Or was she the angel in his dreams. That was it; he was confusing the dream world with the waking world. Her name was Angel and he had dreamed about an angel telling him that his mother was safe in the spirit world. The fresh breeze girl, she couldn't be saying these things, not to him. He squeezed his eyes tightly shut. She touched his eyelashes with her fingertips. He shivered.

"You are cold. I'm going to find more blankets."

"No. Not cold." He reached to stop her. She held his hand and sat on the edge of the bed. He felt her hand trembling.

"Cold?"

"No. I'm scared. I love you so much."

"Angel you can't … I'm not …" He couldn't breathe. He tried to sit up, but the swirling in his head threatened to shut out the light.

"Sh, please lie still. Don't be upset. I shouldn't have told you."

"Angel … I'm going … he's going to … hang me. There's no … time ahead with me."

"No. I won't let him." Sobs broke out in waves. She hid her face on the mattress beside him. "Please get better. Don't leave me. I won't let anyone hurt you ever again."

She felt his arm over her. While he held her she felt him shuddering silently, it stopped her sobs. She whispered, "You won't leave me will you? I mean even when you're well you won't turn away from me."

"I can't."

She woke feeling warm and safe. Rory's arm was still across her shoulders. She lay quietly, not wanting to disturb him, not wanting to ever leave this place beside him. She carefully tilted her head to look at him.

"Are you real?" he asked.

"Yes," she whispered.

He put his hand on the side of her face, his fingers in her hair. Every inch of her skin was suddenly alive with tiny explosions of joy, but her heart was filled with fear for him.

Rory safely passed the next critical days. Angela seldom left his side. He ate and drank a little each hour, gradually building the amounts. After eating he would be seized by the stomach cramps, but he kept everything down. He would tense, drop his head back, pull his knee up and grip the blankets. Angela learned not to let her empathy incapacitate her, to help him take long slow breaths. She wiped the sweat from his face and rubbed his tight sore muscles. She bunched blankets behind his shoulders to raise him up and rested his right leg over another. Rory was too sick and weak to protest the intimacy of she what did for him, and it seemed to both that it was only natural. At night she would lay beside him, he'd put an arm over her and they slept. Just before falling asleep one night Rory said, "Want to ask you something."

"Yes."

"Don't be there."

"Where?" She wondered if he were talking in his sleep.

"When Finch hangs me."

"He won't. We won't go back. Don't talk about it."

He didn't he was asleep.

. . .

One morning he woke and sat up slowly. His arms quivered with the effort, his muscles complained and his head felt like it was spinning. Angel wasn't there. He pushed down the blankets that she had laid across him.

"Hot?" Rose asked from across the room. "Tell her you don't need all those blankets."

He shook his head. He looked around the room for Angela.

"Rosita got her to take some time to take care of herself. She convinced her by telling her to make herself pretty for you," Rose said.

"How many days?"

"How many days? How many days have you been here? Five."

"Five? Her family. Got to get her back."

"She thinks you two are not going back."

"Can't keep her from them. Not right."

"Have you talked to her about this?"

"She won't talk about it."

"She's not about to go without you. You're in for a heap of trouble if you try to make her." She looked at him sharply, "You wouldn't send her away without you would you?"

"No. I'll bring her."

"If you go back you'll be that man's prisoner."

He nodded calmly.

"You might convince her if she's sure she won't lose you."

"Can't. He's going to hang me."

"Don't be so sure. You have a long lifeline. I can't tell you how it'll happen. I just know. You won't break her heart will you?" She felt bad about this last question because she heard his breath catch.

"How can she… care? I have nothing for her."

"What do you mean nothing? Can you hunt, build a home, keep her safe?"

"Yeah."

"You have plenty, brains, skill, love. You do love her?"

He swallowed and looked down. His throat tightened. He couldn't speak.

"Well then if you think you only have a short time you deserve a bit of happiness. Don't you think she deserves to be happy too? Don't push her away thinking you're protecting her. She's a smart young woman. She knows her own heart and mind."

"Can't push her away. Don't have the strength. Can't keep her from family either. Have to take her back."

"You won't be able to force her. She might go back if she's confident in your love. Are you going to make it honest? After all you've been sleeping together," she teased.

"You mean marry? Would she?"

Rose laughed. "She thinks you are the earth and the sun. I guess for her you are. She could do worse."

Rory waited, sitting on the edge of the bed fighting the waves of weakness that threatened to topple him. When Angela came into the cabin, her hair clean and soft, braided down her back and her face lit with happiness at the sight of him sitting up, he almost lost his resolve. She ran to him. "Are you alright? I'm sorry I was away all morning."

"Angel." He took her hand and waited for her to sit on the bed next to him. "We have to go back."

"You can't. Finch is there."

"Your family…"

"I want to be with you not them."

"Think of them. Not knowing if you are … alright. Where you are."

She heard again her mother's scream and saw Ben kicking and striking the Indians, his face stained with tears. She hesitated, then said, "You can't go back. I won't leave you. Maybe we could send them word that I'm fine. We could go far away where Finch won't find you."

He shook his head. "You would be happy?"

"Yes, as long as I can be with you."

He exhaled slowly. "Finch or someone like him will seek me out. I can't let you live … always looking over your shoulder. If they find you with me, they'll think you helped me get away. Your family … I can't be a … wall between you and them. Can't Angel. Not right. You would be sad. I couldn't stand by … seeing you sad."

She saw in his eyes the strength of his determination.

"What are you saying?" she whispered. "I thought…" She couldn't breathe. "You want me to leave?" The black hole was opening again.

"We go back."

"We? Together?"

"Yes."

"You can't. I won't. I won't watch Finch abuse you. And my mother, she'll be horrible. I can't pretend I don't love you. Rory, I won't."

He drew a long shaky breath again. "I told you I won't let anything happen to you. You are better off with your family. I have nothing, not time, nothing."

She couldn't face the meaning of his words. He saw the terrible fear in her eyes and felt sick. He fought a wave of weakness brought on by the power of his feelings for her.

"You have me," she said barely audibly, "if you want me. We can take care of each other."

She was trembling; he couldn't endure it. He put his arms around her. She clung to him tightly her head against his chest, hearing his heartbeat, which seemed to be the source of her own life.

He couldn't move. Finally he kissed the top of her head. "We go back together. Our spirits are already joined?"

She was silent pondering his words for a moment then suddenly comprehending she was overcome with a surge of joy. She hid her happy tears against his chest. "Yes. Don't you believe? "

He took a long breath, "We are together. I don't understand.... Should we ... would you like the ceremony that makes us one?"

They had a simple ceremony with Rose's family. They sat outside, Rory being too weak to stand, while Rose's husband Alex read from the Bible. To both it seemed only a confirmation of what they already knew, yet not quite real at the same time. To Angela it gave strength to their bond. Now no one could separate them. When it was over they were congratulated with toasts and food, but Rory was exhausted. They returned to the little cabin. Rory lay on the bed and let Angela adjust his leg and the blankets without protest. She sat on the edge watching him.

"Sorry," he said, his eyes shut, "not much of a husband."

"Don't say that. You are a wonder to me. How can you say that?" She kissed his forehead.

He smiled the way he did with just the ends of his mouth turning up. "My Grandmother's people ... when they become husband and wife ... they promise to *be* each other."

Angel lay next to him on the bed, her head on his shoulder. "Oh Rory that is beautiful."

Chapter 26

*"Come share of my breath and my
substance
and leave the lost dreams of hard times.
Lead me from tortured dreams
Childhood themes of nights alone."*

*"Pictures at an Exhibition" Emerson,
Lake and Palmer*

Before they found Rory and Angela, Rose and Alex and Rosita had shared the cabin, which they now occupied. The entire clan was crammed into the other for sleeping. But Rose and Alex were in and out of the cabin for things they needed during the day or to work on rainy days. Rose hung blankets from a rope to give them privacy. Angela blushed when she did this.

One morning while they slept, Angela felt Rory's body jolt. He made a sound of surprise and pain. She sat up and studied him anxiously. His shoulder where her head had rested was wet with sweat. His face softened in a smile when his eyes opened on her.

"What's wrong?" she asked.

"Nothing."

"You jumped in your sleep. Do you hurt?"

"No, a dream." He sat up, pushing the blankets down to his waist.

She put her palm on his forehead. "You have a fever. Rory you're doing too much."

"No, hot in here."

She heard Rose moving in the cabin and pushed the blanket aside. "He has a fever again."

Rose came in and felt Rory's forehead. He tried to move away. She laughed. "You're cooking the poor man with all those blankets."

"It's cold at night," Angela protested a little defensively.

"I'm... not used to... being inside, "Rory ducked his head apologetically.

Rose laughed heartily and wagged a finger at Angela. "I told you."

Two nagging concerns plagued Rory and drove him to take interest his own health for the first time since his capture. One was the gap between Angela and her family. He worried that it was widening with each passing day. The other was his uselessness, his inability to repay these people who had taken them in with much trouble to themselves.

First Angel, now these people ... that spirits so kind walked the earth startled him. He forced himself to eat and drink because she wanted him to, dreading the waves of pain and nausea that followed. If he ate only a little at a time he could keep it down. He tried to walk about. His spinning head wouldn't let him get more than a few yards. He had to be content to sit outside, letting the healing powers of the sun and air strengthen his body.

This morning the men were cutting and storing wood for winter. He could at least stack. He started to walk across the clearing, but had to put his hands out to stop the ground rising to meet him. Rose caught him by the arm.

"Honey, where are you trying to get to? How are you going to get better if you don't give yourself time?" She turned him around.

"Can help," he protested.

"You need to rest."

"Got to help. All you've done..."

She started to dismiss his words until she saw the seriousness in his eyes. "Sure we can use all the hands we can get. Here you sit on this stool and I'll bring you work."

Rory was a wonder to Angela more than ever, his beauty, his strength. Her happiness was all the air, the nourishment she required. She never felt tired. His health was the only dark shadow; she was anxious about him pushing his limits. And once in a while the fleeting fear that this was only a dream frightened her, but mostly she felt they were safe, secure in the sanctuary of this family who had enfolded them into their limitless hearts. The women brought him tea or water. They scolded him to rest and left their children to play at his feet when he was sitting outside in the sun. The men stopped to chat or lend an arm.

352

Angela was confident enough to leave his side for short spans knowing the entire clan watched out for him. She and Rosita went to the river to wash clothing and took advantage of the time to bathe themselves.

"Your husband is much stronger," Rosita said.

"Yes. He's better."

"Must be married life."

Angela looked up to see Rosita was grinning at her wickedly.

"Oh we haven't … I mean, …" Her face was hot. "He's ill."

"Soon." Rosita laughed and splashed her. "Like I said, he's getting stronger."

Angela looked away.

"You're not scared are you?" Her tone became serious.

"No. I… I don't know if I'll know … what to do."

"You'll know," Rosita said kindly.

They sat in the river as they had once before on the trail. Angela looked down at her body, something she did not like to do. Although she was amazed by the ways her body reacted to him she was not disappointed by the delay of consummation. He was beautiful, his body sun-kissed and hard, his features finely etched, his hair black with strands of brown running through. Her body was pudgy, her breasts small. She noted now how her body was more taut then it had been before they started on this journey. Her arms, hands and neck were browned making a striking contrast to the rest of her. Would he mind the brown or the white? Would he rather she had more soft weight or did he prefer a lean figure?

One early morning Angela slipped out of bed. Rory stirred.

"Rest," she whispered. "I'll be back in three shakes of a lamb's tail." She padded barefoot outside to relieve herself. Rory was sitting up when she returned. His face registered sleepy confusion.

"Three? Lambs?" He asked.

She giggled. "It's an expression. It means quickly. Are you awake?"

She touched the scar from the rifle butt that trailed down his forehead to his eyebrow.

"Awake," he said.

She stood before him in a thin chemise. The sunlight streaming through the spaces in the walls behind her showed the outline of her figure. She touched a scar on his shoulder, another fading memento from Finch, not permanent, she thought. He shivered.

"Are you ticklish?" She asked.

He shook his head and took the hand she touched him with. He blew out an exhale.

"I didn't mean to wake you." She sat down next to him. "You're not rested." She touched his face.

He turned his head to her touch and kissed her. A different kiss than they had done before; a kiss that melded them together as if they could not be separated. She reached both arms around him, her palms against his shoulder blades. He released the kiss to lay her on the bed. She feared for a moment he would leave to start the day. She reached her arms up to keep him and he lay beside her, leaning on one elbow. She caught his face to bring him close for the kiss again while her fingertips traced over his collarbones brushing light as feathers, over his chest, his ribs, greedy to read him. He shivered, his body tense.

He took her free hand and held it, studying their intertwined fingers. He sucked in his breath when she laid the flat of her other palm against his flat hard stomach. Then he kissed the back of her hand. She wanted that kiss for her lips and she lifted her head to claim it. He ran his fingers down her wrist softly as if she were made of fine bone china that could shatter, down her forearm, up to her shoulder. He traced her neck and chin, the indentation where her neck met her sternum... The kisses changed from not being content to meld to wanting to take each into the other. It was her turn to gasp as his fingers touched her.

Their bodies demanded each other. Still Rory was careful, cautious, gentle. "Alright? He asked.

"Mmm," was all she could say.

It burned a little, but her body screamed for him and she feared she would loose control. Was he feeling the same? His chest was rising and falling, sweat shone lightly along his collarbones. It was exquisitely delicious. How could he bear it? Little sounds came from her.

"Alright?" he asked again before he went deeper. Her back arched and their bodies shuddered.

They lay as one for a while then he rolled to lie beside her, tucking his arm under her head. Tears ran down her face, the entire surface of her body tingled. She wiped the tears lest he misinterpret them. She felt as though they were too far apart now. He was breathing quickly and she was suddenly worried for him. She propped herself up on one elbow. "Are you alright?"

Something flickered in his eyes. Offense? Irritation?

"I mean... it's not too soon? I mean ... you're not too ill?" Oh this wasn't good she didn't want him to think she was implying he wasn't capable of this...

He frowned. She ran her palm lightly over his chest then reached over him to squeeze him closer. "Mine," she said. Then she giggled and hid her face against his shoulder. She felt a little laugh escape him, the first clear laugh she'd ever heard from him.

Later Angela helped the women prepare food for the winter, all the while keeping a protective eye on Rory. When she went to him in the middle of the day she found him deftly sewing hides and she was filled with awe again. Was there anything he could not do? Still she pleaded with him to go inside to rest. Though he didn't want to he would not refuse her. She was glad she insisted because he no sooner hit the bed and he was asleep. She watched him for a while then returned to help the women.

It was a glorious bright day. The women laughed and talked while they worked, the men sang and mocked each other while they built a shelter for the animals.

"Wagon coming!" Alex called out. Angela didn't need to see. Before it worked its way through the trees she knew by the terrible hollow horror in her gut whose it was.

The men set their tools down and went to greet the newcomers. Alex held the horses and Michael helped Lou climbed down. Angela was paralyzed. Rosita stood beside her and put a hand on her arm. Finch emerged, his big red face peering around, then Ben jumped out. Finch caught him by the arm. "Stay here boy."

When her mother and sister cautiously stepped out Angela was poised to flee, before she could Finch caught sight of her. "Hello? There she is!" he shouted.

She ran to the door of the cabin.

"Angela!" Clara cried.

"Wait," Rose held out her arms, "Don't just barge over."

"That's my daughter," Clara said. "You can't keep me from her!"

"No one's trying to keep her from you. I just want you to understand a few things first."

Angela froze before the cabin. She had to keep herself between them and Rory, but now she had almost led them to him.

"Listen to me," Rose was saying. Her husband and sons barred the way to Angela.

"No one here is gonna be forced to do anything they don't wanta," Alex said.

"Forced? What are you talking about?" Clara's voice was shrill. "Angela!"

Barton Finch gave Ben's arm a jerk. He looked past the men's shoulders and feigning politeness called, "Come here girl. You know us. Your poor mother is distraught. Come to her."

"Calm down. Let her come to you," Rose said.

Angela gripped the doorframe. Should she run? Lead them away from Rory?

"Don't frighten her," Rose repeated, "Let her come to you."

"Frighten her? My own daughter? Get out of my way!" Clara demanded.

"I've got to talk to her," Barton insisted. He craned his neck, trying to see around the blockade of bodies. "Come on girl. Where is the prisoner?" he called. "It's important. Tell me."

"Come Angela," Rose beckoned, "Come talk to them. We won't let them make you do anything you don't want to."

Angela walked slowly to Finch and her family, wanting to turn and run with every step, but if she stayed still or went in the cabin they might follow her to him. The protective line yielded.

"Ange!" Ben, free from Finch, hugged her, nearly knocking her over.

Her mother held her at arm's length, looking her up and down. Her eyes moistened. "Are you well? You look well enough."

"I'm fine."

"Are you?" her mother lowered her voice confidentially.

"Yes, mother." Beyond her mother Lillian sat on the wagon's steps crying.

"We've been ill with worry," her mother said, seeing her glance at her sister. "Go to Lillian and reassure her."

Angela went to her sister's arms, dragging Ben who was still attached to her. They held each other.

"What did they do to you?" Lillian asked. "No don't tell me. I don't want to know."

"Nothing, Lilly. They just fed us and gave us a place to sleep."

Angela looked frantically back. Finch was questioning Rose and Alex. Lou stood with them.

"How did you get away from the Indians?" Ben asked. "Where's Prisoner?"

Clara walked to her children. "Did these people save you? Did you tell them what happened to you? I mean when you were with the savages? Remember, you don't have to speak of it, not to anyone. Mr. Finch says …"

"No." Angela shook her head. The questions kept coming and she didn't know how she was going to protect Rory. She had to get between him and them. She blurted, "Rory saved us."

"Rory?" Barton Finch was suddenly there. "Who is Rory? Which one is Rory?" He turned to the family. "Where is…?"

Finch speaking his name was too much for Angela; she sprinted to the cabin door, spun and watched them from that vantage point.

"Ange?" Ben called.

"Stay away!" she yelled.

"Angela? It is your family," Clara called. "Come to us. Everything will be fine."

"They've agreed to come willingly," Rose said, coming between them again. "You all calm down, give them a little time."

"They?" Finch asked losing patience. "What do you mean, 'They'? Where is my prisoner? Is he here or not?"

Angela backed into the doorway.

"Is he in there, girl!" Barton Finch lost all semblance of patience. "Let me through." He shouldered past Rose to the cabin. Clara, Lou and Ben followed him. Angela blocked the doorframe with her body. He was too big; she wouldn't be able to stop him. She reached into the cabin and snatched up the loaded rifle Alex kept ready.

"Stay back. You stay away from him." She pointed the barrel at Finch. "I swear I'll shoot you if you go near him." Her hands and voice shook.

"Angela?" Clara gasped.

After his initial shock, Finch turned to Clara. "Remember what she's been through. It addles the brain." He smiled his cold smile at Angela, "Put down the gun Miss. You've been through a terrible experience, but it's over now. Your people are here."

She raised the rifle. "I mean it. Stay back. He's sick. The Indians made him take poison."

"Angela, put the gun down," her mother ordered.

"No. Stay away. Don't any of you dare go near him."

"You all calm down," Rose said. "They've agreed to go with you. Just back off and give them a little time. Put the gun down honey." She waved for her sons and husband to stay back.

"No," Angela said, "I can't. He will try to take Rory again. You don't know him. He's cruel."

"No one is going to force you or Rory to do anything," Rose tried to convince her. "We won't let them. You trust us."

"You can't believe him. He'll hurt him."

Lou walked right up to Angela while everyone else held back. "No one's gonna hurt him, Miss."

"Put the rifle down before someone gets hurt, and return to your family," Finch smiled.

"Get back! He is my family!"

"Don't be silly," Finch held his hands up. "He's a criminal. You need to return to your family. I'll take him. I promise I won't hurt him."

. . .

A commotion outside the door woke Rory. He got to his feet too quickly; a wave of dizziness dropped him back on the edge of the bed. Before his head cleared, Ben burst into the room and stood before him with a big grin on his face. "Hey."

"Hey," Rory smiled warmly.

"Your name is Rory?"

He nodded. It was good to see the boy.

"You don't look so good. Ange says you're sick. She says the Indians…"

Raised voices in the door interrupted him. Rory jumped to his good leg just as Angela backed into the room, holding a rifle on Finch, who came after. Lou, then the mother and others crowded cautiously in the doorway.

"Angel?" Rory said.

"Rory, sit!" she said, stopping him where he stood. Her eyes were on Finch. The veins in her forearms and hands stood out as she clenched the gun.

"Angel," he reached a hand cautiously to her. He didn't dare push her further, desperate as she was, but he wanted to protect her from her own rashness, calm her.

"Stay there," she said.

He remained where he was to keep her calm. "We talked of this," he reasoned. "We have to go."

"Angela, enough," Clara blurted bluntly. "Put the gun down and come with us."

Angela's eyes flashed angrily at her mother. "We'll come if Rory says we have to. Stay away from him! I mean it!" Finch had shifted his feet.

"Fine, fine, I won't touch him, just put the gun down and come along," he said.

"No! Stay back!"

Finch took a step back. "You can't hold that thing forever. Be reasonable. I'll stay back. You both come along."

Suddenly she realized he was right. She glanced back at Rory. Though he remained on the edge of the bed he was poised to come to her aid in a second. She didn't want him to jump forward giving Finch an excuse to grab for him. How could she protect him day and night? She couldn't hold a gun constantly her arms were tired already. What if she fell asleep at some point? She and Rory had agreed, but they couldn't go. She couldn't see how.

"Get out!" she yelled. "All of you get out!" She fumbled for the rifle's trigger. She didn't know how to fire a rifle, but she would figure it out.

"Easy Miss," Lou moved between Finch and Clara to stand next to her. "I'll make certain he stays clear of the Kid." He spoke low in her ear. "If yer wantin' to come along, I'll help you. If yer comin', it's best we be on our way soon's possible." He recognized a familiarity between her and the Kid. This was more than just her feeling sorry for him. He turned to Finch and Clara. "You all git. Let them figger what they're gonna do." He put his hands on the rifle and spoke quietly to Angela, "Don't worry none, there's enough folks here watchin' out for you," and he took the rifle from her hands. "Go on git!" He motioned with the gun at Finch and Clara.

Clara gasped, "How dare you!"

"I said git!"

"Very well. A moment. We'll give you a moment," Finch said.

When Clara and Finch backed out of the cabin Lou told Rory and Angela, "What you decide is your business."

"We go," Rory said.

"We can't," Angela said. "He's right I can't keep a gun on him day and night."

Rory took both her hands and looked into her eyes. "Angel we have to."

Lou watched them. "These good folks seem to have taken' a liken' to you two. I'll ask 'em if they can spare a weapon, seein' as them Indians took all of ourn. Between you and me," he said to Angela, "we'll make certain Finch minds hisself. Leaves the Kid here alone. He has no weapons no more."

"I'll help too," Ben said. He had stood next to Rory afraid to move, daunted as Rory by his sister's ferocity.

"Come on boy," Lou said. "You and me will go outside and talk to these folks. Let your sister and the Kid talk it over."

Angela followed them to the door.

She could hear her mother appealing to Finch. "What is wrong with her Mr. Finch? Please give me you arm. I feel faint."

"It'll be alright Ange. Lou and me will help," Ben said. "Want me to guard outside?"

"Come on boy," Lou said. He gave her back the rifle. "You keep this. The boy and I'll warn you if Finch comes near."

Angela looked out the door to make sure Finch and her mother were still a safe distance way. They were talking and walking halfway back to the wagon. Rose was with them. Lou went to Alex.

"Angel?"

She went to Rory and he put his arms around her and held her tightly.

360

"I don't want to go. I'm afraid. Please, let's stay here."

"Have to. It'll be alright."

"I'm afraid of what'll happen to you. And … I'm sorry it's so selfish, I'm afraid things will change between us, you'll pull away."

"No, nothing will change."

"You are still my husband?"

"Yeah."

She looked up at him. "Promise you won't do too much. You'll let me take care of you?"

He smiled his soft smile and nodded, brushing her cheekbone with his fingers.

There wasn't much to prepare for leaving. They had only the clothes they came with and one change Rose and Alex had given them. The family surrounded them and gave them gifts, a hairbrush, sinew thread, bone needles for sewing and venison. Rory tightened his jaw and swallowed emotions too intense. The sound of Lou clearing his throat warned them before he came through the safety ring of their adoptive family. He held a rifle and took one of the parcels for them. Ben, close on his heels draped Rory's arm over his own shoulder and helped him to the wagon looming before them. Finch stood before it with her mother and her sister.

"Ridin' with me?" Lou asked.

Rory nodded affirmatively.

"Rory?" Angela asked fearfully. He was leaving her already?

He took her hands and looked in her eyes. "Be with your family. Talk to them."

"You need to rest inside," she said.

"I'll keep a close eye on him," Lou said, "Don't worry."

Rory released her and climbed to his seat. He smiled down on her reassuringly.

Angela entered the wagon last. They sat in silence for a long time. Lillian stared at her through the shadows as if she were an apparition. Finally Ben asked, "What happened? What did those Indians do to Prisoner - I mean Rory? How did you get away? Did he have to kill them?"

"Benjamin, Angela does not have to speak of it," Clara said. "And you should not ask."

361

"You don't want to talk about it?" Ben whispered.

Angela put a finger to her lips.

They sat in silence until Finch began to snore. Angela turned her back on him, her mother and sister to face Ben. She told him the story, ignoring her mother and sister trying to listen in. When she reached the part about marrying Rory, Ben could no longer keep quiet.

"Rory is my brother now?"

"Of course not. Do not be ridiculous, Benjamin," Clara said. "Your sister has been through a terrible ordeal. She needs time to rest and forget. Do not speak of this any more Angela."

"How did you bear it?" Lillian asked. "I would die of fright. I really would die. I'm about ready to now."

Angela turned around. Her sister's eyes looked vacant. She hadn't spent much time with her since the robbery. Lillian had mostly hidden in the wagon day and night. "I was terribly scared, but Rory made me feel safe. He kept saying he wouldn't let anything happen to me. Then the Indians, they treated us like guests. Rory explained we were guests, but we couldn't leave. They gave us food and our own place to stay. It was so interesting being with them I almost forgot to be scared. Their leader was like a king, dignified and wise. And the children were beautiful. You should see the clothes they wear."

"There won't be any more Indians will there?" Lillian peered around the wagon.

"I wish I could have been with you," Ben said wistfully.

"No Ben. It was interesting, but not fun. Rory almost died. If he wasn't so strong ... if Alex and his sons hadn't found us...," she couldn't go on.

"Angela," Clara spoke carefully, "You are confusing your gratitude to him with other emotions. Give yourself time to get over this."

"You and Rory are really married?" Ben asked.

"No, of course she is not," Clara said.

Angela took a deep breath. Instead of retorting, she remembered Rory's quiet words: "Talk to them."

"We are married," she said levelly. "It's not gratitude. I knew how I felt about him before the Indians took us."

"Let's not talk of this anymore," Clara said. "Let's be content that Angela is restored to us."

After having been constant companions for days, the ride's separation seemed endless to Angela. She rushed out first when the wagon stopped. Lou helped Rory down; the ride had taken a toll on him. Ben accompanied them, letting his new brother lean on him. Angela cast anxious glances at Finch. Lou was the only one with a weapon now. He showed it to her by lifting it briefly before going about his work. Finch himself stayed with her mother and sister. He leaned close to Clara talking to her.

Clara did not object when Angela, Ben and Rory stayed together. With Ben as sentry and Lou within sight, Angela prepared a simple meal of biscuit and tea for Rory. The three of them sat together just outside the light of the crackling fire.

When the darkness crept in Clara called, "Angela it is cold. Come inside before the night air makes you ill."

Angela stood up and took Rory's hand.

He shook his head. "I sleep here. Go."

"I'm not leaving you," she said. Fear rose up her throat at the very thought.

"It's cold for you. Be with your family."

"Aren't you and I family?" she asked. She leaned over to wrap his blanket around his shoulders. He drew in a sharp breath as if in pain.

"Rory, you promised if we came things wouldn't change between us."

"They've been without you. I can't go in there. It would … disturb them."

"They know I'm here now. I don't care if they are disturbed or not."

"Angel. I can't."

She looked around. Finch had disappeared inside the tent. Lou, standing before it, nodded at her. "Stay with him," she told Ben. She climbed inside the wagon and found three blankets and a thick rug.

"Angela, are you looking for something?" Lillian asked sleepily.

"No. Go to sleep."

"Angela, come to your blankets," Clara said. She was arranging bedding for her. "Where are you going? Angela! Come here," she called after her.

363

"Thank you Ben," she said when she rejoined them. "You'd better go inside."

"You're sleeping outside? I want to sleep outside too."

"Mother is fretting. Please," she insisted. "You can help by keeping her calm."

She and Rory rolled the rug out. She bunched the blanket she had given him that day so long ago, under his knee and they pulled the others over themselves. He lay on his back; she put her head on his chest and rested to the comforting sound of his heart beating. Later she bolted upright at the sound of footsteps.

"Ben and pup," Rory told her calmly without moving. Ben lay himself on Rory's right side, pulling the blankets to cover himself and Traveler as well.

. . .

Rory hardly dared breathe for fear of disturbing them and shattering this moment that might not be real. The air was tingling cold on his face. The rest of him was warm, too warm, but if he pushed the coverings down Angela and Ben would be cold. They were his to take care of, these two, if only for a short while. A gift he didn't deserve. This time he wouldn't fail.

When Angela awoke in the morning the outside of the blankets was decorated with frost. Cozily warm under the covers, she hated to move. Ben sat up, yawning loudly.

"Sh," she warned, but Rory was already awake. He'd been lying still, trying to decipher if he was dreaming. He thought he couldn't be; all his dreams were nightmares.

"Brr," Ben stood, "Are you coming?" He held out a hand to help Rory.

"Cold?" Rory asked Angela. He slipped his blanket over her.

"No, I was perfectly snug all night."

"Me too," Ben added. "It's much better sleeping outside than in the stuffy old wagon."

Later Angela got Rory his breakfast; his stomach would not have tolerated the coffee or the meat fat and flour mixture that Lou had started for everyone else. He would have quietly set it aside and not

364

eaten at all. The three of them had finished their breakfast together when Clara called to her. "Angela please join us." She and Lillian stood with their satchels of toiletries.

"Go," Rory said softly.

"No."

"Angel, I can't be …between. Please don't put me there," he said. The sadness in his eyes compelled her. He got to his feet with Ben's help. "I'll help Lou."

"You're not well enough. Please rest."

"I'll stay with him," Ben volunteered.

She was loath to leave him. Finch was seated comfortably facing the opposite direction, drinking his coffee.

"Angel, I'll be right there," Rory said. He went to kiss her, saw her mother watching and pulled back. Using Ben for support he walked unsteadily to Lou.

"Yell as loud as you can if you even think Finch is coming near. Promise Ben," she called after them.

"Sure, I can yell very loud. Or I could whistle. Want me to whistle?"

"Whatever is loudest."

Angela joined her mother and sister, but refused to go where she couldn't see Rory.

"I can't do my grooming in plain sight," Lillian complained. Her mother warned her with her eyes to indulge Angela. They went partially behind the wagon. Angela stayed where she could keep both Finch and Rory in her sight.

"Wouldn't you like to wash?" Clara asked.

"We did earlier."

Lillian brushed her hair mechanically, staring at her sister all the while, until Clara took the brush from her and put it up. Angela looked at her mother in question. Clara looked away.

"Lillian are you alright?" she asked her sister.

"Why do you ask? Do I look poorly?"

"No. You look fine."

When Rory and Ben reached Lou, he squinted at them and asked, "What do you think yer doin'?"

"Helping," Rory answered.

"No you don't. You sit by here."

"Got to be good for something," Rory said. He reached to take a horse's lead rope from the older man.

"Stubborn," Lou muttered. He teetered off on his stiff legs to get the other horses.

While he held the horses and helped harness them Rory kept an eye on Finch. Just as Angela watched to make certain the lawman stayed away from him, he was equally wary of the man getting near her. He knew well the depths of Finch's violence through what he did and what he threatened to do to him even to his dead body. Because she was with her mother didn't mean she was safe from him. Finch looked settled where he was, but Rory calculated how long it would take him to get to Angel if Finch was to start in her direction. Bending to pick up a piece of harness a prickle of sweat broke out over the surface of his skin. His breath came quickly. He tried to ignore the growing rock of pain in his gut. When he knew it wasn't possible, he walked away. He slid to the ground behind a large boulder. Ben ran after him. He found him, his back against the rock, his left knee drawn up his head back, fighting the nausea.

"You alright?" Ben hovered over.

"Yeah."

"You don't look alright. Want me to get Ange?"

"No. It will pass."

Ben watched him. "You gonna puke?"

Rory gave a short laugh. After a moment he took a deeper breath, then another. His body relaxed; he rested his head on his arms folded above his knee.

"Ben," he said, trying to get to his feet. Ben grabbed his arms, helped pull him up and then let him lean for support. "Don't tell Angel," Rory continued. "She worries. It comes and goes."

"Is it from the poison? Is it still making you sick?"

"Yeah."

Making their way back to Lou, Ben asked, "How come you call Ange Angel?"

Rory looked at the ground.

"Well?" Ben asked.

"It's the same."

"It does sound the same Angela, Angel," Ben said comparing, "Almost, not exactly."

"Once I thought … my head wasn't clear, … thought there was an angel."

"You mean Angela? You thought she was an angel for real?"

Rory looked away.

Lou was watching for them.

"Rory almost puked," Ben explained.

"Told you to take it easy," he groused. "Can do it myself, always have. You rest over there now. You've given her a scare."

They saw Angela running to them.

"I looked away for a minute and you were gone," her voice quavered.

"I was with him Ange," Ben said. "He was just …" he looked at Rory for a second, "resting."

"Sorry, didn't mean to scare you," Rory said. He studied her face.

"Are you alright?" She felt his forehead.

"Yeah. You?"

"Me? I'm fine." She lifted her chin, trying to appear brave.

When it was time to start, Rory paused in front of Angela before climbing to his seat. "Alright?" he asked.

"Angela," Clara called.

"Don't ask me to ride with them," Angela pleaded.

"Do what makes you happy," he said. "Think of them. They thought … they lost you. Now you're back. You can understand … "

"I can't ride with them. I feel like I'll go mad if I have to. Lillian stares at me like I've grown another head. Mother thinks I'm making everything about us up and that horrible Finch is in there."

"He doesn't bother you does he?"

"No. He hasn't said a word."

"It's hard for you and them. I don't want to be the reason."

"It's not your fault. The only thing I know in all my mistake-filled life, besides God, is that you and I belong together."

He reached to touch her face, but stopped self-consciously as others were near. She didn't care. She hugged him and he wrapped his arms around her. Her head fit under his chin. She believed they must have been designed purposely for each other.

367

During their day's walk together Ben said to her, "Mother will get used to you being married, Ange. Hey? What is your name?"

"Fletcher." she answered and she smiled for the first time in a while.

"Mrs. Fletcher," he tried it out loud. "Angela Fletcher. I like it."

"Mrs. Angela Bear Fighter Fletcher," she said laughing a little.

Chapter 27

"Love, love changes everything
How you live and how you die.
Yes, love changes everything
Now I tremble at your name.
Nothing in the world will ever be the
same."

"Love Changes Everything" Don Black
and Charles Hart, music by Andrew
Lloyd Webber

She hated to disagree with Rory, but walking gave her freedom from her mother's and sister's scrutiny and peace of mind to be able to see him. He and Lou would watch the horizon and exchange a word or two from time to time, neither being a big talker. It touched her to see the old man reminding him to eat and drink the supplies she'd packed for him. Rory wouldn't eat at all if not pressed. She wondered with a pang of regret if he still did not care if he lived or died, if her love wasn't enough. She reasoned it was more likely his sick stomach.

There where times when she would find him and Ben sitting by themselves somewhere or returning to camp after having disappeared. They both assured her he was fine, just resting, but she thought his face looked especially tight. From time to time she'd look up to see Lou leaning over him, talking seriously and Rory was not sitting as straight as he usually did as long as he was awake. When they caught her watching they'd wave as if nothing was wrong.

Every morning, at each stop and in the evenings Clara tried to convince Angela to ride inside. When she refused, her mother attempted to appeal to her emotions. "Angela, think of what we've been through. Your poor sister, you've seen the state she's in."

Angela doubted there was anything she could say to her sister. And if they started saying awful things about Rory, she knew she wouldn't be able to keep her temper. The seed of strength she'd first

369

felt weeks earlier when standing up to Finch had returned and continued to grow. With this strength she did not feel the unsettling eclipse of affection for her mother and sister. There was a familiar fondness, but her energies were focused on Rory. Here was a joy she'd never imagined, that someone so amazing could love her. She saw in his eyes a love and approval she'd never known before. Juxtaposed to her joy was the frightening intensity of this love and her fear for him.

Clara's weapons of emotion failed. She stopped short of ordering her daughter, afraid of setting off another fit, like the gun-wielding scene.

"I fear my daughter has lost her mind," she despaired to Barton Finch when they were bumping along in the wagon.

He frowned as if lost in his own musings then responded slowly, "Yes, it's a common condition with young women captured by Indians. Their minds snap. Sometimes they become unresponsive, just stare into space, and don't speak. Sometimes they form unnatural attachments to their captors, which I believe she has done in an odd way. She has attached herself to the prisoner, him being Indian. You see?"

"Is Angela mad?" Lillian whispered. "Is she?"

"Calm yourself," Clara said to her. She lowered her voice and moved closer to Finch. "I pray it's only temporary. Do you believe she could recover her senses after a few days with her family."

Finch seemed to rouse himself from his deep thoughts. "The continued presence of my prisoner exacerbates her mental derangement. Patience ma'am, we're almost to the end of our travails."

"Are we, Mr. Finch?"

"Reaching our mutual destinations will ease both our difficulties."

"Do they recover? Girls like Angela?"

"Some, but I must tell you some are never right. It depends on the individual." He paused. "You have to admit ma'am, this daughter of yours is by nature difficult."

Clara sighed.

"The longer she goes on like this ... even a week more ... I just don't know. And she's taking that boy of yours along with her."

"Mr. Finch, I don't know what to do. I'd like to force her to stop, but you saw how wild she was. I don't want to make things worse."

"Yes, you are wise. The situation calls for tact. The answer is to remove the prisoner."

"Is that possible?"

"It may be. We're getting close to civilization. I may be able to send word to my employer with a passing rider. If I could arrange for some help ... I could be done with him soon."

"Could you? I hate to make this more difficult for you, but my daughter's health is at stake."

"I would be sad to part from you, but to be free of him and of course to save your daughter; it would be a worthy sacrifice."

"I loathe the idea of finishing this wretched trip without you, Mr. Finch. You have been invaluable. Just the same if you think you can arrange it, it's for the best."

"Yes. I may need your assistance to do this as smoothly. Do you think you can distract your daughter when it comes time?"

"Yes. I can."

"And to get help I'll need a little...something by way of payment. You see I won't get paid for him until I meet with my employer and I must have funds to offer for assistance."

"Oh, I see. I must be careful. Our situation is ... well it is most embarrassing to discuss, but I'm sure I can help somewhat..."

"Whatever you can spare will be fine. It pains me to part from you. I hope we may meet again after all this is over. I have important decisions to make concerning my life's path, but I'd very much like to pay you and your family a social call if circumstances allow."

"We would appreciate that. Before we part I'll give you the address where a letter can reach my brother-in -law. Do try to look us up. I'm not sure where we will be staying. He will know."

Mornings Angela, Rory and Ben would wake to tiny crystal forests of frost on their blankets. Angela did not resent Ben's presence with them even at night. He loved Rory and felt safe with him. Also her courses had started and she would have been embarrassed to have to explain this to Rory if he turned to her for lovemaking.

One afternoon Lou stopped early to soak the hoof of a lame horse. Angela bathed in the river water warmed by the sun, which was a lovely change from splashing icy morning water on her face. Now she sat on the warm earth feeling perfectly decadent.

Rory and Ben were in the water. She sat where she could just see them, but not too close. Ben had reached an age where he wanted privacy from his sister. She could hear him shouting and laughing. Rory as always was quiet. Though she couldn't see his face, she knew his expression. She knew Ben's antics were making him smile gently, his beautiful face lit.

Sounds from camp caught her ear. She stood, shading her eyes. Three riders had come into camp. Lou was somewhere down the creek with the lame horse. Rory was suddenly at her side, dripping wet and pulling on his clothes. Angela gripped his arm.

"Who's that?" Ben asked. He was buttoning his shirt as he came to stand by them.

Neither responded. He followed their example staying where they were and soundlessly watching the three men drink coffee offered by Clara. Finch stood close to them talking intently. Then he shook their hands. With a touch of their hats to Clara and Lillian they rode off.

"What'd them fellas want?" Lou asked when they returned to camp.

"Just travelers passing by," Finch said. "Had to be on their way."

Angela shivered. As innocuous as the three men were, their arrival reminded her of the inevitable intrusion of the world they were fast coming to, a world that meant danger for Rory. She tried not to think about his upcoming trial. Since they left the safety of Rose's family she needed to touch him frequently for reassurance; he was there, he was real. Now, after the arrival of the men reminding her of future perils, she needed reassurance more than ever. Any time he was within reach she touched him, she rested her hand on him, brushed his hair back, pulled his shirt up over his shoulder when it slipped. She feared he would be annoyed by her constant attention. Far from being bothered, Rory sensed her need for reassurance. He frequently took the hand that was touching him and gave it a gentle squeeze or put his arms around her when no one was near.

Two mornings later Angela, Ben and Rory made their way through the frosty grass to a small stream. Their feet melted away the frost and left a darker trail. Wisps of their words to each other lingered in the air.

"Angela."

They were startled to see Clara behind them, at the start of their trail. Tall and thin, wearing a woolen dress and a shawl over her head and shoulders, she looked like ghost.

"Will you help me to the water? I am not feeling well. I would like to splash a little on my face."

Angela went to her. Her mother's hand that grasped hers was cold and bony.

"Benjamin you come with us," Clara called. She waved Rory away. "You go on. We must have our privacy. Come Angela, you and I will go this way."

Angela glanced at Rory and caught the shine of his eyes through the gray light before he turned and walked through the tall grasses to reach the stream's edge.

"It is steeper than I thought," Clara said. "I am afraid I'll fall."

"Want me to help Mother?" Ben asked.

"No. I have changed my mind. Help me back to camp. I will have to be satisfied with old water from a bucket."

When Angela crooked her arm through her mother's she was struck by her frailty. She looked over her shoulder. Ben signaled to her that he would go with Rory. She nodded to him and helped their mother back to the wagon, thinking she would quickly rejoin him and Rory.

Rory had pulled his shirt over his head, rolled his pant legs up and stepped into the water.

"It's freezing!" Ben announced when he touched it. He threw sticks for Traveler, who had overcome her reservations about water. She happily pounced after them, barking exuberantly. "Aren't you afraid you'll get sick in this freezing water?"

Rory was crouched scooping water over his head and face when Traveler's playful bark changed to one of warning. He straightened instantly. The grass rustled and Finch appeared by the edge.

"Ben," Rory took a step toward him and reached out his hands. Before he could catch the boy a man jumped from the bushes behind Ben and grabbed him.

"Hey!" Ben yelled. The man put a hand over his mouth. Rory flew at them, but another jumped out of the brush, knocking him back into the water with the butt end of a rifle to his chest. Rory got to his feet

373

to charge again. The man who knocked him back aimed his gun, but he plowed forward undeterred until the man holding Ben put a pistol to the boy's head. Rory froze.

"Don't move! No one will hurt the boy if you stay smart!" Finch shouted.

Finch waded cautiously behind him, a large knife in his hand. "I know you wouldn't want to see the boy hurt. You have a soft spot for him. Don't you? I tell you what. You come quietly and the boy will be fine."

"Let him go," Rory growled. He stood in the water poised for a fight.

"Ow!" the man holding Ben flapped his hand in the air. "The brat bit me!" He slapped the boy's face. Ben dropped to his knees. Rory launched himself at the man with the rifle who was closest to him. He knocked him down. They fought for the weapon, but Finch splashed behind him and held the knife to his neck. "Don't be stupid. We don't want the boy. Only you."

"Then let him go," Rory hissed. He got to his feet, but stayed ready to take on all three.

Finch stepped back, holding the knife ready. "Hold," he said the to man Rory had fought when he clamored to his feet. "Thinking of putting up a fight?" Finch grinned at Rory. "Think you can take us all don't you? Remember the riders from the other day? How many of them were there? Three. Two are here. Where do you think the third is? Watching your sweetheart. She's just downstream with her mother. Isn't she?"

Rory looked down the winding waters.

"Don't let him run!" Finch warned.

Rory's nearest opponent blocked the way downstream.

"Come on Finch, you and me can take the redskin kid," he said.

"Hold on. He's more trouble than he looks. And I want him alive. I got him this far. You," he addressed Rory, "come with us peaceful and we'll leave your friends alone."

"Finch," Rory growled, "You coward. You wouldn't dare."

"I wouldn't bother children and women, no, but my friends here are impatient types, as you see. Come along and put an end to your friends' predicaments."

"Tell the other to show himself here. I'll come when I see him."

"Just grab him, Finch," the man holding Ben said. "He don't tell us what to do."

"You giving your word? No trouble soon as you see the other fellow isn't near her?"

Rory nodded, "Long as you leave her and the boy alone."

"Mike!" Finch called, "show yourself! You've given your word in front of the boy," he reminded Rory.

Ben kicked and squirmed and tried to shout under the man's hand.

"Want me to hit you again?" His captor shook him.

"Ben, don't fight," Rory said, and the boy stopped struggling.

The third man bushwhacked through the tall grass.

"Here he is. Now give yourself up," Finch said.

"Let the boy go."

"Can't do that," the man holding Ben said, "He's gonna holler."

"No he won't." Finch walked out of the water to them. He smiled down at Ben. "Listen, you don't move or make a sound until we're out of sight. Then you wait longer. Count to three hundred. If you make a sound we will shoot this prisoner dead. If you or anyone tries to follow us we'll shoot him. You got that?"

Ben nodded mutely.

"Let him go," Finch said and the man released him. Rory dropped his defensive stance and let them close in around him. One of the men clubbed him between the shoulder blades, dropping him to his knees.

"Don't knock him out," Finch said. "I want him conscious. Don't want to lug around no dead weight."

They dragged him across the water, into the brush on the other side where their horses were tied, threw him across one, mounted themselves and galloped through bushes.

"Onnne ..." Ben tried to count but he was crying and shaking. He looked back at camp, in the direction the men had gone and at camp again. He wanted to yell, to run, was afraid move, stood helplessly. Then he saw his sister walking briskly towards the water.

"Ange," he rasped. "Ange, they took him. They took him!"

"What are you saying?" She looked around. "Where's Rory?"

"The men and Mr. Finch..." he pointed in the direction they had taken. "They took Rory."

"No, no," she whispered. "Rory!" she shouted. Then desperately to herself, she whispered, "It can't be. No!" She called again, "Rory!"

"Sh, they'll shoot him!" Ben cried, "You have to be quiet."

She ran through the stream calling Rory.

"Ange! Wait!" Ben tried to chase after her on fear wobbly legs. She disappeared from sight, her shouts getting further and further away.

He couldn't see her, couldn't catch her, his legs were too shaky, his voice wouldn't work. He had to get help. He stumbled back into camp where Lou caught him before he fell. "Mr. Finch … the men …, they took Rory! Ange … is running after them."

"Blast him!" Lou cursed. He turned back to the wagon.

"No, she's out there!"

"Can't catch 'em on foot. Got to git a horse."

The old driver grabbed a horse by the lead and gave it to the boy while he got a bridle. He attached rope to the harness bridle for reins, threw it over the beast's head and brought it to the wagon. Ben held the horse while Lou used the wagon's steps to climb on the Goliath's back. "Please hurry," he cried.

"Benjamin? Where's Angela? What has gone wrong?" Clara came as near to the horse as she dared.

Lou leaned over the horse and spoke to Ben. "You stay here. Keep the fire goin'. It's important. Can you do it? I'm dependin' on you son. Stay put. For your sister's sake."

Ben nodded.

"Where is Angela?" Clara demanded.

Lou kicked at the horse's sides and it trotted off.

"Benjamin!" Clara shrieked in his face. "Where is your sister!"

"Mr. Finch and some men … they came … they took Rory. Ange ran after them."

"What? What has she done? Angela! Angela, come back!" She ran to the stream.

"Ben." Lillian peeked out of the wagon. "Are the thieves back?" she whispered.

"No," he cried. "They're gone. Ange is gone. Rory is gone."

"What do you mean?"

Ben sobbed, "I should have fought them. I should have punched and kicked."

Lillian stepped out. She wiped his face. "Don't cry. Ooh Ben you've a bruise. How did you do that?"

376

He walked away from her to the fire and built it up blindly through his tears.

Clara trudged back into camp wringing her hands.

"Mother? Ben has a terrible bruise on his face. He's saying something about Angela. I cannot understand what he is talking about," Lillian said.

Clara went to Ben standing by the fire; she held his face in her hands. "How did this happen? Tell me exactly what happened."

He pulled out of her hands and wiped his face with his sleeve. "I bit the man when he put his hand over my mouth. He hit me. I wish I'd bit him harder."

"He struck you?"

"Yep. I got to keep this fire going. Lou said." He threw dry grass on it.

"Oh, oh," Clara moaned. "This was not supposed to happen. Where is that girl? She was not to be involved. She will be the death of me."

Ben tended the fire vigilantly all day, walking away from it only to look and listen or gather more fuel. If he tried to go to the stream his mother grabbed his arm and appealed to him desperately. She circled the camp with her hands clasped together and pressed to her middle. Lillian asked Ben, "Why is Mother upset?"

"Ange and Rory are out there," he said poking the fire.

"Angela will come back. She is not scared." She smiled and returned to the wagon.

Night fell without any signs of hope. It was a blank world; clouds hid the stars. Ben and Clara stood close to the fire. A frozen mixture of snow and rain fell. They let it glaze their heads and shoulders. Clara heard Ben's teeth tapping against each other. She brought a blanket and put it over him, then sat, her head in her hands.

"What has he done?" she mumbled. "He said nothing would go wrong. It should have been accomplished before she left my side."

"Lou will find them Mother," Ben tried to comfort her, but he prayed silently, "Please, please bring Ange and Rory back safe." The sleet changed to clumps of snow then stopped altogether.

The day lifted dull and dreary. Ben was gathering sticks when the horses nickered. He heard hooves splashing through the stream and ran. Lou came across the water, leading the horse and dragging someone. Ben had to look closely to identify the person as his sister. Her hair hung down, twigs and leaves were caught in it; her dress was wet and torn. She arched back, her fists struck wildly at Lou.

"They're here!" Ben shouted. He and Clara ran to them.

"Git her out of them wet things," Lou said passing her to her mother. His face was gray. "Hang on tight. She keeps tryin' to run off."

"Let me go," she slurred with numb lips. "Got to find him."

Her lips were purple/blue, her face white except for two red spots, one on each cheek. Lou helped lift and push her into the wagon. "Guard the door while I git inta dry things," he told Ben.

Angela fought protesting all the while.

"I cannot hold her!" Clara called. Lou and Ben caught her scrambling out.

"Stop Angela!" Clara shouted. "You must get in dry clothes. You will freeze to death."

They gave up trying to get her undressed, wrapped her in blankets and held her by the fire. She was shaking and crying, but getting easier to restrain.

"Get her some supper. The boy and I can hold her," Lou said. He pulled out his flask with one hand unplugged it with his teeth and held it to her mouth.

Angela's eyes moved to Lou's face as if she were just recognizing him. "Lou help! Help find him! They'll kill him!" She grabbed his arms.

"Easy there," Lou said. "I'll do my best. You got to calm down Miss."

"At once! We've got to go at once!"

"Angela stop!" Clara stood before her. "He is a criminal. You know that. They've simply arrested him. Wait there is something." She felt around in the pockets of her skirt. "The note. Where is the note? Ben hold her."

She produced a piece of paper and held it close to Angela's face. "Look. Look this is from him. He left it for you."

Angela stopped fighting. She stared at the paper.

"Here, I'll read it to you," Clara snatched it away. "It says, 'Angela,

I have to go away to pay for my crimes. You and I do not belong together. Some day you'll meet the right person for you, a person who truly cares. That person is not me. Don't try to find me. Don't blame anyone I brought this on myself. Don't confuse your feelings for something more. It's for the best.

Rory.'"

Ben cringed at the words of the letter. He cast anxious glances at his sister. She sagged in his arms, defeated. It scared him.

"There," Clara said. "He doesn't want you to look for him. He went of his own free will. You see?"

Ben wanted his mother to stop talking. The words were cruel blows to Ange. He didn't know what to do, what to say to soothe her pain. He was stunned himself to hear Rory's words. He let go his hold of her and watched her face.

Then Angela sat a little taller. "Rory didn't write that," she said slowly. Her eyes were fixed on her mother's face.

"Of course he did," Clara said. She crumpled the paper in her hands.

"He doesn't know how to write," Angela said in a strange flat voice.

"Well, Mr. Finch must have written it for him." Clara said.

Ben thought that was odd; he'd never seen Mr. Finch do anything nice for Rory.

It was quiet for a little while. Angela began to shake anew, but now it was more of a deep trembling than a shivering. Ben was disturbed by the change in her, but something she said was giving rise to new thoughts. He looked back and forth from his mother's face to hers.

"He did tell Mr. Finch he'd go," Ben said.

"There you see?" Clara said. "Ben heard him. He went willingly."

"He only said that so the men would leave Ange and me alone," he continued almost to himself.

His sister stared at him. Her eyes scared him.

"Leave you alone? Leave me alone? Who would leave me alone?" she asked.

"The men. The man that was holding you by the water and the one holding me."

"I wasn't at the water. I went back to camp with Mother. What men? Ben, who are you talking about?" Her hands grabbed his arms and she shook him.

"You know Ange, the men that came out of the bushes. One grabbed me. Mr. Finch and another one stood 'round Rory. Mr. Finch had a knife and the other man had a rifle, but they were still afraid of Rory. They kind of stood back after the first time the man stopped him from coming to help me. They didn't dare get too close 'til he said he would go if they left you and me alone. He told them…" Ben worked hard to calm his thoughts and get the words out. "When he saw the man who was guarding you come away he would go with them. When the man came out of the bushes. He let them take him. They hit him even though he said he'd go. He said if they left you and me alone…" Ben was crying.

"There was no one guarding me. He didn't want to go. Finch tricked him. He planned this." Angela got to her feet. She snatched the letter from mother's hands. Running her eyes along it she slowly said, "These are not his words. He doesn't call me Angela."

"No," Ben agreed, "He only calls you Angel. Because he thinks you're kind of like an angel."

She stared at her mother, a terrible realization taking shape. "You knew. You helped Finch. You knew. You knew!"

"Angela it is for your own sake. Stop it. Ben, Lou help me get her inside."

Lou and Ben had to carry her into the wagon while she yelled accusations at her mother and struck and kicked at them. Inside the wagon she refused to submit. Clara and Ben sat with her between them, trying to keep her from crawling away and avoid her fists and feet. Finally Lou agreed to tie a rope around her waist and to the wagon's wall as well.

Lillian hid in the deepest corner she could find and covered her ears. Angela alternated yelling and accusing with pleading long into the night. "Please find him! Lou? Ben?" Clara motioned for Lou to leave. Angela's strength was failing; she pounded the floorboards with her fists. "Please help! Help him!"

"Lou's looking for him," Clara said. "Calm yourself."

Ben looked at his mother. She shook her head in a warning.

380

Angela cried until she couldn't breathe. She gasped for breath against the floorboards.

In the morning her mother and sister led her out like a life sized cloth doll. She seemed insensible until she saw the wagon hitched and ready to go. Her head lifted and she cried, "No can't leave! What if he gets away! I won't leave him out there!" She pulled out of their arms.

Lou caught her. "I'm sorry Miss. There ain't nothin' we can do for him. We got to move on. I'm real sorry. It's a real shame."

"Lou they'll kill him! Help him! Please!"

He didn't have the heart to tell her it was probably too late. "Easy now," he said gently. "He's a smart kid. He might git away and track us. He wouldn't want you to make yourself sick." He lifted her inside.

Curled against the inside wall of the wagon Angela cried and called plaintively for Rory over and over. She struck away food and water.

As days passed she grew weaker and weaker, until she could not stand or lift her head. They pleaded and scolded her to take nourishment. Frightened by her condition, they forced water and broth into her mouth. She fought and choked. The only response she'd make to their appeals to help herself was to chant over and over, "It doesn't matter."

Chapter 28

*"I carry the dust of a journey that
cannot be shaken away."*

*"Pictures at an Exhibition" Emerson,
Lake and Palmer*

"You were correct my friend. A good day's hunt was the cure for what ailed me." Daniel Harrington clapped his nearest companion on the back. "The good air, the thrill of the chase. I feel like a new man." His gray eyes twinkled and his cheeks were ruddy over his trim white beard.

"Been trying to get you out. Always being with the sick is making you old," his friend teased.

"He did well for himself today," A younger companion in a large furred hat said. He tossed game birds tied together by the legs into the back of a flatbed wagon. Daniel smiled broadly.

"Wes, if we hadn't shot a thing I'd still say it wasn't days wasted."

"Better git movin'," Grumbled a fourth hunter, stamping his boots. "I don't like the horses standin' around wet."

"Jeb's right," Daniel agreed. "We'd better get home."

"Come on Albert, bring those horses around," Jeb directed.

The older men, Daniel, William and Jeb rode in the wagon, pulled by a stalwart workhorse. Jeb's son Albert and the young man called Wes rode horses. They were a jovial group of friends laughing, congratulating and taunting each other.

After hours of riding, Wes interrupted the others. "Hold up," he said.

When they stopped to listen they caught the sound of men's voices drifting on the air. After a minute or two Daniel headed the horse in the direction of the voices.

"Where you going? I don't like this. Don't like this at all," Jeb objected.

"We'll just have a look."

383

They approached a grove of firs, through which they caught glimpses of men moving amongst the slim trunks and wispy branches.

"Who's there?" a voice called out.

"Dr. Daniel Harrington and friends," Daniel returned.

"Be off. This is no business of yours." A man appeared between trees.

"Let's move on," Jeb said. "Smells like trouble."

The hunters put their hands on their guns. Daniel flapped the reins and drove to the man. "Easy. Don't make them nervous," he cautioned his companions.

"We don't want any trouble," he said to the man. "Just hunters passing through."

"Then git." The man gestured with a rifle.

"Daniel," William elbowed him, "they've hung a man."

"What's this?" Daniel steered the horse past the sentry and into the center of the grove of firs where there was a little clearing. He pulled the reins. William and Jeb stood up. A group of uneasy men faced them. Three were rough looking men, with wide brimmed hats and rifles in hand. A body hung in the air from a thick rope.

"Now, now, don't worry. Everyone be easy." A large florid faced man spoke to his companions. He huffed up to Daniel and his friends. "This is all on the up and up."

"Yes, all proper and legal," said a small well-dressed man joining him. He held a flask in one hand and a shiny pistol in the other. "We've officially disposed of a criminal. Won't you join us in a drink?"

"Cut him down." Daniel looked past them at the body.

"Let me show you my papers," the big man said reaching slowly into his vest.

"Yes, take a look at his papers to satisfy yourselves," the other said.

Daniel handed the reins to Jeb. He and William got out of the wagon and strode to the suspended man. Wes and Al rode alongside of them.

"Cut the rope," Daniel said.

Wes pulled out his knife, stood in his stirrups and cut the rope. He and Al caught the body and slid it to Daniel and William.

384

"No it's alright," the big man called to three rough looking members of his party.

Daniel kneeled beside the body, took out his knife and cut away the rope encircling the neck. It was difficult work for the rope had dug into the skin and the neck was swelling around it.

"Here," the man waved papers gripped in his beefy hand at the Doctor. "Look for yourself. We've merely cleansed society of a criminal."

Daniel pushed them out of his face. William took the papers and perused them.

"What are you doing?" the fancy dresser asked.

"He's a doctor," William explained.

"Excellent," the man said. "A doctor can verify the death for us. Well doc, is our work complete?"

"Seems so," Daniel said. He carefully felt the neck.

The big man bent his knees and addressed the body. "Ha! You thought you'd get away from me. You were no match for me."

"Well done, a job well done," the other said.

The big man straightened. "It was a long tough job." He sighed. "Toughest one yet."

"Yes well, you did it my friend," the smaller man said. He shook the hands of his companion then offered a gloved hand to Daniel. "Thank you for your assistance Doctor." Daniel ignored him. He took no offense. "Would you like a drink? Any takers? It'll take the nip out of the cold."

Daniel declined as did the rest of the hunting party.

"It was real convenient you coming along like you did," the man with the papers said. "We won't trouble you any further. It's getting dark. I'm sure you want to be on your way."

"Yes, wasn't it," the doctor said. He got to his feet and offered a hand, suddenly friendly. "We might as well dispose of the body for you."

"No, that's quite unnecessary," the big man said, tucking away his papers. "We don't want to burden you."

"Not a problem at all," Daniel insisted.

The man frowned.

"What's taking so long," one of the riflemen barked. "I wanna make camp before it's dark."

385

"Thank you," the man said to the doctor, "but the body must be disposed of properly. It's my responsibility."

"I'm a doctor, I know how to dispose of bodies properly. Besides, I can use it for study."

The smaller man grimaced.

"Well," the big man seemed to like the idea better now, "I guess that'd be alright." He laughed, "He wouldn't like that not at all. He thought the body is sacred, if you cut it in pieces, it's worse than doing it to him living. I suppose that'd be fitting."

The hunters watched guardedly until the hanging party rode out of sight.

"They botched the job," Daniel said to William. "Get blankets and water. Hurry."

William repeated the orders and Wes and Al rushed to obey. William knelt with the doctor and put his head close to the man's face. He heard a high thin wheezing.

It was a young man. His face was cut and bruised and swollen, his clothes torn from a beating. Daniel carefully cut a hole near the base of the man's throat. His body jolted.

"Hold him still. Hold his head William. Al, hold his arms. Easy now, we're friends," he said to the young man.

His eyelids moved, but didn't open. He struggled to force air down his closed throat.

"Easy. Lie quiet. Breathe from here," Daniel closed the young man's mouth and pushed his hand against his abdomen. "Hear me? Feel my hand? Breathe from under it."

The hanging victim moved his head.

"Don't let him move his neck," Daniel said. "Easy now, we'll keep you alive. Listen to me."

Traveling time was passing quickly, but Daniel would not move until he felt his patient respond to his directions. When his breathing steadied, the hunters carried him as Daniel directed and placed him in the wagon. Jeb drove; Daniel and William kept the man as immobile as possible. When the wagon reached Daniel's home well into the night, he leapt out first.

"Al, you support his head and neck. Wes, his shoulders and help with his neck, William his back. Jeb you take his legs. Keep his neck straight. Not yet, wait for me to say." He threw open the front door of

386

the house and ran back to his friends. "Ready? All together, lift now. Up the stairs, first door on the right," he directed.

"Wait," he ordered once they were in the room. He hastily pulled back the coverlet and pushed aside pillows on a bed. "There, set him down carefully."

Daniel wedged the young man's head between two pillows. His arms flailed as if to fight him off.

"Easy, you're safe. Easy. Breathe slowly."

The whistling started again. His neck arched.

"Listen to me. Breathe from here, slowly. Try."

For hours the doctor stood with one hand on the man's middle, the other on his head, encouraging, instructing. His hunting companions quietly withdrew to their own homes. His housekeeper, Mrs. Dunbar, stood ready with medical supplies. When his patient's breathing quieted and he slipped into unconsciousness Daniel seized the opportunity to examine him. He checked the incision he'd made, dressed the rope burn, removed the remains of his clothing and did what repairs he could for the battered body.

"Come downstairs. Have your supper," Mrs. Dunbar said. "Nothin' more you can do tonight."

"Mmm, thank you. You go on to bed. I'll get myself a bite later," he said, studying the man's right leg, which he noticed was lying at an odd angle.

The housekeeper gave a humph of disapproval. She lingered a while longer then went down the stairs, each emphatic footstep stating her opinion.

Mrs. Dunbar woke before the morning light. Throwing on her dressing gown and sliding her feet into her slippers she marched down the dark hall frowning. Just as she suspected, the doctor was asleep in the old chair beside the patient's bed. His eyes opened at the sound of the floorboards creaking. He straightened his knees creakily to check the young man, rubbing the back of his own neck.

"Slept in that chair. Did you eat? I thought not. Go get your breakfast and git some rest. I can sit here as well as you."

Mrs. Dunbar was a tall, strong-boned woman with straight serious eyebrows and a square determined jaw, a formidable woman.

"Thank you, I think I will," Daniel said.

The sound of his voice startled the injured man. He gasped, his head back, neck veins standing out, his lungs instinctively striving to pull air down a tight airway. Daniel held his head. He reached weakly to fight the doctor off

"You're safe. Lie still," the doctor said into the injured man's ear. "Don't move. I don't know how badly your neck is damaged." He pushed the quilt back and pressed his hand over the lungs. "Push against my hand. Breathe from here. Try now. Fight for it. Come, there must be a reason to live."

When his body began to get enough air he ceased struggling. Daniel wet the end of a towel and dripped water into his mouth. Later Mrs. Dunbar returned, fully dressed. The patient slept, but the doctor remained vigilant.

"It is not worth driving yourself to sickness. Now is it? Be sensible for once. You don't even know what kind of person you've got here. Do you?" She peered closer. "Looks like a heathen Indian. He don't want to be helped. I seen him fighting you. What kind of person are you harmin' yourself to fix?"

"A person, Mrs. Dunbar, a person."

The housekeeper padded down the stairs to the kitchen where she had built up the fire in the cook stove and put on water. Preparing a hot breakfast, she saw the unopened letter lying on the table. It was from the doctor's sister-in-law; she recognized the handwriting. She gave it a hard scowl. Burdened as he was she didn't want to bring it to the doctor, but it had been there going on three days. She put it on the tray with a sigh.

Later Daniel sat in the comfortable chair worn to fit his body. He stared at Clara's letter lying unfolded on the little table. He endeavored to clear his thoughts clouded by fatigue. She was due to arrive any day. Here? They were coming here? They had made the long arduous journey. Clara? He had received a letter or two previously. Now he wished he'd paid more attention instead of losing them amidst the chaos of books and papers on his desk. He hadn't believed she would actually make the journey, never mind finish it, not Clara, not once she experienced the difficulties and discomforts of frontier travel.

What had she written? Something about not wanting to be trouble, but one of the daughters was ill. They would go to their own place as soon as arrangements could be made. Their place? He had a least driven out to David's homestead after the first letter. It was an unfinished shell, in disrepair from years of neglect and exposure. He recalled she had mentioned something about hiring someone to manage it. He hadn't understood what she meant. People did not come to the little township looking for work. Folks here worked their own places or moved on. David's place was a few days' ride away, not near anyone, but it was nice land. She was lucky squatters hadn't taken possession of it.

Arrangements? What was he to do? He should have warned Clara about the house. They'd have to stay here. Think, he tapped himself on the forehead with the heel of his hand. Downstairs is the kitchen, the sitting room and my office. Upstairs there are the three small bedrooms, this one, Mrs. Dunbar's room and mine. Clara and the girls can have my room. Will they fit? How big are they now? The boy? He had never seen Ben. "He can sleep on the floor of the sitting room. One of the girls might sleep there as well, on the sofa next to the fireplace. Then Clara and one girl could have my bedroom. I can sleep in my office

It was possible. He watched his patient breathing irregularly. He couldn't leave him for long, nor could he neglect his brother's family. Good Mrs. Dunbar appeared in the doorway, fresh supplies in her arms, towels, clean water, rags for bandages.

"William's downstairs. Should he come up?"

"No, I'll go down."

"William," Daniel greeted his friend. "Good to see you."

"How is he?" William asked with a nod upstairs.

"Alive," Daniel answered. They sat at the table in the kitchen.

"Find out anything about him?"

"No, can't talk."

"You look done in Daniel."

"He won't listen to me," Mrs. Dunbar said. She set plates before them. "Workin' hisself to the bone for some Indian."

"My brother's family has come from back East," Daniel said. "I expect them any day."

"How many of them are there?"

"The widow, two girls and a son."

"Where will you put them?"

"We'll manage. I'm sorry Mrs. Dunbar, I know this puts extra work on you."

"Family is family," she said.

"I can ask around, see if there's someone who can put them up," William suggested. "I could take the boy to my place."

"Thank you. Clara's letter said something about one of the girls being ill. I'd better see to her before any plans are made. Clara's pretty particular and strong-willed. She might not agree to any plans made without her consent."

"I'll git the place ready for em," the housekeeper said. She was rolling out piecrust. "You best rest before they git here."

"She's right Daniel. You should get some sleep. What can I do to help?"

The doctor mused out loud, "I don't know exactly when they'll get here. The next few days will tell with the fellow upstairs. I need to keep a close eye on him, make sure he keeps breathing. It's not fair of me to leave Mrs. Dunbar with all the relatives, but I've got my hands full with him."

"Tell you what," William said. "I'll bring some indoor work from home. May as well work on it here as there. Mrs. Dunbar, mind if I take up a corner of the kitchen table for harness repairs over the next day or two? That way I'll be here to help when the brood drops in."

"Do whatever you please," she said.

"William, you're a godsend. I've got to get back upstairs."

In the sick room Daniel gazed out the window at the dull late autumn scenery, trees were slate colored skeletons. He searched the sky for signs of dangerous weather that might threaten the little family trying to reach the end of their long voyage. He had no time to prepare for them, it was taken up with nagging his resistant patient to fill his lungs, replacing cold compresses on his swollen face and neck, checking bandages and dripping sweetened water into his mouth. Daniel feared he wouldn't last much longer with so little water, no food and no will. He flattened his palms on the sill and leaned his forehead against the cold pane. A house full of children. And Clara. Had she mellowed at all with age?

The patient wheezed, involuntarily trying to draw air. Daniel adjusted the pillows around his head. His eyes flew open; they were dark orbs of alarm. He huffed like a startled deer.

"I'm a doctor. Let me help," Daniel said, "slowly."

The eyes clouded. "No, stay with me. Try. Here," he dripped the sweetened water into his mouth. The hands came up. "Easy," Daniel said. "Can you swallow?"

The eyes closed.

Frustrated, Daniel stared at him. Things could be worse, he wasn't paralyzed and some air was getting through. He would keep the hole in his throat open until he saw the airway was functioning. The other injuries didn't appear life threatening unless there was internal damage, which was certainly possible from the looks of the beating he'd taken.

Chapter 29

"Love is the salutation of the angels to the stars."

<u>Les Miserables</u> *by Victor Hugo*

Noise from the rooms below woke the doctor from an all too brief respite. He looked over his sleeping patient and trudged down the stairs. His sitting room was crowded, every seat was occupied and there were people standing. A tawny dog wandered about, panting through the bodies. He tried to make sense of the confusion. Mrs. Dunbar was speaking. He felt her brush past him into the crowd.

"Trouble here." William's face was in his. He led Daniel to a man in a long dark overcoat standing by near the fire.

"Hello, sir," said the man. "Name's Sam. I work out at the Lassen ranch for Mr. Lassen. Do you know him? The Lassens are famous in these parts."

"Yes, I know the family, been to the ranch myself, helped a few of the daughters into the world," Daniel said. "How can I help you?"

"Well, we was out on an excursion and happened to come upon these folks. Mr. Lassen felt sorry for the terrible time they've had of it an' invited them to stay with him and his missus. It's a real nice place as you know sir. One of Mr. Lassen's relatives was one of the first trail makers out here."

"Yes. I know."

"The lady, Mrs. Harrington, said she needed to get here to you first. Mr. Lassen insisted they use his buggy and had me drive 'em here," Sam continued. "It's a darn sight more comfortable than that contraption they were in. Missus Lassen gets lonely out there. She'd love to have respectable women for company. Mrs. Harrington is considerin' the idea. I can bring 'em out to the ranch if that's what she wants, but I can only wait a day or so, on account of the weather. You never know this time a year what it's gonna do. Would you care to look to the girl sir?"

Daniel turned to the pretty young woman sitting in the chair to his left. Her blond hair was done up with care, but her pale blue eyes seemed to have no light behind them. A vacant smile played on her lips.

"Sir? Over here." Sam stepped right and held a hand out to the sofa. There were two people sitting on it, separated by a pile of dirty blankets.

"Hello, Daniel."

A hand clawed his sleeve. He followed it up the arm to the face: Clara. Under her eyes were dark smudges. Her lips pressed together tightly, her face was gaunt. He took her hand.

"I apologize arriving in such a state." She hesitated then said, "Would you look at Angela? I'm afraid she's made herself seriously ill." She pulled a fold of blanket from the pile beside her.

There was a person wrapped in the blankets. Instantly clear-headed the doctor peeled away layers to find a young woman. Her eyes were half shut; her hair hung stringy and her head seemed too heavy for her slender neck. She leaned against the young boy beside her. The boy's hair was ragged, uneven and overgrown, his face thin and his eyes were those of an older person burdened with worries. He wrapped an arm around the girl.

Daniel felt her forehead. No fever. He pinched her skin between his thumb and forefinger.

"How long has she been like this? Was there a fever? Was there an injury?"

"No, it is not that sort of illness," Clara said. "This wretched trip and the horrible events we experienced, it was just too much for the girls. Their nerves have been shattered." Clara's voice caught.

"Drink your tea," Mrs. Dunbar said. "You're here now. The Doctor and I will take care of you all."

"Daniel," William said, "I'll help these men put the horses in the barn, then bring them to my place for the night."

"Thanks," Daniel said. Glancing over his shoulder he saw an old man behind Sam. He was holding his hat in his hands, turning it round and round. Then he followed William out.

"Mrs. Dunbar," he called, "water please."

When she gave him the cup, he patted the girl's face, "Here you are. Drink." She did not open her lips. Her eyelids lifted half-mast.

394

"She refuses to eat or drink," Clara explained. "She was a fanciful girl to begin with. Now she's taken things too far." She pressed a handkerchief to her mouth. "Dangerously so," she continued. "We've had to force food and drink into her."

The boy inhaled audibly.

"Angela!" Clara shook her. "What could we do? Watch her starve herself? She's doing this to hurt me. She was upset certainly, but now she's trying to hurt me." She shook the girl again. "Angela stop this!"

"Mother, Angela is fine," the young woman in the chair spoke. "You know how she is." She smiled vacuously.

Daniel removed Clara's hands from her daughter. "Mrs. Dunbar, would you take Mrs. Harrington and her family to wash and rest?"

"This way, come with me," the housekeeper said. She took Clara by the arm. Lillian, the blond girl, took her mother's hand when they stopped in front of her.

"Do you have any experience treating over - imaginative girls?" Clara asked before the woman led her out of the room.

"The Doctor will take care of your daughter. You need care yourself," Mrs. Dunbar said, firmly leading her.

The boy stayed on the sofa. "You can go with them," Daniel said. He shook his head. "Let's make her more comfortable," Daniel said. He unwrapped the blankets. The boy stood and helped recline his sister. Daniel put her feet up and took off her shoes. He rubbed her feet and then her hands.

"Can you make her better?" the boy whispered.

"She's very weak. Got to get her to eat and drink."

"I know, but it's awful when they make her. She chokes and cries again. Sometimes I can get her to."

"Can you? Good." Daniel went to the tea tray Mrs. Dunbar had left. He poured a little tea into a cup, filled the rest with cream and passed it to the boy.

"Ange, please drink. Just a little," he pleaded.

She closed her eyes completely.

"Ben? Is that what you go by?" Daniel asked.

The boy nodded. He held the cup to his sister's mouth.

"Why do you think your sister won't eat or drink?"

The boy didn't answer directly. "I know what Mother said." He faced the doctor. "But Ange doesn't want to hurt anyone. She can't

395

stand to see anyone hurt. Please Ange," he tearfully resumed his efforts.

"Let me try." Daniel sat on the edge of the sofa and lifted the girl to rest against his shoulder. Supporting her head he tilted her face towards her brother. "Angela, you are upsetting your brother. He cares about you. Look at him. See how you're hurting him."

Her eyes opened.

"Drink a little to make him feel better."

She swallowed the tea he tipped into her mouth. Then the Doctor lay her down and stepped back. Her eyes were closed. He studied the boy standing by her. "Did you eat?"

The boy wiped his tears with his sleeve and shook his head.

Daniel went to the kitchen and returned with a plate heaped with cold meats, bread, pie, and a cup of milk. He sat Ben in a chair and gave him the food. He closed his eyes to think while the boy ate.

When he saw the boy was nearly finished Daniel said, "Tell me about your sister. Has she always been difficult?"

"Ange isn't difficult. She likes to do stuff."

"Like?"

"Like being outside, seeing new places, animals, plants. She likes taking off her shoes. She isn't fussy like most girls. She takes care of people who are hurt. She always takes care of me when I get a scrape or bump. She doesn't get all white like Mother or faint like Lilly. She's real good at it."

"She is?"

"Yep. I guess it's because she use to help Father. It was when I was a baby."

"How long has she been like this?"

The boy scanned the room. "Since they took Rory," he whispered.

"Rory?"

"Yeah, the men took him. Mother said he wanted to go, but he didn't. I know. I saw them take him. They said they would do something to Ange and me if he didn't come. One hit me." The words came tumbling out, one over the next. Sitting opposite Ben, Daniel leaned forward to catch every one.

"Ange ran after them, but she got lost. Lou had to go find her. No one would help find Rory. Ange kept trying to run away and find him. They tied her up."

"She was upset by this Rory leaving? Why?"

"She loves him. They even got married."

This was a surprising fact. "Why did he get taken away?"

"Mr. Finch said he was bad. He said he was just a criminal and an Indian. Mother didn't like Rory either. That's why she wanted Mr. Finch and those men to take him. She didn't care they were going to hang him."

The words reverberated in Daniel as if a bell had been struck next to his ear.

"Doctor, I know he did some bad things, but he wasn't really bad. He saved me. Two times he saved me." Ben wiped his face with his sleeve again.

"Ben, call me Uncle Daniel." He reached across the space and put a hand on the boy's shoulder.

"He saved Ange from the Indians," Ben continued. "That's when they got married. He was brave too. He wasn't afraid of snakes or bears, Indians or anything. And he never made any noise or cried when Mr. Finch hurt him. Ange loved him a whole lot. He loved her too, I could tell. Rory was good and those men who took him weren't. They helped Mr. Finch take him away to hang him. Lou says there was nothing we could do to help him. He says he's dead by now." A sob stopped the story.

"Rory."

They turned at the sound of the girl speaking. Her head was up, her eyes open.

"Please," she looked up at Daniel, desperation in her eyes. "Help him. Please will you help?" Convulsive sobbing shook her body. "Help," she tried to say.

The doctor went to her and held her as if to keep the sobs from breaking her apart.

"I'm sorry," Ben cried over her. "I didn't mean to upset her. Mother said never to talk about it."

"It's not your fault," Daniel said. "Let her cry."

When the sobs ceased to grip her body and faded to whispered shudders, the Doctor put her hands around a cup of tea. Her anxious brother lifted her hands for her to drink while Daniel tried to steady his flying thoughts. The boy's words were ringing in his head: "hang" and "Indian." He strove to be logical, to calculate the distances, where the family had been on their route, how long ago, where he and his friends had come upon the necktie party.

He went to his office for a towel and basin, which he filled with warm water from the kettle in the kitchen. Should he tell the boy his suspicions? He could take him upstairs and resolve the question now. Should he warn him first? What if it wasn't true? How could he raise the poor boy's hopes and then dash them? Would the shock be too much for the girl?

He walked into the sitting room. The brother sat on the floor holding the cup. The girl lay back, eyes closed. She had to be pulled out of her hopelessness somehow. He began to form a strategy. Ben said she was good at nursing the sick. Whether or not the patient upstairs was this Rory, either way it could be the answer.

He washed her face with the towel and spoke conversationally, not knowing if she was hearing or not. "Your brother tells me you helped your father when you were young. It's hard to find help here. I get tired and discouraged. Hard to keep up with the latest advances in medicine. The journals are months old when I get them, sometimes up to a year. Last thing I read pleased me, though: more doctors are arguing for cleanliness in surgeries, sick rooms and of the patients themselves. I've always thought washing was part of any cure, though some of my fellows scoffed at me. What do you think?"

She didn't respond, but he could see she was watching his face under lowered lids. He continued, "What do you think of bleeding? I've long suspected it weakens patients more than it helps. Same goes for most purgatives. I don't agree with wantonly using them for everything. I know it sounds over-simplified, but I advocate lots of liquids and rest. People these days are excited about water treatments. I'm not sure about them as a cure - all, especially the way they're practiced. I think people need water inside as well as outside to cleanse the systems. Liquids and rest, let the body heal itself as much as possible."

He paused. Was it his imagination, or was she showing interest?

"Not that I'm against medicines, not at all. There are many useful herbs to help the healing and ease suffering. There are many more out there we haven't made use of yet. We've learned about some from the Indians."

He did see a light of interest in her eyes. Sitting on the edge of the sofa, he leaned his chin in his hands. "For all the good of science and medicinal herbs, the human will plays a large part in healing. Take the patient I have upstairs. His injuries are serious, but he could make it if he wanted to. He fights my efforts to help; he won't fight for life. How am I to treat the lack of will to live? What a shame for one so young to give away the gift of life." He looked straight at Angela.

"Your family has been invited to stay at the Lassen's ranch. Your mother would be happy there. It's quite the place, not like the homes back in Boston of course, but for out here it's fancy. Always people coming and going, big parties... It's nice you might like it. Or I wonder if you might be interested in staying on and helping me with my patients?"

Angela blinked.

"I would like it very much if you did."

She was looking at him closely, no question her eyes were brighter.

"My only requirement if you choose to stay, is you must eat and get your strength back. You wouldn't be any help like this and I don't need another patient. You could have my room for now. Mrs. Dunbar is an excellent cook. You are welcome to stay if you wish."

Without waiting for a response Daniel rose. Her head lifted to follow him. "You'll excuse me." He went up the stairs quickly. It had been a long time to leave the young man. He hadn't stopped breathing. Daniel removed the compress and gently washed his face. Hands flew up to push him away. "Easy now, you have guests." The doctor pried a spoon of water between his lips. He tried to turn his head away, but Daniel held him still. "Don't move. Let your neck heal. I don't know what the damage is. Easy now. I'll be back shortly."

In the kitchen Daniel met Mrs. Dunbar.

"The mother and daughter are restin' up on your bed," she informed him. "I put bedding on. I'll make up the cot in your office for you."

"Yes, thank you. I had the same thought."

"Where do you want the boy? The girl can have my bed."

"That's very kind of you, but I think they need to be together for now. I might have them stay in the sitting room."

399

"I guess that'd be alright. I don't want to think about what they've been through," she said pouring herself a cup of tea.

"Why? Did Clara tell you anything?"

"Nope, too worn out. I can see it in their faces. The girl is stunned stupid. That poor woman, so genteel. How's the other girl? I'll tend to her now. What about the boy?"

"No. Thank you Mrs. Dunbar. Sit down and have your tea. I fed the boy. I'm going to try to get his sister to eat. Then I'll settle them in for the night. Please get some rest yourself."

"Her poor mother. What she's putting her through."

"The most important thing right now is for her to eat," he said, preparing a plate. "Please, get some rest yourself."

"I'm going to my room where I can hear if they need me. I think they were asleep before I left the room."

"I think you are right. I didn't hear a sound from the room when I was up there. Good night then."

He took the plate to the sitting room. Angela glanced disinterestedly at the plate her uncle held before her.

"Would you like to see the patient?" he asked. "To see what you're in for if you decide to stay on."

She shrugged.

"Well, first eat a decent amount, then I'll take you."

After she ate all her deprived body could hold, Daniel felt her eyes on him.

"I can't finish," she whispered.

"You did well for the present." He took the unfinished plate. "Come I'll take you to him."

He and Ben helped her up the stairs. The Doctor stopped them outside the doorway. "What are you doing?" his inner voice asked.

Out loud he said, "He's in a bad way. I hope this won't be too difficult for you both."

Ben looked at him curiously. "Stuff doesn't bother Ange or me."

"It's… well … from what Ben told me … You might … well we'll see."

What could he say? Dear Lord, he prayed, don't let this be a mistake. "About the patient, his neck has been injured. It's important he doesn't move. And he can't get too excited or he'll have trouble breathing. Everyone must stay calm. Do you both understand me?"

400

. . .

Angela was led into a small room. She was a dried, dead leaf. She didn't know why she was there except for this man's fleeting suggestion that she might stay here. Her mother and Lillian were going somewhere else? And she would stay here? With them gone maybe she'd have a chance to get away and find Rory.

The shades were drawn, a lamp burned low on a small round table. The walls were white and the floorboards polished. A bed was on the left, its headboard against the interior wall. On the bed there was a quilt giving away the person lying under with its telltale hills. Her pulse quickened for no reason. Her Uncle held back by the door. Leaning on Ben's arm she walked closer to the bed. A large goose down pillow blocked her view of the patient's head. Added to her racing pulse little flickering currents started in her chest and ran down through her limbs. She took a step closer to look down at the face between two pillows.

Reason ceased. Her eyes continued to feed information her brain was unable to explain.

"He looks like Rory," Ben said slowly. "It is. Ange it's Rory!"

"Steady now," their Uncle said. He walked to the bed. "Do you know this man?"

Angela reached with trembling fingers and removed the damp cloth covering his forehead. His eyes opened wide into hers. Her legs gave out; she sat heavily on the bed. He gasped and reached with both arms to touch her face as she reached for his. His lungs fought for air that wheezed down his throat. His chest heaved up and down.

"Rory, it's alright, it's alright," Angela said.

The Doctor leaned over the bed.

"He can't breathe," she said frantically. "What should I do? Help him."

"Breathe slowly," he said to Rory. "Don't move," he warned as the young man tried to raise his head to see Angela. "Breathe like I showed you."

His words weren't reaching Rory, who continued to struggle. His head tilted back, his neck arched. Daniel threw back the quilt and grabbed Angela's hand. "Here," he said to her, "put your hand here.

401

Tell him to push against your hand. Show him how to breathe from here, like this," he demonstrated on himself, putting his hand in the middle of his ribs.

"Rory, feel my hand. Breathe from here," she said applying light pressure. "Slowly. Try please. I'm here. Please try Rory. I'm here."

He shut his eyes and concentrated on expanding his lungs. The Doctor removed the handkerchief from his neck. Angela faltered momentarily at the sight of his neck and the puncture then continued coaching. It took a conscious effort, but his breathing steadied.

Angela smoothed his hair and stroked his face, her tears falling on him, mixing with his own.

"Rory's alive," Ben sang with restrained glee, shifting from one foot to the other.

"Sh," the Doctor cautioned.

"Rory, Ben's here," Angela told the man on the bed. The edges of his mouth turned up.

"Get him to drink this water and then a little broth," her Uncle said. "Don't let him move." He leaned over Rory. "Don't move," he warned, "or they'll have to leave."

Rory let Angela spoon water into his mouth then his face and neck tightened as he swallowed with difficulty. Angela glanced anxiously at her uncle.

"It hurts him to swallow," he explained. "Go on. Who knows when the last time he ate was."

Rory's eyelids drooped heavily. Angela stopped feeding him. He tried to keep them open, lifting them only to have them fall again.

"Sleep. I'm not going anywhere," Angela told him. She leaned over and kissed both closed eyelids.

She pulled the quilt up and sat, drinking him in with all her might.

"Good work. Come, get some rest while he sleeps," Uncle Daniel said.

"No, I'm not leaving. I told him I wouldn't." She examined the hole in his throat and a spasm of pain clenched her own. She gently touched the cuts on his face and cradled one bandaged hand then the other. "His poor hands," she whispered.

"Mmm," whispered the Doctor, "broken bones in both."

Her eyes blurred. "Other injuries?"

"Broken ribs I suspect, mostly banged and bruised up good. His leg…"

"How is his leg?" She went to the foot of the bed and carefully lifted the quilt. "It should be supported."

Suddenly she was all business. Ben sat on a blanket folded at the end of the bed. She yanked it out from under him, ignoring his mild protest. "You could have asked me to move Ange."

She bunched it, placed Rory's leg over it and pulled the quilt back over.

"Have you examined his leg?" she asked the doctor.

"Only a quick look. Haven't been able to do too much. He gets worked up if I fuss."

"Will you please, later?"

"Yes, of course, if you can convince him to let me. You really must rest. You'll need your strength to help him get well. I'll show you where you can sleep."

"No!" she snapped with vigor that surprised him. "I'm staying right here. I will rest here."

"Me too," Ben said. "I can sleep on the floor. I slept with them outside the wagon all the time."

Daniel was too tired to argue with both of them. "Ben come with me. We'll get some blankets and things for your sister."

Ben and his uncle collected blankets, a towel, a wash basin and cup and carried them to Angela. She had pulled the chair to the bed and sat with one hand resting on Rory's lying outside the quilt.

"Do you need anything?" her uncle asked.

She shook her head, not taking her eyes off the sleeper. The Doctor looked him over once.

"I'll be in the sitting room if you need me," he told Angela. "Ben, I don't want you sleeping on the hard floor. Come sleep on the sofa."

"No," Ben protested.

"Sh, please Ben." Angela kissed him on the cheek. "We'll be alright. Go sleep. I'll see you in the morning."

Daniel put an arm around the boy's shoulders and guided him out the door, shutting it behind them.

He put a blanket on the sofa and patted it. "You sleep here. It's softer than the hard ground." For himself he pulled the two chairs

403

together. When he looked across the room he saw the boy sitting upright in the middle of the sofa, his eyes wide open.

"What's wrong?"

"How did Rory get here?"

Daniel explained briefly. Ben was silent, but remained sitting.

"Do you need something?" Daniel asked.

He said, "I'm scared of what Mother will do when she finds out Rory's here."

"You are? Why is that?"

"She won't let Ange be with him. She doesn't believe they're married. If she makes her go away, Ange will get sick again for sure. And who will take care of Rory?"

"Get some sleep. I'll talk to your mother in the morning."

"Mother can raise an awful fuss. What if she finds Mr. Finch and he comes back to kill Rory dead this time?"

"We won't mention Rory to your mother, not until I see how things are with your sister."

"But what if she sees him?"

"I'm going to advise her to accept the Lassen's offer to stay with them. I think she will. Then she won't be around to see him. Leave it to me. Lie down."

In the morning the inhabitants and most of the guests gathered around the table with lamps glowing and the room warm from the cook stove.

"Where is Angela?" Clara asked.

"She's asleep," Daniel said.

"You left her alone? Benjamin!" She stood, pushing her chair back.

"Clara she's fine. I've already checked on her. She can't leave the house without us seeing her. Please sit. I do have some recommendations concerning her if you'd like to hear them."

Clara pulled her chair close to the table. "Go on, Daniel."

"You are welcome to stay here of course, but I think you'd be more comfortable at the Lassen's. David's place is not ready. You won't be able to get to it until Spring. The Lassen's place is not like what you're accustomed to, but very nice for these parts. There are many rooms. They are respectable people, quite famous in these parts.

404

You've already met Cliff. Ellen is a merry woman, who enjoys people. She and her daughters would appreciate the company of a respectable woman and any news you can bring them of the latest styles from the East. It would mean a few more days' travel. I know you've had your fill of it, but they have provided the buggy and driver. Angela needs distraction from her own troubles. I think she should stay here."

"Leave her here?" Clara said the words slowly, but Daniel saw relief creep over the paper-thin skin on her face.

"I'll keep you informed of her progress. There are plenty of soldiers and folks coming and going who can take messages. We have a mail post now. We're getting downright civilized."

"You think it best?" she asked thoughtfully.

"Yes. Mrs. Dunbar and I will keep her busy enough to keep her mind off herself."

"I'll stay with Ange," Ben said.

"Absolutely not, Benjamin. You will come with Lillian and myself."

"No, I want to stay. I can help too," Ben argued. "Please."

"It's up to your mother," Daniel said. "You would like the ranch. The Lassens have children your own age, horses, cows, interesting people coming and going. I'll make sure your sister writes to keep you updated." He winked at the boy.

There was knock at the door. "Hello," William let himself in. He was followed by Sam and the old man from the day before.

"Good morning gentleman. Have you had breakfast?"

"Yes. I fed them," William said.

"You have my sympathies," Daniel smiled at the two men.

"This here is Lou, the guide who brought your family," William introduced the old man. Daniel shook his gnarled hand.

"Mrs. Harrington and I were just discussing plans. Clara have you reached a decision?"

"Yes. We will accept the invitation. Angela will remain with you."

"The Lassen's will be real happy to see you all," Sam said. "If you'll pardon me. I'll go ready the buggy."

Later that morning Clara and Lillian waited in the hall, dressed in their coats and hats.

405

"I must say goodbye to Angela," she said to Daniel. "Take me to her."

"She's still sleeping."

"Still? Well I can't very well leave without a word."

"She shouldn't be disturbed. Sleep is a great healer. I'll convey your words."

"If you think it best. Tell her good bye for us and that we will be praying for her recovery." She buttoned Lillian's coat and led her out the door Daniel held open for them. Ben lingered behind, his head down.

"I need Ben for a minute to help me with something," his uncle called to Clara.

"Come upstairs and say good bye," he said to Ben.

"Please, can't you get her to let me stay?" Ben pleaded as they climbed the stairs.

"I'd like for you to stay. I just don't think we should push your mother any more just yet. You can come back the moment she gives permission." He opened the door. "Go on in."

Ben tiptoed into the room. Angela lay over the arm of the chair, her head and shoulders resting on the bed. Both she and Rory slept.

"Take care Ange. See you soon," Ben whispered. He covered her with a blanket that had slipped to the floor. "Get better, Rory."

Clara and Lillian sat in the Lassen's buggy. Sam held the reins. The old man with the odd wagon approached Daniel and Ben uneasily, his hat in his hands. "The girl gonna be alright?"

"Oh yes, she'll be fine," Daniel said.

"Lou are you coming too?" Ben asked.

"Yep, got to bring all your stuff."

"Can I ride with you?"

"Ok by me," the old man said. "Better ask your mother."

Ben sighed.

"Go ahead," said his uncle, giving him a gentle push toward Lou. "I'll tell her you're riding with Lou."

Walking over to the buggy to inform Clara, Daniel looked back and saw Ben and the old man talking. Lou bent his head to hear the boy, who stood on his toes to whisper. At something the boy said the old man slapped his hat against his thigh enthusiastically. With uncharacteristic agility Lou climbed to the wagon's bench and Ben scrambled up after him. Daniel smiled.

. . .

Rory dreamed. He dreamed he was sleeping under a soft blanket, the sweet earth beneath him. Star upon star filled the great heavens. He lay quiet, controlling his very breathing so as not to wake Angel and Ben, snuggled close on either side of him.

References

The California Trail: An Epic with Many Heroes
George R. Stewart author, McGraw-Hill Book Company

Lawmen of the Old West
James L. Collins author, Franklin Watts NY, London

The Old Trails West
Ralph Moody author, Thomas Y. Crowel Company NY

The Oregon Trail
Francis Parkman

The Prairie Traveler, a handbook for overland expeditions
Randolph B. Macy author, Harper Bros.

Rural America
Suzanne Fremon, Morrow Wilson editors, H. W. Wilson Company

Women of the West
Cathy Luchetti, Carol Olwell authors, Orion Books NY

Women's Diaries of the Westward Journey
Lillian Schlissel, Spoken Books NY

The World of the American Indian
National Geographic Society 1974

Printed in the United States
87485LV00003B/142-165/A